JAN 2 8 1998

W9-BNO-664

F
JOYCE

Joyce, Graham.

The tooth fairy.

$22.95

DATE			

10/03-8x

East Meadow Public Library
1886 Front Street
East Meadow, L.I., N.Y. 11554-1700
8/08-10Y

BAKER & TAYLOR

JAN 28 1948

The Tooth Fairy

Also by Graham Joyce

To Christopher Fowler

The Tooth Fairy

ONE
Pike

Clive was on the far side of the green pond, torturing a king-crested newt. Sam and Terry languished under a vast oak, offering their chubby white feet to the dark water. The sprawling oak leaned out across the mirroring pond, dappling the water's surface with clear reflections of leaf and branch and of acorns ripening slowly in verdant cups.

It was high summer. Pigeons cooed softly in the trees, and Clive's family picnicked nearby. Two older boys fished for perch about thirty yards away. Sam saw the pike briefly. At first he thought he was looking at a submerged log. It hung inches below the surface, utterly still, like something suspended in ice. Green and gold, it was a phantom, a spirit from another world. Sam tried to utter a warning, but the apparition of the pike had him mesmerized. It flashed at the surface of the water as it came up to take away, in a single bite, the two smallest toes of Terry's left foot.

The thing was gone before Terry understood what had happened. He withdrew his foot slowly from the water. Two tiny crimson beads glistened where his toes had been. One of the beads plumped and dripped into the water. Terry turned to Sam with a puzzled smile, as if some joke was being played. As the wound began to sting, his smile vanished and he began to scream.

Clive's mother and father, in charge that afternoon, were lying on the grass, he with his head in her lap. Sam ran to them. Clive's father lifted his head to see what the commotion was all about.

"Terry's been bitten by a green fish," said Sam.

Clive's father scrambled to his feet and raced along the bank. Terry was still screaming, holding his foot. Mr. Rogers kneeled to part Terry's hands, and the color drained from his face. Instinctively he put Terry's tiny foot to his mouth and sucked at the wound.

Clive's mother quickly joined her husband at the scene. The two boys who'd been fishing laid down their rods and wandered over to take a look. "What happened? Did he fall in?"

Clive was still on the other side of the pond. Sam called him over. Mr. Rogers, hands trembling, fumbled for a handkerchief. He tied it around the bleeding foot, lifted Terry in his arms and jogged back toward the housing estate.

Clive arrived, breathless. "What is it?"

"Come on," his mother said sharply, as if Clive were somehow to blame. She gathered up her picnic blanket and marched the boys from the field. The two older boys were still asking what had happened, but she was tight-lipped.

Sam followed behind her, understanding that Terry was only five and life had taken away two of his toes, presumably forever. He hoped for better luck for himself.

Clive's father jogged the half mile to Terry's caravan. There Terry lived with his mother and father and with his twin brothers, who were not yet nine months old. The Morrises inhabited a rust-bucket Bluebird caravan in an untidy garden behind a cottage. They paid a small ground-rent to the owner of the cottage, an old man who never came out of his house. Sam lived in one of a row of semidetached houses running up to the cottage, seven street numbers away from Terry.

The caravan rested on a pile of red housebricks where the wheels should have been. It butted up against a hedge, as far from the cottage as possible. Holes made by various animals and marauding children punctured the hedge, behind which sprawled a scrubby piece of waste ground. Whatever status Mr. Morris had dropped by living in a caravan he reclaimed by owning a sports car. Sam's father certainly couldn't afford a car in those days, and neither could Clive's old man. It seemed to the boys something of an injustice that both Clive's and Sam's fathers worked in a car factory and didn't possess a car, yet Terry's father, whose work was a mystery to everyone, was the proud owner of a spoke-wheeled, soft-top MG glinting in the yard alongside the rusting caravan.

That Sunday afternoon, Eric Rogers carried the still blubbering Terry down from the pond and snatched open the caravan door to find the Morrises engaged in a private act. The twins slumbered in their cot. Mr. Morris swore as Mr. Rogers backed out with his whimpering bundle, yelling that they should come and take care of their son. Chris Morris emerged wild-eyed, struggling with the zip of his trousers. Moments later he'd bundled Terry into the back of the MG and was revving the engine. Mrs. Morris, coitally crimson, stepped out of the caravan in a faded silk dressing gown, her mahogany curls spilling everywhere, insisting she go with them. Then she remembered the twins snoozing in the cot. Mr. and Mrs. Morris started screaming at each other before Mr. Morris sped off to the City General Hospital.

But what could be done? At the casualty ward they dressed Terry's tiny foot and gave him an antitetanus jab. They stroked his golden hair and told him to be a brave soldier. They had no spare toes to offer.

"A pike?" the doctor repeated in disbelief. "A pike, you say?"

Nev Southall, Sam's father, saw the green MG return from the hospital. Having heard the story from Sam, he dithered for fifteen minutes before going round to see how things were with the boy. He found Chris Morris in a state of high agitation, lashing a Stanley knife to a broom handle.

"How's the kid, Chris?"

"Sleeping."

"What are you doing?"

"I'm going up the road and I'm going to get that pike."

Nev looked at the Stanley knife and the pole and at the net Morris had spread out on the floor, and his heart sank. If there was something he knew a thing or two about, it was catching fish. "Not with that thing you won't."

"It's all I've got." Chris slung the pole and the net in the back of his car.

Nev knew it was a hopeless waste of time, that pike number among the most difficult of fish to catch, even with good tackle. But he couldn't let Chris go back up to the pond alone. "Wait. I've got some gear. Let's try to do it properly."

Nev picked up a couple of rods and reels, a good-sized landing net and his basket of equipment. With Sam in the back of the sports car they roared up the lane to the pond. It was already after five o'-clock in the afternoon. The sun had become a pallid yellow disc floating low in the sky, flooding the pond with diffuse light. Sam showed them where the incident had happened.

"You could fish this for years and not get him," Nev said, setting up the rods. Chris Morris wasn't listening. He was staring into the dark waters, landing net poised, as if he thought the pike might oblige by leaping into it.

Sam noticed that his father did all the talking and Terry's father said nothing. He just kept staring into the gloomy pond water. Dusk came. Nev felt he'd made his gesture. He'd had enough of this nonsense.

"Another day, Chris," he said. "Another day."

"You go on home," said Terry's father. "Just leave me the net. I'll drop it back to you."

"You sure?"

"I'm sure."

So Nev and Sam left Chris Morris prowling the darkening bank of the pond and made their way down the lane on foot.

"Will he catch the pike?" Sam said, well after they were out of earshot.

"Not a chance in hell," said his father.

TWO
Teeth

Where Terry limped, Clive flew. Clive, torturer of newts, was what was popularly known as a "gifted" child. If his parents had been nuclear scientists or Oxbridge dons, this "gift" might have seemed less like a curse to his father Eric, who toiled on the assembly line at the Humber works, and to his mother Betty, who served part-time in the local Co-op, slicing bacon and stacking shelves.

Tolerating aggressive correction from anyone younger than oneself is difficult at any time, but Clive's habit of improving his parents' imperfect store of knowledge began when he was four years old, shortly before the time Terry lost two of his toes to a pike. By the time Clive went to school it was widely trumpeted that he could read the daily newspaper. Whether this meant that, like most adults, he dipped into the tabloids every morning while only half awake, or that he scrutinized the quality broadsheets from political comment to sports report and then completed the crossword before breakfast, was not known. But by the time he was five he was said to read newspapers.

At six he entered a competition run by NASA for school-children. Yuri Gagarin had completed the first space orbit; John

Glenn was accomplishing similar things for the Americans; and NASA was consulting six-year-olds in the English industrial Midlands about its space program. How such a competition ever came to Clive's attention at that age is a mystery in itself, but schoolchildren were invited to suggest experiments which might be conducted by presumably bored astronauts as they orbited the planet. Clive suggested that they take spiders into space to see if the condition of weightlessness affected the spinning of webs. NASA went for it.

Because he won the NASA competition, Clive and his parents were to be flown to Cape Canaveral to witness the launch of the next manned space flight. His picture appeared in the *Coventry Evening Telegraph,* looking owlish beside a huge spider's web. What was celebrity in the adult world was the worst kind of notoriety in the school playground. At school he was promptly dubbed "Spiderboy" and kicked by every kid in the yard. He hated the nickname, letting fly a punch in the mouth to anyone who used it on him, and was dealt a few punches in the mouth by way of return.

It was while they were walking home from school one afternoon—Terry, Clive and Sam, led by Terry's older cousin Linda—that Clive gave Sam the dig in the mouth which loosened the milk tooth that was to go on to cause so much confusion.

"Spiderboy!" Sam had said, for no apparent reason.

Clive fisted Sam on the jaw, motivated more by habit than by genuine outrage.

Sam stopped dead in his tracks. Clive, expecting a scuffle, did too. Terry drew up short. "What is it?"

Sam spat a milk incisor, slightly bloodied at the root, into his hand.

"Soz," said Clive, genuinely horrified at what he'd done. They were, after all, friends. "Soz."

"It's all right," said Sam a little shakily. "It was already loose."

Cousin Linda, always ten yards ahead, permanently mortified at having to wet-nurse three small boys, exhorted them to catch up.

"Put it under your pillow," Terry said. "Get a tanner from the Tooth Fairy."

"There's no evidence to suggest," Clive said, "that Tooth Fairies actually exist."

"Every time I lost one I got sixpence," Terry shouted.

"But what did you get when you lost your toes?" Clive argued. "Nothing."

"I got five quid in a bank savings book. Five quid."

"That was from your dad," Sam said. "It's different. Tooth Fairies aren't interested in toes. And, anyway, the pike had the toes."

"Five quid!" Terry was hurt. The pike episode had left him with a limp.

"There is a way to find out," Clive insisted. "Put it under your pillow, but don't say anything to your mum or dad."

"What are you shouting about?" Linda wanted to know when they caught up with her.

"Sam's tooth fell out," Clive said quickly.

"Is there such a thing as a Tooth Fairy?" Sam asked.

Linda quickly redefined the distance between her and the knot of small boys. "Just don't swallow it. Otherwise a tooth tree will grow in your stomach."

"What?" the three boys said at once.

"A tooth tree," she called over her shoulder. "Growing in your gut."

Sam kept his fist tightly closed over the tooth, as if some malignant spirit might want to twist his arm up and force the tooth back into his mouth. He was silent the rest of the way home.

Sam never mentioned the incisor to either his mother or his father. If they thought he was particularly quiet that evening, they reserved comment. In any event, Sam was considered a distracted boy, given to self-absorption and daydreams and unnatural fits of staring.

"Miles away," his mother Connie would often remark. "Miles away. Do you think that boy is autistic?"

"Autistic?" Nev lowered his *Coventry Evening Telegraph*.

"What's autistic?"

Connie tried to recall something she'd read in a magazine. "Well, sort of miles away all the time."

Nev didn't believe in anything he couldn't pronounce. He regarded his son watching television, his own features wrinkling in rough assessment. Sam, always aware of the way in which they talked across him, pretended not to hear.

"Nah," said his father, retreating behind his paper.

That night Sam examined the tooth by the light of his bedside lamp. The ivory peg was stained slightly yellow near the root. The ring of dried blood around the base reminded him acutely of the sensation of it popping from his gum. It was a pain-shaped bloodstain. With his tongue Sam probed the hole the tooth had left behind in his gum. It was identically pain-shaped. He switched off his bedside lamp and slid the tooth under his pillow.

Some hours later he was awoken briefly by his parents coming to bed. His mother looked in on him. Only semiconscious, he was dimly aware of her tucking in the blankets and smoothing his pillow. He rolled over and went back to sleep.

In the middle of the night he woke up feeling stiff with cold. His bedroom window was wide open to the dark of night, and a breath of wind lifted the curtain. The faint crescent of moon offered a little light but no comfort. The breeze brought on its wings a strange odor, familiar yet difficult to identify. It was a composite of smells, among which was that of grass after rain. Yet it hadn't been raining.

Something was wrong. Sam sat upright in bed.

Someone was in the room.

His skin turned inside out like a glove. He blinked at the web of darkness. His white shirt, ready for school next morning, was draped over the back of a hard chair. It floated in the gloom. He stared hard at the shirt. A figure was crouched in shadow behind the chair. The shocking stillness of the room wanted to blister and peel back like a layer of skin.

"I know you're there. I can see you."

The figure stiffened slightly.

Sam was afraid, but deep within his fear he felt curiously composed. Still his voice quavered. "It's no use hiding. I know you're behind the chair."

The figure expelled a brief sigh. Sam couldn't distinguish anything behind the draped shirt. *Burglar,* he thought. *It's a burglar.* The intruder made a decision to come out of hiding. Slowly straightening its back, it stepped from behind the chair. The curtain lifted at the window. Somewhere far off in the night a dog-fox barked, three times. All Sam could discern was the black shadow of what he took to be a small man. The shadow approached the foot of the bed.

The voice came out in a cracked whisper. "Can you see me? Can you?"

Through the window a broken fingernail of moon was visible. It barely illumined the intruder's face, but what Sam could see he didn't like. Two dark eyes, shiny like the green-black carapace of a beetle, flashed at him. The eyes were set deep, each in a squint counterpoised to the other, lurking under a matted shock of black hair. Tangled elf-locks framed high cheek bones and a swarthy complexion. The word "half-caste" came to mind. Sam had heard the term employed by adults but used with an ugliness of meaning beyond the word itself. Now that the figure had come closer, Sam identified the burglar as the source of the smell he'd recognized on waking. It was not streaming through the window at all. It was the smell of the intruder, and in addition to the scent of grass after rain was the odor of horse's sweat, and birdshit, and camomile. The intruder—Sam was unable to tell if it was male or female—suddenly cocked its head to one side and smiled. A row of teeth glimmered in the faint moonbeams, a mouthful of blue light. The teeth were perfect, but, unless he was mistaken, they were sharpened to fine dagger points. At full height the intruder stood little more than four feet tall, or at any rate, just a couple of inches taller than Sam. It was difficult to see what the creature was wearing in the dark, but he could idenfity mustard-and-green striped leggings and heavy, industrial-style boots.

"Yes. I can see you."

"That's bad. Real bad."

Sam nodded a silent yes. He didn't know why it was bad, but he knew it was better to agree.

The intruder was squinting hard at Sam, as if puzzling what to do next. "And you can hear me. Obviously obviously obviously. Bad." The sharpened teeth gleamed electric-blue again in the moonlight. There was a tiny crackle as the figure placed a finger on the bedpost. Sam felt the crackle ride to the nape of his neck and fan his hair. The intruder was discharging static.

Sam suddenly had an idea who the figure was. "You've come for the tooth, haven't you?" He was dismayed by the Tooth Fairy's appearance. If he did have an image of a Tooth Fairy in his head before that night, it was of a fragile lady three inches tall, lace-winged, with an acorn cup for a hat. Not a thug in heavy boots. "You want the tooth, don't you?"

"Shhh! Don't wake the house! How come you were able to see me? How did you spot me? Don't answer. Wait." The Tooth Fairy held up a beautifully manicured hand, five ivory fingers outstretched, a thin silver ring on each. "How many fingers do you see?"

"Five."

"This is bad. Real bad." The Tooth Fairy held a finger and thumb to the bridge of its nose. It seemed to be thinking hard. "This is the worst of all possible situations. The worst."

"Don't you want the tooth?"

"Uh?"

"The tooth. Don't you want it?" Sam held out the tiny incisor in the palm of his hand.

The Tooth Fairy got up and looked at the proffered tooth for a long time before accepting it. Sam felt a tiny prod of static as they touched. The Tooth Fairy retreated to the window, holding the tooth up to the faint light of the moon. "Do you realize how much trouble we're in? Both of us? You've seen me! Do you know what a thing like this means?" The fairy rotated the tooth in the weak light.

"Don't shout! You'll wake Mum and Dad."

"Fuck 'em!"

The venom imparted in this remark shocked Sam to his bowels. "I'll tell them!"

The Tooth Fairy approached the bed. Reaching out a hand toward Sam's face, it closed those long, elegant but strong fingers around the boy's mouth. Again a prod of cold static. The hand twisted the slack flesh of his cheeks violently, the sharp fingernails clawing at his face. "And you'll tell them you saw the Tooth Fairy? They'll think you're fucking crazy. Know what they do with crazies?"

There was a bump from the adjacent room and the sound of bedsprings.

The hand dropped. "Shit!" said the Tooth Fairy, climbing up on the bed and stepping a heavy black boot on the windowsill. "I'm gone."

"Wait! You didn't give me anything! For the tooth!"

The Tooth Fairy looked back, appalled. Darting a glance out of the window, it seemed trapped for a moment, writhing between escape and some unimpeachable contract. They heard footsteps from the next room. Fumbling frantically in a pocket, the fairy produced a silver sixpence and flicked it in the air. It winked in the dull moonlight as it fell, spinning. The sixpence dropped lightly on the pillowcase before disappearing clean through the pillow. Sam slid a hand under the pillow but stopped when the fairy barked violently at him, "Leave it until morning, kiddiwinks. You heard me! Leave it until the morning!"

A door hinge whined, a floorboard creaked. The Tooth Fairy hoisted itself on to the windowsill.

"Will I see you again?" Sam said.

"You'll wish you didn't." The Tooth Fairy leapt out of the window as Sam's bedroom door opened. Light from the hall streamed into the room. It was Sam's mother. She switched on the bedside lamp.

"You all right, Sam? I thought I heard you talking in your sleep. Did you open the window?"

She closed it and drew the curtains. Smoothing his pillow again, she kissed him lightly on the forehead before pulling the blankets up under his chin.

"Go back to sleep," she said.

THREE
Mist

Since her cousin's caravan lay *en route,* Lanky Linda collected
Terry every morning to walk him to school. Terry then insisted on
rounding up first Sam and then Clive for the last half-mile strag-
gle. Linda suffered for this. Almost eleven years old, she sensed
keenly and intuitively the mysterious veil drawing back, the curtain that would give way to the sublime and transcendent state of
adulthood. But this insight made her act strangely. Lately she had
taken to wearing white lace gloved to and from school every day.
Her parents summarized her condition as moody. When she wasn't
known as Lanky Linda she was known as Moody Linda.

It was painful for her, trembling on the threshold of maturity
as she was, to have to escort three ugly, bawling, runny-nosed boys
to school and then back again, so that the prospect and the retro-
spect of the day, and everything between, was sullied. It was like an
exquisite form of punishment meted out by the gods of Ancient
Greece. The boys were always ten or fifteen yards behind her, dragging chains, voicing abuse, spoiling the dazzling purity of her
white, white gloves.

"You'll be late!" Linda screamed through the mist. "Late for
school!"

An early autumn fog draped the fields and the hedgerows and the pavements like fine muslin cloth. The houses, the bus shelters and the telegraph poles had lost all definition. The bloodless silver-gray world needed a transfusion of color. But the hedgerows were jeweled and spangled with spider's webs, gossamer nets dripping silver balls of moisture. Linda made the mistake that morning of bending a twig into a sprung loop, a tool for collecting webbing from the hedgerows. "Look," she said. "Fairy wings."

The three boys were enormously impressed by this trick. Linda felt so encouraged that the boys now realized she had a store of knowledge to offer that she taught them all how to make a twig loop, so they could collect fairy webs for themselves.

"Late! Late! You'll be late!" she screamed again. They were now boisterously intent on thoroughly denuding the webbing from the two-hundred-yard stretch of hedgerow. A kind of competition developed among them, poking and twirling, jabbing and twisting. It was a scene of carnage and plunder, in which the boys were cheerfully responsible for a local ecological catastrophe.

"*Stop!*" Linda bellowed. They ignored her. "STOOOPPPP! STOOOOOOPPPPPPPP!"

They stopped. Linda was red in the face. The boys regarded her with astonishment. But now she'd succeeded in winning their attention she didn't know what to say to them. "If you take too much of that spider's web," she said, "you know what happens."

"What?" said Sam. "What happens?"

Linda was obviously thinking on her feet. "Fairy wings. Nothing left. For fairies. To make their wings."

"Ha!" spat Terry. He flobbed a tiny white ball of spittle and contempt into the gutter.

"And," Linda almost shouted, "spiders catch flies."

"So?" said Clive.

"Then there will be an epidemic of flies. Millions and millions of flies. And you know what *that* means."

"What?" said Sam.

"What?" said Terry.

"Plague." Linda turned on her heels and marched in the direction of school. She stopped after a few yards and turned back. The three boys stared at her with appalled, bulging eyes.

It was Clive who broke the silence. Clive, at moments like this, had a smile like the lace in an old-style football. Anyone could be forgiven for wanting to boot it. "Are you certain?" he challenged.

Linda felt her cheeks flaming. Her white-lace gloves flew to her face. She narrowed her eyes and smiled evilly. "Bubonic plague. If you don't believe me, why don't you just try it? Go on."

But the point had been won. Linda turned again and set off at a brisk pace. The boys hurried behind her in chastened silence. When they reached the sweet shop before taking the turning for the school, they each abandoned their twig loops of gray webbing. In any event the webs had surrendered all of their beauty. They were no longer silver or gossamer or sparkling. As the school hand-bell was heard to ring from the playground, they were discarded at the roadside with the dirty sweet wrappers and the fallen leaves.

F O U R
Eyes

Sam woke up feeling cold. His bedroom window was open, and the chill of autumn had settled on the room like icing sugar. Outside stars were scattered across the sable dark, and the moon was dying into its left-hand cup. Luxuriant odors of night, of the dropped fruit of the damson tree in the garden, of rotting rain-mashed leaves, invaded his bedroom. These smells had marched in on the boots of the figure who sat hunched against the far wall.

Sam shuddered. But the Tooth Fairy seemed exhausted. He or she—and Sam was still unable to discriminate—was hugging one knee. One foot stuck out at the end of the familiar mustard-and-green striped trousers, displaying to Sam the patterned sole of a huge boot. Weak moonlight glimmered in shiny eyes that had been observing Sam for some time.

"We're in a lot of trouble."

Sam sat up. "Why?" Whenever he tried to speak to the Tooth Fairy his heart swelled and his tongue stuck to the roof of his mouth.

"Have you ever been in trouble?"

Sam thought about it. He knew what it was like to hear a raised voice. He even knew what it was like to feel a virile slap hard enough to leave a giant red hand impression on the back of his leg. "Yes."

"I mean big, bad trouble. I mean deep shit."

When the other kids at school used words like "shit," it meant nothing. When he occasionally overheard adults using such language—and the creature in the room talked like an adult even if it didn't look like one—then the words became frightening. They became real.

"I didn't do anything."

The creature snorted. "Didn't do anything," it mimicked nastily. The Tooth Fairy had a habit of choking on its own cynical humor, so that certain words squeezed out with a tiny cough. "You want to know what you did? You *saw* me, that's what you did. You're still seeing me now. That's enough, kiddiwinks. That's enough for anyone."

"I can't help it."

"Fuck."

When the creature said "fuck," its teeth bared. As before, a perfect set of dentures were filed to sharp points. The enamel shone with dull, blue luminosity. The Tooth Fairy spat a tiny white ball of spittle on to the carpet.

"Are you a boy or a girl?"

The Tooth Fairy squinted at him for a long time. "Would you like me to hurt you?"

"I just wanted to know."

"You ask me that again and I'll bite your face off. I mean it."

The Tooth Fairy sat between him and the door. Sam felt his eyes watering. He wanted to shout for his mother, but now he was too afraid of the beast in his room.

"Calm down. I was only pretending to be mad. Shit. I'm sorry. Just calm down. I've got to think of a way out of this for both of us. I meant what I said when I told you we were both in trouble. Bad things are going to happen if we're not careful. Bad things."

The Tooth Fairy scrambled to its feet. It was agitated, moving around the room, touching Sam's things. It stroked a long, elegant and beringed finger across the curve of his football. It twisted the ear of his furry white rabbit. Stumbling against the plastic Crusader fort on the floor, the Tooth Fairy kicked out viciously, sending the fort skittering across the floor, toy soldiers plummeting from its battlements.

"I found my sixpence," Sam tried lamely. "Under the pillow. The morning after you came."

The Tooth Fairy released a thin howl of rage and exasperation, digging the fingernails of one hand into the palm of the other. Sam was terrified to see that the fairy had drawn its own blood. "Fuck! Fuck! Why did you do that? Why? Do you know when I found out you could see me, I nearly put your eyes out? I nearly did that! I could do it now!"

The creature pointed a trembling finger at Sam as it spoke. A mounting rage exploded and it scrambled across the room, leaping on to Sam's bed, pinning him by its bony knees. It leaned across him and exhaled sharply, the full force of the breath striking Sam in the right eye. There was a sharp odor again of bird droppings and horse's stables commingled with damsons and fresh mown grass and a painful, stinging sensation in his eye.

Sam shrieked. It was too much for him. His terror broke. *"Muuuuuummmm!!!! Eeeeeeeeeehhh!!! Daaaaaaaaddddddd!"* His scream turned high-pitched.

The Tooth Fairy leapt back, aghast. "No no no! I shouldn't have done that. I'll have to pay for that! No no no! Stop screaming! Just stop screaming!"

"Eeeeeeeeeeeeeehhhhhh!!!"

Movement could be heard in the next bedroom. A muffled thump.

The fairy placed its ringed fingers across Sam's mouth. "Stop this! If you ever tell them, it will be worse for both of us!"

His parents' bedroom door squealed at the hinge. Footsteps padded on the landing between their room and his. A floorboard creaked. Sam bit hard on the fingers closing his mouth. The Tooth Fairy leapt back in astonishment, staring at the tiny crescent of tooth marks on its finger. It looked at the bedroom door.

"Don't ever tell them!" the creature hissed before leaping on to the windowsill. "Don't ever!" With that it escaped into the night.

Sam's bedroom door opened. Light flooded the room. It was his father, hair tousled, unshaved, eyes like a schoolboy's marbles dug up from the garden. "What's all the shouting about?"

Sam tried to speak but his breath came too short. He tried to say "Tooth Fairy," but all that came from his mouth was a convulsive sob. He was hyperventilating.

"Come on, Sam. You've been having a nightmare. A nightmare. Now it's gone, eh? All right now. All right now." His father stroked his hair. "You're soaked in sweat, old lad. Soaked. You just go back to sleep because it's all right now."

Tucking the sheets in, his father looked up at the window. "It's freezing in here. No wonder." He closed the window, securing the catch.

"Leave the light on," said Sam.

His father hesitated. "I'll leave the hall light on and the door open. Or you'll never get back to sleep."

Sam closed his eyes in an act of compliance, opening them again as soon as his father had gone. He scrambled out of bed and peered through the window. The moon shone palely on the blue-gray slate rooftops of the neighboring houses. He let the curtain fall back and turned to gather up his toy fort. It was broken on one side. His ragged troops of assorted crusaders, U.S. cavalrymen, paratroopers and Red Indians lay scattered across the floor, vanquished by armies of nightmare. He left them to die where they had fallen.

Sam's eye, where the Tooth Fairy had blasted him with noxious vapors, was sore. He climbed back into bed, and after a short while he was asleep again.

The evening following the second appearance of the Tooth Fairy, Sam was sunk in a chair, quietly gazing into a picturebook. He became aware that his mother's gaze was fixed on him. He looked up at her, and her hard stare didn't falter. Neither did she smile, so he let his eyes dip back into the picture book, still aware, at the periphery of his vision, of his mother's attention.

"That boy's got a cast," he heard his mother whisper.

Nev grunted apathetically from behind his newspaper.

"He has," said Connie. "Look."

The newspaper dipped slowly, until Nev's eyes and nose appeared above the headlines. "What?"

Sam pretended blissful unawareness of this attention.

"His right eye. It turns inward slightly."

"So what?"

"It's got to be looked at."

Defeated, Nev let his newspaper dip into his lap. "If that boy's not artistic, then he's autistic, or whatever the bloody word is. And if he's not double-jointed, he's blind in one bloody eye."

"I didn't say he was blind. I said he's got a cast."

"Why don't you leave the kid alone instead of picking and pulling at him all the time?"

Connie wasn't to be placated. "Sam. Put your book down. Put it down. Now look at me. Now look at the door without moving your head."

Sam did as instructed. His mother crouched over him, her eyes owlish and full of overweening concern. His father looked resigned and sympathetic.

"No," Connie insisted. "It's got to be looked at."

FIVE
Friction

Terry's father's occupation continued to be a mystery to the entire neighborhood. When anyone asked he told people—and Terry often repeated the answer—that he was an inventor. But he might as well have declared himself a ufologist or an astrophysicist, so lost in the sky was the idea.

"Inventor of what?" would be the inevitable response.

"Whatever needs inventing," was his stock reply.

Chris Morris worked at this putative inventing in a garage workshop adjacent to his old caravan. If neighbors such as Sam's father Nev or Clive's father Eric ever speculated about the nature of the inventions, perhaps their minds conjured with contraptions poised to outmode the internal combustion engine or turned to space-age devices such as handheld TV sets. In reality, Morris's inventions were more likely to take the form of cut-out cardboard models commissioned for the back of breakfast cereal packets or display units for grocery stores.

"Whatever it is," Clive overheard his father say once, "it can't pay much if they have to live in a rust-bucket caravan."

"Unless he spends it all on other things." Betty Rogers clamped her lips tight, as if she knew something.

"How do you mean?" The men were always asking the women, "How do you mean?"

"Swanning around in a sports car when his kid's shoes are in holes."

Though Clive overheard all this, he was not disillusioned by any of it. Terry's father was Clive's hero. Even though Clive was, by now, only seven years old, he knew he wanted to be an inventor like Terry's father. Despite his mother's assessment, Clive thought Chris Morris looked more like a fox than a swan. Sandy-haired Mr. Morris had an early widow's peak and a way of peering at things that betokened eerie intelligence. His suntanned forearms, so unlike the putty-colored skin of his own father, were forever advertised by his permanently rolled sleeves.

Morris was always tossing out homemade toys or cardboard airplanes. Where Terry had no use for toys, unless they were made of brightly molded plastic and came from Woolworth's, Clive was eternally fascinated by Morris's dexterity and casual can-do. Meanwhile his own father was slow, lumbering and easy-going, just like Terry. More than once he suspected some error, that they'd been given the wrong fathers. Terry, if asked, would have happily embraced that idea. Clive's father had recently bought a television set, and Sam's parents were just about to do the same. Everyone was declaring this the Television Age, while he had to make do with a toy version constructed from cardboard.

Morris's workshop was an Open Sesame to Clive's imagination. Weird specialist tools hung in neat rows on the walls. Shelves were piled with cannibalized bits of engines, sets of old wireless valves, broken penny-arcade machines, springs, pulleys, weights, miles of cable. A genuine propeller blade from an aircraft was suspended from the ceiling, running the length of the roof itself; a double-barreled shotgun was padlocked to the wall at the back of the garage; and a gutted Wurlitzer jukebox sucked dust into itself in the corner, a rack of black vinyl discs waiting under a Perspex canopy for the selection command that would never come.

But Morris was moody. He would hurl things around his

workshop, and language smoked the air like the sparks cascading from his grinding machine. Sometimes he would burst out of the garage, fulminating, scattering children like a prod of lightning, booting stray tricycles or footballs out of his path.

At other times he would soften to Clive's interest, encouraging the boy's attentions. One afternoon, when Linda and the boys had returned from school, he broke off from manipulating bits of cardboard and whipped a tarpaulin cover off a spindly device at the rear of his workshop. Terry had seen it before; bored, he drifted away. Linda too thought she might be asked to get her white gloves dirty, so she went inside the caravan, where her aunt Jane Morris sat with the two-year-old twins, Terry's brother and sister. Sam and Clive were left to blink at the contraption.

A bicycle wheel with its spokes removed was mounted on a frame. Once Morris had set the thing in motion, a series of polished, greased rods were lowered by cunning weights, returning to their original position after making a descent and driving the wheel. It was clever, fiendishly clever. It just didn't seem to *do* anything.

"Perpetual-motion machine," said Morris. "They say it can't be done. But I'm going to do it. I've been working on this for seven years."

"Is it finished?" Clive was mesmerized.

Morris looked at the contrivance sadly. "Naw. After a while it will stop. Friction, boys, friction. That's what's stopping us. All the time. Bloody sodding friction." Morris launched into a wild sermon about how the coal and the oil and the fossil fuel wouldn't last forever, and the scientists had better damn well find an alternative pretty damn quick. He stared at his machine and seemed to be talking to himself. Sam, who couldn't follow any of it, peeled back to go in search of Terry. Clive, who wanted to understand all of it, watched the wheel rotating as if it could at any moment open a door through Time.

Then Jane Morris appeared at the entrance to the garage. She was clutching a piece of paper. Her features were set like iron. Anger had drawn a rude geometry all over her face.

"You'd better get the others and go," Morris said to Clive. "The next world war is about to start."

"The next world war is about to start," Clive told his mother and father that evening.

"Eh?"

"Terry's dad looked at his mum and told me the next war is about to start."

Eric Rogers laughed; Betty pressed her lips together.

They were preparing to go to the library. One of the penalties of spawning a gifted child was the twice-weekly visit to the library. Mr. and Mrs. Rogers suffered in turns the humiliation of being outpaced by their seven-year-old son. They would take five minutes to choose a Western or a romance respectively while Clive demanded the full membership hour. Two days later he would have finished his books, and they'd be compelled to return their own selections unread, just to keep up appearances.

Books, otherwise, would not have figured largely in the Rogers household. Because of Clive's special "gift," however, they had been persuaded by a sharp door-to-door salesman to "invest" in a hugely expensive set of the *Encyclopaedia Britannica*. It was a serious sacrifice. The books came bound in luxurious white leather. Only after they had arrived and lay stacked in the living room like two pillars of an occult temple did Eric Rogers grasp why a teak bookcase was touted as an optional extra. It might have comforted him to know that, because of Clive's rapacious inquiry, theirs was the only set in the city that ever had each and every one of its volumes lifted down from the wall for genuine perusal.

Clive had discovered science fiction, so Eric had tried to discover it with him. Sometimes it was heavy going.

"What's a Geiger counter?"

"Look it up, son. That's why we bought the *Encyclopaedia*."

"What's a positronic tractor beam?"

"Buggered if I know, son. Can't you look it up?"

Dusk was settling as Clive and his father made their way to the library. Huge brown leaves, crisp and dry as parchment, floated down from the birch trees. As they approached the cottage where Terry's caravan was sited, they were distracted by the throaty sound of a roaring engine. Mr. Morris's spoke-wheeled MG spat out of the drive, braking sharply as it hit the road. It was followed down the driveway by Jane Morris, barefoot and running, and wielding a large aluminium saucepan. As the MG sped off, tires shrieking, the saucepan struck the rear fender, bouncing harmlessly into the road. "Wanker!" she screamed. She was puce with rage. Clive blinked at his father through a cloud of exhaust. "You fucking wanker!" Jane Morris shrieked again.

Eric Rogers looked as though he was going to say something. Instead he picked up the pan. The burned remnants of someone's dinner was stuck to the base of it. He handed the pan back to the woman, trying to keep a glint out of his eye. Without a word, Jane Morris retreated to her caravan.

Clive and his father walked the half-mile to the library in silence. Eric could tell that his son's mind was worrying away at something. Even at seven years old he had developed a vertical crease just above the bridge of his nose whenever he was thinking hard. Eric's thoughts were still focused on Jane Morris's outburst.

When they reached the library, his son stopped him from going in. An expression of deep anxiety clouded the boy's face.

"Dad?"

"What is it?"

"What's a radioactive isotope?"

SIX

Bad Influence

At about this time God mysteriously came into the lives of the three boys. God also came into Lanky Linda's life and, simultaneously, into the orbit of five other local children, all younger than the boys. It happened on a morning when Sam had that day no greater expectation of life than a game of football.

After breakfast one Sunday morning Sam found himself being buttoned into a suit of clothes he detested. It was a short-trouser suit woven from some shiny, abrasive, synthetic fiber. He'd been trussed in the suit twice before, once for a wedding and once for a christening. Instructed to root out a pair of elasticated garters to hold up his knee-length, cream-colored stockings, he was then directed to polish his best black shoes until they winked. When he was ready, Connie anointed his head with water and, by dint of overvigorous brushing, proceeded to plaster his hair to his crown.

Sam was ready to protest, or at least to ask what lay behind all this preparation, when there came a knock at the front door. Connie opened the door, and Sam was astonished to see Lanky Linda in a spotless white frock and a white pillbox hat, beaming in at him. He was even more astonished to see, behind her and hovering uncertainly at the gate, a motley entourage of small children gathered from the neighborhood, all groomed, spruced and buffed up in Sunday best. Sam felt an adult hand at his back propelling him outside, and the door was closed—rather too quickly—behind him.

And there was Terry! And there was Clive! Both looking glum and uncomfortable, Clive's neck and ears gleaming livid-pink as if someone had recently set about him with sandpaper.

"What?" said Sam. "What's all this?"

"Come along," said Linda proudly, beckoning them all on with her white glove. "Come along." She set off at a brisk pace but with an air of pride and *hauteur* clearly distinguishing this from any ordinary school day. The smaller children in the ensemble had to run to keep pace with her.

"What is it?" Sam asked Clive and Terry, but either they knew no more than he or they were too disgusted to answer.

"It's a surprise," Linda called over her shoulder, and she marched ahead of her flock, poised and serene, her hands held strangely, like someone carrying an invisible orb and scepter.

They walked for a quarter of a mile up the hill before Linda halted at a gateway. Sam recognized the building at which she'd stopped. It was a modest timbered hall painted black, with a wooden cross mounted on the roof.

"It's a church," said Sam. "A church."

Linda beamed in happy confirmation. She held open the gate, ushering everyone inside. A tiny shiver of apprehension chased around the younger children. Linda soothed them, Linda encouraged them and finally Linda led the way to the church door. Organ music played softly within. The three boys brought up the rear and followed the younger children, who were now huddled together in self-protection, inside.

Sam could not have known, and never would guess at, the small parental conspiracy that had taken place to get them there. One or two parents in the neighborhood, possibly genuinely concerned about the spiritual education of their children, had formed an alliance with those larger number of parents who would welcome the leisure of a Sunday morning unencumbered by their off-spring; and those parents had hatched out the plan to have the very willing Linda march the children up to the mission church of St. Paul. Thus while the kids were listening to the strictures of the Apostle, their mothers and fathers could do in bed what only marriage permitted them to do without burning for it.

Mr. Phillips warmly welcomed Linda and all the children into the Sunday school. There were almost thirty other children inside, some of whom they recognized from school, some they didn't. Mr. Phillips, a man with an easy, slack-jawed smile, glittering blue eyes and a shiny, polished pate, took his place in front of the altar to regale them with stories about a Good Samaritan and a Prodigal Son. Sam listened attentively.

After the service each child was given a stamp and a card on which to stick it. A different stamp, they were assured, was issued each week. That first stamp was an illustration from the doleful tale of the self-same Prodigal Son. The stamps were mildly interesting, but inadequate reward for surrendering a Sunday morning's football. Yet this new Sunday-morning fixture was clearly compulsory, and the boys wore it week after week with reasonable grace. It was, after all, inordinately difficult for any of them to kick up against God.

After the fourth week the boys had gravitated to the back row of seats in the church, where they could smirk and whisper and punch each other while Mr. Phillips smiled and talked enthusiastically at the front. There were hymns, they ploughed the field and scattered, they hunkered down for prayers. Sam dug his knees in the hassock on the polished wood floor and found he could almost drift to sleep during prayers. Only when he heard everyone sliding their bottoms back on to the pews did he sit up.

Terry and Clive were slouched to his right. Sleepily opening his eyes, he was startled to see the grinning Tooth Fairy sitting at his left. He gasped, and froze. The Tooth Fairy put a finger to his lips, and then touched his ear, indicating that Sam should pay attention to the lesson.

"Today I'm going to tell you the story of the Widow's Mite," intoned Mr. Phillips, arms akimbo. He didn't seem to have spotted the Tooth Fairy. Oval patches of sweat darkened the underarms of his white nylon shirt, and his bald head gleamed under the electric light. His eyes glittered with unimpeachable faith, and his head nodded continually in self-affirmation as he spoke. Sam recognized on the faces of Clive and Terry the disguise of dreamy attentiveness. He looked back at the Tooth Fairy, who winked slyly.

The Tooth Fairy winked again, jiggling an eyebrow suggestively. Sam was about to dig Terry in the ribs, when he spotted that the Tooth Fairy was nursing something in his lap. He glanced down and what he saw made him snort. The Tooth Fairy had his cock out. It rested lightly in the palm of his hand, unpleasantly white, its glans swollen like a field-mushroom after a night of warm rain. The Tooth Fairy let his jaw drop, once again exposing teeth filed to sharp points, before winking and nodding playfully at Sam. Sam sniggered loudly. Terry turned to look, as did a few other faces from the seats in front. Sam buried his nose in his handkerchief and blew mightily. When he looked back, the Tooth Fairy had gone.

"So even though the Widow made only a tiny, tiny, tiny offering—" Phillips exhorted the class to understand.

Sam stuck his elbow in Terry's ribs. Terry looked over and Sam winked. Now it was Terry's turn to snigger as he saw Sam's flaccid cock poking from an unzipped fly.

"So it doesn't matter how little it is . . ."

Terry's shoulders started shaking. Clive popped out of his reverie and wanted to know what was going on. In a second all three of them were choking silently, shoulders quivering. Terry stuffed his handkerchief in his mouth, which only induced further snorting and a small explosion at the back of his sinuses, provoking in turn a green worm of snot to rocket from his nostril. Heads were turning. Linda, up at the front in her white pillbox hat, spun round to offer a glare of disapproval. This only exacerbated the situation. Sam dug his fingernails deep into his own flesh, struggling to control himself; Terry gagged on his handkerchief; and the muscles of Clive's cheeks inflated to a critical point.

"And that is the meaning of of of . . . Sam, Terry and Clive, I'd like you to stay behind at the end . . . the meaning of the story of the Widow's Mite."

The head was cut of all laughter. Sam shuffled uncomfortably, trying to work his cock back inside his trousers before anyone else noticed. The way Phillips had looked at him intimated that he knew. *He knew* Sam had been holding his cock. *He knew* because God had told him. God had told Mr. Phillips, and Mr. Phillips would tell Linda, and Linda would tell his mother, and his mother would tell his father, and his father would take off his leather belt with the brass buckle and give him a pasting.

This was how God worked.

After Sunday school Mr. Phillips lined up the three of them in the vestry as the other children filed out of the south door. They were afraid of Mr. Phillips, his geniality and deep-down kindness notwithstanding. His connections with vaster powers intimidated them; and after the event they—at least Sam and Terry—were terrified by the gravity of their offense, specifically by the certainty of its becoming public knowledge.

"He knows," Sam said as they waited for the others to leave. The vestry smelled of beeswax polish and lavender. On the wall opposite was a painting of Jesus crucified between two thieves.

"He doesn't," said Clive. "He can't."

"I think he knows," said Terry. "I think he does."

"Don't say anything," said Clive.

The door opened and Phillips came in. The catch clicked gently as he closed the door behind him. Standing over them with hands on hips, he took off his glasses. "Right. I would like to know what it was you found so funny today."

Silence.

"Yes, well, I'm quite prepared to stand here all day until you give me an explanation. All day."

Silence.

"I'm waiting." They all sensed that Phillips had already lost. "Come along, Clive, you're the most sensible one of the three. Giggling like silly little girls. I'm still waiting."

Clive cleared his throat. "Sorry, sir."

"I'm not sure I want "sorry." I want an explanation."

Clive cleared his throat a second time. "I think," he said, parroting a phrase he'd heard adults use, "that we must have found something amusing."

"Oh. You think you must have found something amusing, did you?"

"Yes, sir."

"I see. And what about Jesus?"

"Sir?"

"I said, what about Jesus?"

"Sir?"

"Yes, what about Him? What about Him when He was dying on the cross for our sins. That's your sins and my sins. Do you suppose He must have found something amusing?"

The Tooth Fairy also taught Sam how to hyperventilate. It was a trick he took to school. The story even got into the local newspaper.

It was a fine, dry afternoon during the school lunchbreak, about ten minutes before the bell was scheduled to call everyone back to class. An airplane flew by overhead, surprisingly low, almost low enough to see the pilot in the cockpit. Sam stood watching after it, squinting into the sky, still mesmerized by the loud, cylindrical drone of the plane long after all the other children had forgotten it. He stood at the edge of the playground and suddenly remembered what the Tooth Fairy had shown him during the night.

Turning back to the playground he caught Clive by the arm. "Hey, watch this." Designating two other boys to be ready to catch him, he plugged his ears with his fingers and inhaled deeply, very rapidly, until he fainted clean away. The boys caught him, and within a few seconds he recovered consciousness.

"Hey!" said Clive, and he too wanted to try. The same thing happened. Then the other two boys each had a go, followed by Terry, and within moments they had an audience of ten or fifteen kids, all waiting to take a turn at the new game. The audience doubled, tripled, until the entire playground was full of kids watching.

Then a strange thing happened. Sandra Porter from Sam's class suddenly fainted without even hyperventilating. The same thing happened to Janet Burrows and to Wendy Cooper, followed by Mick Carpenter, and then three other girls, and four more boys, until they were all fainting clean away, the entire playground full of kids, over one hundred and sixty on the school roll, all drifting to the ground like petals from a blown rose.

Sam saw teachers running from the school building. Terry and Clive were among the last to fall, and Sam thought he'd better go down with them. He heard the teachers moving among the bodies crying, "Stop this!" and "Stop this at once!" But it was fully three minutes or so before the first children started to recover. Sam opened his eyes briefly and saw, sitting on the fence ringing the school yard and grinning with satisfaction, the Tooth Fairy. Then he was gone.

When the children started to recover, no one seemed able to offer the teachers any explanation for what had happened. It just became The Day Everyone Fainted. The incident was written up in the *Coventry Evening Telegraph* and described as a case of mass hysteria.

Somehow the episode was never traced back to Sam.

SEVEN
The Cage

It was a day off school when he preferred not to have a day off school. Life in the Unusual Objects Society was becoming progressively more interesting, and now he was going to have to miss a session when Terry had promised to bring along an unexploded cartridge from his father's twelve-bore shotgun. Clive had formed the Unusual Objects Society only the week before, recruiting Sam and Terry into membership by producing a Nazi armband: blood-red with a black swastika sewn on to a white disc, it had fallen into Eric Rogers's possession during the war. Conditions of membership required the production, on a daily basis, of an item of equal or similar interest. Terry, on his day, had brandished a cat's-eye road reflector, stolen from his father's workshop. Sam delivered an Egyptian temple token, which, according to *his* father, had come from Christ-knew-where. Terry had promised to produce the shotgun cartridge on the day Sam's appointment at the eye hospital came up.

To get to the eye hospital required a modest walk to the bus stop, a tedious bus ride into the city and then another considerable hike to reach the hospital. Then back again. Sam's mother was in no mood for nonsense. When Sam complained for the fifth time that he didn't want to go to the eye hospital, she trussed him in his duffel coat, stuffed his head inside its hood and shook the hood until his head spun. He was standing at the bus stop before the world settled down again.

Before the bus arrived, Chris Morris's souped-up MG Midget scorched past, exhaust cracking out an inordinate roar, heading in the direction of town. Thirty yards beyond the stop the Midget squealed to a halt, paused and reversed back toward them at high speed. The passenger door flipped open and Morris leaned across to offer them a death's-head smile. Fingering the steering wheel, he revved the accelerator aggressively. Connie looked doubtful.

"It's a lift," Sam said to his mother, as if the sudden appearance of the sports car was a portent requiring expert interpretation.

Sam climbed into the well behind the driver while his mother did her best to lower herself into the bucket seat with some kind of dignity. As Morris set off at speed she was pressed back into the seat, fumbling at her skirt with her knees in the air. They were halfway into town before Morris said anything.

"She's mad, you know," he declared in a very quiet, controlled voice.

"Who?" said Connie.

"She is. Completely mad. Barking. Expect she's given you all her side of the story. What women do, isn't it?" Morris slammed to a stop at a red light but only at the last moment.

"She hasn't said anything to me."

Sam sat in the back, looking from his mother's face to Morris's. The adults conducted their conversation with eyes glued to the road in front of them. The lights changed, Morris slipped into gear and Connie's knees went up in the air again.

"Anything she says is a lie. I expect you know that. You women. You know how people are."

"Yes."

"ALL RIGHT IN THE BACK THERE?" Morris suddenly bellowed at Sam, as if they were cruising at altitude in an open airplane. "ALL RIGHT?"

"Yes," Sam answered happily.

"He's all right," Morris said, his eerie, quiet voice taking over again. "He's all right." His fingers gripped the steering wheel. "At least."

"Just here would be nice," said Connie.

"Huh?"

"Drop us just here."

After they climbed out of the car, Connie gripped Sam's hand, watching the Midget zoom toward the top of the town. "Fast," said Sam. "Mr. Morris drives fast. Where's he going?"

"Straight to hell," said Connie. "Don't you push me in that car again."

Mr. Morris's lift had made them early for the hospital appointment, so Connie took Sam to the top of the town, to see the hour strike. Under the clock in Broadgate a set of doors flipped open, and a curious, mechanical Lady Godiva, following a horseshoe track, made unsteady passage. Above her head a second mechanical window revealed a wide-eyed Peeping Tom stealing a forbidden glance. Sam was more fascinated by Tom than by the wobbling naked lady. The clock struck.

"Blinded," said Connie.

"Why?"

"Looking when he shouldn't have been looking."

They made their way from Broadgate to the hospital. Sam's heart was heavy. He wondered if he too was being blinded for having seen things he should not have seen. Perhaps he was sharing Tom's punishment for having seen the Tooth Fairy.

On the way, Connie stopped at one of the surviving gates of medieval Coventry. A gargoyle leered at them from the gothic arch overhead. Its teeth were sharpened to points. Sam took Connie's hand. As they passed through the gate, he was afraid that when he emerged from the arch on the other side, the world might be irredeemably changed.

———

"Is Mickey in the cage or out of the cage? In or out?" The fat nurse was becoming irritated. She'd put this question to Sam three times, and he was finding himself unable to answer truthfully.

He didn't like the eye hospital. The waiting room was full of people with patched, plastered or bandaged eyes. Intimidating wall posters admonished people to PROTECT YOUR EYES: NO SPARES. From there he was frog-marched into a small, darkened room where he had to read an eye chart, and thence to a Stygian cavern where a fiendish, metal-mask contraption was settled on the bridge of his nose, and where he was instructed to report on the performance of tiny, winking red and green lights.

"Are they going to let me go?"

"Of course they are," Connie soothed. "Not long now."

Later he was bullied into another, lighter room, where the fat nurse pushed him into a seat before a table bearing a black box. Fat nurse pressed a switch and the black box was suddenly illuminated, presenting him with an image of Mickey Mouse and an iron cage. Fat nurse held a card at his eye.

"Is Mickey in the cage or out of the cage?"

A species of binoculars was clamped to the front of the black box. Sam was commanded to look through the binoculars. They had an evil smell, of rubber and metal. Fat nurse did something to make the left glass of the binoculars go blank.

"Is Mickey in or out?"

Sam was so afraid that his answer was, "Yes."

The nurse sighed deeply. "In or out?"

"In. Yes."

The left glass opened again. "Is Mickey in or out of the cage?"

Sam hesitated. The question presented a problem, in that Mickey was both in *and* out of the cage. He could see two Mickeys, one clearly out of the cage and a second image, slightly hazier but recognizable, inside the cage.

"I don't know."

"Either," said the fat nurse, "he's in or he's out. Is Mickey in or out?"

Sam held his breath. He knew it was crucially important not to cry. Where was his mother?

He bit his lip and waited. The nurse slammed her pen down on the table. "In or out?" she said. "For goodness' sake, in or out?"

"In."

The nurse seemed satisfied. She picked up her pen and ticked a box on her clipboard paper. She changed the glass. "Now?"

"In."

"Now?"

"In."

"That's better. Easy, isn't it?" The nurse's mood had swung dramatically. Sam secretly sighed with relief. "In" seemed to be the correct answer, the one which won everybody's approval. After a while he was allowed to go.

He was given a seat in an empty corridor and told to wait while Connie spoke with the doctor. A young nurse passed and smiled at him. The minutes passed. Someone sat on the chair next to him, but Sam, lost in his own thoughts, didn't look up.

"I feel bad about it," said the figure next to him. "I feel bad, so I've got something for you."

Sam glanced up. It was the Tooth Fairy. Sam identified the smell from his bedroom when the Tooth Fairy had visited, varied only slightly. Now it was a smell of hay and leather and horse's sweat. In the daylight the Tooth Fairy looked slightly uglier. Its squint was pronounced, and its short physique seemed tougher, like something made of wire and coiled springs. "You're a boy," said Sam.

The Tooth Fairy clicked his teeth in irritation. "You won't always see me this way. Only for now. Look, I feel bad about putting you through all this. I mean this thing with your eye. I've come to give you something."

"What? What do you mean?"

"That little friend of yours. The one with the limp."

"Terry?"

"He's marked. But listen. Saturday it is. You damn well find a way, right? You damn well find a way to keep that kid at your place, eh? Saturday night." The Tooth Fairy prodded Sam's shoulder with a hard, bony finger. "I've given you this and we're quits. I'm clean again. You sodding well make damn sure. Now I'm gone."

The Tooth Fairy got up from his chair and ambled down the hospital corridor, aggressively pushing a trolley out of his way before turning a corner out of sight. His head appeared briefly around the corner, glaring back at Sam.

"Sam! Sam! Can't you hear me when I'm talking to you?" It was his mother. She grabbed his arm and pulled him from his chair. "Let's go. You've got to have glasses."

EIGHT

Television

On Saturday, delivered in an impressively large cardboard box, the Southalls' first television set arrived. It was a momentous day all round, since it was also the day Sam was taken to the optician's to collect his prescription National Health spectacles. He would be able, everyone remarked pointedly, to watch the new television in his new glasses. The circular lenses framed by thin blue wire made his head feel large and top-heavy.

Nev Southall had consulted Clive's father Eric, who already had a set, and Eric had told him that a signal aerial erected in the attic would suffice. It would also save a fair few quid and the trouble of mounting it on the roof, Eric pointed out. The delivery man had disagreed. Tugging his earlobe and clicking his ballpoint pen, he told them they lived in a "depression" on the wrong side of the transmitting station and needed a roof-mounted aerial.

"Nothing," said Connie.

"Nothing," chimed Sam.

"What about that?" shouted his father.

"What about that?" echoed Sam.

"No good," said Connie.

"No good," called Sam.

Sam had been posted at the top of the stairs. Nev, manipulating the aerial up in the attic, couldn't hear Connie, gamely twiddling the dials of the new TV in the living room, and vice versa. Sam's job was to stand under the open loft door, relaying communications between the two of them.

"Better." Connie.

"Better." Sam.

"Gone again."

"Gone again."

To his credit, Nev endured a full quarter-hour of this before he started to lose his temper.

"What's happening down there?"

"What's happening down there?"

"No good."

"No good."

Nev's disembodied and inverted head appeared, framed in the black hole giving way to the attic. He growled. Sam thought better of repeating the growl before his father's legs swung down and dropped lightly to the top of the stairs. He could feel a slap to the ear coming on, and through no fault of his own. He remained upstairs as the dispute swelled in the living room. His father bounced up the stairs again and scrambled back into the attic, whereupon the entire process was repeated. Finally, with Sam losing interest and timing, and with the volley of his father's curses augmenting in the attic, he found himself banished from the house.

He discovered Clive at Terry's place, loitering in the doorway of Mr. Morris's workshop. Mr. Morris was in a state of agitation, hurling things into a crate. He was clearing junk associated with his inventions, counting off his failures to Clive before binning them with unnecessary force.

". . . waste of time, Clive, waste of time." Sam joined Clive at the door of the workshop as a guitar-shaped object was dashed into the crate. Morris pulled another contraption from a shelf. There was something vaguely theatrical about his behavior, as though he wanted someone to step in and stop him from doing this. "The Mechanical Butler. Another disaster. A machine for answering the telephone. No one interested." Crash. They saw a perfectly good tape recorder discarded as the Mechanical Butler was flung into the crate. Sam peered into the crate after it. Whatever it had been, in its short life, the instrument was now trashed beyond all possible repair.

Then, "Oh, yes, here's a good one: the Nightmare Interceptor. I made this one for Terry." Morris displayed an electrical clock trailing a mess of wires. Sam noticed a fleck of white spittle on Morris's chin. "He had nightmares after that pike took his toes. Still gets 'em. So I made this. See that thing? It's a thermal sensor— detects heat. When you get a nightmare, you start breathing heavily, so you fix this on—" He snapped a metal crocodile clip on Clive's nose.

"Ow!" said Clive.

"And when you start breathing heavily through your nose the sensor trips a switch which makes the alarm clock come on. So you wake up and no more nightmare. Simple, eh?"

"Does it work?" Clive wanted to know.

"Never had a nightmare while using this did you?" Mr. Morris shouted to Terry.

Terry was standing under the apple trees at a short distance, whacking the last of the fallen Bramleys over the hedge with a cricket bat. "No."

"No," Morris said bitterly. "Couldn't get to sleep with all these wires up your nose, could you?" Morris unclipped the peg from Clive's nostril and flung the device into the crate.

The failure of the Nightmare Interceptor seemed to make Morris sad. He clamped his lips together and appeared to have nothing left to say to the boys. More unfinished devices followed the others into the crate. Such a frightening degree of violence accompanied his actions that Clive and Sam drifted away to join Terry. The apples mushed by his cricket bat laid a sharp tang of cider on the air, already sharp with the decline of autumn.

"How's your television?" Terry wanted to know.

"Can't get a good picture," said Sam, bowling Terry an apple.
"Why not?"

"Because we're all depressed."

A rickety and rotting table stood under the apple tree, draped with golden leaves and laden with bruised fallers. A jamjar wasp trap rested on the table, set there by Morris. Narrow holes had been poked in the lid; eight or nine wasps crawled across the inside of the glass. Sam put his eye as near to the jar as he dared. The glass vibrated with angry activity as the wasps searched for a way out. The furious energy inside the glass seemed almost enough to crack it.

After a while Morris's large face appeared next to Sam's. The boy could smell tobacco and the rot of alcohol on the man's breath. Though Morris himself had set the wasp trap, he behaved as if he was seeing it now for the first time.

"You see," he said to Sam very quietly, "they can find a way in, but they can't find a way out."

Morris made Sam feel uneasy as he continued to stare into the jar of angry wasps. Sam peeled away. Morris covered his eyes with his hand, and Sam saw that his shoulders were shaking. Then the other boys saw it too. After a moment Morris returned to his work-shop, closing the doors behind him.

It was Terry who suggested they should go. While they waited for him to collect his coat from the caravan, Sam glanced through the dusty glass windowpanes of the garage-workshop. With his back to the doors, Morris was seated at his workdesk. His hands grasped the desk and he seemed to be staring dead ahead at the wall. But as he looked Sam saw a familiar shadow whispering to Morris. The figure, a little over four feet tall, worked its pink tongue close to Morris's ear, back and forth, back and forth.

"Hey," Terry said quietly. "Let's go."

They sat up by the pond where Terry had lost two of his toes. The boys spent many hours there, ostensibly looking for the pike without ever seeing it. Terry had a small penknife, stolen from his father's workshop. Whenever he was at the pond he opened and closed it more out of nervous habit than in any readiness for action should the pike choose to appear. After a while Clive went home. Sam hung on with Terry, knowing his friend was reluctant to return to the caravan. That day his fiddling with the penknife was more agitated than usual.

"Do you think it's still there?" Sam wanted to know.

Terry stared into the water. Luminous green duckweed stippled the dark, mirror-like surface of the water. "Getting fatter and bigger every year."

Sam saw Terry's face reflected there. Suddenly, looming out of the depths alongside Terry's reflection was another face. Familiar and frightening, squinting back at him, the pink tongue working back and forth, reminding him. Sam jumped back from the side of the pond.

"What is it?" shouted Terry.

"Tonight," Sam gasped.

"What about tonight?" Terry closed his penknife and stood up.

"Television. We've got a television."

"You told me that already."

"You've got to come and watch it. Tonight."

Terry smiled. "Great."

"No! You've got to stay over! You've got to stay at our house. You can sleep in my room."

Terry was puzzled but flattered by Sam's urgency. "My mum won't let me."

"She will. She's got to. My mum will tell her." Sam was up and running.

Terry darted a glance back at the black waters of the pond. Then he ran to catch up with Sam.

"It's practically next door," said Connie when Sam asked her if Terry could stay overnight. "Why?"

"Television!" was all Sam could think of saying.

"So, he can watch television, and then he can go home."

"No! He's got to stay. First television night!"

Connie looked at her boy. His eyes were moist, his fists were clenched. He was normally such an undemanding child. She couldn't understand why he was so insistent. Terry hung back, knowing when to stay out of an argument; Connie looked at him and was flushed with a wave of sympathy for her neighbor's son. She'd spent the afternoon baking apple pies; she'd iced cakes. Maybe it was a special day. "I'll see what Mrs. Morris has to say about it."

Nev had fixed the TV aerial, approximately. He, Connie, Sam and Terry watched the screen that Saturday evening in awed and almost spiritual silence. They watched, through a moderate blizzard dogged by a screen ghost, an early episode of *Doctor Who and the Daleks*. So astonished were they by what they'd seen, the two boys were convinced the world outside must surely be a changed place. They were also amazed that Sam's mother had the courage to venture all the way to Terry's caravan to have a word with Mrs. Morris about his staying overnight. When she returned, bearing his pyjamas and a toothbrush, the boys made joyful fists at each other.

"Cut it with a knife," Sam overheard his mother say to Nev. The boys were permitted to stay up to watch a game show and half of an incomprehensible drama before being packed off to bed. Finally they were settled, head-to-toe in Sam's bed, before the light was switched off. Muffled voices and signature tunes from the television carried to the bedroom. It was a new and comforting sound.

Sam woke at about one o'clock in the morning. The window was ajar and the room was cold. He lifted his head from the pillow. At first he thought a Dalek might have come into his room, metal gleaming, death-ray leveled at his head. Blinking back sleep, he saw it was the Tooth Fairy. Somewhere in the night, not far away, he heard two very loud bangs. He looked into the Tooth Fairy's eyes.

The Tooth Fairy was somehow diminished. His coal-black hair was wet and matted, and his face was a pale, dirty ivory. He

was shivering and hugging himself. Then there was a third bang.
And a fourth.

The Tooth Fairy nodded his head slowly at Sam. He seemed
to be crying. Then he faded.

"Terry! Terry!"

Terry woke up. His eyelashes flickered. "It's cold in here."

Sam closed the window. "Did you see him?"

"Who?"

"He was here!" Sam had never previously mentioned the
Tooth Fairy to either Terry or Clive. He was highly excited that the
fairy had made an appearance in the presence of Terry. Because
Terry *didn't* see him, it didn't mean that he *couldn't.*

They heard someone get up. The bangs had also disturbed
Sam's father. Nev put his head round the door. "Go back to sleep,
you boys."

"I heard some bangs."

"A car backfiring. Go back to sleep."

In the morning, while the boys were having their breakfast, Nev
came in and shouted for Connie. He cast a glance at Terry as Connie came hurrying down the stairs. Something in his father's eye
frightened Sam. Nev ushered Connie through to the lounge and
closed the door.

When they came out, Nev said, "Get your coat on, Terry. I'm
taking you up to your Aunt Dot's house."

"Why?"

Nev floundered for words. He looked ghastly. "Because it's a
good idea right now."

Sam went to the window. A police car had parked outside the
gateway to the cottage behind which Terry's caravan was sited. As
he watched, an ambulance arrived and turned into the yard. It was
followed by a second police car.

Connie got Terry's coat and buttoned it on for him. Her lips
clamped tight together. Sam could see her fingers trembling on

Terry's buttons. She hugged Terry before Nev took him by the hand and led him away.

"Oh, my God," said Connie after they'd gone. "Oh, my God." She was crying now. There was to be no Sunday school that morning, she told Sam. Then she hugged him and with unnecessary severity ordered him upstairs to tidy his bedroom.

NINE

The Nightmare Interceptor

It was three weeks before Sam went near the Morrises' caravan. When he finally did so, he approached it from behind, via the apron of wasteland to the rear, so that the old man who lived in the cottage wouldn't spot him. It wasn't that he was afraid of the old man, an amiable, shuffling octogenarian with whom he'd spoken many times: it was that he was ashamed of becoming a ghoul.

There had been many ghouls poking around the caravan during the first two weeks: hatchet-faced photographers from newspapers; brittle journalists who had knocked on his door; casual sightseers loitering. Sam knew they were ghouls because that's what his father had called them. They looked like ordinary people, with overcoats and polished shoes, but Sam knew that beneath the human disguise these ghouls leaked luminous gray slime from ear and nostril. He didn't want to become a ghoul, but the caravan summoned him.

It called to him.

Terry had been spirited away, by his Aunt Dot, to another aunt's house in Cromer on the east coast and hadn't yet returned. This had precipitated a debate in the Southall household about whether the right or the wrong thing had been done by Terry.

"Isn't right," Connie declared. "That boy should have been here."

"What good would it do?" Nev argued. "Why put him through more of it? Poor little sod's had enough."

"He shoulda been here to see it through. She was his mother and he was his father, whatever happened. He shoulda been at that funeral to see it, end to end. Now it'll always weigh."

"I don't know, love. I don't know."

Connie had sniffed. She knew.

The curtains at the caravan windows were drawn. By climbing on the coupling bar Sam was able to squint through a chink in one of the sets of curtains, and he could see that the interior had been scrubbed and cleared. All surfaces had been wiped clean. He jumped down from the bar. A lot of the Morrises' property still littered the yard: Terry's bike; his cricket bat propped against the apple tree, russet fallers putrefying around it; the wasp-trap jamjar, its victims shriveled to dried beads inside the glass.

The door to Morris's workshop was securely padlocked. Between the side of the garage and an adjacent privet hedge there was a twelve-inch gap. Sam squeezed into the gap, working his way to a cobwebbed window. Terry had once demonstrated to him how the entire window frame swung outward. He tested it now. Putting his eye to the glass, Sam could see that the workshop lay untouched since he'd been present on the afternoon before Morris had done the deed. It was waiting to be cleared. Presumably no one knew what to do with all the paraphernalia Morris had amassed. Sam swung the window frame open and climbed inside.

Morris's masculine smell pervaded the workshop: traces of tobacco flake, whisky or beer, hair oil and an indefinable locker-room odor Sam always associated with the gusto of Morris's mind working at speed. It was there whenever Morris was agitated or aroused, a warning discharge, a dangerous leak. It was there now.

Sam paused in the shadows, his heart hammering. The workshop was still vibrating with the shock of what had happened. He had no purpose in being there. He'd simply been propelled to get inside the workshop in order to listen to the echo of events. With the caravan locked, the garage had offered the next best thing. Sunlight filtering through the leaves outside the window cast spangled light over the floor and across Morris's desk. A tiny red mite was making an epic journey across Sam's hand. His own blood sported in his veins. Then the thumping of his heart began to level off, and he breathed.

He stood in the shadows, motionless as a gargoyle, absorbing the silence, until he felt the garage had forgiven his intrusion. No one had told him what, or how, or why, but he'd managed to absorb enough kaleidoscopic information to construct a picture. It was also easy to assemble Morris's ghost out of hair oil and tobacco odors, until the man himself sat there before Sam, laboring at his workshop desk, measuring minuscule distances with a microrule, shaking his head, muttering incomprehensibly.

The kaleidoscope slipped.

Somehow the light had changed outside. Day was night; the sun had been transmuted into a left-hand cup of moon tilted at a dread angle, and Sam knew that his own corporeal body was asleep a few houses away, sharing a bed, head-to-toe, with Terry, and that the time was out of joint.

"It won't work. It won't work," whispered Morris, laying down his microrule with exhausted finality. He pushed back his chair, got up and turned away from the desk. For a moment he seemed to see Sam staring at him. Running a mechanical hand across his hair, he looked directly through the boy.

Then Morris was gone, and the light had changed back again. The sun angled through the window, flooding the desk. Sam approached, touching the swivel chair where moments earlier Morris's ghost had been sitting. Everything was in place just as the tidy-minded inventor had left it on his final evening, jars of pens and pin-sharp pencils, pots of paintbrushes, blades and scissors.

The crate where Morris had junked his failed inventions was overspilling. Sam moved some wooden blocks and pulleys aside, shifted a set of greased, interlocking cogs and saw the discarded tape recorder, the device Morris had called the Mechanical Butler. He instinctively wanted to steal the tape machine. It was too highly conceived to abandon to some uncaring person charged with the task of clearing out Morris's shed. He considered taking it but knew there was no way he could hide it from his parents. They would find it and make him return it. His eyes fell instead on the Nightmare Interceptor, the modest electrical clock trailing wires. It was small enough to be secreted in his bedroom, he reasoned, and not likely to be considered valuable by anyone who ever found it. He reached into the box and grabbed the clock. The trailing wires snagged on something deep in the junk. He tugged again, but the wires wouldn't release.

Sam reached down into the high crate, inching his fingers along the length of the wire, trying to find the crocodile-clip-sensor he knew to be located at the cables' extremity. His footing slipped, and he felt his hand twist beneath the stacked weight of heavy metal objects. The wire looped around his wrist. He jerked his hand back and felt a sharp pain as the wire bit into his flesh.

He tugged again. His glasses came loose, and he fumbled at them with his free hand, winding the thin metal frame around his ear. He yanked his arm again, hard, his breathing coming short. He was ensnared. He realized he was stuck, with no possibility of calling for help. There was a moment when his stomach dropped away. He panicked. He couldn't pull his hand free.

Something quivered in the crate. Objects shivered and tumbled aside. Some black, unpleasantly warm, hairy thing brushed against his hand, sweeping along his arm. He wrenched back violently, wincing at the pain to his wrist, kicking out at the crate. It was useless. The black furry thing inched farther up his arm.

Even as it moved, the black thing seemed to take its shape and form from the box of objects itself. Black trailing wires resolved themselves into hair. Interlocking cogs became a face. Pieces of wood, cardboard and metal accreted to the thing as it shook itself free of the other objects in the box, until spitting and snarling, still gripping his wrist in a handcuff of wire, it was the Tooth Fairy.

"Stop kicking! Stop fucking struggling!"

The Tooth Fairy climbed out of the crate, his arms and legs for a moment assembling themselves from bits of tape recorder and metal cubes and pipes, and from pulleys and cog wheels and cardboard offcuts, until they resolved themselves into the Tooth Fairy's normal, terrifying form. His face looked dirty, greasy, angry. He shook himself, and he roared, as if in pain.

"You're hurting me," Sam whimpered.

"Hurting? Hurting?" The Tooth Fairy wound the wire tighter, pulling the boy toward him, thrusting his face in Sam's, grabbing Sam's hair. "Want to know what pisses me off?"

Sam got a full face of the Tooth Fairy's breath. It was a sweet rot, a decay like the putrefaction of apples, of moldering grass, of cabbage, of drains.

"You hear me, four-eyes? See them fucking goggles you got? They make you look dumb, boy. Ugly and dumb. A freak. Half-boy, half-frog. You want to know what pisses me off about you? You're always *looking at things*. Always looking at *things you shouldn't be looking at!* You gonna stop? You gonna stop looking at things you shoont be looking at? Gonna stop seeing things, you google-eyed fuck?"

Sam winced in pain. His hair was being ripped away at the scalp. The smell of the Tooth Fairy's breath made him faint. At last the Tooth Fairy released the wires and pushed Sam crashing back against the garage wall. Then he spat, fully. The thick gob of phlegm hung from the side of Sam's head.

"You hear what I say? You hear? Stop seeing, you little shit. You hear me?"

Sam could hardly form an answer. "Yes . . . yes."

The Tooth Fairy staggered before the workshop desk, leaning against the wall as if exhausted. He buried his head in his hands. "I've got to think this out," he muttered. "I've just got to think this through."

Sam was still holding the Nightmare Interceptor, its leads and crocodile clip trailing at his feet. He wanted to get out. The Tooth

Fairy seemed preoccupied. Sam made a break for it, swinging open the window and trying to cock a leg over the sill.

"Not so fast!" bellowed the Tooth Fairy, springing forward to grab Sam by the foot. Sam wailed and kicked. He was half in and half out of the garage. Lashing out with his leg, he caught the Tooth Fairy under the chin with his boot. The blow lacked the force to dislodge the Tooth Fairy's grip; Sam grabbed his opponent's hair and pulled hard. The Fairy swore, releasing the leg only to snatch at Sam's hand. In the struggle the window slammed back and the glass pane broke, half of it falling inside the garage.

"Remember me with this," the Tooth Fairy said, twisting Sam's arm up at the broken glass and searing it along the exposed edge. The jagged glass bit deep into flesh. Sam screamed and fell backward out of the garage. Still screaming, and still clutching the Nightmare Interceptor, he ran home, with the vile taunts of the Tooth Fairy ringing in his ears.

TEN
Vandals

"How long does it take?" Terry wanted to know.

"How long is a piece of string?" said Clive. It was a smart answer he'd picked up from one of his teachers at the new school.

"It's getting a bit sore," Sam complained.

"Just keep at it," Clive coaxed helpfully.

The pond had been infilled to half its original size and the surrounding land bulldozed to make way for a football pitch. The Heads-Looked-At Boys sat on the newly created mudbank of the reduced pond with an inarticulated sense of grievance. A yellow JCB digger with caterpillar tracks lodged in the damp clay at a prodigious angle, like a casualty of war, along with a dumper truck, both abandoned for the Saturday afternoon.

A few small perch and tench floated on the scummy surface of the water. There had been the usual speculation about the whereabouts of the pike. It was conceded that he'd still got plenty of water to swim in and that there was still time to catch him. But favorite trees had been felled, bushes had been uprooted and a sheltered, hidden bank had been collapsed into the pond. For Terry, a keen footballer struggling against some loss of balance since losing his two toes, the change to the landscape was regrettable but inevitable; footballing opportunities would open up, and in one sense the infill of the pond was a blow against the ravening pike. To Sam and Clive, however, who felt that things would never be the same again, it was an unforgivable violation.

It had been two years since the appalling Morris incident, when Terry was sent away to the east coast, and when Sam had his arm sliced by broken glass. Sam still bore the scar. When he'd returned home that day, bleeding profusely, he'd been rushed to the hospital for tetanus inoculations and deep interrogation. Everything about the Tooth Fairy had come blubbering incomprehensibly out of him, the entire history, all the early encounters and the violent grapple resulting in the slashed arm. Connie had been shocked and had discussed with doctors—within earshot of Sam—the need for him to "have his head looked at."

Connie was genuinely worried, and after three months when Sam had persisted with his monstrous stories, Connie dragged him to the local GP, who in turn arranged for Sam to see a specialist. Oddly, during this period Sam lost sight of the Tooth Fairy, except for one occasion, his birthday, when it suddenly appeared, naked, sitting on the corner of his bed, warning darkly against his saying any more to anyone.

"You start telling shrinks about us and we're in deeper shit than we already were—are. It won't help." The Tooth Fairy exuded a sweet, unpleasant, mushroom-like odor. Sam couldn't take his eyes from the creature's erect cock. Straining from the swart bush of black curls, it was unpleasantly white and marbled with prominent veins. Sam was mesmerized into wanting to touch it and yet simultaneously repulsed by the terrifying organ.

The Tooth Fairy suddenly noticed the focus of Sam's attention, and it made him swagger. Dragging a hand through his dark locks, he tilted his head to one side and narrowed his eyes. "Wanna touch it?"

"No."

The Tooth Fairy ran a moist, raspberry-colored tongue across his lips, smiling provocatively. "Go on. You know you want to."

Sam's eyes locked again on the marbled cock. In stark contrast to the white stalk of the penis, the head was damson and black-currant, almost splitting at the skin, ready to puncture.

"Want to kiss it?"

"No."

"Just a lick. One sweet lick."

"No."

"Go on. Make it pop."

"No."

"Don't know what it's for, do you?" The Tooth Fairy sneered. "Shit-scared of it, aren't you?"

Sam looked into the Tooth Fairy's eyes. For a few moments they held each other's unblinking gaze. At last the Tooth Fairy sighed, and Sam felt a critical moment had passed. The Tooth Fairy folded his arms, and the monstrous erection began to subside. "Listen while I tell you why I'm here. It's about the shrink. Find a way out, or things will take a dive. I'm warning you."

"You cut my arm."

"For which I'm deeply sorry. Things got out of hand, and you had no right to be in that place. But those shrinks are going to put a mark on you much worse than that little scratch on your arm. Believe me. I haven't lied to you yet."

Leaving out the erotic element of the encounter, Sam reported this conversation verbatim to the specialist, an imposing but hearty Caledonian with butter-colored hair and nicotine-stained fingertips. The Tooth Fairy chose that moment to make a brief appearance at the psychiatrist's window, shaking his head in dismay, an event Sam had considered it wiser to leave out of his report.

Sam stared glumly into the pond. "How long did you say this takes?"

Terry sat to his right, his right cheek muscle twitching slightly as diligently he worked away. Clive sat on his left, eyes closed, a distant expression of studied concentration molding his features. "As long as it takes," said Clive.

Terry had returned from his six weeks on the east coast looking strangely diminished and with a faint burr lodged in his accent. Some profound change had taken place in the boy, which Sam and Clive could detect but not identify. Often in moments of laughter Terry would seem to "catch" himself and would be overtaken by a strange, self-conscious fluttering of the eyelashes, after which his eyebrows would knit fiercely, as if he were persecuted by a brief but intense migraine. These flashing visits of *petit mal* would cause his pals to look away in embarrassment; though they sensed their origins, both the cause and the condition were off-limits for discussion, even for boys who would normally ruthlessly attack any weakness in the scramble for advantage known as growing up. No one ever told Clive and Sam that what happened to Terry's parents was a taboo subject. They understood that the matter was not open for debate in the same way in which you understand your friend's eyes are not for gouging nor his belly for disemboweling.

The arrangement for Terry to stay with his Aunt Dot and cousin Linda was put on an apparently permanent basis, though the other two boys never questioned Terry about this either. Meanwhile Terry had brought back from the east coast a new harvest of nightmares. The old bad dreams had been replaced by new ones, and the new ones were bad enough to precipitate his own crisis. Night after night, he awoke screaming, inconsolable, terrified, until he too was taken to his local GP, who bounced him in turn into the consulting room of a specialist. Terry too was having his head looked at, and it was a matter of considerable joy to the two boys to find out that their heads were being looked at by the very same Aran-sweatered, nicotine-sallowed psychiatrist, Skelton.

And then Clive too had to have his head looked at, but for different reasons and by a different specialist. Clive's abilities as a "gifted child" proved to be more and more disruptive in the classroom. Teachers did not take kindly either to being corrected or to having their arguments amplified. Clive was examined, tested, interviewed and tested again. His reward for demonstrating exceptional intelligence was to be taken away from his dearest friends and placed in a special school, run, it was said, by more specialists.

It was Clive who had come up with the new group name. Both Terry's Aunt Dot and Sam's mother had separately advised them, in lowered tones, not to mention to anyone about seeing specialists. Clive, however, made it a badge of honor. "We've all had our heads looked at. We're the Heads-Looked-At Boys."

And they were.

"Goons! They're all freaks and goons!" Clive had protested after his first week at the Epstein Foundation for Gifted Children. He was truly appalled. If this was what it meant to be gifted, he understood instantly that there was neither honor nor pride in it. "Freaks and goons! They've all got glasses and—sorry, Sam, not like yours, I mean thick glass like at the bottom of a pop bottle and some of 'em even have brown lenses in their glasses—and long fingers, I've noticed they've all got fingers probably nine inches long. Then there's this kid called Frank, who's ten years old with a beard, honest."

This bearded Frank had told Clive about wanking, and Clive had immediately passed on the information to the other Heads-Looked-At Boys, a gift from the school of gifted children.

"Mine's starting to feel a bit sore," Sam complained.

"And mine," said Terry. His right cheek muscle continued to flex, as if attached by some mysterious ligament to the cock he was busily stroking. Clive, meanwhile, continued to pump at his own cock while mentally engaged in some esoteric form of astral travel.

"And it's gone a purplish-reddish color."

"Mine's more pinkish-brownish."

Without missing a stroke, Clive opened his eyes and said, "Frank says if you keep at it long enough, then this white spunk squirts three feet in the air, and it absolutely kills you and—"

"If it kills you, what's the point?" Terry asked, reasonably.

"Not kills you, that is, it doesn't *kill* you, but it kills you in a way that feels incredible, Frank says."

"I'm not sure about this Frank. He sounds like a—"

Sam's words were cut off when they heard a rustle in the grass behind them. "What are you doing?" said a girl's voice. The three boys toppled forward, squirming on the ground at the pond's edge, stuffing themselves back in their trousers, clutching at their midriffs.

It was Lanky Linda, or rather Moody Linda; less lanky now that, approaching fourteen, she was filling out her height but increasingly disposed toward moodiness. Terry kept up a running report on her moods for the other two, plus a steady commentary on her bra size, underwear and sanitary towels.

Linda had become a *teenager*. It was a word which all the adults around seemed, when uttering it, to underline. There was a frisson, exasperation and a note of distaste in the word. A *teenager*. Something clearly happened to you when you became a *teenager*. You carried this word like a hump on your back; it was a mark of infamy. "Now that she's a *teenager* . . ." they would say, as if what they really meant was "Now that she's a vampire . . ." or "Now that she's a werewolf . . ."

And the white gloves had been discarded in favor of miniskirts, and patent-leather shoes, and American-tan tights, and belts with huge buckles; and her sleek, black hair was styled in a Jean Shrimpton cut that had literally made her father weep. There were also reports from Terry of boyfriends, potential or otherwise, hovering in the background. Names were named, and the thought of Linda necking with these people left the boys uncertain whether to giggle or puke. And now here Linda was, her face made up to an astonishing wax finish, her eyelids painted marine-blue, her lips a peelable, cherry-pink gloss, demanding to know what they were doing, the query put in a way which answers itself, the tone betraying that the poser of the question can see the answer perfectly well, and would rather not, but feels compelled to say something, anything to mask an evident surprise. Linda's dog Titch, a whippet-cross, stood with its head on one side, as if it too was looking for sensible answers to reasonable questions.

"Having a pee," Clive said quickly, scrambling to his feet.

"Having a pee sitting down?" For one horrible moment it seemed that Linda was going to insist on debating the point. Sam got up and affected to be fascinated by the high-pressure valve on one of the wheels of the dumper truck. Clive and Terry turned away, cheeks flaming. Mercifully, Linda changed the subject by addressing Terry. "Dad says he wants you to come and wheelbarrow some sand."

Terry's Uncle Charlie was building an extension to their house, chiefly to give Terry a room of his own since he currently shared with Linda's two younger brothers. "I'll be along in a minute." He couldn't look his cousin in the eye.

Linda surveyed the ploughed field and the partially in-filled pond. "Shame," she said. "Shame they did this." Then she turned and walked back the way she came.

The boys were silent for a minute or two. Clive sniggered. Sam, fiddling with the valve on the dumper wheel, snorted too. Then came a mighty blast of pressurized air from the valve as it opened, spraying a fan of white foam at Sam's face. The other two boys shouted and cheered at the sudden release of pressure. Clive picked up a rock and tossed it at the cab window of the JCB, webbing the thick glass. Terry found an old newspaper in the cab. He stuffed it under the driver's seat, took a box of matches from his pocket and ignited the paper.

"Let's help Terry move that sand," said Clive.

They sprinted home.

ELEVEN
In the Saddle

After the eleven-plus they transferred their attentions from the football-club changing rooms to the gymkhana pavilion. Over the past two years they'd poked out the football club's windows on a regular basis, gouged holes in the door, committed the offense of breaking and entering in order to scribble on the nude pin-ups tacked to the walls and wrecked the internal plumbing of the showers.

Perhaps it was the eleven-plus itself that provoked this change in policy. Sam and Terry had sat the exam side by side. "If you pass, you go to Thomas Aquinas Grammar School," Terry reasoned, "which has a shit football team. Fail, and you go to Redstone Secondary, which cleaned up the A, B and C leagues last season."

Sam found a question which asked them to *Describe a recent holiday you have taken with your family*. Before setting out to answer it, he looked over at his friend. Terry had laid down his pen and his eyelashes fluttered furiously. Sam passed, Terry failed. Clive, having breezed the eleven-plus exam when he was only seven, had no need to sit it again. He was to stay on at the Epstein Foundation.

"With the geeks and the freaks," he said, staring grimly into the pond. They sat with their backs to the football pitch. The football club kept in readiness a net on a long pole for hooking the ball out of the water.

"So that's it then," Terry said. "I'm thick, so I go to Redstone. You're bright, so you go to Epstein, and Sam's—"

"Mediocre," said Clive, "so he goes to grammar school."

"Fuck off, Epstein egghead," said Sam.

"You fuck off."

"You fuck off."

"Let's leave the football buildings," Terry broke into the gay banter, "and give the gymkhana pavilion some hammer instead."

"Why?"

Terry rubbed his chin judiciously. Now that it was settled he was going to Redstone Secondary, he was aware that one or two of the senior boys played for Redstone Football Club, and that one day he might too. "Football is for ordinary folk. Gymkhana is for the snotty bastards. We play football."

"I don't play fucking football," Clive objected. "You two play fucking football, but I don't."

"No," Terry agreed. "You play three-dimensional chess while composing music along with boys from another planet. Fucking egghead."

"Fuck off."

"You fuck off."

"You fuck off."

"Fair enough," said Sam. "We move on to gymkhana."

"So your reasons are proto-political," said Clive.

"Fuck off."

"You fuck off."

"You're outvoted," said Terry. "It's decided."

"Who said this is a democracy? It isn't. Heard of intelocracy?"

"?"

"Government by the brains," Clive continued. "I get three votes. Sam gets two votes. Terry, with his school for turnip-toppers, gets one vote."

"Have you heard of punch-in-the-mouth-ocracy?"

"Fuck off."

"You fuck off."

"You fuck off."

But power in this group, true power, rested in the hands of the one who had the stamina to say, "Fuck off" more times and more vigorously than the next man. Clive, who didn't give a hoot whether they wrecked the football rooms or the gymkhana pavilion, surrendered early to the new political order.

The sun made intermittent stabs between wind-chased clouds. The gymkhana ring was just two fields away. They ducked under the barbed wire dividing the fields, crossing between the crimson and white and black and white painted poles of the show jumps. Stepping around the ramshackle wooden toilets, they paused to squint through knotholes large enough, it was remarked, to watch women taking a piss if the opportunity arose. Beyond that was the large timber pavilion, with its stainless-steel tea urn and storage area to the rear. The pavilion backed on to marshy, soot-colored ancient woods, a close-knit copse breathing odors of fungus and decomposed leaf into the Saturday afternoon sky.

"And a big hand for Abigail," cheered Clive as they passed the empty commentary box, before drawing abreast of the pavilion.

Forcing an entry was easy. Terry, standing on Sam's shoulders, broke a pane of glass and reached in to release a small horizontally opening window. Scrambling inside, he opened a larger window at the side of the pavilion, through which the other two followed. Working on a scale of one to five, they had just agreed on some level-two vandalism before a Land-Rover sped through the open gate at the uppermost corner of the field. The vehicle revved its engine through the mud and bumped across the grass toward the pavilion.

The boys froze. Then thawed, and there was an ecstatic scurrying as they buried themselves under the painted poles and simulated brick-blocks at the back of the storage area. They scrambled into holes only rats could have found. The dust was still settling when the padlocked door was rattled from the other side. A heavy bolt shot back, and they heard a man's deep voice. Sam's range of vision was restricted to a pair of muddy green wellingtons and the knees of corduroy trousers, followed by a pair of slender legs in jodhpurs and riding boots. A pile of sticks tied with cloth pennants tumbled to the ground. The two pairs of legs went out again but returned in the space of a few heartbeats. A pile of plastic hoops clattered to the floor. Sam's glasses were hanging off his head, suspended by one ear.

"Hello," said the man's voice. "What's this, then? I see it. They've broken the swining window."

"Did they get in?" said a girl's voice.

"Look at that! Little swines! Wish I could catch 'em. I'd make 'em into pulp! I would! Make 'em into pulp!"

There was the sound of the entry window being bumped shut. Then the heavy wellingtons trooped out again, and there was a manly shout from outside. The jodhpurs and boots trotted after the wellingtons. Then the riding boots came back in again, and the jodhpurs kneeled on the ground as a pile of numbered armbands with string-ties slithered to the floor. A girl not much older than Sam collected the armbands and shuffled them into a neat pile. She was wearing a baggy woolen jumper, threadbare at both elbows. Her long, dark hair was tied behind her head. She looked up and her slate-blue eyes locked with Sam's.

Sam was wedged behind a pole painted with black and white hoops. He knew that only the band of his eyes was visible. If he blinked, she would recognize what she was seeing, and if he closed his eyes he would give them all away. He tried to make himself black and white, to conjure a badger's stripes across his face, feel himself as a piece of painted wood. The Tooth Fairy, he knew, could have accomplished such a trick. Still on her knees, the girl continued to stare back at him. In her eyes he identified both confusion and recognition. Sam felt an insect, perhaps a wood louse or a spider, crawl inside his collar and down his back.

The driver of the Land-Rover sounded his horn. The girl scrambled to her feet and went out. The bolt shot in its cradle, and the sound was followed by the rattle of hasp and padlock. Then the Land-Rover moved off, the sound of its engine diminishing slowly.

"Could be a trap," Sam warned the others in a low whisper.

Five breathless, heart-stopped, insect-crawled minutes passed before Sam exploded from his bolt-hole, snorting dust, scattering poles and tearing off his shirt.

"Close," said Terry, emerging from the pile, face streaked with pitch.

"Too close," said Clive, escaping from a crate. Sam was still twisting and clawing at his bare back. "At least they didn't see us."

The next day they returned to the scene of their almost-crime to pour scorn on the gymkhana. They had to pass the Sunday school on their way. Mr. Phillips was just emerging from the gate, looking rather pleased with himself. "Hello! Haven't seen you chaps in a good while!" The boys' answer was to smirk and to avoid eye contact as they passed. Each of them sensed Mr. Phillips watching their necks a good way up the road.

It was a dry, blustery day, and the early-morning rain had not discouraged the fifty or sixty pony-riders who'd spread their horse-boxes and towing vehicles around the gymkhana ring like pioneers of the Western prairie. Some kind of game was in progress, involving the pennanted sticks Sam had seen, from his hiding place, dumped on the pavilion floor.

Most of the pony-riders were either younger than the boys or in their early teens. Terry thought it was hilarious to go from cluster to cluster of the girl riders asking for a fictitious Abigail.

"Excuse me, have you seen Abigail?" Very polite.

"No," they would reply, already looking suspicious, twitching their reins. "Abigail who?"

"Well, if you see Abigail, could you tell her not, under any circumstances, to use the toilets over there?"

"STAND!" they would bark at their nervous ponies. "Stand! Why?"

"It's just that there are some boys going round looking through the holes in the wood when people are using the toilets. I think she ought to know—I mean, it's not very nice, is it?—so I'd be grateful if you'd tell her. Thanks very much."

The girls would flick a glance at the toilets and then look back at Terry as he walked away, and he would sense—rather, he would *know*—that the girls would be calculating when they last used the toilets or when they would next need to. Although the novelty of this exercise quickly wore off for Sam and Clive, Terry could have cheerfully continued the game all afternoon.

They bought lemonade from the refreshments counter inside the pavilion. "You've got a broken window," Clive observed to the lady engaged in serving.

"Vandals," she said, opening the till.

"I wish I could get 'em," said a red-faced man with a cloth cap and green wellington boots. Purple veins in his cheeks seemed set to explode. "I'd make 'em into pulp."

"It's so senseless," Clive pointed out, accepting his change.

"They must be sick," Sam added.

They slurped their lemonade and watched the competitors without interest. The commentator's disembodied voice requested a big hand for Lucinda on Shandy. Terry left them to go to the toilet. While pissing he glanced up and saw an eye looking at him through a knothole. The eye disappeared, to be replaced by another one.

When he came out two girls in jodhpurs, holding their riding hats in their hands, were giggling at him. "Fucking perverts," he growled.

He found the other two standing near a practice jump, hoping to see someone fall off. Ponies cantered up in regular order to leap the bales of straw. Terry was about to tell them about the giggling girls when he heard pounding hooves accelerating behind them. "Out of the way!" a rider screamed. The boys scattered as a horse twice the size of most of the ponies galloped between them and cleared the practice jump by at least three feet. The rider reined in the horse, turned it in a circle and walked it back toward them.

It was a girl. She wore cream-colored jodhpurs and a tweed

hacking jacket. Her long, dark hair was stuffed into a net under her peaked riding hat. Her cheeks were flushed, her eyes blazed.

"Could have killed us!" bellowed Clive.

"Then *don't* stand in the *middle* of the practice ring, *stupid!*"

The horse loomed overhead. She sat six feet above them, twisting in her saddle, struggling to restrain the excited, wall-eyed animal. Sam recognized the girl with whom he had locked eyes when he was hiding in the pavilion. He instinctively took off his glasses, and then put them back on again. "Just watch where you're going."

"You stay there if you're *dumb* enough to want to get *trampled.*" She spurred on the horse with the heels of her gleaming black riding boots, and the boys had to part a second time to get out of her way.

"Bitch," shouted one of the boys, but she was already cantering away.

"Slut!"

"Tart!"

"Slag!"

They were silent, gazing after her as she disappeared inside the competition ring.

"She's fucking gorgeous," breathed Sam.

"Yeah," Terry agreed, still in awe.

"Yes," said Clive, doubtfully.

TWELVE
Gun

"How long have I been seeing you now?" Skelton made a cursory flick through the file in his hands.

Sam shrugged. He wasn't certain if it was three years or four. Terry had stopped seeing Skelton after the first year, when his nightmares began to subside. Sam, however, had taken Clive's advice.

Indeed, Sam had never objected at all to having his head looked at. It meant, after you'd endured an hour answering pointless questions and drawing pictures for the nicotine-stained psychiatrist, a respite from school. When Terry had been "cured," thereby losing his bonus holiday, Clive had advised Sam how to secure a day off school indefinitely. "Next time he asks you, draw a picture of your own gravestone."

So Sam had done just that. After the usual round of tedious and baffling questions about his mother and father, Skelton had given him a pencil and a large sheet of cartridge paper, instructing him to draw a scene "with water." Sam had hastily scribbled a picture of a pond surrounded by trees, under which was beautifully rendered a Celtic-cross gravestone, shadowed with lush moss and tangled with ivy. His name was engraved in the stone.

SAMUEL SOUTHALL

REST IN PEACE

GNAWED TO DEATH BY A TOOTH FAIRY

For good measure, Sam had included a bat swooping toward the headstone and a skull pierced by a dagger resting alongside the grave mound. Skelton had taken the sheet of paper and studied it closely. "Good," he'd said in a disturbingly quiet voice, "good, very good." Then he'd made extensive notes as Sam sat playing with his thumbs. Appointments had quickened in frequency after that offering and had then thinned out to one meeting every twelve weeks over the last three years. With Skelton now flicking through the manila folder and asking him how long it had been, Sam wondered if it was time to sketch another gothic picture.

Placing the folder flat on the large, polished oak desk, Skelton came from behind it to plump heavily in the armchair next to Sam. Crossing his legs, he placed his fingertips together, prayer-like, under his chin. He exuded stale tobacco. "Are we still seeing the Tooth Fairy?"

Sam croaked an answer. He had to say it again. "Yes."

"How often?" Skelton's answer was met with a shrug. The Scotsman thrust out his jaw, exposing the yellowing, stone tablets of his own lower teeth. He seemed barely to have enough room in his mouth for them. "Often, occasionally or rarely?"

"Occasionally."

"And does he still instruct you not to tell me about him?"

"Yes."

"Always?"

"Yes."

Skelton tilted his head radically to one side, fluttering his eyes closed, as if listening to faraway music. Suddenly he jerked upright. "What?"

"I didn't say anything," Sam insisted, pushing his glasses up the bridge of his nose.

"Quite. I think it's time we said goodbye to this Tooth Fairy, don't you?" Sam shrugged another answer. Skelton mimicked with a return shrug. "Yes, farewell to the *spiritus dentatus,* methinks, Godspeed, safe journey, *bon voyage,* mind how ye go, be on yer way, old chap, only goodbye. What say you? Hmmm?"

Sam looked at his shoelaces.

Skelton reached behind him and snatched a pencil from a pot on the table. He held it up for Sam to see. "Look at this, laddie." The pencil had been sharpened to a needle point. Skelton held the pencil aloft, carefully displaying it as though about to perform some conjuring trick. Suddenly he snapped it into two pieces, a clean break. He looked deep into Sam's eyes.

Sam looked back, trying to match Skelton for deepness. It had been a perfectly good pencil.

"See that?" said the psychiatrist. "Easy." He reached over and plucked another from the pot. "Can you do it?" He presented the pencil to the boy with both hands, proffering it as if it were Excalibur.

Sam snapped the pencil in two and handed it back.

Skelton accepted the broken pencil. "Yes, yes, yes, and farewell to the Tooth Fairy. Don't you agree? We've had enough of him. There are important changes going on in your life. Changes, Sam. Things you don't even know about. Hormones, good God. No room for this Tooth Fairy. We've got to make space for other things. What other things? I hear you ask. Well, girls, life, beer and skittles. Understand me?"

Sam nodded briefly. Skelton placed the broken bits of pencil on his desk. "Suppose I freely give you a gun. Here it is. Take it." The psychiatrist held out an empty hand. "Go on, lad, take it, don't be afraid. It won't go off in your hand. Take it!"

Sam held out his hand, and Skelton clapped it with the leathery palm of his own in an aggressive handshake. "Good. Feel its weight, that's it. Aim it, go on. NO! NOT AT ME! That's better, point it over there. That thing is loaded with a silver bullet, which is what you need for dispatching Tooth Fairies and the like. Right, so you know what to do next time this wretched Tooth Fairy appears. You know what to do, yes?"

"What?"

Skelton pointed another imaginary gun at the door and fired off a round. "You kill him, laddie. You kill him."

Sam looked at the door and then back at Skelton.

Skelton blew smoke from the barrel of his own imaginary gun and offered an evil, conspiratorial smile.

Since Clive had demonstrated the art of masturbation by the pond, Sam developed an easy facility for the habit in the privacy of his bed. His imagination, he discovered, offered considerable aid and encouragement to the practice. Female volunteers were numerous. Actresses were easily persuaded to step forward from the TV screen, their enthusiasm matched by one or two of the prettier female teachers at Thomas Aquinas Grammar, and indeed some of the older girls seen around the school were equally pliant. He did make the occasional concession to the girls who were his immediate contemporaries, in that he would stand on a table before a small, energized crowd of them and masturbate for their enjoyment and edification; they in turn would gaze back in awed fascination and amusement, daring each other to touch the object of interest. It was during the performance of these fantasies that he could achieve the unspeakably satisfying throb Clive had earlier described. But it was a dry throb and not at all the fountain to which Clive had attested.

Then one night *it* came.

Sam was asleep and dreaming. He was hiding in the gymkhana pavilion. The doors of the pavilion had been blasted away by a bomb, and the girl in jodhpurs and riding boots was searching for him. Outside the pavilion a huge white horse grazed noisily. Beyond the horse he could see the woods and the pond, gleaming in a yellow light, all strangely out of proportion. The girl spotted him through the chink between the crossed poles of his hiding place, and their eyes locked. She put a hand to her mouth, backing away slowly, reaching for the reins of the grazing horse. Mounting the horse, she kicked it on. At first the animal resisted, until finally she urged it inside the pavilion. Suddenly the horse jumped, its forelegs stretching toward him. Miraculously it passed through the three-inch gap into his hiding place.

And he was awake, back in his own bed; but the horse had completed its jump through the open window of his bedroom. Still on its back, the girl rider steadied the horse before slipping down from the saddle, shimmying slightly to advertise the sword-like slimness of her thighs in her tight, tight jodhpurs. She took off her riding hat, swishing her long, dark hair like a horse's tail as it fell free. Only then did Sam become aware that his own hand was grasping his swollen cock in a vise-like grip. Fire scourged his bowels, and there was a lazy tickling in his testicles. Something ominous was about to happen.

"This is a dream," he told himself.

Then he woke up, and the girl and the horse were gone. His window was open to the night air. Someone was watching him at the foot of the bed. The Tooth Fairy, after a long absence, was back.

Sam was astonished at how the Tooth Fairy had changed. The outfit was almost the same, with mustard and green striped tights and heavy boots. But the face was completely remodeled. It was less heavy; the features were finer, the eyes softer. And when the Tooth Fairy smiled at him, the teeth, although still filed to sharp points, were whiter and smaller. The Tooth Fairy had grown taller and yet had lost weight, exhibiting a trim, lithe frame except around the hips and the buttocks, which had plumped considerably. And even as he looked, Sam saw the unmistakable paired cupolas straining under the tight-fitting black tunic.

"You're a . . ."

The Tooth Fairy's long eyelashes blinked at him. "I'm a what?"

"I mean you're . . . but I thought you were a . . ."

"Talk sense or don't talk at all." The voice hadn't got any higher, but it was now a purr instead of a growl.

"You're a girl!"

The smile vanished from the Tooth Fairy's face. "I swear I'm going to kill you one day for the things you say."

"But I always thought—"

"Stop! Don't say another word!"

"It's just that—"

This time the Tooth Fairy stepped up to him and placed her fingers against his mouth. "You can be so hurtful, Sam. So hurtful." She sat down on the side of the bed, crossing her legs, her nylon tights hissing as one leg brushed another. Sam smelled a new perfume on her fingertips. It was a fragrance he associated with the moist earth at springtime, with woodland bluebells; and there was another, more ambiguous, marine odor.

The Tooth Fairy took her hand from his mouth and looked at him hard, her dark eyes squinting slightly. She quickly removed her tunic, letting her full breasts fall free. Sam looked at the dark buds of her nipples and the surrounding bruise-colored aureoles. The question was settled beyond dispute. One breast was slightly smaller than the other, and the strange new scent streamed from her body. His breath came shorter. It was the closest the Tooth Fairy had ever been, and he was simultaneously attracted and repelled by her physicality. She was grotesquely beautiful.

"You've got something I want," she said.

His mouth dried.

"Yes," she said. "Something Skelton gave to you. I can't tell you how important it is that you give it to me."

"Skelton?" He remembered the imaginary gun.

"That old bastard knows nothing. Believe me, I know everything you two say to each other. I have to have it, Sam. I have to have it." She was almost pleading with him. "Give it to me."

"You're too dangerous."

"Anything I've ever done to you, I didn't mean it, Sam. It's just the way it works out sometimes."

"I haven't got it. Skelton just gave me an imaginary—"

"You're hiding it under the bedclothes, Sam."

"I'm not."

"Let me see. I'm going to have a look."

Sam was paralyzed as she slowly peeled back the bedclothes. She leaned closer so she could see in the dark, and that mysterious new scent broke like a soft wave, a cloying musk, an admixture of tidal odors, marsh gas, mushrooms dipped in honey, an intoxicating smell of corruption and inspiration commingled. He thought he would faint.

"My God," she said, peering at the swollen penis still gripped in his fist. "My God. So that time has come."

Sam cringed with terror and humiliation, but his cock responded to the threat of her proximity by engorging still further inside his closed fist. He could feel her breath condensing on his face. Still gazing at his cock with fascination, she extended her little finger toward it. Sam tried to shrink back from the long, manicured, polished fingernail. His breath came shorter, and still shorter, as contact between her fingernail and his cock seemed imminent.

Did she touch? Did the outstretched fingernail make contact? He never knew. The moment was blotted out by a booming thunderclap of the heart. Some exquisitely fine elasticity linking brain and bowel snapped and a canal opened, flooding like the slow-fast, fast-slow lava flow of some primeval subterranean pool, pumping from the agonized cock still squeezed in his fist. The explosion blew the Tooth Fairy clean out of the window, shattering the glass and the window frame together. There was a long, aching moment of void, before a spiced wind rushed to fill the vacuum, reassembling the window frame and all the glass, fragment by fragment, like a film playing backward but without the Tooth Fairy.

Sam lay in the dark, feeling in his hand the hot sting of his first seed. Slowly his breath came back to him. He lifted his hand to the pencil-beam of moonlight stealing through the crack in the curtains. It glowed dully, silvery. He blew gently on his hand to cool his fingers.

THIRTEEN
Incrimination

"I didn't do it!" Sam swore. He was close to tears. "It wasn't us."

"Because if I thought you had done it . . ." Nev Southall fingered his belt buckle to show Sam what to expect. Saturday morning's ritual bacon, eggs and black pudding had been spoiled. The greasy odor of smoked rashers turned cold in the frying pan hung in the air.

"Bringing the police to the door!" Connie's voice was shrill.

"It wasn't us!" Sam repeated for the ninth or tenth time.

Meanwhile a similar scene was taking place at Terry's house. Moody Linda was washing up at the kitchen sink while her mother and father gave her adopted cousin a grilling.

"I swear it wasn't us," Terry said, saucer-eyed with innocence. "I swear it."

"Because I'd knock you through that bloody wall if you did." Uncle Charlie wasn't fooling.

"I didn't! We didn't!"

Moody Linda, growing more beautiful by the day, turned from the washing-up and stunned Terry by saying, "It couldn't have been Terry, Clive or Sam, because all three of them were here with me that afternoon."

Terry's Aunt Dot turned and looked at her with astonishment. "Well, why didn't you say that? Why didn't you speak up when the police were here?"

The twice-played scene was ready to be repeated at the Rogers household. Betty answered the door to two bookend police detectives, both with darts-player physiques. "Mornin'," one said cheerfully, bringing in the milk and newspapers. Eric had yesterday's *Sporting Life* spread across the breakfast table. He paused in the act of marking form with a ballpoint pen.

The two police officers accepted chairs at the kitchen table, but passed up the offer of a mug of tea. "Just had a brew at Mr. and Mrs. Southall's. Lovely cup, eh, Jim?"

"Lovely cup."

Five minutes later Eric planted himself at the foot of the stairs and bawled up at Clive. "Get dressed and get down here, NOW!"

Clive appeared, hair a-quiff, rubbing sleep from his eyes. He blinked at the two strangers staring at him and looked back at his father with a quizzical expression.

"You little sod!" Eric threatened a backhand.

Clive ducked. "What? What?"

Betty, recognizing that Eric was likely to hang their son in the morning before trying him in the afternoon, intervened. "Where were you Sunday afternoon? What were you doing?"

"Just dossing about," Clive protested.

"Dossin' about? Dossin' about?" Certain of Clive's teenage expressions were guaranteed to pitch Eric into a frenzy, and this was one of them. "I don't want to hear dossin' a-bloody-bout! I want to know where you were, who you were with and what you were doing. Now, I want an answer!"

Clive squinted at the two detectives. They were saying nothing. Both sat back on their chairs, heads tilted slightly to one side, looking at him from beneath eyebrows cocked high and ready to disbelieve his every word. He struggled to remember. "I was with Sam and Terry."

"And?"

"We were just . . ." He was about to say "dossing around" but he changed his mind. "We were here. Then we were at Terry's. I don't remember . . . it was raining."

"Did you go up the gymkhana field?"

"Not last Sunday, no. There was no gymkhana last Sunday."

"No," said Eric. "And some little bastards smashed the gymkhana hut to smithereens, didn't they? Smashed it all up. Broke all the equipment. Burned the jumps. Wrecked all the canteen crockery and poked out every single window in the place. Twenty-six windows."

"Twenty-eight," corrected one of the officers helpfully.

"It wasn't us!" shouted Clive.

"You were SEEN!" Eric jabbed a finger dangerously near Clive's face. "Your names were given to the POLICE!"

"Who did? Who gave our names? It wasn't US! It wasn't!"

And so the scene which began at Sam's house and was repeated at Terry's was replicated exactly at Clive's. The policemen said almost nothing, surrendering it all to the boys' parents. Whether the boys had actually been spotted *in flagrante* in the act of vandalism or whether general inquiries had simply turned up their names was never clarified. Perhaps they had no hard evidence, or conceivably all they wanted to do was to scare the boys into yielding still further information. Whatever their strategy, they remained quiet spectators and then simply withdrew at an appropriate moment, in each case leaving the boys to a further hour on the parental griddle.

"The thing that gets me," Terry said later as the three made their way together up to the pond, "is that after a while I started to think that we *had* done it."

"Me too."

"And me."

There was a long pause before Sam said, "We didn't do it, did we?"

Terry and Clive stopped dead and looked at him. "Don't be stupid. What do you mean?"

"Of course we didn't do it. Not unless you did it on your own."

"No," said Sam. "What I meant was: is there a way we might have done it without knowing we did it?"

Terry walked on in disgust. "Somebody look at his head."

"Yeah," said Clive, "somebody look at his head."

"So who did do it?" Sam wanted to know.

"Good question."

"Shall we go to the gymkhana field and take a look?" Clive suggested.

"That's fucking stupid," Terry spat. "That's what they mean by returning to the scene of the crime."

"But we're not!" Clive defended. "That's exactly it. We didn't do it! So how can we be returning to the scene of the crime, since we weren't there in the first place?"

"I know that. You know that. We all know that. But *they* think we did it. So to *them* we'll be returning to the scene of the crime."

"But that's the point! If you think like that, then you're playing their game. They want us to stay away, knowing we wouldn't return to the scene of the crime. It's like a double-bluff. Inside another double-bluff."

"Oh, fuck off," said Terry.

"You don't get it, do you?" Clive was puce in the face. "We didn't do it, but we may as well have done. It's all about who decides what really happens. Or what happened. Even if something altogether different happened."

"Oh, fuck off."

"You fuck off."

"No, you fuck off."

"Why don't you both fuck off?" said Sam.

"What I want to know," Terry said, "is who gave our names to the police?"

A horse rider, smart in white jodhpurs, tweed hacking jacket and peaked riding hat, approached on a skewbald mare. The rider advanced at a trot, passing by with her nose in the air. The boys recognized her as the girl from the gymkhana field. Sam also identified her from the day they hid in the pavilion—and from his dream. They watched her cross the road. She swung in her saddle to open a field gate and cantered across a buttercup meadow toward the woods.

"Me too," said Sam.

FOURTEEN
Tenderfoots

Connie, Betty and Terry's Aunt Dot put their heads together, as they had done over the matter of Sunday school some years ago, and came up with an idea. To be accurate, it was Moody Linda who came up with the idea when Aunt Dot privately expressed dismay over Terry's alleged delinquency. Although the charge of smashing up the gymkhana pavilion had never been proved, the arrival at the door of the local police was incrimination enough.

"Our Terry's going off the rails. Off the rails."

Moody Linda stood before her bedroom mirror, adjusting a pristine white lanyard. Her royal-blue skirt and blouse were starched and ironed to such crisp perfection that her patrol leader's badge and stripes were hardly necessary to signal authority. "Scouts," she said, tugging her beret at an efficient angle.

Dot placed her hands together. "Hadn't thought of that. Wednesdays, isn't it? And you'd be there to keep an eye on them."

Linda closed her eyes, shuddering at the thought of what she'd just done. Pride of the Coventry Forty-fifths, troopleader and processional flag bearer, Linda had made dizzying progress in her three years as a Guide. It was for her a private and perfect world, insulated from the tangles and disorders of the home front, a painstakingly regimented, well-drilled environment where neatly pressed uniforms and snow-white lanyards garnered respect, loyalty and appreciation.

There was only one minor flaw to a perfect evening spent in the sisterly company of the Forty-fifths, and that was the occasional childish behavior of the Coventry Thirty-ninth Scout troop, who convened their meetings on the same evenings, and at the same school, and who considered it amusing to spend half the evening banging on the door or knocking on the windows before running away, so that there was never anyone there when you answered, and who, if you tried to ignore them altogether, would resort to more extreme methods of distraction, like lowering their trousers and pressing their bottoms against the glass window. It occurred to Linda, as she tugged at her beret, that she had possibly just recruited Terry, Sam and Clive into the ranks of her persecutors.

"No," she said, fumbling with her silver whistle, "on second thought, I don't think they'd like it."

"I don't know," said Dot. "I think they'd get a lot out of it."

Which is how Moody Linda, just turned sixteen and resplendent in her blue uniform, came to be walking seven paces ahead of three twelve-year-old boys mobbed up in a collection of secondhand Scout uniforms Connie had rummaged from the neighborhood. Sam's shorts were too long; Clive's shorts were too short; and Terry's shirt could once have fitted the fattest Boy Scout in Coventry. Only a little pressure had had to be applied to get them to go along. Sam's instincts in particular had resisted, but now, as they stepped smartly to keep up with Linda's brisk stride, they paced out like three conscripts cheerfully resigned to circumstance.

Inside the school gates Linda did a military right-wheel, airily waving them away in the opposite direction. Across the playground they could see a small knot of Scouts gathered under the gymnasium wall. As they made to present themselves, their pace reduced the closer they got to the gym wall. What slowed them was the aggressive, contemptuous collective gaze of the six regular Scouts huddled there, older boys, all smoking cigarettes. The three pulled up at a distance of a few yards. Nothing was said. Clive scratched his sock-top. Terry pretended to tie up his shoelace. Sam folded his arms, and then quickly unfolded them.

"What do you fucking want?" said the biggest of the gang, a boy with cropped hair and eyes narrowed to a porcine squint. His huge, meaty legs strained the seams of his short khaki trousers. The gray-pink skin of his thighs looked chafed and raw. Sam shifted his weight from one leg to the other.

"Yeah, what do you fucking want?" said a tall, thin boy with shockingly bad teeth, stubbing out a cigarette on the heel of his shoe.

"Fuck off," said the first Scout.

"Yeah, fuck off," said his lieutenant.

Terry, Sam and Clive did exactly as instructed. Turning uneasily, they made agonizingly slow progress back across the playground. Still feeling six pairs of eyes burning into their backs, it was a long, long walk.

They hovered nervously at the school gates for five minutes or so and were about to leave when a grown man, in full Scouting uniform, sped through the gates on a bicycle. Applying his brakes, he skidded to a halt. "New boys? You the three new boys?"

The question carved them an island. They swam to it, gathering round the bicycle. The man lifted a hairy leg over the crossbar, wheeling the bicycle back across the playground. The boys followed, covering old ground to find that the smoking Scouts had vanished. The man had a toothbrush moustache and a florid complexion, plus a way of smiling which involved baring his clenched teeth. He introduced himself as Skip. He chatted amiably, learning their names immediately.

Wheeling his bike through a back entrance to the school, Skip led them down a corridor and opened a door to a classroom where almost thirty Scouts were busy unpacking boxes and unloading equipment. He pushed his bike into the classroom, leaning it against the chalk-dusted blackboard rail. Then he turned to press an industrial-sized forefinger flat against the center of Clive's fore-

head. "Falcon," he whispered, with mystical intensity. Slowly with-
drawing his finger to leave a white mark on the flushed skin of
Clive's brow, he let the finger float toward Sam's forehead. "Eagle."
Terry was the last to be anointed. "Merlin."

Skip bared his teeth before propelling first Sam, then Terry
and finally Clive into different corners of the room, where small
clusters of Scouts were still busy with a ritual of unpacking a battered suitcase, checking off the equipment therein and restoring it
to its original position. Sam's group turned from their task and
looked at him with a mixture of pity and contempt. Sam found
himself face to face with the brawny, cropped, fat-faced boy they'd
encountered under the gym wall.

"What do you want?"

"Eagle," spluttered Sam. "Eagle."

The boy's lip curled, miraculously ammonite-like. "Fuck."

Skip sauntered over. "Show him the ropes now, Tooley. Be a
good mother."

The boy's sneer disappeared. With an alacrity quite alarming,
he jumped up and offered his Scoutleader, and then Sam, a winning smile. "I'm Tooley. Eagle PL. Best patrol in the troop. Welcome aboard."

"That's the stuff," Skip said, baring his teeth before wheeling
away to facilitate similar introductions elsewhere.

After he'd gone, Sam was pushed into a chair and given a short
piece of rope to hold. Then he was ignored for three quarters of an
hour. When the equipment was packed back into its box, someone
snatched the rope out of his hands and stowed it. Skip came round
and inspected the box that had been unpacked, checked and
packed again.

"All correct?"

"Yes, Skip."

The next section of the evening comprised games. Skip stood
on a chair with a whistle shouting, "Port," "Starboard," "Freeze,"
"Thaw" and one or two other commands. Scouts charged back
and forth in tumult. Sam, like Clive and Terry, tried to imitate
what the others were doing, but without really grasping the rules

they were all eliminated early. They stood around for twenty minutes until a winner was declared; whereupon the game was repeated, all three again making an early exit.

The third slice of the evening was set aside for Badge Work. This involved free association with other patrols while Skip and his assistant leader were kept busy testing people in various arcane skills. Suddenly Sam found himself roughly bundled against the wall and lifted clean off his feet by Tooley. He was covered by his friend Lance, the boy with the appalling teeth, who stood close but with his back to them, keeping watch for Skip. "Those other two new boys. Friends of yours?"

"Yes."

Tooley let him down, pretending to dust off his shirt. "Eagles chin Merlins, Falcons and Owls, don't we, Lance?"

"Yep. Chin 'em hard."

"You're going to start with your pals."

"What?"

Tooley put his ugly face very close. Sam could smell tobacco on his breath. "Never 'what' me, right? Never 'what' me. Yes, Tooley. No, Tooley. But never 'what.' Right?"

"Yes, Tooley."

"What's his name? Your mate with the stick-out ears."

"Clive."

"Right. You chin him before the evening is out, right?"

"No!"

"Please yourself. If you don't, we're going to pull your shorts down, and my friend Lance is gonna fuck you up your arse, right, Lance?"

"Right."

"Remember: before the evening is out." Tooley turned from his ministrations, and both he and Lance blended effortlessly back into Badge Work. Sam looked at Terry, who was seated on a chair looking slightly pale, and at Clive who, in being taught how to tie a knot, seemed happy enough. Lance looked up and gave Sam a gorgeous flash of green-and-black dentures.

Sam felt faint. Skip came by. "Everything all right?"

"Yes," Sam said weakly. "Yes."

"That's the stuff. All seems strange at first, but you'll get used to it."

The appointed hour was approaching fast. Sam felt increasingly dizzy, what with Tooley squeezing past him every few minutes to tap his wristwatch and Lance intermittently beaming him beautiful mouthfuls of rotting teeth. When Skip stepped out of the classroom for a moment, Sam recognized all the signs of an engineered diversion. He stepped across the room toward Clive, fists clenched. Terry meanwhile beckoned him over, but he was not to be distracted. Clive had his back turned. He tapped Clive on the shoulder, but before he could do anything, a small fist hit him stingingly hard in the side of the mouth. Terry stood back, his fist still raised. Clive instantly looked up and punched Terry hard, and not in revenge for the blow inflicted on Sam, at the exact moment Sam landed a sharp blow to the side of Clive's nose.

Skip came back into the room to see all Scouts busy but for three new tenderfoots dazed and confused in the middle of the room. "All right, lads? That's the stuff, back to your patrols. Time for the flag."

Sam, Terry and Clive lined up at the rear of their respective patrols, each nursing a sore, bruised face as the Union Jack was unfurled. They saluted along with everyone else. All Scouts enthusiastically chanted the Scout Law. "I promise on my honor to do my best to do my duty to serve God, Queen and country and at all times to obey the Scout Law."

Then it was all over, and Moody Linda was waiting for them outside, resplendent in her blue uniform, slightly flushed with the small pleasures that a successful evening of Guiding can bring to a girl.

"See you next week, lads," shouted Skip, switching off the classroom lights with an extravagant sweep of his arm. "See you next week."

FIFTEEN
Wide Games

They did return to Scouts the following week but only because Wide Games were promised "to take advantage of the Indian summer." As for the intimidation from the likes of Tooley and his cohorts, everyone assured them they'd simply been initiated.

"They're just seeing what you're made of," Eric told Clive.

"They're simply teasing you all," Nev assured Sam.

"It's a kind of test, which you've passed," said Terry's Uncle Charlie.

So they went to the Wide Games, which were organized at Wistman's Woods. The stipulation had been that they should gather at the end of the track leading to the wood rather than at the school where meetings were usually held. Terry, Clive and Sam donned their ill-fitting uniforms and took the road which passed the pond and the gymkhana field. It was a warm September evening, and the bronze disc of the sun was already low in the sky. Clouds of gnats flared in the yellow light, a thousand winged creatures individually aflame. As they approached the woods, a horse rider came trotting out between the trees. It was the girl from the gymkhana. Drawing abreast of them, she reined her mare and stopped. The horse seemed to want to walk on the spot. They too stopped.

Her eyes were shadowed by the peak of her riding hat. She looked down at them with an expression of haughty amusement. "Boy Scouts," she said, landing a cynical emphasis on the "boy." There was both irony and contempt in her voice. *"Boy* Scouts." Without warning, she urged her horse and cantered clear, leaving the three to gaze stupidly after her. None of them could think of anything to say.

"Come on," Clive said at last. "Let's find these games."

The activities were to be commenced in daylight and finished in darkness, they were told. A campfire would be lit. A command point was established, and colors were distributed. They were joined by Scouts in the unusual green shirts of the Coventry Forty-eighth, and all boys present were divided into three groups. Each group was given "honors" in the form of a colored flag "to be placed up a tree." The object of the game was for each group to acquire, by cunning and stealth, all three flags.

"By cunning and stealth," Skip repeated frequently, intoning the words.

Sam followed his Eagle patrol and three members of the Forty-eighth who had the good fortune to be assigned to it, and together this "Blue Team" went off into the woods. Five minutes into the game, Tooley stopped everyone dead and turned on one of the members of the Forty-eighth. "We need a decoy," he said.

The young Scout was bundled to the floor, gagged, his hands tied behind his back and his legs lashed together at the ankles. His two comrades looked ready to object, but sizing up Tooley made them think better of it. The blue flag was stuffed halfway into the boy's breast pocket, a rope was tossed over a tree branch and he was hoisted by his feet to dangle, upside down, eight feet from the ground. Then the rope was lashed to the trunk of a fallen tree. The blue flag hung invitingly from his breast pocket.

"Now we hide," said Tooley.

The group took cover behind toppled, rotting logs and dense bushes. Tooley crouched near Sam. They waited in silence. After a moment, Sam cleared his throat, and Tooley rewarded him with a stinging slap to the ear. Tooley bared his teeth. They waited several minutes. Sam, kneeling, developed a cramp in his leg but dared not risk another slap from his Patrol Leader. He crouched in agony.

Eventually a pigeon broke through the trees, followed by the shrill clucket of a disturbed blackbird. Tooley's muscles coiled like springs. Two young Scouts appeared, stalking the path. Sam recognized them as Falcons from his own troop. They stopped dead when they saw the gagged Scout hanging upside down from the rope. Both glanced round nervously before approaching further.

Obviously they had been dispatched to gather information and report back; now they whispered to each other, as if trying to come to a decision. One of them seemed to sense something. The blue flag was obviously theirs for the taking, if they could just reach it. They approached gingerly. One of the boys jumped up for the flag but couldn't quite make it. It was just inches from his fingers. They looked around again. It was not until one had climbed upon the other's back and was groping for the flag that Tooley released an unearthly cry and charged from behind the thicket. He felled the two Scouts with a rugby tackle. There was a brief scuffle in the leaves before the two were subdued by the other Scouts hard on Tooley's heels. The victims were gagged instantly. One of them was stripped naked, lashed by the ankles and hoisted upside down alongside the decoy scout.

"Did you bring the pen?" shouted Tooley, breathing hard from his exertions.

"Here it is." Lance produced a fat blue felt-tip marker. The luckless Scout was hoisted to eye-level, so that Tooley could draw a large T on either buttock. Then he drew a horizontal arrow across each T. Lance smiled thinly at Sam. "Tooley's sign," he said by way of helpful explanation.

"Let's get out of here," Tooley commanded.

They dragged the second Scout to his feet and pushed him down the path. Someone retrieved the blue flag.

"What about our friend?" protested one of the Forty-eighth.

Tooley looked up at the decoy scout, still twitching on the end of his rope. "Yeh," he said generously, "let him down."

"The rules say we should leave the flag in the same tree for the duration of the game."

Tooley grabbed the Forty-eighth trooper by the collar. "I'm Tooley. I make the fucking rules. Now cut him down and let's go."

Crouched behind a fallen silver birch, the light beginning to dim around him, Sam saw the next two victims approaching. The second abducted Scout had been blindfolded and strung up with the Blue's colors dangling from his belt. The three Scouts from the Forty-eighth troop had slipped away some minutes before, the decoy Scout strangely silent, still dazed from his ordeal. Sam bit into his own knuckles when he saw the identity of one of the two Scouts drawing near. It was Clive.

Sam had a moment of crisis. He could alert his friend to the danger, or he could squat in silence and leave him to his fate. He knew that if he betrayed the ambush, he was certain to suffer even worse treatment at the hands of Tooley, Lance and their hobgoblin cohort. Sam had a shrewd idea that if more hostages were not taken soon, he would be the next to be swinging by the rope.

He stayed silent.

Two minutes later Clive and his comrade were wrestled to the ground and gagged. Sam hung back, hoping his friend wouldn't identify him as an assailant. There was an ugly enthusiasm in the way the rest of the Eagles ripped off Clive's Scouting uniform. While the melee was going on, Sam inched back and made his escape, rejoining the path and jogging out of sight.

Dusk gathered like soot on the branches of the trees. Sam stopped to recapture his breath, leaning against a tree. The woods had taken on a murky gloam, and he had a sick weight in his stomach. The trees around him seemed to be closing in. A hand touched his collar from behind. "Going somewhere?"

"Terry! Am I glad to see you! Christ, am I glad to see you!"

"I've had enough," said Terry. "There's too many weird things happening."

"Don't I know it. Listen, they've got Clive and they're stringing him up. I couldn't help him."

"How many are there?"

"Too many. If they catch either of us, we'll get the same treatment."

"They're not getting me," said Terry defiantly. He held up his fist. It was clenched round a Swiss Army knife, biggest blade exposed.

Sam could see from Terry's eyes he was serious. He wondered what Terry's experience of the Wide Game might have been. "We could cut him down after they've gone. They leave you dangling bollock-naked with a sign on your arse. But we could get him down if we wait until they've gone."

So Sam led Terry back to the place where Clive had been abducted. They were terrified should a branch snap under their boots. Terry told Sam something he'd read in the Scouting Handbook about rolling your feet as you walked. They heard Tooley barking orders, followed by Lance's high-pitched giggle, and were able to observe from behind a sprawling clump of holly.

Clive was naked, staked out on the ground, nose downward. He was red-faced from the exertion of useless struggle. Tooley's sign had been scribbled on his bare buttocks. The other Scout was gagged and blindfolded and held in an armlock.

"Where's that fucking four-eyed little squirt?" Sam heard Tooley shout. "Anybody see him go? What's his name, the four-eyed squirt?"

Sam had obviously made such an impression on the Eagles that no one could remember his name. Tooley dispatched two Eagles to go in search of Sam, with the instructions to "bring him back on a pole." Sam fumbled with his glasses, taking them off and wiping them on his khaki shirt.

"Don't worry," said Terry. He was still clenching his Swiss Army knife.

"Go to that clearing by the hollow," Tooley told the others. "I'll finish up here and join you in a minute."

"I'll wait with you," Lance giggled.

Tooley slapped Lance's ear, hard. "Do as you're fucking told!"

"Don't hit me! You never hit me before! Don't hit me!"

"So do as you're told!"

Lance scurried after the others, who'd taken their prisoner with them. This left only Clive, and Tooley, and the blindfolded second decoy Scout who through all this activity had been left to swing from the rope. Tooley watched his patrol mates disappearing through the trees. After he was certain they had gone he took up a position behind Clive, gazing down at his helpless victim. Tooley jerked off his beret and wiped the sweat from his forehead. His chest rose and fell and he was perspiring heavily. He spat into the dead leaves before placing his beret back on his head. Glancing around him briefly, he lowered his shorts.

"Oh, no," Sam whispered as Tooley's livid, engorged cock sprang free. "Oh, no."

"What's he doing?" said Terry. "He's . . . No, he can't." Terry looked at Sam, and Sam nodded. "We've got to stop him," said Terry.

"How?"

"Christ! What's he doing?" Tooley was kneeling on the grass behind Clive. "Look, you run at him, and while he's fighting you I'm gonna stab the bastard."

"You can't!"

"Just watch me. Come on. Run at him, Sam! Run at the fat bastard!"

"He'll kill me! He'll flatten me!"

"You've got to do it!"

"I'm too scared, Terry! I'm too scared!"

Tooley pressed Clive's legs apart.

"That's it," said Terry. "I'll rush him. *You* stab him. It's one way or the other, Sam. We can't let Clive down! We can't! Now what's it to be? One way or the other."

Sam looked at the Swiss Army knife in horror and then at the sight of Tooley's bobbing, erect penis. He held out a hand and then withdrew it.

"Fuck," said Terry. He slapped the handle of the knife into Sam's hand, scrambled to his feet and launched himself full-pelt at Tooley, screaming as he ran. Alerted, Tooley scrambled up on one knee. Terry tried to grab Tooley by the throat, but he was easily shaken off. The big Scout struggled to his feet and, letting fly with his huge ham of a fist, caught Terry in the mouth, sending the younger boy sprawling unconscious.

Sam was paralyzed. His thigh muscles had turned to slush. Then there was a vacuum as time stood still. There came a roaring in his ears, and the light in the woods flooded red, and he began running toward Tooley, imitating Terry's ineffective assault.

But Sam never made it. He was bundled off his feet by a force striking him from behind like a buffeting wind. As he sprawled in the dead leaves he looked up and saw a huge white horse leaping over him. Its rider was the Tooth Fairy, her mouth distorted in a hideous, high-pitched scream. The vicious blades of her filed teeth were bloody in her mouth. She was pointing at Sam and shrieking incomprehensible words. The horse whinnied, rearing up and powering its hooves down upon the head of the astonished Tooley. He was felled instantly. The horse reared again, landing a full clattering weight of metal hooves on Tooley's chest, and then again and again in frenzied stomping. The Tooth Fairy spat something and kicked at the horse, driving it between the trees, ducking under a branch as the horse galloped them both out of sight.

There was a moment of blackness. Sam felt a coursing in his veins and the red light returned, and faded again. His vision oozed. Then his head cleared and he saw Tooley sprawled on the ground in a broken and bloody bundle. Clive was screaming through his gag. Terry was back on his feet, shaking his head in an effort to clear his own vision.

"Jesus!" said Terry. "Jesus!" He snatched the knife from Sam. The blade was blood-soaked. Tooley's blood on the knife shone darkly in the gloaming of the woods. Terry ran over to Clive and cut the ropes staking him. Clive scrambled to his feet, dragging off his gag. Seeing Tooley sprawled on the leaves, he ran across and kicked the supine Scout in the face. And again. And again.

Then some instinct stopped him from inflicting further punishment.

Terry came over with Clive's uniform. Clive quickly pulled his clothes on. Bending down, he prodded the older Scout with a stick. Tooley made no movement. Clive rolled him over. His chest was scored with innumerable small gashes, each leaking black blood on to the khaki shirt. Clive leaned over his chest listening for a heartbeat, and then for a sign of breath. Nothing.

"What did you do?" said Terry in a subdued voice.

"Nothing," whispered Sam.

"I'm not blaming you. Clive, Tooley was going to fuck you. He deserved it. Nobody could blame Sam for this."

"Are you certain he's—"

"See for yourself," said Terry, and Clive took a turn again at listening for a heartbeat, breathing, any life-sign.

The three boys stood looking at each other, darkness settling on their shoulders like strange cloaks. Then Sam got closer, eyes bulging, trying to inspect the wounds. He traced crescent shapes in the punctures. "Hooves. A horse's hooves did this."

"What are you talking about?"

"Nobody's going to believe that," said Clive.

"It doesn't matter," said Sam. "That's what did it."

"You're in a state of shock," said Clive. He looked at Terry. "He's in shock."

"Here's your glasses," said Terry. "They fell off." The glasses were broken.

They were dazed, stunned; and now they were in awe of Sam. Clive called them to order. "Grab a leg," he said at last.

They dragged Tooley deeper into the undergrowth. Terry found the cracked hollow of an oak stump. Tooley was a dead weight. Sweating, shivering, teeth clenched, the three boys managed to lift Tooley and drop him into the hollow. By now his lips had turned gray. They piled leaves over the body, and dragged branches across the rotten tree stump.

They had to go back to get the knife. Terry found it, wiped and closed the blade and put it in his pocket. They uprooted the stakes and scattered leaves to disguise any signs of struggle. It was only as they made to leave they heard a muffled cry from above their heads.

A Scout was still dangling silently over them. He'd been there all the time, blindfolded and gagged. Clive wanted to leave him, but Terry wouldn't. They gently lowered the Scout and cut the ropes from around his legs without a word. His hands were still tied behind his back, but before leaving him they took his gag away so that he could shout for help.

Then they left the scene. By now the woods were pitch-dark. They decided to exit the woods by the north side. On their way they had to scatter from the path to avoid an advancing gang of Scouts hurrying along with a lighted candle in a jar. The Scouts all had a piece of string tied round their arms. A new Wide Game had begun.

They broke out from the woods and sprinted across a ploughed field. Eventually they reached the gymkhana ring. By the time they drew alongside the pond, they were breathless.

"Get rid of the knife," said Clive.

Terry pulled the Swiss Army knife from his pocket. He looked at it sadly.

"Get rid of it," Clive said again. Sam hadn't spoken since the incident.

Terry flung the knife into the middle of the pond. The black water glooped, sucking the knife into itself. "That's the last time I go to Scouts," Terry said.

"No. We have to go next week. As if everything is normal." Clive was already thinking everything through.

Then they went home. Connie and Nev were watching TV when Sam got back. They gave him hell for breaking his glasses.

SIXTEEN
Blood Dream

That night Sam dreamed. She came to him, beautiful and re-
pulsive, her lips stained the color of a broken damson, her face
whited, the black grapes of her nipples and the goblet-breasts visible through her stretched bodice. Her striped leggings were torn
at the top of her fleshy thighs to reveal an unguarded zone of white
skin and a tight, autumnal thicket of pubic curls streaming an un-
holy hedgerow scent of earth, fire, nightshade in flower, as she
swung a supple leg across him, straddling him, poised, hovering
over him, holding off the moment, her vicious and tender gaze
pinioning him, moon's catchlight in her eyes terrorizing him, ah-
ah, and he knew it no longer mattered whether she/he/it was
dream or substance, since she had now shown herself beyond the
limits of his dreamed room, in that gloaming in the woods, in the
forest, in the dark, the blade-thing, saving and protecting, borne on
a wild-eyed horse, ah-ah, and as the moon spun red outside his
window her pale face reflected its red sheen and her coiling,
corkscrew fingernails of years and years of uncut growth teased his
boy's chest, a blade, a threat, a promise, but he knew she could at
any time gently reach a hand inside his flesh and take a part of
him, the thing she wanted, didn't even have to lower herself on to

him, she could hover above him, pulling at his innards as he rose up, trying to leap at her open crotch until he felt the vulcan wave break, course, flow, slip, ruby to silver, cadmium to mercury, blood to molten metal, strange whiff of alchemy, the smell of her shivering insubstantial body, drawing him in with her unfleshy succubus divinity, feeding from him, syphoning, leeching, bleeding him until he knew he would never be free of her, never wanted to be free of her, that he was wedded to the Tooth Fairy, and now she had broken free of the bedroom and found her way into the woods she would keep coming and coming and coming.

SEVENTEEN

Thunderland

Sam's first term at Thomas Aquinas Grammar passed in a per-petual twilight. If Connie and Nev noticed that their son had be-come withdrawn, they attributed it to the new school. Certainly they didn't guess that their twelve-year-old was suffering a burden of guilt entirely appropriate for a first-time murderer.

All three of the boys had, since the incident, kept well away not only from Wistman's Woods but also from the gymkhana field, the football field and the pond. Sam knew for certain that it was only a matter of time before Tooley's body would be discovered, and their crime would find them out. Every day he got off the school bus outside his home expecting to see a police car parked on the grass verge and to find those same two book-end detectives drink-ing tea in the kitchen of his home. Every evening before doing his homework he scoured the pages of the *Coventry Evening Telegraph* for reports of a decomposing body unearthed in Wistman's Woods. That weeks and months went by with no such report did nothing to make the burden more bearable; it only made the knock on the door ultimately more inevitable.

Anticipation of that knock on the door came regularly at three o'clock every morning. Sam would wake up, bathed in perspiration, as the cast-iron knocker fell in the dead of night. He would lie awake in the dark, waiting for his parents to stir or for a second knock to sound through the sleeping household; but they never would, and it never did. Meanwhile, his studies suffered.

Terry and Sam had returned to Scouts the week following the slaying of Tooley, pale, nervous, but motivated by Clive, who had drilled them on their story. It became possible, in the company of the other two boys, for Sam actually to believe what they had rehearsed over and over. It was only when he was alone that the truth of the event regathered its shape and returned to torment him.

That first week after the Wide Game, Clive had directed Sam to inquire cheerfully after the whereabouts of Tooley. When he failed, Clive himself marched across to the Eagles' corner of the schoolroom and put the question directly.

"He ain't been around," said Lance sullenly. "Why do you want to know?"

In a way which deeply impressed Sam, Clive made his eyes shine with naïve enthusiasm. "I had to give him a cigarette."

"Give it me. I'll pass it on."

Clive produced a battered fag from his shirt pocket and handed it over.

"Now piss off."

Later Sam plucked up courage to ask again. The question, coming from one of his devoted patrol members, was not unnatural. "Probably fucked off to London," said Lance, swelling in the job of Acting Patrol Leader. Sam gleaned from Lance that Tooley lived with his grandfather, an old man suffering from Alzheimer's disease. It was the grandfather who had suggested that Tooley had gone off to London, though his testimony was flawed in that he occasionally couldn't remember Tooley's name or even who Tooley was. The story squared with Lance's view, since Tooley had often claimed he would one day jump on a train to Euston station and from there find a job as a drummer in a rock 'n' roll band. "He was going to take me with him," Lance added sadly.

The weeks passed, and the boys attended Scouts faithfully.

Only Linda suspected that something unpleasant had happened. The walk to and from Scouts every Tuesday evening was now a dispiriting trudge, conducted mostly in silence. Linda, in her starched, immaculate blues, would try to lighten them with conversation or questions about what they'd accomplished that evening, but it was hard going. Their extreme reticence struck her as odd. It seemed to her that in attending Scouts there was no joy whatsoever for them but that they persisted for some dour and unfathomable purpose. She could never guess, as she tried to make jokes about woggles or to inquire about reef knots, what lay in their hearts.

Lance soon dropped out, and two other boys from the Eagle patrol were promoted to Leader and Second. New boys joined, and Sam found himself bounced up the patrol pecking order. Then came investiture evening. The three were invested together after having passed all their Tenderfoot tests of Observation, Knotting and Firelighting. They were given badges; they made oaths before the flag of the realm; and they were saluted by the rest of the troop.

"That's it," Clive said quietly on the way home that night. "Two more evenings."

"Why?"

"I overheard Skip moaning to one of the Scouters that most of the kids drop out shortly after they've been invested. Two more meetings and that's our lot. We're done."

"What's that you were saying?" Linda wanted to know, waiting for them to catch up with her.

"Scouts," Terry said quickly. "We were just saying these meetings are a lot of fun."

The Christmas holidays approached. Sam stood in the ragged queue of schoolchildren waiting for the bus home after school. His mind, as usual, was not on the present scene of bawling and jostling kids. He wondered if tonight might be the night when the two detectives would be sipping at their second cups of tea the moment he walked in; and he speculated on why the Tooth Fairy had failed to revisit him since the extraordinary night following the murder of Tooley. Suddenly he was buffeted from behind.

His glasses fell off. Luckily he caught them in a reflex movement. "Excuse me," a sarcastic female voice said, overloudly, in his ear. By the time he'd replaced his glasses, all he could see was a girl making her way to the back of the disorderly queue. When she reached the snaking tail of the queue, she turned and looked back at him from under a long fringe of brown hair.

It was the girl from the gymkhana. The horse rider. She looked different, younger in her school uniform. Her hair, released from its ponytail, cascaded over her shoulders, and her fringe was cut in a straight line above her dark eyebrows. The hem of her regulation pleated gray skirt stopped at a non-regulation point several inches above the knee, and when she drew her blazer aside to place a lazy, elegant hand on her hip, the action seemed to advertise a line of thigh just a little too skinny for her black nylons. The expression on her face as she gazed back at Sam was neither hostile nor friendly.

Sam looked away. Instinctively he touched his fingers to his ears, feeling them flame. He had turned, he knew, pink with self-consciousness. It was a relief when the transport arrived, and he was able to join the mêlée pressing to get on to the bus. He took his seat wondering what she was doing there. He knew all the usual faces on the school bus and hers wasn't one of them.

When her turn came to board the bus she paused in the gangway. For an awful moment Sam thought she was going to sit beside him. Instead she dipped her head toward him, putting her face close to his. She had high cheekbones and pale blue eyes, deeply set. Her long hair lightly brushed his arm as she spoke in his ear. "I saw you that day."

Then she was gone, making her way further down the bus.

The girl alighted one stop before Sam's, about a quarter of a mile away from his home. Struggling but failing to resist the temptation, Sam stared through the window at her as the bus pulled away. But her back was turned as, satchel slung across her shoulder, she walked away in the opposite direction.

Skelton's concession to Christmas decoration took the form of one tired rope of green glitter pinned to the wall in a slack wave behind his head. A single Christmas card was displayed on his desk. He was smoking a pipe, gazing out of his window when Sam went in.

"Sit, laddie, sit."

Skelton had a habit of biting hard on his pipe stem, thus baring his teeth. Some days he wore a tweed suit and some days a baggy, off-white Aran sweater. Today he seemed to be in an informal mood, because it was an Aran-sweater day. His cheeks were swollen and ruddy, his neck the color of poached lobster. He swayed slightly as he moved across from the window before hoisting himself on to the edge of his large, polished desk, his feet a-dangle, and exposing an inch of hairy leg between his Argyle socks and his corduroy trousers.

"Biters and bedwetters," he said through a mouthful of pipe stem.

Sam looked up.

"Biters and bedwetters. Which are you?"

Sam looked down.

"That's what comes to me, laddie. The one lot goes on to become your common-or-garden psychopath; the other lot become poets, God help us all. Wet your bed recently? Bitten anybody's face lately?"

"No."

"No? The boy says no. Do I believe him? Aye. Why not? He's never lied to me yet." Skelton waved his pipe stem at an imaginary audience. Sam was so convinced he had to look over his shoulder to check that no one else was in the room. "Now then, there's a young fellow, Timmy Turtle—not his real name, don't go telling your ma—he was here just yesterday. Stand up and have a look at the chair you're sitting on. Stand and look." Sam did as he was told. A broad stain darkened the upholstery. "Don't worry, it's dry now. This Timmy Turtle, fourteen years old and still pissing the bed every night. And just when I'm talking to him about it, nice, friendly chat like we're having now, he pisses his pants again. On my chair."

Skelton clamped his jaws on his pipe. His teeth clacked against the stem, and he puffed thoughtfully. He snatched his pipe from his mouth and said, "Then there's Mickey the Muncher. Bit his mother—doesn't have a father, see—then bit his sister, his brother, his aunt, his nurse, his teacher. Then because I wouldn't let him take a chunk out of me, he had a go at my table leg." He pointed with the stem of his pipe. Sam could clearly see marks where the veneer of the table had been bitten down to the internal wood.

"So, laddie, why am I telling you this? Because I'm thinking, if the lad's not a biter and he's not a bedwetter, and he doesn't fit one or two other minor categories I've drawn up over the years, then why in God's blithering name is he coming to see me?" Skelton leaned forward, putting his face within inches of Sam's. The boy got a sweet-rotten blast of whisky and tobacco. The psychiatrist's eyes were bloodshot. Broken purple veins stood up either side of his nose. "Can you answer that for me?"

"No."

"No, he says. No. You see, there's Mickey the Muncher. Now, sure as God made little green apples, our Mickey has got a great future ahead of him as a homicidal maniac. Nothing I can do is going to change that. It's already encrypted. And Timmy Turtle is going to be a whining versifier, which is even worse in my book. I'd lock up all the sniveling poets with the killers if I had my way. But, there again, I can't do anything about it. So the point is, laddie, if I know what the problem is with these two boys, and I can't do anything about it, what am I supposed to do with you, whose problem I know nothing about?"

"Don't know," Sam said helpfully.

Skelton reached behind him, grabbing a manila file. He flicked through, almost uninterested. "Seen this fairy chappie recently?"

"No."

"Hmmm. What about lasses?"

"Pardon?"

"Lasses. Any lasses on the scene yet? Any sign of 'em?"

Sam shrugged.

"Girls," said Skelton. He pronounced the word "girruls," bit-ing hard on his pipe. "You see, I think all your problems will be over as soon as those naughty wee lasses come into play." Then he stared hard and long at Sam, so hard and long that Sam was forced to look away.

The discomfort was relieved by the appearance of Skelton's secretary, bearing a tea tray with biscuits. "Is there an extra ginger snap for the boy, Mrs. Marsh? It is Christmas, after all, and me and young Sam here are having a bit of a heart-to-heart. Facts of life, isn't that right, Sam?"

Mrs. Marsh laid down her tray and looked at Sam as if he'd been caught stealing apples. Sam colored.

"Thank you, Mrs. Marsh, thank you." After his secretary had left the room, Skelton resumed. "So no lasses, eh? You might think about getting a move on in that department. Advice, laddie: he who hesitates is lost."

"I want to confess," said Sam.

"Eh? What? Confess what?"

"I want to confess to a murder."

"What? You're a murderer now?" He poured the tea and gave Sam a cup. Then he reached into his desk drawer, and as his hand withdrew, it passed across his own cup. Sam heard a small splash of liquid.

"Yes."

"Hold on, laddie. Don't misunderstand me. Just because you don't bite people or puddle your bed doesn't make you an inferior person. You don't get ten points and a gold star with me for being a murderer."

"No. I killed someone."

Skelton chuckled. "I'm on to you, Sonny Jim. You don't think

I was fooled by that lovely Celtic cross and the bat coming out of your grave, do you? We call that attention-seeking round here. But, you see, I knew that you knew that I knew. The reason I kept you on is that I want to know why you're busy *pretending* to be disturbed. "Rest in peace," indeed. That's a Catholic song, and you're no more a left-footer than I am!"

"It's true. I killed someone."

The psychiatrist folded his arms and bit hard on his pipe. "Right then. Let's be hearing it."

Sam felt a sudden weight fold in on him. The room darkened slightly. The clock on the mantelpiece ticked louder. He focused on the exposed, hairy inch of leg above Skelton's Argyle socks and thought of Tooley lying buried under leaves in a tree hollow in the woods. He had come today determined to tell Skelton all about it. But now, as he looked at the hairy flesh and listened to the sound of him chomping on his pipe, it suddenly seemed less than a convincing idea.

He looked up at the window, half expecting, half hoping to see the Tooth Fairy, ready with advice. But there was no help from any quarter. The Tooth Fairy, who had watched him through the same window on previous occasions, wasn't there. "You gave me the gun," Sam said suddenly.

"What? I gave you what?"

"A gun. You gave it to me last time I was here."

Skelton suddenly tired of the game. "Laddie, I've never given you a gun in my life. What in God's name are you jabbering about?"

"Last time I was here!" Sam protested, loud with indignation.

Skelton, taken aback by Sam's outburst, scratched his head. "You mean . . ." He blew the smoke from an imaginary gun.

"Yes!"

"Aha! And it worked, by golly! You shot and killed him?"

"Her."

"Her?"

"He became a she."

"Aha! Aha! And she's dead now? Killed by a silver bullet?"
Sam shook his head. "She came back. Worse than ever."

Skelton looked defeated. He checked his watch and buzzed through to his secretary. "Mrs. Marsh, make another appointment for this boy. He's cleverer than we thought." He turned back to Sam. "I was hoping to send you away from here for the last time. But listen, laddie. I'm on to you. Hear that? Skelton is on to you."

The door opened and Mrs. Marsh stood waiting, the usual signal for him to leave. She was still looking at Sam as if he'd been caught doing something really quite forgivable.

"And have yourself a nice Christmas," Skelton called. Sam turned in time to see Skelton bite on his pipe and reach a hand into his desk drawer.

Mrs. Marsh closed the door behind him.

EIGHTEEN
Odor of the Female

It was the last day of term before the Christmas break. Sam stood in the bus queue, braced and ready for the girl to jolt him with her satchel. Every day for the last week she had bumped him from behind, hissing, "I saw you," in his ear before taking her place further along the line. Today he was waiting for her. He was ready to bump back.

It was not as if Sam was going to make a fight of it. In any case, the bumping had been rather restrained, but there was still something intimidating about the girl. All he knew of her was that she was in the study year above him, and whenever she pushed into him and whispered those three words, he felt more disconcerted than threatened. What discomfited him most was not what she said, nor even the accusing way she looked at him. It was something else. It was the smell of her.

There was always a whiff of shampoo in her long hair, then a deeper, second smell, like a scent which was nothing like the flowery perfumes used by his mother or, these days, by Linda. It was perhaps more like sweet yogurt, he decided; then, no, he thought it had more of a salty tang; but, no, it was like a yeast extract; no no no, the task of pinpointing it was maddening, but whatever it was like, it possessed the extraordinary power to arrest him, to make his muscles seize and his body stiffen. And because of that, because he was always momentarily paralyzed by these actions of hers *en passant,* he was inevitably too slow to respond and was consequently left feeling foolish. But today he was ready for her.

She didn't come. The day before he had also been ready for her, and yet in the one moment when he'd slackened his guard and looked away, that was when she'd bumped him from behind. But today she didn't seem to be around. Sam relaxed. The bus arrived; he climbed aboard and took a seat. As the bus was about to leave the girl jumped on and swung into the seat next to Sam.

Every sinew went into a state of alert, every muscle locked instantly. For an inflated moment Sam stopped breathing. He knew it was ridiculous, but he felt himself in the presence of abstract danger. The girl kept her eyes averted, fumbling with the straps of her satchel, putting away her bus pass. Flicking her hair from her eyes, she turned to him. "Where's the short trousers?"

His ears burned. "Where's the pratty jodhpurs and the kiddie's rosette?"

"Touchy."

Her unruly scent drove him crazy. It made his blood itch. He caught himself scratching his arm. Her satchel had rucked her skirt up around her thighs. He hated her proximity; he wanted to jump out of the seat and climb over her. He felt trapped. "Actually I don't go any more."

"To Scouts? Excitement too much, was it?"

"You could say that."

They sat in silence for some distance. She started stroking her long hair, one handful over the other. It streamed perfume. Looking into her lap, she said, very softly, "I saw you." The tip of her tongue tapped her upper lip. "In the hut. Hiding."

He waited a while before answering. At least it was not the incident in the woods she had seen. "I didn't do it."

Now she looked up at him. Her pale, slate-blue eyes were unblinking. "But I saw you."

"I know you did. But I didn't do it. Why have you started taking this bus?"

"Pardon me. You're not the only one allowed to take the bus."

"I only wondered . . ."

"Well, don't."

Silence. They stared ahead. The bus crunched through its gears.

"Are you going to tell anyone?" said Sam.

"Tell anyone?"

"About seeing me. In the gymkhana hut."

"I thought you said you didn't do it."

"I did say that. Are you going to?"

"I don't know. I might. It all depends."

"Depends on what?"

"On you. It all depends on you." She got up out of her seat, swinging her satchel over her shoulder, and rang the bell for the bus to stop. After getting off, she didn't glance back at Sam, who looked hard at her through the window.

After they'd stopped attending Scouts, everyone became disgusted with the Heads-Looked-At Boys.

"I don't know what's the matter with you lot," Eric Rogers complained. "You mope around, you never go anywhere. What's got into you?"

"Good money thrown away on perfectly good Scout uniforms," Connie Southall protested. "And you were doing so well. I don't understand any of you."

"What's happened to you lot?" said Terry's Uncle Charlie with irritating cheeriness. "I've never seen you so miserable. Terry's like a wet weekend; Sam's got a face as long as a gasman's mackintosh; and Clive looks like a Cleethorpes donkey on Bank Holiday Monday. What a moody bunch! What happened? Did somebody die?"

"Leave them," said Linda, certain now that something untoward had happened at Scouts. "It's just a phase." Linda was no longer Moody Linda. She was blossoming by the day into something gorgeous, something special. She had left her moods behind her; indeed, it could be said she had passed on the baton of moodiness to the boys. She was preparing, too, to turn her back on the Guides. She was sixteen and rumors of boyfriends smoked the air. Somehow in all that she had taken on the mantle of defender, interpreter and apologist for the three boys who, all her life, had been a vexation. "A phase they're going through."

It was Saturday morning. Uncle Charlie offered to take the boys to Highfield Road to see Coventry City play Wolverhampton Wanderers, but only Terry showed any enthusiasm. When Aunt Dot enjoined them to help Terry tidy his room, Clive and Sam made their excuses.

Outside the house Sam said, "What shall we do now?"

"I'm going home," Clive said sullenly.

"That's right," Sam said disparagingly, "go and play with your chemistry set."

"Fuck off."

"You fuck off."

"No, you fuck off."

Clive went home, leaving Sam to mope alone. Not wanting to return home himself, he shuffled dispiritedly up the lane. The pond had recently been fenced off from the road after the land had been bought outright by Redstone Football Club. Golden, pine-scented and unseasoned timber had already dulled to become a drab yellow fence ringing the land. It was another violation, another marking off of the boundaries of childhood geography. Together the three boys had tried to kick a part of the fence down, but it proved too sturdy for their efforts.

Someone was sitting on the new fence as Sam approached. He stopped in his tracks. The Tooth Fairy was there, her feet hooked on to the lower bars of the fence, her hands held limply between her thighs. Sam felt the claw in the pit of his stomach, a dredging in his bowels. The familiar flutter of fear whenever the Tooth Fairy appeared coated his mouth. It squeezed his heart. Each encounter always seemed worse than the last, and each meeting with her left him more in dread of the next.

He was about to retreat, to turn away, when a flicker of movement from the figure on the fence made him gasp. He was mistaken. It wasn't the Tooth Fairy at all. It was the girl, the girl on the school bus. She was looking at him. How could he have been mistaken?

She saw him hesitate. Now he had to go on. He couldn't let her think that the sight of her was enough to make him turn back. He proceeded slowly, avoiding eye contact, but he knew she was staring at him. As he drew abreast of her he looked up, self-consciously nodding in recognition. Coolly, she nodded back. Not until he'd gone several yards past her did she call out to him.

"Where are you going?"

He stopped and turned, having nothing to say. He tried to think of a clever remark, but none came to him.

"Don't you know? Don't you know where you're going? That seems dumb!" He shrugged. "Come here," she said.

He found himself stupidly obeying. When he reached the fence, she cocked her head to one side, squinting at him through her long hair. She wore jeans and baseball boots and a leather jacket with fringes hanging from the arms. "Aren't you going to tell me where you're going?"

"I'm not going to smash up the gymkhana hut, if that's what you mean."

"I didn't mean that."

"I didn't do it. It wasn't me."

"I know you didn't. Want a ciggie?" She held out a box of Craven A, with a black cat on it. Sam, who detested cigarettes, having sampled a few along with Clive and Terry, found himself taking one from the box and accepting a light. He climbed up on the fence beside her and put the lighted cigarette to his mouth.

"You didn't inhale. It's pointless if you don't inhale." She almost seemed to want the cigarette back. Just to demonstrate, she gave a passionate suck on her own cigarette, held down the smoke, tilted her head back and exhaled a vertical stream. Sam took another drag, inhaling as much as he could bear.

A car came by, and they instinctively held the cigarettes behind their backs. She jumped off the fence. "Let's go down to the pond. You can't be seen from the road."

Sam showed her the tiny sheltered bank where he and the others had dragged the back seat of a wrecked Morris Minor. The leather of the seat was torn and coiled springs had burst through the upholstery.

"Is this where your gang meets?"

"What gang?"

"I knew this was here," she said, slumping on the seat.

He sat down next to her. It felt strange. He could smell the same mysterious scent which had confounded and perplexed him before. He sat close to her, yet the tiny space between them might have been a high-voltage electrified fence. The space was skirted with the same respect. It was a cold afternoon, too cold for anyone but dispossessed teenagers to sit outside. The sun was a diffuse yellow disc in the sky, gleaming benevolently through the trees and across the cold, green water of the pond. They smoked their cigarettes in silence. Whoever this girl was, Sam felt both terrified and happy to be with her.

"Alice," she said at last. "I'm Alice."

"Sam."

"I know."

"How do you know?"

"I just know."

They sucked their cigarettes right down to the filters. Something glooped and splashed in the water. "There's a big pike in this pond. A monster."

"You've seen it?"

"Know my friend Terry? When he was a little kid this pike came up out of the water and bit his toes off. Now he walks with a limp."

"Yeah. I've seen that."

"We've been trying to catch the pike for years. It's too clever."

"How do you know it's still there?"

He looked at her. His observation had been slightly wrong first time, he decided. Alice's eyes were the blue-gray of slate on a pitched and sunlit roof after rain. "It's there. And I'll know when it's not."

"What were you doing," she asked, "the day I saw you?"

"We were about to smash up the hut. But then you came in the Land-Rover and that stopped us. We didn't do it."

"I know that. I already told you."

"How did you know?"

"Because *I* did it."

"You? You did it?" She blinked her cloudy eyes at him in affirmation. "Shit! We had the police round our place for that!"

"I know. I put 'em on to you."

"So! Because of you we all had to start going to the fucking Scouts. And it was because we went to Scouts that . . ."

"What?"

Sam took off his glasses and looked at her. Suddenly he saw in her the cause of a long cycle of events, the extent of which was too overwhelming for him to feel anything more than exasperation. "Nothing. Never mind."

"What were you saying about Scouts?"

"Look, why did you put the police on to us?"

"To take attention away from me, dummy."

"So why did you smash up the place? I mean, when you're one of the Jolly Jodhpurs set."

"I got my reasons."

Sam was suddenly suspicious. He narrowed his eyes. "How come you started catching the school bus out of nowhere?"

"My mum and dad split up. I moved up here with my mum. We live behind those woods."

"Oh, yeah? Show me your teeth."

"Huh?"

"Just do it."

She flashed him a set of neat white pearls. "What's that for?"
"Just testing."

"You're weird," she said. "Really weird. Have another Black Cat."

Sam accepted his second cigarette of the day. He liked the way Alice tucked her long hair behind her ear before lighting up. He liked the rose-flush on her high cheekbones. He liked the way she stroked her match so lightly against the abrasive side of the matchbox it seemed as if it could never possibly ignite, yet it did.

"You stare at people," Alice said, blowing out smoke.

"People are strange." He couldn't tell her what he felt: that she fascinated him, that he wanted to creep a little closer to her, close enough to breathe in again that perplexing scent so suggestive of bare, sun-warmed skin, but that the only way he dared approach was by looking at her, searching her person as if she were a riddle with the answer concealed somewhere about her.

She seemed to read his mind. "Change jackets," she said suddenly. "Come on, change." She whipped off her own leather jerkin and waited for him to hand over his blue denim jacket. They held each other's cigarettes while they tried on the jackets, and he contrived to switch the cigarettes so he could taste her lips on the filter. If she noticed, she said nothing. With the leather jacket he had what he wanted. Impregnated in the pliable fabric was that maddening scent of hers. Even though he couldn't say what it was, he knew it acted on him the way an apparently silent whistle set at a high frequency acts upon a dog.

Alice got up suddenly. "You out tomorrow?"
"Sure."
"Here. Tomorrow. One o'clock."
"Wait. I'll walk down with you."
"No. I'm going the other way. See you!"

She was already gone before Sam had scrambled to his feet. The temperature had dropped sharply, and the sky was darkening. The pond, which moments earlier had seemed such an ideal and favored place, now looked cold and lorn, apt to draw the darkness into its unpleasant depths. He zipped up the leather jacket and was arrested in the act of turning up its Alice-scented collar. Someone was watching him from the other side of the pond. Poised in the twilight, half-hidden among the bushes and trees, the Tooth Fairy stood with one foot in the water and one on the clay bank, shoulders hunched, arms folded tightly. She wore the bright scarlet neckerchief of the Coventry Thirty-ninth. Sam felt a wave of spiteful and poisonous disapproval. The Tooth Fairy met his eyes, then spat into the pond. Sam sank deeper into the collar of Alice's jacket and left.

"Where's your good denim coat?" Connie wanted to know when he got home. It was the first time she'd referred to it as "good."

"I swapped it."

"What?"

"Only for a day."

Connie flicked at the fringe dangling from the worn leather sleeves. "Well," she sniffed, "I don't think much of that one."

NINETEEN
Redstone Moodies

A hand placed over his mouth woke Sam in the middle of the night. The chill from the Tooth Fairy's body swept across his skin like a contagion. She was naked. Her clothes lay on the floor in an untidy heap. Blue with cold, her skin glittered with hoarfrost. When she decided he wasn't about to cry out, she reduced the pressure of her hand on his mouth. But she began to explore his lips with her fingers. Her fingers were long and elegant ivory carvings, but her sharp, tapered fingernails were fetid and filthy, black with earth or other dirt upon which he preferred not to speculate. He wished she would keep them away from his mouth. As if guessing his thoughts, she pressed inside his mouth, seeming to count his teeth with loving slowness, teasing the vulnerability of his gums with her nails.

"I know what you did," she breathed. "In the woods. I know what you did."

"It was you," Sam tried to whisper through his crowded mouth. "You did it."

She withdrew her fingers, squeezing his cheeks in her strong hand. "Oh, no. I couldn't have done it without you. We were partners. Just remember that. You let me down and I'll let you down. I might just tell someone what you did to that poor Scout."

She slipped between the sheets, pressing her chilled flesh against his. The cold pleasure of her body stung his skin. Still squeezing his cheeks, she crouched over him, forcing her free hand down on his chest and pressing her lips to his, kissing him deeply. He was aware of her sharply filed teeth as she mashed her lips on his. Then her tongue explored inside his mouth, probing, slippery, like a live fish. She pulled back from him and released his face. "Keep away from her. She's no good."

"Who?" said Sam. "Alice?"

"She's no good."

"You say everyone is no good. You said Skelton is no good. You always say that."

"She'll hurt you, Sam. Believe me. Aren't I enough for you?" She smoothed her hand across his belly, reaching for his cock.

"You're not real."

The Tooth Fairy jackknifed upright, releasing his cock and lashing out at his head with her hand. He managed to avert his face, but not quickly enough to stop her flailing fingernails tearing a thin track of skin from the line of his jaw.

She was already out of his bed, dressing hurriedly, spitting with rage. "I know what you did! I know! I could tell someone at any time!"

Sam was left nursing the torn flesh on his face.

"I'm going to leave you something," she hissed. "Something for you to show the shrink."

Then she left by the window.

The next morning Sam woke early, dressed at speed and slipped out of the house wearing Alice's leather jacket before his mother and father were awake. He didn't want any questions about the three-inch scratch down the side of his face. He didn't want to invite further comment about his jacket.

There had been a freeze overnight. The grass and trees and the pavement were sprinkled with white powder-frost. A pallid sun was up, already unpicking the glittering lacework. Sam's sleep had been disturbed by elusive dreams in which his bedroom window swung open and closed, open and closed; and when the window opened it admitted a chilling voice calling to him from varying and unknown distances. A kind of dream residue still clung to his mind like streamers from a bad party. He dug his hands into the jacket pockets and, with hours to kill, stared gloomily at the frost.

The bottoms of the pockets of Alice's leather jacket were peppered with debris. From one he pulled out strands of tobacco, crumbling nuggets of horse feed, a torn cinema ticket and a twisted fragment of gold foil bearing the italicized word—readable after he'd straightened out the foil—*Gossamer.* He let it all fall to the frozen ground while rummaging in the other pocket. Here he found some torn scraps of what had once been a letter. The slivers of paper were too small and too few to comprise the full letter, but a few words could still be deciphered. He returned the scraps to the pocket and set off for the Bridgewood newsagent's, one and a half miles away.

He needed to buy cigarettes so that he could casually flip open a box and offer one to Alice, as if it was something he did every day. There was, of course, a nearer shop, but the small detail that Sam was buying cigarettes was certain to get back to his mother. Parents, and mothers in particular, Terry had once observed, were inclined to squawk loudly whenever a teenage boy did anything other than stand still with arms folded. Having scuffed or unpolished shoes, for example, would merit Low Squawk. Borrowing someone else's jacket would engender Medium-low Squawk. Smashing up the gymkhana hut was Ultra-high Squawk. Smoking cigarettes at the age of twelve was Ultra-high Squawk. Brutally murdering a fellow Scout was rather off the scale.

Thus Sam found himself waiting behind a perfumed young woman who was also buying cigarettes at Bridgewood newsagent's. When she turned from the counter, she accidentally bundled into Sam and, on seeing him, she dropped her own just purchased cigarettes. "Sam!"

For a moment Sam failed to recognize the young woman. Her

hair was brushed back from her face, and she wore a revealing, low-cut minidress. A pendant dangled above her breasts, and her thigh-length boots drew attention to a deliciously brief expanse of flesh between their tops and the hem of her skirt. "Linda!"

"You didn't see me!" she hissed.

"Weren't you supposed to be leading some parade today?"

She blushed. "Promise you didn't see me!" she repeated. "Promise!" Without waiting for an answer, Linda picked up her cigarettes, swept out of the shop and climbed into a waiting black Austin Mini. Sam peered out of the shop window between the cardboard display units. He didn't know the driver, but he did see Linda's Guide uniform neatly folded on the back seat of the car.

"Twenty Craven A tipped," said Sam to the shopkeeper after the car had roared off, belching exhaust fumes.

"For your dad, are they?"

"Yes. And a box of matches."

What was Linda up to? Sam had plenty of time to speculate as he wandered the one and a half miles back to Redstone. Wasn't she supposed to be leading the Forty-fifths that morning in some kind of Commonwealth parade culminating in a service in Coventry Cathedral? He thought of Linda leading them to school in white gloves, and then leading them to church in white gloves, and then to Scouts, still in white gloves, and he hoped she knew what she was doing.

Sam had to pass by St. Paul's mission church on his way back from Bridgewood. Folk were just leaving after the morning service. He saw Mr. Phillips, his old Sunday-school teacher, shaking hands with the last of the departing congregation. Phillips then went back inside the church, closing the door behind him. Sam remembered his dream and immediately thought of Tooley's body wedged in the hollow of a tree in the woods, decomposing. Every time he thought of Tooley's body, he thought of crows pecking out its eyes or of foxes feasting on Tooley's beefy thighs. He found himself venturing inside the gate.

"Sam! How are you? Didn't recognize you in your Wild West

gear!" It was Phillips, appearing from the other side of the church. Sam realized he was referring to the fringed leather jacket.

"Hello, Mr. Phillips."

"Were you looking for someone?"

"Yes. No. I mean . . ."

Phillips waited patiently. "I don't expect you were looking for me, were you?"

"No. I . . ."

Phillips smiled, then wrinkled his brow, puzzled. He tried to help Sam, saying, "How are those rascally friends of yours? Terry and Clive? How are they doing?"

"I'm sorry about that day."

"Pardon? What day was that?"

"That's what I came to say. That day. We were being stupid. Completely stupid. Childish."

Phillips blinked but plainly at nothing in particular. "What day?"

"We were just messing around, that's all. Nothing personal."

"I'm not quite with you, Sam."

"Mr. Phillips, is it true you're like a doctor, and anything anyone says to you can't go any further, like to the police or parents or anybody? Is that true? I heard that you're not allowed to tell anyone things other people tell you."

"You mean at confession? Yes, the thing is, Sam, I'm a lay preacher—do you know what that means?"

"Oh?"

"But I mean . . . yes, if there was something you wanted to tell me, or to talk about in confidence, then of course that would just be between me and you. Have you scratched yourself?"

Sam took his glasses off and turned away. He didn't want Phillips to see the tears that had formed in his eyes.

"Anyway," Phillips laughed, resting a gentle hand on the boy's shoulder, "what can be that bad? I'd only have to tell someone if you were to confess to a murder! So cheer up. Come on, Sam."

"No. I just came to say sorry about that day. I have to go now. I've got an appointment."

"An appointment! Sounds important!"

"Not really. 'Bye."

Sam felt Phillips watching him all the way to the gate. After he'd gone a dozen yards or so he looked round. Phillips was still regarding him carefully.

The pond seemed to be the only place where he could get away from the complications of friend's cousins, parents, Sunday-school teachers, so he went there, hopelessly early for his appointment with Alice. He sat on the battered car seat, smoking (or, rather, occasionally holding a lighted cigarette to his lips rather than genuinely smoking, since he still didn't really enjoy the things) and trying to decipher the tiny fragments of the torn letter he'd found in the pocket of Alice's jacket.

On one piece he discerned the words *you never said* and on another *memories I have* and then *loving you will not* and then *not married* and then *fucking*—yes, yes, it clearly said *fucking*—and *crying all night.* There were other words and half words out of which it was impossible to construct phrases or any sense. He tried piecing them all together, placing the scraps side by side like a jigsaw, but most of the letter was missing. Whoever had torn up the letter had made a thorough job of it.

Sam threw the letter fragments into the pond, where they fell like tiny leaves, floating on the cold surface without breaking the skin of the water. He searched through the pockets again, looking for more information about Alice. All he found was a comb in the inside pocket. A few hairs were attached to the comb. He took the hairs from the comb, twining the long, fine strands around a matchstick. It was while he was putting the matchstick in a pocket of his jeans that he caught a flash of something moving on the water at the periphery of his vision. There was a "gloop" and a brief flash of green and gold as a large fish came up and took the fragments of paper from the surface of the water.

Then it was gone.

Sam scrambled to the edge of the pond, peering into the wintry blackness, seeing only the shadows of fronds and the deeper darkness. Two cool, soft hands reached from behind him, covering his eyes, and he knew from the scent that came with them that it was Alice. Too soon the hands were removed.

"The pike. I just saw it."

"I don't believe you!"

Oh, yes, he wanted to say, it just ate the last pieces of your love letter. Her head was tilted at a shy angle, but her eyes mocked. Alice's eyes subtly changed color depending on the time of day, or the condition of the sky, or the brightness of the light on the water. She wore his denim jacket and yards of multi-colored scarf. She collapsed on to the old car seat. "I nearly didn't come. My horse has gone lame, and I couldn't ride this morning. Hey, did you scratch yourself? Then I thought you wouldn't speak to me again on the school bus if I didn't come."

"Makes no difference to me," said Sam. "I was coming here anyway." He flipped open his box of ciggies, offering them.

They sat together, smoking and playing "Do You Know Him?", as Alice named all the people she knew at school and Sam named the few he pretended to know. Sam had no sense of time passing. Though Alice's presence made him jumpy, and he felt his nerves straining and popping every time she spoke or he had to answer, he was happy in her company in a way he could never have predicted.

There was a scuffling in the trees, and Terry and Clive broke through the bushes. They stopped dead when they saw Alice sitting with Sam. Terry blinked stupidly, a half-smile twitching across his face. He looked at Sam's cigarette. Clive had, the day before, been inflicted with a severe haircut, making his ears and neck seem excessively pink. His eyes widened at Alice, who merely crossed her legs and took a cool drag on her cigarette. Clive looked as though he felt he'd been tricked but in a way he couldn't quite figure out. He picked up a stone and flung it into the pond with unnecessary force.

"Where's your pony?" said Terry.

"It's not a pony. It's a horse."

"You look a twat in that jacket," said Clive.

"Fuck off," said Sam.

"You fuck off, scarface."

"No, you fuck off."

"Is this what passes for wit in your little gang?" said Alice.

All three boys looked at her, as if they all wanted to say the same thing and she'd just taken it away from all of them. "We're not a little gang," said Clive.

"A little Boy Scout gang."

"No more than you with your Pony Club. Deborahs and Abigails."

"And Jemimas," Terry put in supportively.

"She knows," said Sam, "who smashed up the gymkhana hut."

"Who was it?" said Terry.

Alice narrowed her eyes at Sam. "I *know*. But I'm not *saying*. Crash the ash, Sam." Sam took out his cigarettes and offered them round with desperate nonchalance. Clive and Terry took one each. "So. What do you call your little gang?"

"We're the Heads-Looked-At Boys," said Terry.

"No," Sam cut in quickly. "That's in the past."

"Or the Moodies," said Terry. "That's what my Uncle Charlie calls us. The Moodies."

"That fits," said Alice. "The Redstone Moodies."

Sam was about to protest when Clive barked a mirthless laugh. "Yeah. That's us. The Redstone Moodies." Then he tossed another stone in the pond, but more gently this time.

"What do you have to do to join? Wear shorts? Tie a reef knot?"

"Strip naked and jump in that pond," said Terry. "For full membership."

Alice stood up and offered to take off her jacket. "Come on, then. We'll do it together."

Terry looked less than keen.

"You have to suck my dick," said Clive.

"Right. I'll suck your dick while you suck Sam's."

"Ha!" laughed Terry, jabbing a finger at Clive. "Ha!"

"All talk," said Alice. "You're all talk. I'll match anything you do. But that's just it. You won't do anything."

"You don't have to *do* anything," Sam said acidly. "You just have to be fucked up in the head."

"Good." She took off the denim jacket and lobbed it at Sam. "Now give me my leather back. I've got to go."

Reluctantly Sam handed Alice's jacket back to her. She put it on, pushed her way through the bushes and was gone, leaving behind her a unique silence, a rippling silence like the one that follows a stone tossed in a pond.

"Who is she, then?" Terry said after a while.

"Alice," said Sam.

TWENTY
Deep Mood

The following morning, on the first day of the school's Christmas holidays, Sam lay abed consulting a dictionary.

> **Gossamer** n. & adj. light, filmy substance; the webs of small spiders, floating in calm air or over grass; a thread of this; something flimsy; delicate gauze

He heard from downstairs a knocking at the back door. After a moment his mother came into his bedroom. "Terry's here for you."

Sam dressed, went to the bathroom, squashed a wet flannel against his face and went downstairs, still blinking. Terry stood in the hallway, wearing gloves and scarf, his left foot turned inward. "You won't believe this," he whispered. He fidgeted nervously while Sam ate a dish of breakfast cereal.

"What is it?" said Sam when they'd got outside.

"See for yourself."

Terry led him toward Clive's house. After two hundred yards they passed a tall, white-painted picket fence. Sam stopped in his tracks. Daubed in red paint, in broad letters three feet high, were the words REDSTONE MOODIES.

"Who . . . ?" said Sam.

"There's more. Follow me." On the bus shelter farther along the street, the same words: REDSTONE MOODIES. Then again a little farther, on the white-painted side of the local pub, the Gate Hangs Well. And on the brick wall running beneath the window of the newsagent's. And on another garden fence. What's more, the large sign outside the library was overpainted with the words YOU ARE NOW ENTERING FREE REDSTONE.

"Jesus!"

"It doesn't stop here," said Terry.

The graffiti ran on for half a mile. The artist, or the author, had obviously got bored at some point and started to introduce variations in the language. Royle's sweetshop was particularly targeted, splashed with the words DEEP MOOD and FINE MOOD. The same slogans cropped up intermittently, so the perpetrator, running out of walls and windows, had painted the pavement. Even the church was daubed DEEP MOOD.

"Why," Sam wailed, "do I think this is going to come back on us?"

"Uncle Charlie saw it this morning. He questioned me about it, but then he said he didn't think that even we were stupid enough to do it right on our own doorstep."

"I don't feel we should even be out on the streets."

"Why? You didn't do it. Did you?"

" 'Course I didn't do it."

"You certain?"

Sam stopped Terry with a look. "You think I did it?"

"No, I suppose not."

"You think Clive did it?"

"No."

They were unable to call on Clive because he wasn't home. They knew he was spending that day, even though he was still not quite thirteen years old, sitting a degree-level examination.

"Perhaps you're right," said Terry. "We shouldn't be on the streets. They'll all think it was us."

"I'm not going home."

"All right, we'll go to my place."

But when they got back to Terry's house, there were recriminations of another order, and for once the boys were not the target of parental outrage. In the lounge, Linda was in tears. Charlie and Dot stood over her, looking wronged, angry and bewildered all at the same time. The chief Guide had called to say how disappointed she'd been that Linda hadn't turned up to lead the Commonwealth parade, and how everyone had missed her, and was everything all right? Dot and Charlie, who only the day before had seen her leave the house in her Guiding gear, and had indeed welcomed her return that evening in the same smart uniform, were dumbfounded.

Then it had all come out.

Linda's head was buried under cushions. She was weeping bitterly. Charlie was shouting irrationally. "You can't have boyfriends," he stammered, "if you're going to study! You can't!" Linda was, that year, preparing to sit her O-level exams. It had been widely assumed that she would stay on at school for A-levels.

"We don't know anything about this boyfriend!" Terry's Aunt Dot's voice was raised to a queer pitch. "Nothing at all!"

"I'm sick of the Guides!" Linda shrieked through her cushions and her hot tears. "Sick of the Guides!"

"You can't be a scholar *and* have boyfriends!" Charlie bawled again. There was something odd about the way he brandished the antiquated word "scholar," as if the sitting of A-levels implicated the taking of certain vows. "You just can't do it!"

"Nothing's been said about this boyfriend! We know nothing about him!" Dot turned to Terry and Sam, who were observing all this from the hallway. Her eyes bulged like those of a frightened horse. "Do you two know anything about this boyfriend?"

"No," they said together.

"And who carried the flag?" Dot wanted to know. "At the parade, who was it that carried the flag?"

No one seemed to know whether the argument was about the

Guides, Boyfriends, Completing One's Studies or Carrying the Flag. Linda swept away the cushions and ran out of the room, shouldering Terry and Sam aside. She stomped upstairs and slammed her bedroom door behind her. Charlie ran halfway up the stairs after her. "You can't! You can't do it!" He came back down the stairs, nostrils flaring, eyes rolling. He wagged a trembling finger at the boys. "You can't be a scholar and have boyfriends!"

"We don't want boyfriends," Terry said. He had to step back smartly to avoid Uncle Charlie's backhand.

Charlie stormed back into the lounge, snatched up a newspaper and slumped into an armchair. The newspaper practically ignited in his hands.

"Do you know anything about this boyfriend?" Dot asked them again. "Do you know anything?"

"Of course I didn't do it," said Alice. "What do you think I am?"

"You admitted to me you smashed up the gymkhana hut that time," Sam put it to her.

"I had a reason. You told me you smashed the football pavilion, right? Does that prove you painted 'Redstone Moodies' all over the place? Anyway, why would I? I'm not one of your gang."

"Yes, you are."

"Who said?"

"I said."

Alice shook her head.

This conversation took place three days after the morning the graffiti had been discovered. Both Sam and Terry had received another visit from the police—this time by the local uniformed bobbie called Sykes—as had Clive. Sykes had turned up on a bicycle, wanting to know what Sam knew about the incident.

"Do you know this girl called Alice?" Sykes had asked.

"Yes."

"Has she got anything to do with it?"

"No."

Nev Southall, listening and with his arms folded very tight, put in, "It's hardly likely to be a *girl* now, is it?"

"Hardly," said Sykes, pocketing a notepad on which he'd written nothing. "But Sam's friend Clive said it would be this Alice."

"Clive said that?" Sam bridled.

"Oh, yes. But that was only after we'd found the paint."

"What paint?"

"We found the tin of red paint at the bottom of Clive's garden."

So that was that. Clive was found out, fair cop. He was officially cautioned, though not charged with an offense. Sykes told him he was lucky not to be dragged before a juvenile court and sent to Borstal. He also told him that the reason why he personally wasn't going to give Clive a bloody good hiding was because Eric Rogers had done the job already, judging by the bruise on Clive's cheekbone. Sam never told Alice anything about Clive trying to switch the blame to her, but he did wonder why Clive—clever, clever Clive—could have been so inexpressibly dumb as to leave the incriminating paint at the bottom of his garden. He was certain Clive wouldn't have done that. But then he believed Alice too.

"Swear it wasn't you."

"What?" said Alice. "All right! I swear on all that's holy! I swear on anything you want me to swear on! Is that enough for you?"

They sat by the pond, sharing a cigarette. The water had formed a thin skin of ice. They both agreed it was too cold to sit around, so they went to their respective homes. It was the last time Sam was to see Alice until after Christmas. She was going with her mother to stay with relatives.

"See you after, then," said Sam.

"Sure." She flicked her long fringe out of her eyes. He thought her eyes were slightly red-rimmed. "See you after."

He watched her walk across the frosted field, hands dug deep, deep into the pockets of her leather jacket.

TWENTY-ONE

Christmas Eve

"Someone put it there," Clive said bitterly. The bruise on his cheek had changed hue to plum and marmalade.

"Stitched up like a kipper," said Terry. It was a phrase he'd heard on TV.

"But who would do that?" said Sam. "Who would deliberately leave the paint in your garden?"

"Yeah," Clive said. "Who?"

They stood under the Corporation bus shelter, waiting for the bus into town. The words DEEP MOOD sprayed on the side of the shelter didn't help. No one had made any effort to get rid of the graffiti, and indeed most of them would stay untouched for eighteen months or more. Clive was scandalized that the police, or the municipality, or the parish council, or the community itself hadn't made strenuous efforts to clean up. He almost felt like cleaning the place up or painting over the words himself, he said.

"Why?" said Terry.

"Because," he spat, "everyone thinks I did it. And every time they walk past it they think of me."

"So why don't you?" said Sam.

"Terrific! So if I clean up, then that would be like *admitting* to the thing, wouldn't it? It don't matter if I leave the paint or if I clean it up: I'm dead in the water either way."

"You could explain to people," Sam said.

"Sure," Clive said sarcastically. "I could put a note through everyone's door saying I didn't do it, but because of my devotion to the neighborhood I'm going to put it all right. Great idea!"

Sam adjusted his glasses on his nose. Terry said, "Here comes the bus."

By the time they'd got into the city, a twenty-minute bus ride later, each of them was disgusted with the company of the other. Terry was angling to go to a department store, where a Coventry City footballer was appearing in public to open a new sports department. Only out of decency did he invite the other two along.

"I'd rather watch snot congeal," said Clive.

"You got plenty of that lately," Terry fired over his shoulder, already gone.

Clive had his own appointment with a visiting Russian Grand Master of chess. The Russian was in town to play twenty-four local challengers simultaneously, and Clive had earned the right to be one of them. Thus Sam was abandoned. He stood at the top of the town under the Lady Godiva clock, wondering where to go. He'd come here expressly to accomplish the tedious chore of Christmas shopping. It was a bitterly cold day. Tiny flurries of wind-blown frost never quite graduated to what might have been called snow.

On the stroke of noon, the clock above him began to strike. The mechanical Lady Godiva whirred forth precariously, but the third stroke of the timepiece clonked hollowly as Lady Godiva wobbled to an unexpected halt. Sam looked up. Godiva's enamel buff skin seemed to chafe visibly in the cold air. Peeping Tom had just managed to insert a nose between his half-opened shutters. The mechanism, either frozen or failed, continued to clonk ineffectively until, before the job was completed, it too gave up the ghost.

Sam looked around. No crowd had gathered. Shoppers marched briskly past, huddled into heavy coats, faces deranged by the imperative of seasonal spending. No one seemed particularly dismayed by the dysfunction of Lady Godiva and Peeping Tom or even of the town clock. The public simply proceeded, with appalling dedication.

Sam was astonished. Why did no one rush out to fix the clock? Why didn't crowds of outraged and stubborn Coventrians form a large, unruly scrum and demand an immediate restoration of the city's timepiece? But that was it. If something was wrong, they simply put their heads down and went on without righting it. He was appalled by humanity's capacity to allow a broken thing to go unfixed.

"It's just a clock," said a voice behind him.

Sam turned. Sitting on the steps of the bank beneath the clock, her knees drawn up under her chin, was the Tooth Fairy. Sam felt a compression in his bowels and, for a moment, a painful ringing in his ears. The street tilted slightly.

"Did you ask them? About the telescope?" She was wearing a red and white Santa cap, and she had acquired a leather motorcycle jacket, several sizes too big. Huddled inside the jacket, her gloved fists pressed against her face and her nose blue with cold, she looked up at him, waiting for an answer. Her striped leggings were holed at the thigh. A disc of white flesh bulged from the hole in the stretched fabric. Sam gazed back up at the stopped clock, squeezed his eyes shut and then looked back at her. She was still there.

"Well?"

The Tooth Fairy had appeared one night with a request. She wanted Sam to ask his parents for a telescope for Christmas. She didn't insist; she merely pointed out that she had abetted him in the woods. For that, she said, Sam owed her something, and that something was a telescope. On the contrary, she suggested, if a telescope didn't arrive, she would prepare a spectacular means of exposing Sam's crime.

She shivered. "I'm freezing. Can't we go inside somewhere?"

Sam ignored her and walked away, very fast, toward the pedestrianized shopping precinct. She trotted at his heels. "Did you ask for it? The telescope? Did you?"

Sam didn't look back.

"Because if you didn't, you know what's going to happen. I'm going to tell everyone about your dirty little secret in the woods. Christmas Eve. On the stroke of midnight. I'm going to tell your folks. What a Christmas Box that would be! That's what I'm going to do."

Sam swung sharp left into a large department store, where the air inside was stale and warm. "That's better," she said.

"Mum, Dad, Aunt Madge, Uncle Bill, Aunt Mary, Aunt Bettie." He chanted his Christmas shopping list like a rhyme or prayer for holding off his fear. Hastily selecting a gift from a counter, he paid for it and moved on quickly before taking an escalator to the next floor. He carefully avoided the floor displaying the telescopes. Connie had already priced them for him, and they were prohibitively expensive. Sam was sensitive to his parents' limited means. There was no conceivable way he could ask his parents about it a second time.

"I could help you choose your presents," said the Tooth Fairy, jogging to keep pace. "I've got loads of ideas."

"Dad, Aunt Madge, Uncle Bill . . ."

"Look at that! You know, that kind of thing really makes me want to do something violent! Just *look* at that!" The Tooth Fairy had stopped dead and was jabbing an angry finger at the corner of the store. A huge Christmas tree dominated one end of the store, resplendent with lights and shimmering baubles and golden bows. At the top of the tree a Barbie-doll fairy in a white crinoline waved a mechanical starred wand benevolently over the heads of shoppers passing obliviously beneath. The Barbie-fairy seemed to be the focus for this outburst.

The Tooth Fairy was puce in the face, spitting with rage. "I feel like going over there and pulling the whole thing down. I could too! I could pull the whole thing down!" She jabbed a corkscrewed fingernail in the direction of the tree. Sam saw that her fingers were stained red.

"Red paint!" Sam gasped.

"What?" Puzzled, the Tooth Fairy looked at her hands. "My hands are just cold."

"Why are you fucking up my life?" Sam hissed. "Why? Why?"

An elderly lady loaded with shopping bags stopped and stared at him, openmouthed. He bustled away, putting a distance between himself and the Tooth Fairy.

"Where are you going?" she shouted. "Telescopes are on the next floor."

"Aunt Mary, Aunt Bettie, Mum, Dad, Aunt Madge . . ."

"You wait, you little shit! You just fucking wait!" She bellowed across the department store. "Midnight on Christmas Eve! I'm going to tell them all! I'm going to tell them everything."

The weathermen predicted a white Christmas that year, but the Tooth Fairy woke Sam in the middle of the night just to tell him that the weathermen were wrong, and by Christmas Eve it still hadn't snowed. The house was full of seasonal favorites: tangerines, Brazil nuts, boxes of chocolate liqueurs with glossy foil wrappings, tins of biscuits, packets of "Eat Me" dates which wouldn't be touched until late February. A nylon tree had been decorated and placed in the front window.

"What a sad-looking thing!" Connie looked doubtfully at their own fairy. Half of her blonde hair had fallen in tufts from her head, her white dress was yellowing with age and her wings had been creased in storage. "Perhaps we'll have to get you a new dress," she said, stroking it affectionately.

"Don't talk to it," Sam said in disgust.

"Got to talk to Fairy, haven't we, Fairy? Fairy's been in her box all year, so we love to have a little talk, don't we, Fairy? Don't we?"

"Can't we have a star instead?"

"Oh, Sam! We can't just throw Fairy away like that. You've been on the tree since I was a little girl, haven't you, darling?"

"Stop talking to it!"

Which only encouraged Connie to launch into a nauseating dialogue while holding the fairy like a glove-puppet. She even affected a squeaking, wheedling voice for the fairy, which made Sam grit his teeth. He was rescued from wanting to do violence to the tree fairy by the rap of the cast-iron knocker at the front door. A taste of gray cinders came into his mouth as he thought of the Tooth Fairy's threat to reveal his crime that very evening.

Christmas saw a string of visitors, mostly relatives, some of whom elicited a warmer welcome than others. There were large, perfume-drenched aunts in floral-print dresses who imprinted red lipstick on Sam's blushing cheeks, and thin, whey-faced aunts in catalogue frocks who preferred, thank you, to sit on a hard-backed chair. They arrived with fat and thin uncles, often but not always the converse of themselves. The fat uncles might unbutton their waistcoats and let their opinions spread all across the room. The thin ones might have very little to say between consulting their wristwatches.

It was Connie's sister Aunt Bettie and Uncle Harold who'd arrived, bearing gifts and the ebullience of a little alcohol. Along with sandwiches and pickles, Bettie accepted a cup of tea; Harold, his bald head as smooth and shiny as one of the pink baubles on Connie's tree, preferred a glass of whisky. Sam was handed a neatly wrapped gift. "Not to be opened until Christmas Day!" shrieked Bettie as if reading what, every year, she scribbled on the label. Kisses were exchanged. Though his Aunt Bettie was very much one of his favorites, the challenge not to wipe the wet kiss off his face remained until after she had gone.

Sam tried but failed to slip upstairs unnoticed and was summoned back as his school progress, shoe and collar size were publicly addressed by the four adults. The issue of Sam fundamentally structured the visit. The adults might wander from the subject, catch up on gossip about other relatives; or Harold in particular might insert some remark inscrutable to Sam which brought mirth to the company; but the topic of conversation would always return to Sam.

And with every minute urging the evening on to midnight, the leather football of anxiety inflating in Sam's stomach was pumped still further. He knew that the Tooth Fairy could begin the proceedings at any moment. He also knew that she was awaiting the opportunity of his greatest humiliation.

The matter of the graffiti came up. Everyone was becalmed, regarding him steadily until Bettie broke the silence with a lament on the degeneration of the nation's youth. "Anyone with hair over their ears," she ventured, referring to the growing fashion, "should be thrown in jail."

"You've got hair over your ears," Harold pointed out, winking at the company and making everyone but Sam laugh.

Bettie slapped his leg playfully. "Any man, I mean. Teenage boys goin' around looking like girls."

Sam was just about included in this category. "Yes," said Harold. "You don't know whether to love 'em or hate 'em."

More laughter. They regarded Sam steadily again, as if deciding whether to love him or hate him. Bettie asked, "Is he still seeing that chap?"

Bettie was one of the few aunts in whom Connie had confided that her son occasionally had to see a psychiatrist, and in parlor-speak the psychiatrist had become encoded as "that chap." In Sam's ears, however, the phrase was always delivered with a certain ominous ring far worse than the actual word it avoided.

"What chap?" Harold wanted to know. Bettie gave him a look. "Oh, that chap," Harold said, cottoning on. He winked at Sam. "Waste of time. Sam don't need to see no chap."

"Go upstairs and get your presents for Auntie Bettie and Uncle Harold," said Connie.

Even though he knew this was a cue for Connie to brief Bettie on the latest from that chap, Sam was grateful for the opportunity to make a break. It was a while before he returned with their Christmas gifts, by which time his aunt and uncle were struggling into their coats.

"Merry Christmas, merry Christmas. Are you going to midnight mass?" Bettie wanted to know.

"Yes," said Connie.

"No," said Sam.

Bettie grabbed him and saturated him with more kisses. "Oh, you *must* go to midnight mass! Promise me you'll go to midnight mass, sweetheart!" Bettie was of a religious bent. She was the sort who, without remembering a word of scripture, dressed the church every Harvest Festival and cried when everyone told her how beautiful it was. She kissed him again. "I'm not going to let you go till you say you'll go with your mother. I'm going to keep kissing you till you say yes."

She meant what she said. "There's only one way out." Harold laughed.

Then it occurred to him that perhaps church was the only safe place to be at midnight. He would be protected. The Tooth Fairy wouldn't make a move while the congregation celebrated midnight mass. Not in a church full of people. Not in a place of hymns and prayers and sermons and candles and light. The Tooth Fairy wouldn't dare. The Tooth Fairy would be neutralized. She might even be banished to hell.

"Maybe," said Sam, and then, "yes, yes, all right."

Nev, as usual, declined to join them at midnight mass. He lay on the couch watching TV, a glass of amber ale at hand, and cracking Brazil nuts with a silver implement as they prepared to leave the house. He cheerfully admitted to lacking Connie's religious instincts. Sam thought he caught a trace of irony in his father's voice just before they left. "Have a lovely time," he said, and loudly cracked another Brazil nut.

Midnight mass began at eleven-thirty, and it was bitterly cold when Sam and Connie walked up to the church. A thick canvas of frost had rolled across the world in a single, perfect sheet. It laminated the cars parked in the street; it stretched across the road and the curbstones and the garden fences and over the hedgerow. The night was black and moonless, muffled in the freezing mist, barely penetrated by the street lights sparkling faintly on the frozen pavements.

A few cars had drawn up by the church, and folk were chatting by the gate before going in. Yellow light blazed from the windows, the only bright color available in the evening's silvery darkness. Mr. Phillips, who as well as being a Sunday-school teacher was sidesman to the vicar conducting the service, greeted them warmly as they entered. He seemed genuinely pleased to see Sam. An unmistakable aura of anticipation was gathering over the congregation, as if they genuinely expected something to happen.

No sooner had they taken their seats than the organ pulsed on a deep, resounding note. There was the sound of kneejoints cracking as everyone rose to their feet and took up the first hymn, "Hark! the Herald Angels Sing." Connie, scrambling to find the page in the hymnbook, sang in a high, tremulous voice. Sam, by contrast, occasionally opened and closed his mouth with an approximation of the words.

The service was conducted by the Reverend Peter Evington, resplendent in his vestments, lisping slightly, his bald head glistening under the overhead lights. After a few words the congregation stood again for "O Come, All Ye Faithful." Halfway into the first verse Sam, hearing a tapping from overhead, looked up at the skylight directly above him.

A leaden cloud passed across his heart. Don't do this, he thought. Not here. Not tonight. For the Tooth Fairy had the side of her face pressed flat against the skylight, her sooty curls tumbling over her head. Her mouth was open and her filed teeth reflected the light from inside the church. Meanwhile her fingers, with their extraordinary corkscrewing nails, cantered over the glass like the fall of a horse's hooves. Sam saw one or two people in front of him crane their necks upward, still singing throatily, to see where the tapping came from. Sam buried his red face deeper in his hymnbook.

The crescendo of the carol drowned out the noise from the roof. Before the next verse started up, it had disappeared. He looked up. The Tooth Fairy had gone. She had gone. Thank God, he thought. Thank God.

But as the next verse progressed there came a loud and impressive banging, this time not from overhead but at a window not more than six feet away. She was back, hammering hard on the glass, grimacing at him. Worse, she'd been joined by others like herself. Sam could see, across the Tooth Fairy's shoulder, two or three other sooty forms, vaguely female, with laughing eyes and toothy, open mouths, urging her on, pointing provocatively and flicking back their lank, black hair. One of them leaned across her and rapped hard, with white knuckles, on the window.

Several members of the congregation stopped singing and lowered their hymnbooks, looking around to see where the disturbance was coming from. Sam didn't know if they could see what he could see. Perhaps they just didn't know where to look . . . But the consternation of the disturbed worshippers cut through the carol like a ghost ship through a safe harbor. The carol began to die out all across the church as the rapping continued. Now everyone was sweeping the roof with their eyes, trying to detect the source of the noise. The organ stopped.

The rapping on the glass came louder and still louder. The congregation fell deadly silent. Of all those present only Sam seemed able to see who was responsible for the disruption.

Then the organ started up again, and, with someone bravely leading from the front, the singing recommenced. Everyone joined in with augmented vigor. By effort of conjoined wills and mighty lungpower, it seemed, the congregation succeeded in obliterating the commotion, for when they reached the end of the carol there was no more disturbance. Everyone stood in silence for an unnecessary length of time, waiting, listening, straining, before, on the given signal, they resumed their seats in a shuffling and fluttering of coat hems that sounded like wind among leaves.

There was a cough, and another, before the Reverend Peter

Evington, jowls sagging slightly, a little pink from the exertion of singing, began to sermonize. Sam looked at his watch. It was a minute or so before twelve. Although the service tended not to register the precise moment of midnight and the manifestation of the Holy Spirit in this world, Sam had a dread feeling that he knew someone who would. A reptile claw dragged at his bowels.

Sam checked the windows. The urchin faces had all gone, banished by the freezing cold. Frost had formed on all the external glass. The sky outside seemed as malignant as the breath of an ice-giant. The vicar's words, however, offered little warmth. His educated vowels were shrill against the comfort of his congregation's regional accents; his story seemed numb, hollowed by repetition; and the exhausted cadences of his speech paralyzed the magic of the midnight ritual. Sam lost focus on the words spoken but was brought to his senses by renewed hammering, this time on the church door.

This was no tapping or rapping, but a deep, resonant booming, loud and violent against the oak. Sam glanced at his mother. She looked more afraid than he'd ever known her to be. So too did other members of the congregation. A sudden contagion of fear was in the air.

The Reverend Peter Evington stopped abruptly. Mr. Phillips and another grim-faced man hurried to the door and went outside. In a few minutes they returned, the grim-faced man closing the door securely behind him as Phillips went forward and spoke a few words in the vicar's ear. He coughed into his hand before resuming his sidesman's position.

"A few children, we think," said Evington evenly, "possibly another creed, attempting to disrupt our service."

Sam tried to offer his mother a reassuring smile. Connie clutched the collars of her coat and glanced around nervously. Evington was still speaking when the banging recommenced, louder this time. The church walls shuddered. Exasperated, Evington gave a signal to the organist. All stood to sing another hymn, loudly and at a slightly hysterical pitch. But the banging on the door did not abate. It resounded through the church like muffled cannon, penetrating the currents of the hymn with deep, doomy, slow thumping. Mr. Phillips and some more men went outside again as the singers redoubled their efforts. The banging continued, even after some of the men had returned, shaking their heads.

Sam knew in his heart that he could stop it. All he had to do was to walk to the front of the church, stand before the altar and confess. There was blood on his hands. He had to bow his head and admit to them that he had murdered another boy in the woods. He would confess to them where it had happened. He would lead them to the place. Then it would all be over. The Tooth Fairy would no longer have this terrible power over him, and she and her cohorts would stop what they were doing.

He would do it. Now. He would lay down his hymnbook and walk to the altar. He looked at his mother's set and frightened face. She trilled the hymn neurotically along with the rest of the congregation. As he stepped into the aisle, she looked up from her hymnbook. Something in his deathly expression made her stop singing instantly and caused her own face to turn white. She reached out and touched his arm, offering him a quizzical expression.

"The telescope," he croaked. "Did you get it?"

Appalled and confused by the condition of her son, Connie nodded. Then she pulled him back into the pew beside her, returning to her singing with desperately augmented vigor. Sam felt faint. He put his nose back into his hymnbook and made his jaw work along with everyone else's, trying to lose himself in the singing, letting his weak voice rise like thin smoke to the rafters.

The booming became fainter and fainter. Finally it disappeared altogether.

There was no repetition of the disturbance, and the rest of the service continued in peace. At the end everyone shook hands and wished each other a happy Christmas. They filed out one by one, and Evington shook everyone's hand, simultaneously grasping their forearms with his left hand in a way that made Sam wince.

No one commented on what had happened. It was as if they preferred not to admit that anything unusual had taken place. But Sam knew everything was out of kilter. There was a curve of panic, a disguised hysteria in the voices of the Christmas well-wishers before they went home.

"Well," said his mother when they'd cleared the church gate. They walked home together in silence.

"How was it?" Nev Southall asked sleepily. A dish of Brazil-nut shells lay broken in front of him and the room had a beery tang.

"Teenagers," said Connie darkly. *"Teenagers."*

TWENTY-TWO
Boxing Day

After a disastrous Christmas Day, one package remained unopened. It had appeared under the tree with all the other gift-
wrapped presents and packages. It came in unusual pale green and
yellow striped wrapping paper, and the most distinctive thing
about it was the invisibility of any folds. Sam's own gifts to other
folk, despite his best efforts, were invariably scruffy parcels, ragged
and uneven at the extremities, lashed together with so much Sell-
otape that a pair of shears was usually required just to get them
open. But the paper around this particular package, a rectangular
box, showed signs of being neither folded nor stuck.

It was a gift for Sam, sure enough. His name was spelled out
on the paper but with each letter written in tiny crosses. Something about the parcel made him feel instantly uneasy, so he spirited it upstairs and hid it under his bed. Then he came back down
for the ceremonial unwrapping of the presents, which is where
things began to go wrong.

"What did he do with it?" Clive wanted to know. He was
drawing on a sheet of cartridge paper with Terry's new Spirograph,
a toy that produced mindlessly beautiful spirals.

"He wore it for a while, as if it was a great joke," Sam recounted glumly, "but after ten minutes he said it made his head sweat." They were sitting on the floor in Terry's room, Charlie and Dot being the most tolerant of the three sets of parents on a day when it was too bitterly cold outside to consider their normal, purposeless trawl of the streets. Downstairs Dot and Charlie were watching an afternoon film on television in the company of Linda and her boyfriend, Derek, who was an astonishing twenty years old, four full years older than Linda. Dot and Charlie had revised their early outrage, deciding that it was better to welcome Derek into their home, where they could keep an eye on the pair, rather than have them driving around and parking his Mini in country lanes at night. Clive and Sam made sure they got a good look at this Derek when they came in. He was a tall, stooping character with long sideburns, a large nose and a fairly extravagant sense of dress. He referred to himself as a Mod. Charlie used the word "dandy." When they later remarked they couldn't see what Linda saw in him, it was Terry who pointed out that he'd "got a Mini" after all. Now, downstairs, Derek was looking somewhat uncomfortable holding hands with Linda, watching TV with his hipster jeans crossed at the ankles and still wearing a paper hat from a Boxing Day cracker.

"So for Christmas," Clive taunted, "you bought your dad a plastic Beatle wig?"

"It's true: they make your head sweat," Terry said helpfully. "I've tried one."

"The thing is—" Sam began.

"And you got your mum a moustache mug? Wow."

"I just don't know how they got mixed up."

"But," Terry cut in, "whose presents did they get mixed up with?"

"What?"

"If you reckon they got mixed up, they musta got mixed up with things you intended for someone else."

"No," Sam said unhappily. "Nothing was what I bought. I remember getting bath oil for Mum and Argyle socks for Dad.

Then someone changed them for a plastic Beatle wig and a moustache mug."

"Has your mum got a moustache?" said Clive.

"Fuck off."

"You fuck off."

"So who changed them?" Terry asked, reasonably.

Sam couldn't shake off the picture of his mother's face. Connie
had unwrapped her moustache mug and looked up at her son with
such a mixture of bafflement and disappointment, wanting to
laugh but her instincts checked by sensitive restraint and dismay,
that her expression would be branded on his memory for the rest
of his days. Nev, too, had been made momentarily speechless by his
gift but had tried hard to rescue the situation by squeezing the
shiny black plastic wig over the crown of his head and mouthing,
inaccurately, the words to "Love, Love Me Do."

How long this might have gone on was anyone's guess, but the
moment was interrupted when Aunt Madge and Uncle Bill arrived, on their way to Christmas dinner with their daughter's family. It was just before they got up to leave that Madge, sixty-eight
that year and not too sprightly on her feet, thanked Sam for the
"thoughtful" gift she'd opened that morning.

"What was it?" Connie asked pointedly.

Madge said that though she'd never played the guitar, and indeed didn't have a guitar, there was a first time for everything, and
the book would surely come in handy one day. "What was it
called?" Madge often needed help from Bill in remembering
things.

"Bert Weedon Invites You to Play Guitar in a Day," Bill recalled
precisely. Bill, who as an RAF pilot had been shot down in the
war, also thanked Sam for his Christmas gift. "Scout neckerchief
and woggle. Colors of the Coventry Thirty-ninth, unless I'm mistaken." He said this without blinking and with no trace of evalu-
ation in his voice.

Before visiting, it emerged, Bill and Madge had called in
on Sam's Aunt Bettie and Uncle Harold, with whom Sam had

exchanged gifts on Christmas Eve. Bald Uncle Harold had received from Sam a hairnet. Bettie, a silent dog whistle. This last, they all agreed, would have been a useful gift but for one problem: no dog.

As they were departing, Uncle Bill pulled Sam aside and secretly pressed the neckerchief into his hand. "I'm a bit old for Scouts, Sam, but thank you all the same," he whispered. Bewildered, Sam looked at the neckerchief in his hand and quickly stuffed it into his pocket.

After Bill and Madge had departed, Connie and Nev stared hard at their son, whose only recourse was to blink back at them, until Nev took off his plastic Beatle wig. "This is making my head itch," he said. "Let's get on with dinner."

Sam took off upstairs to examine the neckerchief. Unlike his own abandoned neckerchief, resting there on the wardrobe shelf, lovingly washed and pressed by Connie, this one was grubby and sweat-soiled. The gold embossment on the leather woggle had been effaced by use. It was, without doubt, Tooley's neckerchief. It bore his smell.

It was a warning from the Tooth Fairy. A reminder.

He took the neckerchief outside. While Nev carved the turkey and Connie made the gravy, he doused the neckerchief in paraffin and burned it at the top of the garden. The charred woggle he threw into the dustbin.

Sam himself had better luck with Christmas gifts received. Among other things, Connie and Nev had, indeed, bought him a sizable telescope which he set up in his bedroom, angled at Mars. Terry, meanwhile, had new football boots and a full Coventry City FC football strip, the shirt of which he now wore. Clive had a chemistry set so big it had to be rigged up in the shed outside, which Eric Rogers was already calling the Stink Box. Clive was still a little swollen-headed after his rub with the Russian Grand Master, with whom he had come close to forcing a draw. The Grand Master, having simultaneously eliminated most of the players in the first half-hour, striding rapidly from table to table and moving his pieces almost without thinking, had congratulated Clive and had something to say to the boy.

"He said," Clive reported to the others, " 'Don't underestimate your opponents, but don't overestimate them either.' "

"What did he mean by that?" asked Terry.

"It means," said Sam, "that Clive tries to outsmart himself."

Clive stopped twiddling with the Spirograph. "Are you seeing that tart over the holidays?"

"What?" said Sam.

"That tart. Are you seeing her?"

"You mean Alice?"

"That's the tart's name, isn't it?"

"She's not a tart."

"She's a bit of all right," put in Terry. "I certainly wouldn't mind."

"I haven't seen her. She hasn't been around."

"She's a tart," Clive said again, nastily. "A slag."

"No she's not," said Sam.

"A *bag*. A *slut*. A *dog*."

"Cut it out!"

"Why?"

"Just cut it out!"

"Come on," said Terry, not liking the way things were developing. "Let's go downstairs and give Derek a hard time."

TWENTY-THREE

Demise of the Purple Thistle Club

The heart-piercing cold weather of Christmas translated itself into snow for New Year's Eve. It fell outside Sam's window, at first in wind-blown whorls and spirals and curlicues and finally in large, soft, slowly falling flakes. Sam lay on his bed for most of the morning, watching it. Occasionally his attention turned to the unwrapped Christmas gift. He ran his fingers across the green and yellow foil, searching for a seam, a flap, a way in without tearing the paper. Then he would look out again at the deep feathering and the crumpled clouds promising more snow.

"Every new snowflake is ridden by a Tooth Fairy," a perverse voice said, somewhere inside him.

By early afternoon the wind had swept the snow into impressive, narcotic drifts. Then it stopped. Sam hid the unwrapped gift back under his bed and dressed for the outdoors. He tied a scarf around his neck, pulled on his coat and set out.

Connie called him back. "Where you going?"

"Out."

"Not in those shoes you're not."

He was grateful no one was around to see him wearing rubber boots. The boots squeaked against the snow as he trudged up the lane. There was no other sound. The snow numbed the earth, muffled it and drained it of all color, making everything simple. He felt exhilarated with nothing to feel excited about, courageous with nowhere to go.

The frozen pond was deceptively carpeted with snow. He thought about the pike trapped under it and tried, but failed, to kick a hole in the ice with the heel of his rubber boot. Looking across the field, he saw the dense, dark woods beyond. It had been a long time since he'd been in the woods.

At the edge of the trees, his feet broke through snow-covered tangles of dead bramble, bracken and leaf mold. The earth under the snow was moist and brown, rich and curranty like a cake beneath a layer of marzipan. Breaking through the outlying trees, he found the woods made anew. Nothing stirred, and all noise from beyond the woods was baffled by the density of snow on the trees. The woods were stunned. It was a moment in closed time, a dream of ecstatic paralysis, a phase of Creation in which the trees waited impatiently to take on color, sound, texture.

Sam felt like an intruder offered a glimpse of the miraculous. He stumbled along like a dreamer, trying to follow paths he should have known easily, losing his way, finding it again. A fire burned in the middle of the woods, and he was looking for it. Not a fire with orange flames, crackling and smoking as it burned, not that sort of fire, but one burning with tender rage, flames invisible, heat impalpable: the fire of something in a state of slow decay.

Then he found it. A hollow in the stump of an oak, obscured by bushes, partially covered over by brambles and broken branches, as if someone had dragged a pile of woodland debris across the tree hollow to hide something . . .

He gasped, and his breath came out like a low bark because at first it seemed as if there *were* orange flames, three feet high, licking from the hollow, wavering against the white snow. Then he realized he was looking not at fire but at the brilliant orange winter coat of a dog-fox, balanced on the rim of the stump, dipping its muzzle into the hollow, chewing vaguely and without interest.

Sam's rasping bark made it turn around. The fox looked over its shoulder at him with yellow, conspiratorial eyes, hardly startled. It skipped off the stump before trotting nimbly through the snow, disappearing behind the scrub.

Sam looked back at the hollow trunk, his heart hammering. Had the fox uncovered the thing he feared most? He dithered between approaching the tree stump and running away: he felt he should cover anything exposed by the fox and yet dared not bring himself to look.

"Hey! What are you doing?"

He spun round. It was Alice. She wore her leather jacket and suede mittens and a long scarf wound round and round her neck. Her nose was pinched and blue. Sam felt he was going to retch.

"Fancy meeting you here!"

"Fancy," Sam said.

"You all right? You look sort of funny."

She was huddled inside her jacket. Her cheeks were ruddy, and her blue eyes were bright with reflected chips of ice. Sam saw she was still wearing baseball boots, and all he could think of saying was, "Bumpers."

"So?"

"I can't believe you're wearing Bumpers in the snow."

"So? I can't believe you're wearing wellingtons."

Sam still felt as if he might be violently sick. "Got any ciggies?"

"Plenty!"

The nausea began to subside. "Come on. Let's go back up by the pond."

Sam was relieved to get out of the woods. They walked side by side, talking about what they did over Christmas, where they'd been, what presents they'd been given. When they reached the pond, the car seat was covered with six inches of snow. They didn't bother to clear it before sitting down and lighting up.

"What were you doing in the woods?" Alice wanted to know.

"Walking," said Sam.

"Me too. Sometimes I like it. Just walking. On my own. Mostly on my own."

He exhaled a thick blue plume of smoke.

"That's good: you're smoking properly now. When I first met you, you didn't even know how to smoke. Anyway, I don't mean you. I was glad to see you in the woods. I just mean, there you are, walking on your own in the woods, and you don't know who you're going to see. It could be anyone. Or anything. But I'm glad it was you."

"When did you get back?"

"Yesterday. We were supposed to stay over New Year, but my mum had an argument with my uncle. So here I am."

"What did they fall out about?"

Alice shrugged irritably, blew smoke and stood up. "Something about cooking. It's too cold to sit around," she said, stamping her feet. "What are you doing tonight?"

"Nothing."

"It's New Year's Eve."

"So?"

"Aren't your folks going out?"

Sam knew that Connie and Nev would be cheering in the New Year at the Working Men's Social Club. Every year, for as long as he could remember, they had come home giddy about half an hour after midnight, wearing cardboard policemen's or pirates' hats, and Nev would jog through the house holding aloft a piece of coal and a penny. "Probably."

"I could come round." So startled was Sam by the idea that he just looked at her. She tossed away her cigarette butt. It hissed in the snow. "Not unless you want me to."

"No. It's okay."

"I'll bring a bottle of Woodpecker."

"Great."

"See you later, then."

The sky was already shading from turquoise to mauve as Alice left. Sam trudged home through the snow in a state of blended terror and excitement. He kicked off his boots and went straight upstairs to his room, lying down flat on his bed to compose himself. After a few moments he reached under the bed for the unwrapped package, turning it this way and that under the yellow glare of his bedside light.

Alice is coming, an inner voice kept saying, *Alice is coming.*

Tea was early that evening. Connie bustled around, trying to get ready in time so they could "get up there and get a seat." She accused Nev of taking too long in the bath, and Nev blamed her for taking too long at the mirror. Sam kept his head down as his parents infected the household with an hysterical level of personal preparation. Connie finally appeared in a pink nimbus of scent and hairspray. Nev's skin had about it a strange, scrubbed sheen.

"Make yourself a sandwich," called Connie, simultaneously spotting a ladder in her stocking and thundering back upstairs to change it. "We'll never get a seat. You can watch *The Purple Thistle Club* on TV. You like that."

"Help yourself to a glass of ginger wine," Nev shouted from the hallway, giving his hair oil a last-minute check in the mirror, "while you're watching *The Purple Thistle Club.*"

"Clive or Terry might pop round," Sam said lightly.

Nev came in from the hall and thrust a huge, scrubbed forefinger between Sam's eyes. "No messing," he said, repeating the phrase to cover all possibilities. "And that means *No Messing.*"

"They might not come," Sam said innocently. "But they might."

"Get on," said Connie, opening the front door, "or we won't get a seat."

The door closed behind them.

Sam scratched his head. He switched on the TV, and switched

it off again. He plumped up a couple of cushions on the sofa. Then he found two tall glasses, placed them at the ready and sat with a straight back, hands resting on his knees, waiting.

After half an hour he began to feel self-conscious. He went upstairs to the bathroom and found Nev's aftershave, liberally splashing his face with the disgracefully pungent lotion. After that he stripped off his shirt and sponged his armpits. The doorbell rang.

Buttoning on his shirt, he ran to the front window and, looking down, he saw Clive and Terry staring expectantly at the door. He waited. Terry leaned forward and rang the doorbell a second time. Sam glanced at the clock. It was eight-thirty.

Sam had made no arrangement to see either of them that evening but had a fair idea they would show up. He moved back through the bedroom and waited silently at the top of the stairs, holding his breath. The letterbox flap was pushed open and Sam heard Terry call his name. He heard them discussing where he might be as their voices trailed away. He prayed they wouldn't run into Alice on her way there.

By nine-thirty he decided she wasn't coming. He poured himself a glass of ginger wine, switched on the TV and felt a deep draught of loneliness. On screen *The Purple Thistle Club Hosts Hogmanay* would be at it for hours. A bale of straw had been dragged into the studio, somehow to denote the Caledonian flavor of the evening, and he was staring uninterestedly at the antics of a grown man in a kilt when there came a gentle tapping at the window. He drew back the curtains. Alice was at the window, framed by the snow and the wintry dark.

"I nearly didn't come," she said, handing him a bottle of Woodpecker.

"Shall I take your coat?"

"No. First my mum was going out. Then she wasn't. Then she was. Then she wasn't. Then someone rang to beg her, which was what she really wanted, so she went out. I was going to phone you and tell you."

"We don't have a phone. Did she go to the Working Men's Club?"

"You're joking." She slumped on the sofa and flicked back her long hair. "She wouldn't be seen dead in such a place. God, you're not watching *that,* are you?"

They switched off *The Purple Thistle Club* and Alice showed Sam how to find the waveband of the pirate station Radio Caroline on the radio. Alice sat on the edge of the sofa, her arms dangling between her legs, looking like she might get up and leave at any moment. Sam produced the glasses, but she waved them away. "Tastes better from the bottle," she said, demonstrating with a hefty swig before passing the cider to him.

After a while she relaxed back into the sofa but always keeping an eye on him. She had a habit of cocking her head to one side. Then she released her long brown hair from its ponytail. Her hair fell over her face, and she watched him from behind it with sparkling pale-blue eyes. "Want a ciggie?"

"Naw. My folks don't smoke. They'd smell it when they get back. High Squawk."

"We'll go and stand outside."

They went out to the back garden and lit up. All clouds had been chased from the sky, and the snow was made blue-white by a brilliant three-quarter moon. It was cold. Sam felt the air icy on his lungs. They stood in the snow and smoked.

When they came in again, Alice took off her jacket and reached for the cider. Her lips popped on the mouth of the bottle. The Kinks came on the radio playing "Waterloo Sunset." "I love this," said Alice.

"Yeah," said Sam. He'd never heard it before.

"You're slow, aren't you?"

"What do you mean?"

"Never mind. You're just slow. You're all right, though. Just slow."

Sam told Alice about his unopened package.

"You don't know who it's from?"

"No."

"Well, open it."

Sam went and fetched the package from upstairs. He sat next to her on the sofa and showed her how it appeared to have no folds and no flaps. "That's nothing. They have a machine, in a shop in the town, does that. It's no big deal."

Sam was disappointed. "I didn't know that." He could smell her hair, her skin. Yogurt. Salt. Yeast. The scent of her, the proximity, made his hands tremble fractionally.

"Aren't you gonna open it?"

"I dunno. I—"

"Want me to open it?"

"No, I'll do it." He fumbled with the paper, ultimately tearing it. Inside was a beat-up gray cardboard box. He opened it, and the contents slid into his hand.

"Looks like a bomb," said Alice.

"No," said Sam, staring at the contraption. "It's not a bomb. It's a Nightmare Interceptor."

Sam tried to explain to her what the machine was supposed to do. He even clipped the sensor to his nose by way of demonstration. What he couldn't explain was who had found it, wrapped it and left it under the Christmas tree.

"Weird," laughed Alice. "Bit like you, really. Weird. Pass the cider."

Sam learned a bit more about Alice and her mother as the Radio Caroline DJ burbled happily. Her mother, according to Alice, was an alcoholic who had once worked in the chorus line at the Hippodrome Theatre but who had driven Alice's father away. Her old man was a telecommunications engineer who traveled to places like Saudi Arabia. It all sounded fabulously exotic and sordid at the same time. Since her parents' divorce, money had become a lot tighter, and inevitably her horse-riding was threatened. She and her mother were unable to maintain her horse any longer. "That's why I wrecked the gymkhana that time. I was so upset, I went crazy for a while. But I'm all right now. I get to ride other people's horses. It's not so bad."

When they'd finished the cider, they polished off the bottle of ginger wine. Sam had an attack of the hiccups.

"I know how to cure that," Alice said.

"I'm not standing on my head."

"No, it's not that. Want me to show you?"

"Sure."

"Keep still. Ready?"

"Yes."

She reached across and pressed her hand hard on his crotch. The hiccups stopped instantly. He gazed into her eyes. Her face was neutral, impassive.

The Radio Caroline DJ suddenly became ebullient, announcing the countdown to midnight. Alice jumped out of her seat. "Got to get home before Mum does, or I'll get hell." She threw on her coat, and Sam followed her to the door. When she opened it, an icy blast of crisp midnight air blew inside the house.

"That's the New Year in," said Sam.

She turned back to him, grabbing the collar of his shirt, cocking her head on one side. "Do I get a New Year kiss?" Without waiting for an answer, she pressed her mouth lightly on his. Sam felt his lips tingle. Then, only for a second, she pressed her tongue gently into his mouth. An instant later she was gone, hurrying down the snow-covered path.

"Happy New Year," Sam told her departing shadow.

TWENTY-FOUR
Ad Astra

"Aren't you afraid to look at her? Not just a little bit?"

"No," said Sam, trying to focus.

"I would be. You look at the Medusa and she turns you to stone. Anyway, you're way out. You need to move closer to the zenith."

Sam squinted into the eyepiece and elevated the angle of his telescope at the constellation of Perseus, looking for Algol, the "Demon Star."

"You're still way out. The eclipse will have happened before you get there."

"How can you tell?"

"Because the stars are my sisters and brothers."

"No, I meant how can you tell from where you're sitting?"

The Tooth Fairy sat cross-legged on Sam's bed, picking at the ever-widening hole in her striped leggings. Her heavy boots had left an imprint of February rain and decomposed leaf on his clean bedspread. "I've told you before: I have a map of the night sky tattooed on the inside of my skin." She scrambled off the bed and joined him at the window, gently moving him aside. Without looking into the eyepiece, she elevated the telescope another degree.

Sighting through the telescope again, Sam felt her arm settle gently on his shoulder. "Is that it?"

"That's it. Be patient. Any moment now."

Sam watched, waiting patiently. Finally Algol, the binary star representing the head of Medusa, moved into eclipse and faded to minimum light. It was like heaven winking back at him. "Wow!" said Sam.

"She's dangerous, Sam."

"It's just mythology!"

"I'm not talking about Algol. I'm talking about Alice."

"Alice?" Sam drew back from the telescope and looked at the Tooth Fairy in surprise. Her eyes swam with starlight. "Don't you like her?"

In the weeks since Alice had kissed him, Sam had been visited by the Tooth Fairy many times, and almost invariably on the occasions when he looked through the telescope in the quiet of his room. At these times the Tooth Fairy seemed to reflect his mood exactly; he discovered that if he could be relaxed with her, she could be with him. Though he remained afraid of her volatile and unpredictable nature, he was learning how not to provoke her, while she was capable of surprising tenderness, and even affection, toward him.

"I'm not saying that. I'm not saying I don't like her. In fact, there are many things about her I do like. But she's dangerous, and that's the point."

"*You're* dangerous! What about that stunt you pulled at Christmas?"

"You still haven't forgiven me for that? So your uncle got a hairnet. So what?"

"I'm not talking about the presents. I mean what happened at the church."

Unexpectedly the Tooth Fairy looked sad. "You have no idea how lonely it is at Christmas." She changed the subject hurriedly. "Come on. Angle your telescope toward the southern horizon. Sirius is gleaming."

The Tooth Fairy's eyes were turned up to the night sky, but her renewed interest in the stars was fake. She was grieving over something about which she could never speak, and Sam surprised himself when his heart squeezed for her. He put his eye to the glass.

"Sirius is Greek. It means the 'Shining One' or the 'Scorching One.' I never told you before—it's my star name. Sirius." As she uttered her name, Sam thought he saw the star glimmer with needles of ultraviolet, golden and crimson light. She sighed. "There's too much light. All of this unnatural electrical light streaming from your cities, it pollutes the night sky. You suffer. You all suffer without knowing it."

"Suffer from what?"

"From loss of stars."

Sam felt intimidated by the Tooth Fairy when she was in this mood. He drew back from his telescope and made notes in the journal he'd been keeping since he'd started using the telescope. He looked at his wristwatch and noted what he'd seen. "I've got to see Skelton again," he told her.

"The head-shrink man? He's a star-killer too. He's a real fucking Medusa. There are snakes coming out of his head. You can't see them, but I can."

"He's all right. Mum and Dad told him what happened with the Christmas gifts. He's made an extra appointment."

"So I brought that on, did I? I never wanted that. Listen: I fear him, that one. I fear him more than Alice. Between them they're coming for me."

"Will you always be around?"

"No. Because you don't want me. You make it easy for them." She turned her eyes skyward, and he saw that she was crying. The faint light from the sky starbursted on a tear.

Suddenly there was something appallingly human about her. Her tights were ripped and holed, exposing small areas of white, fleshy thigh, and the wool of her bodice was unraveling under her tunic. Her boots were scuffed, and it occurred to him that, apart from the Santa cap and motorcycle jacket that day in Coventry, she'd worn the same clothes from the moment he first saw her and that the garments were slowly disintegrating.

"I didn't mean to make you sad."

"I'm dying, Sam," she said. "I'm dying."

"I'm sorry," he tried again. "I honestly never meant to make you sad."

He reached out to touch her shoulder, but she stiffened, tossing her head back like a horse. Quickly wiping away her tears, she bared her pointed teeth at him, snarling, "Fuck you. Get away from me." Without warning, she sprang on to the windowsill, sending his telescope clattering. Sam scrambled to catch the telescope as she opened the window, able only to watch her leap into the blackness of the night. He leaned out into the sharp February air to see where she'd gone, but there was no sign of her, neither down nor up.

Sam slammed his window shut. His heart hammered. Reaching under his bed, he found the box containing the Nightmare Interceptor. He clipped the sensor to his nostril and hyperventilated through his nose until the alarm clock was triggered. He switched it off quickly so as not to alert his parents.

He disconnected the crocodile clip from his nose and went over to his astronomical journal, which was lying open on the table. Underneath the date he'd written: *In the constellation of Perseus, Algol eclipsed at 11.45 p.m. Sirius brilliant in colors. Can we recover from Loss of Stars?* On his bedcover was a sooty bootprint.

So he hadn't been dreaming. The Nightmare Interceptor had proved that. Unless he'd been dreaming about using the Nightmare Interceptor. He closed the curtains and climbed into bed. Before settling down to sleep, he reached out and pulled the curtain aside to look out again at the night sky.

Sirius dulled on the southern horizon.

TWENTY-FIVE
The Truth Room

Meanwhile the kiss hung in the air for months, like an aerial spirit. Offered at midnight betokening a new year, with Alice's tongue inserted between his lips at some hazy time dividing the first and the last radio-broadcast chimes of Big Ben, it neither belonged to the dying old year nor yet was it properly born into the celebratory nascence of the new. So it hung, frozen in time, over the threshold of Sam's house, neither in nor out, unacknowledged, the unhatched kiss.

It was never spoken of. Sam certainly never mentioned it to either Terry or Clive. In any event, Terry would have waggled his eyebrows suggestively, and Clive would have curled his lip. Despite the fact that Alice and he sat together most days on the bus to school and back, discussing many things, the subject was never broached. The magical kiss was like the Brazil nuts and the "Eat Me" dates: it seemed to have no place in the world beyond its seasonal novelty.

But again it wasn't a dream. She *had* kissed him. His tongue *had* tingled. His hand *did* tremble. Though the issue could grow no further, the moment could never be taken away. So Sam lived with it, this mystical halfway state of being kissed; and he developed, every time he saw Alice, the nervous habit of pushing his spectacles higher up the bridge of his nose.

The most extraordinary thing was the way in which some of the people around him seemed to suspect vaguely or to guess exactly. Connie had taken to watching him very closely since the holiday season. He might turn suddenly and catch his mother staring at him, her face etched with concern. Then one evening at Terry's house Linda had said something to him that caused him to blush outright. Not that this was unusual. Lovely Linda's unfolding beauty was unstoppable. She wore pink lipstick and enticing perfume even around the house; her increasingly short skirts trumpeted her dazzling, sword-slim thighs; and her full breasts, straining against the white cotton of her blouse, provoked a pang every time he saw her. Sam didn't know how Terry could bear to live so close to her. Each time he saw Linda in a new outfit he would eventually be compelled to return home and go to his room for a frenzied bout of masturbation.

"You look different somehow." Linda had laid a light and fragrant finger on his reddening cheek. She was wearing thigh-length patent-leather boots and a black leather miniskirt. "What have you been up to?"

"Sam always looks like he's found a quid and lost a fiver," chuckled Terry's Uncle Charlie.

"That's right," Linda said thoughtfully, still looking hard at Sam. "You look like you found something and then lost it again."

Sam stood up, pushing his glasses higher up the bridge of his nose. "I have to be getting back home."

"Ask her if she's got a friend for Terry," said Linda. Sam turned furiously. "Joke," she said.

But Skelton was the worst, and the most perceptive.

Sam's next appointment with Skelton was brought forward because of the Christmas-gifts fiasco. Connie had complained to her GP that Sam's visits to the psychiatrist were proving useless. The local doctor had responded to this complaint by arranging an extra session of uselessness, which, oddly enough, appeared to satisfy Connie.

Skelton too seemed to have gone through subtle but discernible changes in the holiday period. He sat behind his desk, licking his finger and slowly turning the pages in a file when Sam was shown into the familiar office. His face was pink with capillaries exploded at the surface of his skin, and his flaxen hair was brushed up in a greasy quiff. His ivory and nicotine-stained teeth jutted out farther than ever when he spoke.

"Tsk, tsk, tsk. Sam, my boy, what have I told you about not buying your uncle a hairnet for Christmas? Eh?"

"Nothing," Sam said, suddenly emboldened.

Skelton glanced up from the file. "Correct! I've told you nothing. Was that unfair of me, laddie? Not warning you about that, I mean. Not telling you not to buy a hairnet for your uncle's tonsure?"

"No."

"Right. Right. So what's all this bloody nonsense about dog whistles and bloody Beatle wigs?"

"It wasn't my fault. Someone switched them on me. Switched the presents, I mean. I bought socks for people and bath salts and all the usual stuff. Then they got switched."

"Oh, I see. A kind of joke. And who, Sam, in your estimable opinion, did the switching?"

Sam shrugged. "Probably the same person who left me the Interceptor."

"The Interceptor?"

"Yes. The Nightmare Interceptor."

Skelton tossed aside his file and folded his hands together. "Tell me about this Nightmare Interceptor."

So Sam told him at length how he'd first been shown the contraption by Chris Morris, Terry's dead father who'd shot himself and his wife and babies because of the wasps in the jamjar; and how Sam had broken into the shed and tried to steal the Nightmare Interceptor the day the Tooth Fairy slashed his arm; and how for a while he'd used the Nightmare Interceptor whenever the Tooth Fairy came around, to test for dreaming, but it always failed, proving conclusively that the Tooth Fairy wasn't a dream.

After Sam had finished Skelton regarded him steadily, thrusting out his jaw and baring his lower teeth. "Can I see this contraption?"

"No," said Sam.

"Aha! So it's like the Tooth Fairy? Only you can see it?"

"No. I mean, I don't want you to see it."

"Why not?"

"I'm going to patent it one day and sell it. It might make me some money. So I don't want every Tom, Dick and Harry having a look at it."

Skelton's eyes widened. Then he smiled to himself. "There is no bloody Nightmare bloody Interceptor is there, laddie?"

"Yes there is."

"Admit it."

"There is."

"Admit there's no such thing."

"There is. It's not like the Tooth Fairy."

"Ah! So you admit there's no Tooth Fairy?"

"That's not what I meant. I knew that you were thinking about what I was thinking. The Tooth Fairy is real, but only I can see it. Anyone can see the Nightmare Interceptor."

Skelton got up out of his chair. "Laddie, there's something changed about you. Now what is it, I wonder?"

Skelton prowled back and forth in a half-circle behind Sam's chair. Sam felt his neck flushing hot. Skelton leaned his ruddy face over Sam's shoulder, seeming to sniff the region of his neck. Sam got a whiff of whisky and pipe tobacco.

Skelton's nostrils twitched vigorously. "Hmmmmmm." He made a low humming sound, "Hmmmmmm. That's it! That's it! I should have known! There's a *girrul!* Admit it to me, wee man, there's a *girrul!* I can smell her, this *girrul!*"

Sam said nothing.

Skelton withdrew his face. "Tee-hee-hee! A *girrul!* Tee-hee-hee! Am I right? Don't be bashful, young Sam, there's no one more pleased than me. I disapprove not in the slightest. Hear me? Not in the slightest! On the contrary, me and this lovely *girrul* together can put an end to your problems. Me and this *girrul* can kick that Tooth Fairy into touch! Now, could you just give her a name for me?"

Silence.

"Please? Pretty please?"

"Alice."

"Alice! Hurrah for Alice! This calls for a celebration!" Skelton marched to his door, flung it open and called to his secretary. "No disturbances now, Mrs. Marsh. See to it, please!" Closing the door, he went to his desk drawer, taking out a half-bottle of whisky and two sticky-looking tumblers. "A wee nip only for a young lad like you, but this is an important occasion, man to man." He poured two glasses, splashing a larger measure for himself, pushing the smaller glass into Sam's hand. "Here's to all the *girruls,* from this first one to the last one, all those lovely, lovely *girruls* who save us boys from the rack and thumbscrew of ourselves. Drink, laddie, drink!"

Sam took his cue from Skelton and sank the whisky in a single gulp. The amber fluid scorched his throat and squeezed tears from his eyes, but he wanted to show the hoary psychiatrist that he could respond to being treated like an adult.

"See all those books?" Skelton waved his empty tumbler at the rows of psychiatric journals and psychoanalytical textbooks. "There's not one of 'em can do anything for you, right now, that a good *girrul* can't do. In your case. I'm not saying that's true in all the cases that come before me, understand, but in your case.

"Now, then, you do know what it's for? Hmmm? You've worked out for yourself that it's not for stirring your tea with? Not for measuring your pastry, what? Well, my advice to you is to get this lovely . . . Alice was it? . . . get this lovely Alice and stick it in, with her consent, of course, as often as she'll allow. Now, do you know what a johnny is?"

Sam screwed up his face.

"What? Thirteen years old and you don't know what a johnny

is? Here. Look at this." Skelton rooted through his drawer, fishing from it a small, foil package. He waved the thing under Sam's nose. Then he laid it on the desk. Sam could see the word "Gossamer" scripted on the foil, exactly like something he'd found in Alice's jacket.

"Now, laddie, I can't give you this. I would, but if your mammy found out, all hell would break loose, and I'd be drummed out of the Brownies and no mistake. Why? Because you're only thirteen years old. Now, I know, and you know, that you're perfectly ready for this. That's the truth. I'm paid to find the truth. It's my job to find the truth. But the trouble with my job is that after finding the truth, I'm under an obligation not to tell it to anyone. They—that is, those outside this room—don't want to hear the truth. But this is the Truth Room, which is why I'm telling you this. The Truth Room.

"I'll tell you where you can get one of these for yourself. You could get these at a chemist's, but you'd only go in there and come out with a bottle of Lucozade, so here's what you do. You wait until your mammy and daddy are out, you go up to their bedroom and you slide your hand between the mattress and the base of the bed, somewhere up the top toward the pillow. Right? You'll find 'em, sure as eggs is eggs."

"How do you know?"

"Got any brothers or sisters?"

"No."

"Then you'll find 'em. Take one and one only—they tend to come in packs of three, God knows why, as if three jumps a night is some kind of national sporting average. Anyway, your old man will just think he miscounted. That's all. Off you go now. And not a word about this to anyone else, understand? Not a bloody word."

Sam realized that somewhere among the appalling information imparted to him Skelton had suddenly stopped treating him like a boy. In his mind, perplexity and gratitude struggled for supremacy. "I understand."

"Good. Now clear off. I've got to think up some bloody silly big words to write about you in this here file." Sam was out of the door before Skelton called him back. "Hey. If you have a change of heart about that contraption you mentioned, that Nightmare thing, I'd like to see it. That is, if the object actually exists."

"It does exist."

"Well, I'd like a squint. And I promise not to tell anyone."

Sam said nothing, gently closing the door behind him. Mrs. Marsh looked up at him with her irritating smile of faint disapproval. Sam opened his mouth and burped whisky at her.

At the earliest opportunity Sam tested Skelton's advice. Having waited until his parents were out, he entered their bedroom, kneeled at the side of the bed, plunged both hands between mattress and base and ran his splayed fingers to right and left. The fingers of his left hand closed around a small cardboard wallet.

Skelton was correct.

There was one foil package left in the wallet. Sam dithered. He examined the package and read the instructions. He was unsure whether to risk taking the only remaining condom. The front door slammed as his parents returned. Sam stuffed the condom in the wallet, shoving it back under the mattress before getting out of the room.

Some days after that Sam found himself in the woods, on his way to see Alice. Ever since the day on which he'd observed the fox chewing at the snow-covered tree hollow, Alice had encouraged him to meet with her there in the woods. He had resisted, for obvious reasons. But she'd been particularly insistent, pressing even. She'd promised a surprise for him. They had arranged to rendezvous at a clearing where they'd once shared a cigarette.

The moment Sam passed into the fringes of the woods he sensed that something was wrong. Tempted at that point to turn back, Sam found Alice's allure to be stronger than his anxiety, and he pressed on. The snow had completely gone, and the crisp, cold wind had dried the debris-strewn paths between the oaks and the birches. It was mid-afternoon. The sky seemed to have darkened early, and the woods were already absorbing a sooty endowment of darkness to come.

Up ahead he could see Alice waiting for him at the edge of the clearing. She wore her leather jacket and her scarf and mittens. She leaned her back against an oak, and one knee was drawn up so that the heel and sole of her shoe was pressed flat against the bark of the tree. On spotting him, she took a nervous pull on her cigarette.

"Hi," she said overloudly. "How are you today?"

There was something stilted and unnatural about the question: as if it actually required an answer. Sam stopped in his tracks. Alice didn't seem to want to look him in the eye. She flicked her fringe and took another drag on her cigarette.

"What's this about a surprise?" said Sam.

"Come here. I'll show you." She stubbed her cigarette butt out on the tree. Her face was flushed. The light about her gloamed lilac, a warning.

Sam stepped closer. "What's the surprise?"

Two shadowy figures stepped from behind a tree. "We are," said one of them.

It was Tooley. He was dressed in his Scout uniform, as was his companion. Only the red neckerchief was missing. Tooley's face was hideously scarred. A livid crescent deformed his cheek as if a horseshoe, still red and glowing from the furnace, had branded its mark there. His dark eyes smoked with hatred.

Sam turned quickly, running directly into the arms of Lance and another youth. "No, you don't," said Lance. He flashed Sam a familiar smile, exposing his appalling crooked and blackened teeth. Sam kicked out wildly, but Tooley leapt at him, grabbing his hair. They easily wrestled him to the ground.

"I see you've met my old friend Alice," said Tooley.

"Strip him," said Alice.

The four Scouts stripped him naked. Alice watched almost with uninterest as they tied him to an oak tree. When they finished, Alice came over and made a contemptuous examination of Sam's cock, curling her lip at what she saw, flicking it hard with her sprung finger before turning away.

Alice delved into her pocket for a packet of cigarettes. She gave one to each of them, offering each a light in turn. They all sucked hard on the cigarettes.

"Get a nice hot red cone," Tooley instructed, examining the lighted end of his own cigarette before giving it another passionate suck. "A nice red tip."

Understanding what they were about to do, Sam pissed himself with fright. Together they advanced on him, lighted cigarettes held like darts and leveled at his face, chest and genitals.

"Wait," said Alice. Holding her own cigarette aside, she cupped his balls in the palm of her free hand. Then she smiled. Her teeth gleamed silver in the strange, lilac light. They were filed to wickedly sharp points. Opening her jaws, she leaned into his crotch to bite, and as she did so Sam heard an alarm bell ringing far, far away.

He woke up, still hyperventilating. The crocodile clip slipped from his nostril as he sat upright in bed. He silenced the alarm of the Nightmare Interceptor.

It was the same appalling dream. He'd had the dream several times before, and he knew he would have it again. Then in shame he realized he'd pissed the bed in his sleep. He despaired.

TWENTY-SIX

Autopergamene

Sam spent many evening hours in his bedroom observing the winter skies through his telescope. Connie thought he spent too much time up there. In ways she was unable to articulate, she thought it wasn't good for him. Nev retorted by asking her why they'd bought him such a damned expensive telescope for Christmas if they didn't want him to use it.

But then they didn't know he had company.

When he watched the stars the Tooth Fairy was always subdued, languid, affectionate. She would lean against his side, draping an arm over his shoulder or resting a hand on his leg, gently stroking his thigh with her long fingernails. And she would instruct him in the wiles of the coursing stars.

"Castor, the white one, and Pollux, the orange one. The Gemini twins, who are not twins at all. And if you had a bigger telescope, you'd see that Castor is a beautiful double star. Now swing right over to the west because it's time to say goodbye to Pegasus for a while before she dips below the horizon."

Sam would gaze in silence and in splendid awe.

"And Andromeda?"

"In three nights Andromeda will be well placed."

Often Sam would sit naked at the window of his darkened room, and as the stars made passage across the night sky her hand would stray and dip toward his genitals, teasing his balls or brushing against his cock. And, as the stars blazed, his cock would engorge with barely solicited blood, until it too pointed at the stars. Trembling, with his eye squeezed against the viewer, he would be seized by an image of the Tooth Fairy, naked. And though he might try to shut it out of his mind, the image would eclipse even the stars in the lens. He would scent her sitting next to him, and he might detect a slight flexing of her limbs, and he would know that she knew. And often he would imagine, against some complaining instinct within him, slowly undressing the Tooth Fairy, his hands and limbs almost paralyzed with anticipation of the revelation lying beneath her clothes.

"You want to see me naked?" she murmured shyly on one occasion.

He leaned back from the telescope, staring directly ahead without answer, which for her was answer enough. There was a whisper of garments slowly removed, a toss of her hair, the hiss of nylon as it rolled along her slender thighs and a slight shimmy at the periphery of his vision as she stepped free of her underwear. Then he looked at her.

Sam was deeply shocked. He was also intimidated by her raw physicality, as she shifted her weight very slightly from one foot to the other, gently pushing her pelvis toward him, measuring his reaction. The dense, dark bush at the top of her legs, in contrast with her creamy flesh, was a stellar explosion in negative light. The coils and curlicues of her pubic hair launched like twisting flares scattered by an energy burst at the carnal source of this astonishing black light. Her aggressively offered cunt was appalling, beautiful, devouring. He felt momentarily blinded.

It was as if a third force had entered the room. First there was him, and then there was the Tooth Fairy, and then she'd undressed and unleashed into the room this ravenous power, this insatiable maw; and he understood for the first time that one's initial impression of the locus of a person residing in their face, their eyes, their talking mouth was childish and staggeringly incorrect, that a brute third force was guiding and misguiding them. Voracious carnality lived and fed and thrived in the shadows, under the water. The insight tolled in him like a bell, and it made him afraid. He was paralyzed by the vulgarity of the truth, but he understood dimly that what he was afraid of was life itself.

On that first occasion her cool fingers closed deftly around his erect cock, and she led him, like a creature on a chain, to his bed. She seemed to reach a decision, softening her brutal assault on him. "Who do you want me to be? I'll be anyone but Alice."

"You're jealous."

"She takes you away from me."

"Can you be anyone?"

"For you, yes."

"Be Linda."

"Linda? You want me to be Linda?"

"Yes."

And she would be Linda, lying back on his bed, naked, smiling, open to him. She would smell the way Linda smelled, and she would take on the voice of Linda. He would lie down on top of her and ease himself inside her, ejaculating almost as soon as he felt the warmth of her thighs under him. And always, after he had come, the Tooth Fairy would be gone, leaving only the indentation in the pillow where her head had been and the sheets glistening wet with starlike semen.

Clive peeled back a piece of skin from his fingertip. He'd punctured the skin repeatedly with a pin until he had enough purchase to roll back a fragment half the size of a postage stamp. Now he had to draw some blood to write his initials on the skin. He pricked his thumb with the pin. Sam and Terry watched with appalled fascination.

Around the time Clive had been scheduled to take his special exam, his face exploded in a distressing case of acne. Various people were full of advice about what he should do, how he should wash more diligently and what he should or should not eat. Someone at his school had even told him that his acne was caused by excessive masturbation. Clive, however, had the good sense to consult Terry and Sam about this last matter, both of whom were acne-free and yet admitted openly and candidly that they had become chronic masturbators.

Despite his levelheadedness over this particular matter, Clive held certain irrational views. He blamed his acne, for example, on attendance at the Epstein School. "Three-quarters of the pupils at Epstein have got terrible acne," he said bitterly, tossing a pebble in the pond. "Three-quarters!"

The pond was fringed with snowdrops, and the sky was a bleached blue. The depths of the pond had taken on a bracken color, and a gentle breeze brought with it a premonition of spring.

"It's just hormones," said Terry.

"That's just a word. You and Sam have got hormones. No, it's that fucking school. It's all boys, for one thing, and that don't help. You two go to mixed schools and look: no fucking acne."

"We got loads of kids with zits in our school!"

But Clive wouldn't listen. "It's what's inside you, trying to find a way out. If you've got something wrong inside, believe me, it'll find a way out."

"And writing your name in blood on a piece of skin is going to cure your acne?" Sam asked unsympathetically.

"It's called an *autopergamene,* not that I expect you to know that. It means 'self-parchment'."

Clive was an unhappy boy. He was due to sit an early Oxford entry examination to demonstrate that he was capable of entering university six years ahead of everyone else. Then a teacher at his school had remarked drily that the main advantage of going to either Oxford or Cambridge was that they taught you how to sneer at other people without their ever suspecting.

"You already do that," Terry had said, when Clive reported this perception. "So I'd say you should go."

The remark had stung Clive. He was acutely self-conscious

about the way in which he had been partitioned from his two
friends, even though they themselves attended different schools.
He felt he had lost something. He was perplexed by the ease with
which Terry and Sam related to people outside their circle. He en-
vied the way they could be relaxed around girls. He was puzzled
by the way they could both talk to Alice without immediately exciting conflict because he couldn't.

Clive drew blood from his thumb on the end of the pin and
wrote his initials on the flake of skin. When the job was completed,
he buried the *autopergamene* in the earth at the side of the pond.
"I'm prepared to try anything," he said.

Sam woke one morning and found a Scout's beret in the middle of
the floor. He felt a dredger move across his heart. He picked up the
beret, and the room tilted precariously.

It was not his own Scout's beret. He didn't need—to be certain
it wasn't his—to check the wardrobe shelf where his own green
beret, khaki shirt and shorts and red neckerchief lay neatly and ob-
solescently folded, even though that was exactly what he did. In any
event, the beret which had appeared on the floor was of a larger
size than his. It was grubbier, the leather rim cracked and split. It
smelled distinctly of hair oil, of decomposing leaf and woodland
mulch. It reeked, unspeakably, overwhelmingly, heart-stoppingly,
of the dead Scout.

It was Tooley's beret.

Sam looked across at the window. It was ajar. He remembered
the Tooth Fairy threatening that she would one day leave something to "show the shrink." His next instinct was to burn the thing,
exactly as he had done with the neckerchief. He hid the beret under
his bed until he was able to steal more paraffin from his father's
toolshed. He took the fuel in a lemonade bottle up to the pond.
There, alone, he burned the beret to a crisp and kicked the cinders
into the water.

"Eat that," he told the pike.

Meanwhile no day went by, on the bus and from school, when Sam didn't look into Alice's eyes to try to divine a hint of special intimacy. He knew she hadn't forgotten the kiss. His intuition informed him that she knew how keenly he waited for some sign from her and that she even knew that he took pathetic comfort from every smile she gave him. His intuition also told him that something external was acting as a block.

One Friday afternoon, on the bus home from school, it came out.

"What're you doing this weekend?"

Alice yawned and looked out of the window. "Seeing my boyfriend."

Sam recovered quickly. "You never said you had a boyfriend."

"You never asked."

The news was crushing and humiliating. The journey continued in silence for some way, until Sam, clinging to a shred of dignity by trying to sound only vaguely interested, said, "Anyone I know?"

"No." Then after a while Alice volunteered some information. "He works in London. I only see him occasionally. When he gets to drive up this way."

When he gets to drive up this way? thought Sam. Here was Alice, fourteen years old, merely a year older than himself, and she had a *regular boyfriend* who *worked* in *London* and *drove* a car. "How bloody old is he?"

"Twenty-two."

Sam was disgusted. How could she think of going with someone so cadaverously *old?* His mind flashed back to the scraps of letter he'd found in the pocket of her leather jacket and to a crumpled piece of foil. "Light filmy substance?" he said.

"What?"

"Webs of small spiders? Something flimsy?"

"What are you talking about?"

"Wouldn't you like to know?"

"You're mad. Totally insane." She rang the bell to stop the bus. "Do you want to come to my place?"

Alice's place? Sam had only ever seen Alice's house from the outside. "When?"

"Tomorrow. Come round in the afternoon."

"I thought you were seeing your boyfriend?"

"Come anyway."

So Sam finally got to meet Alice's mother. Alice was the only person Sam knew who lived in a detached cottage with an impressive, tree-lined gravel driveway. The cottage, however, was in need of renovation. Closer inspection revealed a roof in disarray and patches of rendering on the side of the house that had fallen. When he arrived at the place a Jaguar sports model in racing green stood smarting on the gravel. The wrought-iron knocker in the shape of a dog's head rapped weakly on the door. Alice answered.

Sam had for some time been curious about the character of Alice's mother, June. A former chorus-line dancer, she was now a writer, Alice had said. She made a living from composing the rhymes inside greeting cards. Sam felt slightly intimidated by the idea of meeting a writer. It was like being forewarned that the person you are about to encounter has a hunched back or one eye and a withered hand.

The room into which he was shown, however, was disappointing. He'd anticipated an exhibition of overt bohemianism in the writer's habitat; at least there should have been a human skull on the mantelpiece or an Egyptian sarcophagus in the hallway. Instead there were acres of chintz, flock wallpaper and a mahogany upright piano standing against the wall. June Brennan satisfied some expectations, in that although her face was heavily rendered with makeup, she hadn't yet managed to clamber out of her nightdress. She was reclining on the sofa, sipping white wine from a glass flute. Her bare feet rested on the lap of a young man.

"Who's this?" she asked, not altogether unfriendly. The young

man looked up at Sam. He had tight, blond curls and a Mediter-
ranean suntan. A humorless smile bent his lips slightly as Alice introduced them.

"This is Sam."

"We're honored, Samuel," said June, raising her glass. There
was a slur in her voice. "She doesn't usually bring her boyfriends
heyah." This last word cracked like a whip on a horse's flanks.
Whatever meaning was in it was lost on Sam. It was two o'clock on
Saturday afternoon, he noted, and Alice's mother was sloshed.
"Take Samuel upstairs, Alice. Go and play Monopoly or whatever."

"Come on," Alice said glumly.

Sam had never before had a good look inside a girl's bedroom.
Terry and he had once snooped inside Linda's boudoir, but they'd
been caught and unceremoniously bundled out. Alice's walls were
covered with color-magazine pop-star pinups: Animals, Kinks,
Yardbirds, the Who, some white-haired guy called Heinz. Her
dressing table was festooned with riding rosettes and small tro-
phies. A box record player lay open on the floor, a disc already on
the turntable. Alice set the stylus, turned up the volume and closed
her bedroom door. The Troggs belted out "With a Girl Like You"
as she and Sam squatted on the floor.

"Take no notice. She's always like that."

"Always pissed?"

"Mostly. That's why I haven't brought you here before."

"So why did you today?" Alice shrugged. She turned to the
dressing-table mirror and began brushing her hair vigorously. "For
a minute," said Sam, "I thought that bloke downstairs was your
boyfriend."

"He is."

"Really?" Sam blurted. "Looked more like your mother's
boyfriend."

Alice's eyes blazed briefly in the mirror. She let the brush fall
into her lap. "It's complicated. She doesn't know."

The record stopped, and in the silence Sam heard the ratchets of his own mind figuring out the complication. Alice leaned across and lifted the record arm from above the spindle, so that the same disc could repeat. "I like to play the same one over and over. It really gets on her nerves."

"Why don't you get a boyfriend more your own age?"

"What? From somewhere round here? Everyone in Redstone is backward."

He had to agree. Everyone in Redstone was backward. He also had a pretty good idea why he'd been paraded that afternoon. "Do you?"

"Do I what?"

"Light filmy substance. Something flimsy."

"What?"

"Not worth crying all night over."

"I hate it when you talk like this."

He wanted to tell her he'd read the fragments of her letter to—he suspected—the young man downstairs. Instead he said, "Do you know what an *autopergamene* is?"

"No."

"Got a pin? I'll show you." The record stopped, the stylus arm lifted and returned. There were a few seconds of empty vinyl hiss before the record started over again.

Alice held her *autopergamene* up to the light with a pair of tweezers. Her initials ALB were finely traced in blood on the fragment of skin. It was fascinating, for about fifteen seconds. Then she carefully laid it down on the dressing table. "I'll make us some coffee." She got up and bounced down the stairs.

Sam took a matchbox from his pocket and, with tweezers, he pressed the two scraps of skin together. Then he dropped them in the matchbox. After that he opened a window. He would tell Alice a breeze had blown the "self-parchment" away. The Tooth Fairy stole teeth from him, and she stole semen. He would steal skin and blood from Alice. It crossed his mind that the Tooth Fairy might not like this act of magic, this blasphemous *autopergamene.* She might be angry. He shivered.

Alice returned with two mugs of instant coffee. "I just heard something on the news," she said. "On the television. Downstairs. It was in the woods. They just found a body in Wistman's Woods. Hey! Are you all right? Sam, are you all right?"

TWENTY-SEVEN
Nemesis

After Sam left Alice, he went directly to Clive's house. His hand trembled as he let the knocker fall at the front door. No lights were on in the house, and it was rather obvious that no one was home. Despite this, he knocked loudly three times. Finally he went around to the back of the house, desperately thinking how he might leave Clive a warning message. He leaned his head against the wall, pressing his face to the rough pebble-dash, thinking he was going to be sick. The angle of the wall tilted precariously.

He looked up. The small window of Clive's bedroom was propped open. It occurred to him that if he climbed on to the flat roof below the bedroom, he might squeeze inside the window and leave a note for Clive. Finding some housebricks in the garden, he carefully piled them one on top of the other. By stepping up on the housebricks, he was able to hoist his chin over the lip of the flat roof. Then the housebricks toppled under his feet, his chin slamming against the roof. He fell back, spitting blood and nursing his jaw. A loosened canine wobbled in his mouth.

He gave up on the idea of breaking into Clive's bedroom. Careful to conceal any signs of his visit, he returned the bricks to where he'd found them, closed the gate behind him and made for Terry's house. His legs seemed to act independently of him, moving him along in jerky, inept strides. A passing stranger gave him a sidelong glance.

At Terry's house he'd been trained to use the back entrance. There stood Terry's Aunt Dot with the door wide open, flapping at kitchen smoke with a tea towel. A chip pan had almost caught fire. Dot didn't have much time for him: didn't he know Terry had gone to the football match? With Dot still slapping her tea towel Sam backed away.

Expecting to see a squadron of police cars drawn up outside his house, blue rotary lights quartering the air, he was shivering violently by the time he got home. He tried to slip up to his bedroom unnoticed but met Connie on her way downstairs. He stood paralyzed, one foot set on the bottom step.

"You're back," Connie said.

"Have they been?"

"Who?"

"Anyone."

Connie suddenly noticed he was shivering. She put a hand on his brow. "You've got a temperature. You're burning up. Get up them stairs and let's get you into bed. What have you been doing all day?"

Connie made Sam climb into bed. She brought him a hot drink and two aspirin tablets. He pretended to fall asleep immediately. Connie looked in on him and touched his brow again before turning off the light. She closed the door softly behind her and went downstairs. Sam lay shivering in the dark for some time.

Then the Tooth Fairy came.

And the Tooth Fairy had changed.

It manifested as a scintillating light on the floor, a few feet from Sam's bed. Sam recognized it as the Tooth Fairy in diminutive form, no more than an inch high. His fever raced as he beheld the sparkling vision. Then the light died, and the figure ballooned rapidly, a shadow filling out the available space, its head and shoulders impacting heavily against the bedroom ceiling. Its female form had gone.

The androgynous shadow regarded him steadily with a glittering, baleful eye. The black tangle of corkscrew locks quivered in the dark. The old smell was back, the rancid odor of the childhood fairy, smells of the stables and the fields, but with a new, chemical odor, a smell of corrosion, a whiff of burning. The Tooth Fairy's clothes hung in rags, the striped leggings barely visible.

The Tooth Fairy—no longer could it be referred to as she—moved across the room, reaching its huge head toward him. In the diminishing space of the room the filed teeth gleamed, menacing, predatory, moving closer. Sam felt the venomous breathing on his neck. "You shouldn't have done that."

"Done what?"

"*Autopergamene.* Blood-and-skin thing. Shouldn't have done that. Haven't I looked after you?" The Tooth Fairy clutched the matchbox in which Sam kept the *autopergamene* and the twist of hair stolen from Alice's comb. "Haven't I?"

"Yes."

"Haven't I protected you? Haven't I been the one?"

"Yes."

"I'm going to tell them you did it. Did you get the beret?"

"Please don't."

"Then you're going to have to pay. It's my turn."

"No. Please."

"Blood and skin, Sam. Blood and skin."

"Please!"

The Tooth Fairy reached out with a poisonous, claw-like hand, grasping him by the windpipe, forcing his head back on to the pillow. Sam kicked, and the Tooth Fairy placed a huge choking knee on his chest near his throat. Sam couldn't breathe. His throat rasped. He couldn't cry out. The Tooth Fairy reached inside his mouth with putrid fingers, grabbing at a loose tooth with thumb and forefinger. A searing white-heat of pain exploded in his head as tooth root snagged on nerve. Sam tried to scream as the Tooth Fairy waggled the tooth violently back and forth, but the grip on his windpipe stopped all but the faintest gasp. Pain detonated in shock waves again and again, each beat an electrically charged microflash of agony.

Then the tooth erupted, in a hideous ejaculation, into the Tooth Fairy's hand. Cold air rushed to fill the gum cavity left behind. The Tooth Fairy's fist closed around the bloody tooth before it was consigned to the matchbox. Sam heard a roaring wind and saw the Fairy slavering in triumph before he lost consciousness.

"Laryngitis," said the doctor breezily, stuffing the tentacles of a stethoscope into his battered leather bag. Sam lay in bed with his eyes closed while the doctor spoke to Connie. "He's got laryngitis. That's why his throat is so inflamed and his voice is hoarse. Try to get him to drink as much as possible. Don't worry if he starts babbling. He's slightly delirious, but the antibiotics will eventually bring down his temperature." The doctor had been in the house under a minute, and now he was gone, leaving Connie and Nev looking at each other. "I suppose they don't like being called out on a Sunday," said Connie.

Sam spent the rest of the day slithering helplessly between sleeping and waking. Each time he came to consciousness he pressed his tongue to the new cavity in his mouth, waiting for the police to knock on the door. He was tormented by images of himself and the other boys interrogated by the book-end detectives, dragged through the courts and dispatched to a juvenile detention center. Now it was impossible to reach either Terry or Clive before the police arrived. It was only a matter of time. He surrendered to the inevitable.

Monday passed, and nothing happened. Sam spent Tuesday in bed waiting, waiting for the knock on the door. But it was not until early Wednesday evening that anybody came. Sam heard voices downstairs, and though he strained to hear, he couldn't determine who it was or what was being said.

Then the bedroom door opened slowly and the moon-like faces of Clive and Terry appeared. They looked ghastly; stiff and uncomfortable. Escorted by Connie, the boys crept into the room. "Your friends have come to see you," she said. "I told them they could just say hello, even though you're not well enough to have visitors yet."

Terry's eyes bulged. Clive's eyes burned. Connie stood over them as they stood by the bed, shifting their weight uncomfortably from one foot to the other. "How are you?" said Terry.

"Yeah," said Clive. "How are you?"

Sam desperately tried to read the frantic codes and signals and messages behind their unblinking eyes. He looked at his mother standing over them with her hands on her hips. She showed no sign of moving. "Not too good."

"Not too good. It looks bad," said Clive.

"Oh," said Connie. "It's not that bad. He'll be up and about in a day or two."

"You'll be *out of the woods in no time.*" Terry hitched up an eyebrow.

Clive agreed. *"Out of the woods."*

Sam seemed to shrink.

"We'd best leave him," said Connie. "You'll come again in a day or two, won't you, boys?"

"Yeah," said Clive. "Best not talk with laryngitis. Best say nothing."

"Best say nothing at all," said Terry. "Not a word."

"Gosh! You make it sound worse than it is." Connie laughed, shepherding them out of the room. "He's not dying, you know."

Sam heard the front door close and lay staring at the ceiling. *Out of the woods. Best say nothing. Out of the woods.* The words echoed down a dark shaft. *Out of the woods.* He felt himself riding soft, black earth, itself shifting and tumbling beneath him into the steep-sided shaft, a pit reeking of strangely comforting leaf mold and tree root, until the bottom of the world blew outward in a slow, silent explosion and he was falling, falling through space, amid stars, stars that looked upon him with interest, but with cold energy.

TWENTY-EIGHT
Out of the Woods

By Thursday Sam was recovering. His high temperature had disappeared, his voice was back to normal and he was sitting up in bed. A get-well card had been delivered by hand, and Connie left it, unopened, by his bedside. Sam waited until Connie had returned downstairs before tearing open the envelope.

It was from Terry and Clive. Terry had written, "Don't Worry," and had printed his name. Clive had written, "Everything Will be All Right," signatured with a flourish. Then there were messages from people with bogus names like Tom Chum and Billy Wellbeing, along with slogans such as "One Hundred Per Cent" and "Happy Days." Sam winced at the Martian code. His eyes strayed to the dreadful rhyme printed in italic script and wondered if it had been composed by Alice's mother.

Late on Friday afternoon Clive and Terry visited again. Sam was up and about, and Connie let them go up to Sam's bedroom to talk. Terry closed the door as Clive switched on a transistor radio.

"What's been happening?" asked Sam.

"They found a body in the woods," said Clive.

"I know. I heard on Saturday. I tried to tell you before I got ill."

"Someone said they saw you trying to break into our house. One of the neighbors."

"I was trying to leave a message."

"Anyway, neither me nor Terry heard anything about it until Sunday night. We tried to get to you, but your mum wouldn't let us near you. That day we came round, we were trying to warn you, to tell you just to deny all knowledge. To say nothing. We were going out of our minds. By then they still hadn't identified the body."

"There was a police statement," put in Terry. "The body had decomposed."

Sam remembered stalking through the snow-covered woods and seeing the fox chewing on something in the hollow stump.

"We had it all planned out," said Clive. "We'd played the Wide Game until we'd got bored, and then we'd made our own way home. The simplest stories are the best and the easiest to stick to. Then there was another police statement."

"The body they found," said Terry, "had been there for seven or eight years."

"You mean it wasn't . . . ?"

"No," said Clive. "It wasn't *our* body."

Sam tilted his head at the implication. "Who was it?"

"They still don't know."

"God! Jesus! What a relief!" The other two nodded. Then something else dawned on Sam. "But that means . . . it means—"

"It means our body is still there," Clive cut in.

"Waiting to be found."

"I've thought about that too. But I figure we should just carry on, say nothing, know nothing. Even if it did get found, there's nothing to link us with it. We just got bored the night of the Wide Games and we went home. Only us three know any different."

Sam looked at the wall.

"That's true, isn't it?" said Clive. "Only we three?"

"Pretty much."

"Pretty much? What's that supposed to mean?"

"I might have mentioned it to Alice."

"*Mentioned it?* You might have *mentioned* it?"

"Keep your voice down," Terry hissed.

"You *told* that stupid tart? You fucking idiot fucking weasel-faced fucking toe-rag—"

"She told me about the body. I was so shocked, it just came out!"

"Moron! Brain of a fucking blowfly! Why are we sticking up for you? You're the one who did it!"

"He was helping you, Clive!" Terry protested. "Or would you have preferred Tooley to—"

"Maggots for fucking brains! Worms! You intestinal piece of dog shit!"

The door burst open. It was Connie, and she was livid. "What's all this shouting? I've never heard such language in my life! I'll not have it in my house! You hear? Not in my house!"

Clive pushed past Connie and went thumping down the stairs. The front door slammed.

"What's going on? What's got into that boy?"

"He's upset," Terry tried. "He had an important exam this week and he messed up. Then Sam said the wrong thing and Clive got upset."

"No excuse!" Connie turned and followed Clive down the stairs. "I'm not having language in this house!"

They could hear Connie downstairs, still talking to herself five minutes later.

"Was that true about Clive's exam?" said Sam.

"Yes. He had to do this poxy Oxford thing, remember? Well, it was on the Monday after we heard about the body being found. Something weird happened. He went into the exam and wrote his name over and over and over for the entire duration of the exam and handed it in."

"He cracked up," said Sam.

"He said he had this voice talking in his ear the whole time he was sitting the exam."

The Tooth Fairy popped into Sam's mind. *It's spilling over,* he thought, *it's spilling over.*

"He said," Terry continued, "there was this weird, scruffy girl with metal teeth sitting behind him, whispering, telling him what to write."

"He'll be all right. We've just got to keep our heads."

"That's great. The Heads-Looked-At Boys have got to keep their heads."

Terry swiveled the telescope on its tripod. It was possible to train it on Wistman's Woods in the distance. He squinted into the eyepiece, trying to focus on the trees. "He's right though, Sam. It was a pretty stupid thing, telling Alice."

"I know. But I don't think she believed me."

"Let's hope not. How does this work?"

"Especially now they found that other body. She'll think I was just making up stories to impress her."

Terry was still fiddling with the focusing ring. "Is that what you do to impress her? Hey! What's that?" Terry focused on a black dot at the edge of the woods; something high in the branches of a tree. The black dot resolved into a white face. The face was smiling, looking back across the half-mile distance directly into the telescope. The face grew larger, smiling malevolently at Terry. He made out a head of sooty, corkscrew curls and a grinning mouth, exposing what appeared to be a set of teeth sharpened to vicious needle points. Suddenly the face ballooned massively and came speeding toward the telescope.

"Look out!" Terry flung himself back from the impending impact. There was a tiny splitting sound.

"What is it?" shouted Sam.

Terry dropped into a crouch, hands held up to protect his face. Recovering only when the anticipated crash failed to arrive, he looked nervously across the top of the telescope. There was nothing. "I saw something," he breathed, "something coming at me."

Sam put his eye to the viewer. All he could see was a milky cloud. He fiddled with the focusing ring, but the milky cloud failed to resolve or clear. Swinging the telescope round, he peered at the master lens. It was shattered, without having falling apart, into a thousand tiny points of glass. "It's broken," he murmured.

"What's going on?" Terry said unhappily. "What's going on?"

TWENTY-NINE
Alice's Party

Sam suddenly had another friend to sit with on the bus to and from school. Clive's transfer from the Epstein Foundation to the more democratic Thomas Aquinas Grammar School was effected with extraordinary swiftness. Eric Rogers had been emphatic. The Epstein Foundation, he opined after being informed of Clive's disastrous exam performance, had done nothing but turn his ordinary little boy into an opinionated brat who knew better than everyone about all things under the sun and who employed fantastical language to tell them so.

He was as modest about Clive's intellectual abilities as he was about his own. "You can't pour a quart into a pint pot," he told everyone. "Look what happens." And though Clive didn't particularly like to think of himself as a pint pot (some of the elitist froth of the Epstein Foundation was still clinging to the lip of the vessel) when his father demanded he be returned to a "normal school for normal boys," he didn't object. He even believed, in his overcrowded thoughts, that the change might cure his terrible acne.

When Clive appeared in a pristine Thomas Aquinas black blazer for his first morning at his new school, it presented Sam with a dilemma. Should he sit with his old childhood pal, to whom he was loyal even to the point of murdering another human being, or with the sexually precocious, incitingly fragrant, heart-squeezing Alice? On the way into school that morning, he could do nothing other than lower himself into the seat next to Clive, even though, when Alice climbed aboard the bus one stop farther down the road, he saw her falter very slightly on seeing Clive. It was like experiencing a heart skipping half a beat, or perhaps a quarter-beat. But he felt he solved the problem by slipping in beside Alice for the return journey, leaving Clive to take the seat in front of them. While Alice talked happily, Clive gazed sullenly out of the window all the way home. This arrangement became the daily pattern; it never varied, nor was it ever commented upon.

It was bluebell time when the police became interested in Wistman's Woods all over again. Sam, Alice and Clive sat up by the pond one Sunday afternoon, enjoying some fine spring weather. Terry was waiting to play football in the field behind them. Already outstripping his contemporaries in schoolboy football, he'd made the subs' bench for the Redstone Village B team, the youngest player ever to put on the Redstone claret and blue. The sky was cloudless, and mayflies were skimming the surface of the pond. With the shouts of the footballers volleying behind them, Alice explained what she'd heard.

"They're going to make a new search of the woods. It said so in last night's *Telegraph*."

The police had made no progress in identifying the corpse unearthed in the woods. Appeals for information had yielded nothing. A new search was to be made in the hope that it would provide further clues.

Sam and Clive stared into the water. The still pond perfectly reflected the overhanging trees and the bushes and bluebells growing near the bank; the skin on the water could almost have been rolled up like a tapestry picture, stolen and taken home. Alice watched them keenly. "Does it make you nervous?"

Neither gave her an answer.

"Well?"

"Why should it make us nervous?" said Clive.

"Sam told me."

"Told you what?"

"You know. And I know he told you he told me."

"What's she on about, Sam?"

"Dunno."

A whistle blew. There were cheers. A goal had gone in.

"She's on about that time," said Sam, "when I was pulling her leg."

"Oh, that," said Clive. "Some people believe anything you tell 'em."

"I saw Sam's face that day. I don't think he was joking."

"Sure, Alice."

"Anything you say, Alice."

"You're going to have to move it."

Sam and Clive turned to look at her. The sky was reflected in her sincere and immaculate eyes. She stood up and, leaning her back against a tree trunk, she lit a cigarette, blowing the smoke vertically.

"You know your trouble, Alice?" said Sam, pretending to laugh. "You can't tell the difference between fantasy and reality. That's your trouble."

"I can help you," she said softly. "If you'll let me."

When the final whistle blew, they strolled over to the football pitch. The players were trooping toward the changing rooms. Terry was shaking hands with the opposition. Clive marched ahead. "Did you get a game?" he demanded within earshot of the team coach, a costive, overweight little man in a cloth cap.

"Last two minutes," said Terry, jogging away with the other players.

"Two minutes?" Clive spat in disgust. "It's not worth showering after that!"

"The lad's only thirteen years old," the coach barked back. "These are grown men."

"He can run rings round any of your players! He could tactically humiliate all of you! You won't see a finer talent in Redstone, ever!" Clive walked away, with Sam and Alice following. The coach stared after them, lip curled in an expression of speechless contempt.

"What do you know about football?" smirked Sam.

Clive stopped in his tracks. "Nothing. But I believe in Terry. Totally. I believe in my friends, in everything they do. I believe in Terry. I believe in you, Sam. And I believe in you, Alice." Clive stalked away in the direction of the changing rooms to look for Terry.

"Looks like you just got admission to the gang," Sam told Alice.

Alice looked uncertain whether she still wanted membership.

"We've got to move the body before the police find it," said Clive.

Terry sat on the leather Morris seat, head in hands, hair still wet from his post-match shower. Sam sat on a low bough, legs kicking nervously. Alice had gone home.

"Maybe it's better," Sam tried weakly, "if we don't touch anything. Say nothing. Know nothing. Keep our heads down."

"It's only a matter of time," said Clive, "before they find it. Then they'll go to the Scouts. Then they'll come to us."

"What's your idea?" said Terry.

Clive let out a deep sigh. "We get a tarpaulin. Wrap it round the body. Carry it back here. Tie some weights to it." Then he picked up a rock and tossed it into the middle of the pond. It splashed noisily, dispatching concentric ripples toward the edge of the pond. "I reckon it's pretty deep. And we know there are things in there that eat flesh. Pike and things."

"Oh God, oh God!" moaned Terry.

"We do it at night," Clive continued. "Late."

"This isn't going to work," Sam whined.

"Isn't there anything else we can do?" moaned Terry.

"Like what? We can't bury the thing in the woods. The police dogs will sniff it out. The only other option, as I see it, is to turn ourselves in." No one liked that idea. "So that's agreed, then?"

"What about Alice?" said Sam.

"Absolutely not."

"I'm not sure we can manage on our own. She could help us carry it."

"No."

"Has she offered to help?" Terry wanted to know.

"Yes. She'd be useful. In all sorts of ways. For a start, we're going to need some explaining to be done."

"Absolutely not," Clive insisted. "I won't consider it for a moment."

"Clive, you're outvoted," said Terry. "Tonight. We do it tonight."

Sam told his mother and father that both Clive's and Terry's folks had said it was okay, and that if they refused, he stood to appear childish and could never look his friends in the face again. Clive and Terry used the same line. All three boys produced Alice's telephone number, since Alice's mother had offered to reassure anyone with anxieties about the enterprise. Nev and Connie had no telephone, however. Terry's Aunt Dot and Uncle Charlie had just had one installed, and since both hated using it, they got Linda to telephone for them. A very eloquently spoken lady declaring herself to be Alice's mother convinced Linda that there was plenty of room at the house for the boys to sleep over at Alice's birthday party. Linda was sent to tell Connie and Nev that everything was fine.

"Does she drink?" Linda whispered to Sam. "She sounded half-cut, and it's only six-thirty."

Eric and Betty Rogers were more obdurate, however, and for a while it seemed as though Clive was going to have to fall back on the expedient of climbing from his bedroom in the dead of night. But then a well-timed tantrum, blaming all of his misfortunes and misery on the Epstein Foundation and the fact that he'd never been allowed a whiff of normality, unlike Terry and Sam, who were being allowed to stay overnight at Alice's house, neatly steered his parents round.

"It's not as if they're going to get up to anything at their age," Betty reasoned. Eric, having no illusions about what thirteen-year-olds could or couldn't do, preferred not to answer. Betty, who'd been baking all afternoon, thoughtfully iced a cake with Alice's name and insisted that Clive take it to Alice's party.

The whole idea had been Alice's. After the boys had gone to her house, she'd whisked them up to her bedroom and played loud music while her mother readied her face for a night on the town. Alice knew from experience that June wouldn't get back until two or three in the morning, rapturous with gin. Any phone calls after six o'clock could be dealt with by Alice's impersonation while the genuine article soaked in her perfumed bathtub as Vivaldi blasted, with cannons, from the bedroom.

So it was that at eight-thirty the three boys arrived at Alice's house, each toting a sleeping bag and a bottle of Woodpecker cider. Clive in addition sheepishly supplied a large iced cake, Sam a packet of cigarettes and Terry a disconcerting, frozen smile reflecting an admiration for Alice that was growing by the minute.

They played records. They drank the cider and smoked cigarettes. They ate the cake.

At midnight the three boys waited, crouching behind a hedgerow beside a five-bar gate. The gate opened on to the field adjacent to Wistman's Woods. A large canvas tarpaulin had been pillaged from a nearby building site, where things had already started to go wrong. While cutting the ropes that lashed the canvas to some building materials, Clive had gashed his hand with his penknife. Then the canvas was so incredibly heavy that it took two of them to carry it away. They were grimy and exhausted before they had even entered the woods.

A gibbous moon illuminated the field and the road beside the hedgerow, the kind of moon they didn't want. A few scudding clouds were not enough to dull its lantern.

"What if she doesn't come?" said Clive, sucking his wound.

"She'll be here."

"I've been wondering about this other body they found in the woods," said Clive. "The police said it had been there about seven or eight years."

"So what?" Terry said uneasily.

"Well, I've been figuring out how old we were at the time. I figure that person, whoever it was, would have been killed around the period that . . . about the time when . . ."

Clive's voice trailed off when he saw Terry's face. Terry's eyes were closed, and his eyelids fluttered wildly.

"Shut it!" Sam hissed. "Just shut it!"

A car's headlights appeared along the road, and they flung themselves full length to the ground until long after it had passed. After some minutes they heard a horse snorting, and Alice appeared in the moonlight, her leather jacket gleaming. She was leading the skewbald mare across the grassy field on the other side of the road. Girl and horse seemed to glide noiselessly through the field. Mist rose from the grass under her feet and beneath the horse's hooves.

"She's here! She's done it!"

She stopped at a gate on the other side of the road, fumbling with the latch. The horse tossed its head, its breath a silver plume in the night air. Suddenly another car's headlamps appeared in the road, speeding toward them. "Get back!" cried Sam. "Get back!"

Alice ducked back, tugging sharply at the horse's reins, trotting it away from the gate. The boys flung themselves on the ground again.

But the car didn't roar past, as expected. It slowed as it approached, stopped in the middle of the road and then eased into the gateway entrance, its headlamps sweeping across the field, throwing the trees at the edge of Wistman's Woods into sharp relief. They heard the ratchet of the handbrake applied before the lights dimmed and the engine was switched off. The car had come to a halt on the other side of the hedge, not nine feet away from where the boys lay sprawled.

They kept their heads down for some time. After a few minutes, a whimper issued from inside the car, followed by a deep sigh.

Clive, with the side of his face pressed against the earth, mouthed a blasphemy. It was a courting couple. "They could be here for hours."

"Depends," Terry whispered through gritted teeth.

"On what?" Sam was thinking of Alice trying to keep the horse quiet on the other side of the road.

"On whether she gives out."

They waited. A little squeal of protest sounded from the car's interior. Then there was quiet again. Terry got to his knees, prepared to take a squint into the car. "Careful," said Clive. *"Careful."*

Terry crawled across the ditch, pushing his head through the hedgerow. The car's windows were misted with condensation, but there was no mistaking the shape, in the passenger seat, of a woman's breasts exposed to the moonlight. The driver put his head to the bared breasts, taking a strong erect nipple between his lips. "Hey!" said Terry. "Hey!" Suddenly he stiffened. "I don't believe it!" he hissed. He pushed his head farther into the tangled hedgerow. "It's Linda! Linda and Derek!"

The other two boys scrambled up and pressed their faces into the hedge, close to Terry's. In an instant, Linda had turned and was vigorously wiping away the condensation from the passenger window. The boys retreated slightly, trying to draw branches across their faces. They froze as she appeared to stare right through them. The muffled conversation from within the car was easily audible.

"I heard something," they could hear Linda saying. "Then I thought I saw three horrible, dirty faces in the bushes. Like demons. It was horrible." She was still trying to wipe the window.

"Want me to take a look?" Derek's muffled voice offered.

"No, don't."

"It's all right. I'll get out and take a look round."

"No. I'm frightened. Let's go."

"Come on!" Derek made another dive for her nipple.

"Get off!" Linda buttoned herself. "I want to go."

"Shit!" Amid complaints from Derek, the engine sparked to life. The headlamps blazed and the car reversed out of its parking spot. Tires screeched as they accelerated away, red taillights disappearing down the lane.

They breathed a collective sigh. Then Alice called from the other side of the road.

"Come on, Alice! It's clear."

Alice led the horse to the gate again, but she couldn't get it open. Sam darted across the road to help her. It was tied with baling twine. "I'll get Clive's knife."

"Forget it," said Alice. "Get out of the way."

Though there was no saddle on the horse, Alice leapt up on its back. She trotted the mare several yards away, reined it round and broke into a sprightly canter back toward the gate. Sam scrambled out of the way as the horse launched into the air. He saw five, six, seven horses in a single but staggered image, making a bridge through the air from takeoff to landing point, in a vision brittle with moonlight. It was a moment of inspiration, charged with force. They cleared the gate easily, Alice's hair streaming behind her as they arced through the air. The horse came to a halt just a few paces on the other side of the gate. Alice slipped off its back and led it across the road. Clive and Terry held the second gate open.

Without a word, Alice led the horse to the edge of Wistman's Woods. The boys fell in behind, hauling the tarpaulin. "Right," she said. "In you go. And don't be long about it. Remember we've got to get back before my mother does."

The plan had been that the boys would recover the body and drag it to the edge of the woods in the tarpaulin. They would throw the corpse over the horse's back and take it to the pond. There they had already assembled ropes and a collection of heavy weights to lodge the thing on the bottom of the pond. Meanwhile the horse tossed its head, its breath steaming in the night air. The boys dithered, looking for leadership.

"Get going!" Alice hissed.

The three stepped inside the woods. Moonlight probed as far

as the second or third depth of trees, silver on the vulnerable clusters of bluebells at the edge of the woods, but beyond that it dimmed, leaving barely enough light to pick out the winding pathway through the trees. It had been nightfall when they were last in the woods together, on the evening of the Wide Games. Sam led the way; Clive and Terry followed closely in single file.

An owl screeched somewhere in the depths of the woods. Sam stopped to listen. Within the darkness of the trees, slender silver birches reached above the treetops to act like conduits, slender tubes of faint luminescence channeling dull blue moonlight down into the blackness. The exhalation of the trees was everywhere, a watchful presence, attentive, waiting. He continued, and the other two followed.

"We're going the wrong way," Clive said after a while.

"No." Sam was confident he knew where the hollow stump stood. He quickened his pace, sure that the others would follow.

At the junction of two pathways Sam was surprised by a sudden whiff of something familiar, a smell with such a precise character that it caused him to stumble from the path in the dark. Ferns whispered under his feet.

"You're taking us the wrong way!" Clive tried again. "It's way over there!"

"This way!" Sam insisted.

"I think Clive's right," Terry cut in. "I don't remember any of this."

"That's because we're in the wrong neck of the woods!" Now that he'd recruited Terry to his opinion, Clive was furious with Sam. "It's nowhere near here!"

"How would you know? You were tied down with your arse in the air when it happened."

"Look," said Terry reasonably. "If you were about to have Tooley's fat, diseased, swollen dick shoved up your arse, you'd probably remember exactly where it happened, wouldn't you?"

"That's just it. If I was about to have Tooley's fat, diseased, swollen dick up my arse, I wouldn't be making a note of the exact compass coordinates, now would I?"

"Fuck off, both of you!" Clive bellowed, not happy at being reminded of the experience which he'd narrowly been spared. "Follow me."

Terry shrugged and waved Sam along with a gesture. They marched behind Clive for ten minutes or so, Sam growing more convinced with each step that his first instincts were correct. The screech owl sounded closer. "It's around here somewhere," Clive murmured.

Sam caught a whiff again of something close, of something dangerous in the dark. He looked back down the path. Each tree offered a cloak of blackness behind which anyone could hide. "Someone's following us," he hissed.

Clive and Terry stopped and looked back. They strained to listen. "Alice?" said Terry.

"No, not Alice."

"Are you sure?" Clive said.

"Yes. I think so. Maybe. I mean, I'm sure it's not Alice."

"You're spooking us," Terry said.

The screech owl called, loud and shrill, only yards away. Sam saw it sitting on a high branch, looking down at them.

Clive pressed on. They came to a small clearing. "This is it," Clive announced. "That's the tree where the Scout was hanging. I was tied up over there. We dumped Tooley's body in that hollow stump."

Sam felt sure Clive was mistaken. But Terry was nodding, sizing up the boughs of the tree. Together they shuffled across to the hollow designated by Clive. It was half filled with dead leaves, rotting branches and other woodland debris. No one was ready to lift any of it clear. "Right," said Clive.

Terry was first, and the other two joined in. Slowly at first, and then with mounting hysteria, they flung the debris clear of the hollow, until their fingernails dug into the soft, organic matter beneath.

"Ugh!" said Terry.

Clive pulled up a handful of the stuff. Sam too.

"It's just earth," said Sam. "Leaf mold. There's nothing here."

"It's been moved," Clive breathed.

"No. This isn't the place. You've brought us to the wrong place! Look at that tree! You couldn't hang the skinniest Scout from that tree! And where were Terry and me supposed to be hiding? This just isn't the place, you dumb bastard!"

Terry was scratching his head, looking round. "Sam's right," he conceded.

"I can't believe it! I just can't believe it!"

Sam got a blast of that overpowering smell again. Bird shit; rain-mashed leaves; tree lichen; fungus; rotting hay; wild bulbs waiting to flower. He knew they were in the presence of a power. The hair bristled on his neck. "Never mind, Clive. We were led here. We were tricked."

"What do you mean?"

Sam looked up. The screech owl left its branch and flew overhead, going north. He knew they wouldn't find anything that night. When he looked back, the other two were staring at him with appalled fascination.

"Tell him to shut his fucking mouth," said Clive.

"Yes," said Terry. "You'd better button it, Sam."

Sam led them in silence back to the place where he'd first intended they should go, to the clearing where he'd seen the fox in the winter snow. Its features were similar to those of Clive's venue: but the tree was a more likely candidate, the cover was better, the hollow stump was much deeper. It was also artificially piled with uprooted bushes and broken sticks. After they'd uncovered it in a second frenzy, the results were no different from their initial endeavors.

Clive sank to the earth, his face blackened with dirt and sweat. He wept with frustration. Then he stopped suddenly, simply staring ahead of him.

Sam helped him to his feet. "Come on. Alice will be going out of her mind."

They trooped dispiritedly to the edge of the woods, Terry and Sam dragging the useless tarpaulin. Alice was crouched on the ground, hugging herself for warmth, smoking a cigarette down to its filter. There was no need for anyone to explain. The failure of the enterprise was apparent.

They led the horse across the field and over the road. Alice jumped the gate again, and they climbed into the field behind her. "I'll see you back at my house in about fifteen minutes. Sam, can you ride bareback? Jump up behind me."

But Sam was distracted. Over Terry's shoulder, sitting on the gate, was the Tooth Fairy, watching them. The moon reflected balefully on its white face. It smiled at him with evil satisfaction.

"You wouldn't allow us to find it, would you?" Sam murmured, so softly that the others, standing a few yards off, did not hear him. "You wouldn't want that, would you?"

Terry dropped his end of the tarpaulin and pushed past Sam. "I'll come if Sam won't!" He was up on the horse behind Alice in a second. Sam spun round. He saw Terry's arms fold around Alice's waist. Alice dug her heels into the horse's flanks, and they were away, cantering across fields streaming with mist and flooded with moonlight.

THIRTY
Premonition

"What a good thing," said Alice.

Alice and the three boys studied a planning-application notice posted on the football-field gate. Redstone Football Club, having purchased the land outright, was proposing to level the ground to construct a second pitch. The enterprise would require infilling half of the pond.

"I mean, what a good thing you three never found anything that night in the woods. They might dredge the pond."

Over a year had passed since the disastrous project to recover the body of the dead Scout from Wistman's Woods, and this was the first time the abortive effort had been mentioned. There had been sleepless nights immediately afterward, and dreams of bodies composed entirely of leaf mold rising from the paths through the trees; but the police had made their threatened renewed search of the woods with no more success than the boys'. Now, as they read the planning application pasted on a wooden board, the implications of what might have happened had they been successful that night were dawning on all of them. None of them knew whether the infilling of a pond would cause a submerged body to surface or seal the matter forever.

"Anyway," said Sam, and the word "anyway" temporarily infilled the gaping nightmare for all of them, "anyway, they *can't* just come and fill in half of what's left of the pond!"

"Why not?"

"Because it's *our* pond! It's always been our pond. It's been our pond since we were little kids. They can't do it!"

"They can and they will."

"Well, they shouldn't be allowed to get away with it." Sam looked across the water, a distance from bank to bank of about seventy or eighty yards. "They're going to reduce it to the size of a mere puddle."

"A *mere* spit," said Clive.

"A *mere* flob," said Terry.

This was the current delight among the Redstone Moodies: anyone foolish enough to try out a word drawn from beyond their immediate range of vocabulary would have it gleefully and mercilessly bounced back at them.

"Someone ought to bomb the football club off the face of the earth," said Sam.

"Easily done," said Clive. "What sort of bomb do you want?"

"Are you serious?"

"I could serve you up a nice Molotov cocktail in under a minute; a more cultured device might take me a full day." Clive's garden-shed chemistry set was capable of anything.

"Cultured," Sam said in a thin, reedy voice.

"Hmmm, I say, *cultured,"* Terry echoed.

"Or I could knock up a pipe bomb in ten minutes."

They turned from the notice on the gate and made toward the pond. "Really? Would it blow up the football club?" Sam wanted to know.

"Not exactly. But it would blow a decent hole in the door."

Terry scratched his head. Football had stopped for the summer, but he was hoping to get a regular first-team place with Redstone FC for the new season. "I don't think you should do that."

"All you need," Clive chirped happily, "is a length of pipe, a couple of rags, sugar and sodium chlorate. Weed-killer to you."

"Gosh."

"No," said Terry. "Do the gymkhana instead."

"Keep your hands off the gymkhana," Alice said fiercely.

"Hey! What's happened here?" Sam shouted when they reached their usual hideaway in the bushes alongside the pond. The leather Morris Minor seat had been slashed; an old stool had been thrown in the pond; their tarpaulin shelter had been pulled down; and some empty cider bottles had been smashed on the ground.

"Kids from the estate!" said Terry.

"Little bastards!" said Alice.

"Wish I could get my hands on them," said Clive. "I'd make 'em into pulp."

"This is ingenious! Damned ingenious!" Skelton, his large, hairy hands pressed against his thighs, sat on one side of his polished mahogany desk while Sam perched on the chair opposite. The psychiatrist's sleeves were rolled to his elbows. His window stood open to the warm June air. Between them, in the center of the desk, stood the Nightmare Interceptor. Sam had finally conceded to Skelton's requests to bring it in, partly because of Skelton's scepticism about whether the thing actually existed and partly because he wanted someone in authority to assess its value.

Skelton's teeth were like a row of weathered clothes pegs left on a washing line, and he bared them proudly in a huge grin. He put his eyes close to the device, poring over its working parts as if it was too fragile and precious to touch, not merely an old alarm clock attached by wire to a thermostatic switch and a crocodile clip. "And you're certain it works?"

"For all ordinary nightmares, yes. For what you call Tooth Fairy nightmares, no."

Skelton waved away the distinction. "Do you realize, lad, how many people in this country suffer—I mean, really *suffer*—from the terror of nightmare? About eight million. Not just bad dreams but sweating, weeping, screaming, paralyzing, terrifying night-mares. People who are afraid to go to bed at night. This could help them. Really help them. With a few refinements, of course. And it's so accursedly *simple!*"

"It hurts your nose a bit."

"May I?" Skelton jabbed a finger at the crocodile clip. Sam shrugged. Skelton delicately plucked it up, opened the spring and let it snap on to his nose. "Ow! You're right."

"You have to put bits of cotton wool between the clip and your nose. Otherwise you can't get to sleep to have a nightmare in the first place."

"I see. I see. So the sensor is here on the clip, is it? Right. Now then. Let's have a go." Skelton proceeded to hyperventilate through his nose. In a few moments the alarm triggered. He tore the clip from his nose and shouted, "Hallelujah!" He got up. With his hands clasped behind his back, he proceeded to walk around and around his desk, chuckling to himself. "What we need is someone who can develop this thing. Develop and refine, eh? Develop and refine. I'm going to get in touch with one or two people. We'll get it patented."

"It'll still belong to me," Sam said stubbornly.

Skelton stopped in his tracks. He leaned across and put his face uncomfortably close to Sam's, close enough for Sam to see a jaundiced halo round each eyeball. He was not pleased. "Listen to me, lad. I may be a damned lousy psychiatrist. I may even admit to taking the occasional drink. What I'm not, however, is a bloody thief. What am I not?"

"A bloody thief."

Skelton seemed satisfied. He nodded grimly before returning to his chair, grinning all over again. "No, this is your toy. We'll get it patented in your name, Sam. But I've got to find someone to take the idea and make it into something more compact and more comfortable."

They sat and talked about the Nightmare Interceptor for some time. Sam finally realized that Skelton wasn't at all interested in stealing the idea; his fascination was genuinely motivated by the potential psychological benefits for some of his patients. Eventually Mrs. Marsh put her head round the door and reminded Skelton he was running well over time.

"Golly! You'd better go, lad. Take your toy with you for now. Make another appointment with Mrs. Marsh." Sam was halfway out of the door before Skelton seemed to remember something. "Oh! Now then, before you go, is everything all right with you?"

"In what sense?"

"In the sense of your bloody mental health and well-being."

"Suppose so."

"No fairies?"

"Not for a long while."

"Good. Carry on."

Shortly after his deliberations with Skelton over the potential of the Nightmare Interceptor, Sam and Terry passed by the cottage behind which Terry used to live. The caravan had been towed away long ago, but the garage workshop remained padlocked and, as far as Sam could tell, untouched since Morris had shot himself, his wife and his baby twins.

"Don't you ever want to look in there?" Sam asked Terry.

Terry colored and spoke very quietly. "Nothing to look at."

"But there might be stuff in there. Stuff you could use. It belonged to your . . ." Terry never made reference to his father, and Sam couldn't bring himself to either. "I mean, those things belong to you."

"They sold off all the good tools and things when they flogged the caravan," Terry said. "Uncle Charlie said that only junk and clutter got left behind. I'm not bothered."

But Sam found himself drawn again to the workshop, even though his last visit to the place had resulted in a gashed wrist, the scar of which he still bore. The place contained demons he had to exorcise, ghosts he needed to lay.

He knew he was in no danger of being spotted by the old man

still living in the cottage. One warm evening Sam squeezed down the side of the garage, looking for the loose window where he had cut his arm all those years ago. The broken pane of glass had never been replaced. The window frame easily swung open, as before. He cocked a leg over the window frame and pushed his head inside. The interior smelled of warm wood and mold. Even the darkness smelled of dust. As far as he could tell, most of Morris's equipment had been removed, but a few of the old features remained: the airplane propeller blade was still strung to the roof; the gutted jukebox rested in the corner along with the husks of penny-arcade machines. But Sam was afraid to climb in. He hung there for a while, half in, half out, unable to overcome either his fear or his memories entirely.

He pulled himself out of the garage and slipped away, nursing a sense of defeat.

Midsummer's Eve, and Redstone and District Social Club were hosting the annual Midsummer Queen beauty competition. Judging was scheduled for seven o'clock that evening. A cash prize of £100 was on offer, plus a weekend holiday for two. The judges were the editor of the *Coventry Evening Telegraph;* George Crabb, the Coventry City Football Club top goalscorer, and someone or other who manufactured light aircraft.

Linda had entered.

Competitors had to appear in daywear, evening wear and swimwear. Because Linda had entered, Clive, Sam and Alice, along with Terry and Linda's boyfriend Derek, were dragooned into the living room to be an audience on which she could practice and parade her change of clothes. The Social Club conducted its business in a dirty nicotine fug where the tang of sour beer was sharp enough to sting the nostrils. It made no sense to sport swimwear in such a venue, Sam thought, and he said so.

"Don't be ridiculous," said Alice.

"Killjoy," said Terry.

Only Derek agreed with Sam, but the argument was hushed when Linda shyly entered the room modeling her daywear and performed a twirl. Clive and Terry put their fingers in their mouths and wolf-whistled. Linda blushed and smiled. Her face had been carefully made up by Dot, and she wore extraordinarily long false eyelashes and a simple miniskirt. Sam blushed too. Linda was stunning. She was heart-stoppingly desirable and utterly unattainable to him. She saw his blush, and she met his eyes for a moment before he looked away.

Linda went out and reappeared in a sky-blue swimsuit and white high heels. Sam remembered the shape of Linda's breasts, purple nipples erect in the moonlight as they had spied on Derek's Mini from the hedgerow that night. His eyes strayed to the soft mound of her pubis under the stretched sky-blue cotton of the swimsuit. A cirrus of stray pubic hair was visible at the groin; he wanted to suggest she do something about it, but couldn't possibly draw attention to such a thing. His cock fattened in his trousers and he shifted uncomfortably in his chair, glancing guiltily at Derek, but Linda's boyfriend only seemed nonplussed by the whole business.

"Good choice of color!" Terry bawled. "That'll get George Crabb going!"

After she'd modeled her evening wear, the show closed. Derek went out to fiddle with his Mini, getting ready to drive Linda up to the Social Club. "She's gorgeous," said Alice. "She's breathtaking."

Terry said, "You should enter too, Alice."

"Ha ha ha. No chance of that."

Sam looked hard at her. Alice too was lovely but in a different way. She had beautiful bone structure. Yet her good looks intrigued, where Linda's comforted. "Terry's right, you know."

"No," said Alice firmly. "Linda's the one."

And Alice was right. Linda was the one. All competition withered before her, and Linda was crowned Midsummer Queen. She was photographed wearing a sash and a coronet and again with George Crabb mashing his thick lips against her cheek.

"George Crabb asked her for a date," Terry reported the following day, as they waited for the carnival parade to pass. "Derek was not happy about that at all. Not at all!"

"Did she say yes?" Clive wanted to know.

"Christ, no. He's one ugly footballer, that George Crabb. He looks like he ran into the Main Stand chasing a ball."

"I knew she'd win," Alice said with a sigh. "Men would die for someone like Linda."

"Then there's area finals and regional finals and national finals," Terry said. "People said she could go all the way."

"All the way where?"

Sam's question wasn't answered, as the first lorry appeared, moving slowly in first gear, like a ship chugging between the small crowd of people fringing either side of the main street through Redstone on its way to Coventry. It was a great day. Redstone had hosted the competition and Redstone had provided the winner. The local girl had beaten all comers. The sky was blue, and all was fair. A dozen vehicles lumbered slowly through the street, coal trucks and lemonade lorries and haulage wagons commandeered by disorderly rabbles in fancy dress, this one with a Spanish theme, this one a science fiction spoof, this one unguessable.

"What are *they* meant to be?"

"Dunno. Something."

And the penultimate lorry, beautifully decked with satin drapes and vast bunches of gladioli, fluttering streamers and bunting a-flapping and a hundred helium-filled, sky-blue balloons, bore Linda, the summer Goddess of Love enthroned, happily waving to all the folk lining the street, her coronet glinting in the sunlight, flanked by her handmaidens of second and third place, waving, all waving, waving. And, seeing her mother and father—Dot and Charlie—and Terry and Derek and the others, Linda got out of her throne and moved to the edge of the lorry to shriek and blow kisses and wave and accept the cheers and the whistles and the acclamation.

Sam, waving and whistling with the others, stopped suddenly, feeling his smile collapsing and his face falling and some dread part of him inside crumbling to a foul black dust. "Don't," he said, very faintly. "Don't."

"What is it?" said Alice, seeing Sam. All other eyes were turned on Linda.

Sam raised a finger close to his face, pointing it in horror at the passing carnival float. Because he saw on the throne the Tooth Fairy, a sooty shadow lolling on the vacated gilded chair. She had resumed her female form again, but her face was a hideous mask, and she wore a crown of ivy leaves and a sash of a thousand beaded teeth, a hollow mockery of the beauty queen waving in innocence to the cheerful crowd.

"I don't see anything," said Alice.

But even as Alice tried to make sense of Sam's behavior, he saw the Tooth Fairy reach out a fetid hand from within its own shadow, extended to touch Linda on the shoulder, ready at any moment to infect her immaculate beauty and her moment of triumph. "Leave her alone," he whispered. "Not Linda. Leave her alone."

But the float had already passed on, leaving Sam gazing after it in horror and Alice staring at Sam in dismay.

THIRTY-ONE

Blim-blam Boys

BLAM! Sam practically saw black printer's-block letters and an exclamation mark bent across the cloud of smoke as the bomb exploded. The noise of the explosion volleyed across the football field and seemed to die somewhere in the neighboring woods. Gray-white smoke hung in the air for a while, like buds of cotton.

It was after six o'clock in the evening, and no one else was around. The football teams had long gone home, and it was too early for courting couples to park their cars in the lane. Impressed by the noise of Clive's weed-killer pipe bomb, the Moodies emerged from behind the bushes by the pond and strolled over to inspect the damage to the door of the football changing rooms.

Clive got there first. The bomb had left an acrid smell in the air and a dirty scorch mark on the flagstone under the door. The wooden door itself, though, had sustained no more damage than a nine-inch split in the wood just above the center of the explosion.

"It's hardly touched it!" said Sam.

"I thought," said Alice, "it was going to blow the door off its hinges."

"Here's the casing," said Terry, kicking at a still smoking length of gutted pipe. Terry was still ambivalent about the idea of bombing the football club. The season had started, and he'd been passed over for selection when the team coach chose his own son to play in what, everyone acknowledged, was rightfully Terry's position. The coach had counted Terry's toes in the showers at the end of the last season and had expressed doubts, never previously mentioned, about Terry's balance.

"Right," Clive had said on hearing of this instance of appalling injustice and pretext for nepotism, "we bomb the football club."

"Seconded," Sam concurred.

"Seems fair," Alice had agreed. Terry wasn't sure about all this, but, seriously aggrieved, he went along with the others.

Clive inspected the pipe. He was slightly apologetic for the ineffectualness of the device. Most of its force seemed to have been concentrated in ripping the pipe open. "I don't know what you expected," he said. "It was only a thin piece of pipe."

"Make another, then," said Sam.

"We'll all make one," was Clive's answer. "See if you can do better."

The following afternoon they gathered in the shed behind Clive's house. Eric and Betty Rogers were accustomed to Clive and his friends locking themselves in the shed, supposedly meddling with chemistry equipment which, in reality, hadn't been touched for over a year. It was a regular Moodie venue, with a one-bar electric fire, where they could gather for a cigarette without too much risk of being disturbed. Clive showed them how to use a hacksaw to open a detonation point, how to pack the pipe and how to close the extremities. "You have to be particularly careful here," Clive said seriously, "because if you hammer the ends too hard, a spark can explode the thing in your face."

Apart from Alice, who wouldn't have anything to do with making the devices, they'd all found bits of pipe which they hacksawed into equal lengths. Clive mixed the weed-killer and sugar, and filled a separate bag for fuses. When the pipe ends were squeezed shut in a vise they each had a bomb. Clive suggested they personalize the things. He took a pot of white paint and a small brush and painted the words DEEP MOOD on his bomb. Then he looked up at Alice.

Sam grabbed the brush and painted the words BLIM-BLAM BOY on his. "What's that?" the others wanted to know. Sam shrugged. Alice looked at his pipe. "Yours is a bit thin," she said. Suddenly everyone was sniggering. "Terry's is the thickest."

Terry took the brush and just about squeezed the words ALICE IN THUNDERLAND on to his pipe. He looked up at Alice. She blushed.

At the onset of dusk they walked to the football field, and after checking no one was around, they crept over to the changing rooms and wedged their individual bombs under the door. Clive laid powder fuses of equal lengths along the ground.

Alice, invited to ignite the fuses, declined, so the boys lit their own simultaneously. The fuses burned sluggishly with yellow, moth-like flames. The four of them hurried across the field, took cover behind the bushes around the pond and waited. Two of the bombs detonated within a split second of each other, a double blast which seemed to echo back from the low-lying clouds. After an interval of a few seconds the third pipe bomb made a different sound, a sharp, concentrated crack.

The Moodies giggled uncontrollably as they ran across the grass to inspect the results. This time the door had been blown off its lower hinge and the nethermost panel had been blasted away. Smoke hung around in the twilight air like ectoplasmic spirits. Clive nodded in satisfaction. He was about to say something when a car pulled up in the gateway to the field, obstructed by the closed gate itself. The four dived behind the building as the car's headlamps flicked on to full beam. The car reversed slightly and inched forward again to play the headlamps at a different angle, and then again, shining them directly at the building. The four crouched in heart-stopping silence, squeezed into the shadows, inches from the searching beam of light.

After several minutes the car reversed into the road and drove away. They emerged from hiding, sighing and shaking their cramped limbs. "That was close," said Clive. His face was smeared with charcoal or soot from something he'd pressed his cheek against in the dark. They all started giggling again, hysterically.

"Let's go to my place and play some records," Alice said. Elated, they walked to Alice's, all talking simultaneously. The bombs had exalted them. They stumbled across the dark fields in an afterglow. Then Sam, bringing up the rear, stopped talking.

He saw that Terry had his left arm around Alice's shoulders. Alice was making no effort to resist. She even seemed to lean toward Terry, staggering through the long grass. Terry's hand resting on her left shoulder gleamed pale and white in the dark, like some alien thing not attached to his arm, an insect or a creature with a life of its own, maggoty, flexing occasionally and unpleasantly. They crossed barbed-wire fences and a stream to get to Alice's house, and after each obstacle Terry's arm found its way back around Alice's shoulders.

In the dark, throughout the buoyant journey, none of the others noticed Sam's silence.

A different kind of explosion was happening at Terry's house, and it was happening around Linda. Things had moved so rapidly after the triumph of the Midsummer Queen beauty competition that Charlie and Dot were reeling. They went around in an abstracted daze, not knowing quite how to share Linda's excitement. On the one hand, they clearly appreciated what a compliment to them it was to have bred such a beautiful and personable daughter; on the other they realized that their only reward for this achievement was to have her snatched, prematurely it seemed, away from them.

Linda was going to leave home. Linda was going to live in London.

Three weeks after the citywide competition staged at Redstone Social Club, Linda walked away with the area trophy. And then in August she carried off the regional crown. Her photograph, having appeared in several newspapers both near and far, attracted many eyes. All kinds of "work" seemed to come with the beauty-queen territory: snipping ribbons to open new shops; kicking off footballs to commence charity games; pushing piles of pennies over the bar in public. Everyone wanted Linda. Linda Linda Linda. What's more, they were prepared to pay good money to get her.

The American company Chrysler had bought out Humber and were launching a new car that autumn. Linda was contracted to stand by the new saloon in a miniskirt while press and company photographers aimed their cameras. Ironically her father, working in the paintshop at the car factory, had sprayed the very same vehicle before the assembly line began to turn them out in quantity. Charlie went with her to watch her receive all this attention. He felt self-conscious and uncomfortable in collar and tie in the executive lounge and showroom, standing with his manager and all his middle-ranking factory superiors as the cameras flashed and the male jokes ricocheted off the polished body of the gleaming new saloon. For three hours of this "work" Linda was paid almost the equivalent of Charlie's wage packet for a month. The irony was not lost on Linda, who tried to make a gift of the entire check to Charlie and Dot, though they refused to accept it.

Then, a few weeks before the Moodies began their bombing campaign, Linda was invited to model some clothes in London. She was asked by the illustrious Pippa Hamilton Modeling Agency to spend three days in the capital, accommodated in a hotel at their expense. Linda was on her way.

"It's all too fast," Charlie complained. "It's all happening too fast."

"It's an opportunity, Dad!"

"Your studies are going to suffer!" Dot whined.

Linda, having completed her A-levels, was set to attend teacher-training college in Derby within a couple of weeks. "But this job might lead to even more work. Who knows?"

"That's not real work," countered Charlie.

"But look at the letter, Dad! For three days' work they want to pay me half what you earn in a year!"

Linda regretted saying this as soon as it was out. She hadn't meant to demean, merely to persuade, to recruit her father's support. But Charlie had no answer. He looked away, and Dot looked at Linda and Linda looked at the floor. "Anyway, I want you and Mum to come to London with me."

Charlie cheered up, and relented. "No, my sweetheart. But you and your mum can go to London and have a nice time. And don't come back without a whole weight of shopping bags."

Linda squealed with delight and ran to the telephone to let Derek in on the good news. Charlie went upstairs to his and his wife's bedroom, where he closed the door behind him. He lay down on the bed and wept for the first time in eighteen years, since the day Linda had been born.

The expedition to London was a great success. Linda met Pippa Hamilton in person, and though Dot thought the woman a gorgon, Linda was bowled over. A letter soon followed, in which Pippa raved and raved about some photographs and in which Linda was invited to place herself on the agency's books. Pippa would personally oversee her career, it said, and if the answer was yes, then Linda should waste no time in making arrangements to move to London.

"What about college?" said Derek.

"It can be put off for a year, can't it, Derek?" Linda asked.

"Yep," Derek said glumly. Derek knew it was all over bar the shouting, and the crying, and the talk of how much she could earn for doing so little, and the cancellation of a place at teacher-training college in Derby. Linda was London-bound.

"Don't brood on it," said the Tooth Fairy. "I told you she'd hurt you."

Sam lay on his bed, staring at the ceiling. It was a warm Sunday afternoon. The others would be up by the pond, smoking cigarettes, cracking thin jokes. He wanted to be there, to be close to Alice, but he couldn't bear to witness her burgeoning relationship with Terry. He felt disemboweled every time Terry's hand was allowed to stray casually across her clothes, to stroke her hair, to brush the exposed skin of her arm. So far he'd managed to conceal his feelings entirely. No one knew how he was suffering.

Except the Tooth Fairy.

"At least you know now what it's like," she said. "Now you know what it is to feel jealousy."

"Jealousy?" Sam said bitterly. "Why should you feel jealous?"

"Because you're all I have. You make me come here, and then you want someone else! I never want to come here: it's like a bad dream for me. And when you want Alice or Linda instead of me, I feel like I'm dying. I get sick inside. I choke. I sob. I bleed for you. My life ebbs away. What do you expect me to do? You're all I have here!"

Sam couldn't understand her when she railed against him like this.

She softened. "Am I forgiven?" The Tooth Fairy's female aspect had been restored. She sat on the bed, her long fingers laid upon his thigh. She was revitalized, renewed. Those black eyes shone like a beetle's carapace again; her pale skin was clear and unblemished. Her mass of black curls seemed full of stars as, awaiting an answer, she moistened her lips with her tongue.

Suddenly it dawned on him. "You use my teeth to heal yourself, don't you?" said Sam. "That's how it works, isn't it? You take something of mine and it helps you."

"Yours or someone else's. I'm sorry. I didn't mean to hurt you. There are different sides to me. It's not even something which I control. You have to understand that. The first time, the first tooth, is supposed to put an end to it. But you saw me—I don't know how. You saw me, and we were both doomed." She got up and trained his telescope on the woods. Fiddling with the focusing ring, she said, "I've always had your interests at heart, Sam."

"You're so fucking generous." He was becoming bolder in his dealings with the Tooth Fairy. "I don't know why you care."

"This is not a one-way thing, you know. You may think I'm your nightmare, but you in turn are my nightmare. It's your moods that pull me here. So is it too much if I ask you to love me instead of Alice? Is that too much? There! Found it!"

"Found what?"

"Stop playing with your cock and come and look."

Sam got off the bed and dragged himself over to the telescope. He squinted through the eyepiece as the Tooth Fairy held the instrument steady. She had focused on a spot among the trees in Wistman's Woods. All Sam could see was a blur of branches and a brown shadow in the center of the lens. "What is it?"

"Keep looking."

At last the trees became more defined, and the brown shadow began to assume shape, changing hue as it did so. Finally it resolved. Sam was looking at a strange, long-stemmed woodland plant with a purple trumpet-flower. It looked vaguely poisonous. Growing inside the sinister purple trumpet was a fat, erect stamen, white and tuber-like, waving slightly in the breeze.

"Very rare," said the Tooth Fairy. "In fact, those babes only grow where there's a corpse in the soil. To fertilize it. Honest."

Sam looked hard at the base of the plant. It was growing out of a hollow trunk stuffed with ferns and branches. "What sort of plant is it?"

"It's got lots of names. We call it a carrion flower." She giggled. "But I think I'd call it Tooley's Revenge."

Sam pushed past her and returned to his bed. He lay down and thought of Terry's arm draped around Alice and of his hand on her shoulder.

"Don't brood," said the Tooth Fairy. "It hurts me when you brood."

The bombing campaign was stepped up in the weeks leading up to Linda's departure. The football club's changing rooms were the target of two more bombs (one called PLUG and the other called SKUNK, both inexplicably). Others were detonated in various venues, such as under the railway bridge, in the gymkhana field's commentary box and, most pointlessly of all, in a half-oildrum floated on the pond.

Sam kept a watchful eye on signs of a quickening relationship between Terry and Alice. What he saw was difficult to interpret. The hand—the dread hand of his friend—would occasionally scuttle around her shoulder and would rest there for as long as Alice allowed it. And at these times there was no doubting the special intimacy developing between the two. But at other times Alice would squeeze up against Sam, rest an ivory finger on his thigh, provocatively share a cigarette. It was as if she was telling him he wasn't excluded or perhaps that she had yet to make her choice. Only Clive seemed to exist outside this troublesome formula, and then even his resolve collapsed.

In trying to throw off the quirky character and geeky scent smeared on him by the Epstein Foundation, Clive took to wearing blue jeans and baseball boots, outsmoking all three of them and doing hard-case things to show how mean he was. Like embedding razor blades in the trees' branches to booby-trap their "den" against the kids from the estate who'd roughed up the place. Alice objected, and she and Terry privately went around afterward taking out as many as they could find. And it was no coincidence, given Alice's deep interest in pop music, that Clive became fascinated by, and authoritative on, the subject. He exchanged discs with Alice and dropped names like Syd Barrett and Captain Beefheart, names Sam and Terry had never heard of. But when he turned up with a pipe bomb one day and was wearing a fringed leather jacket just like Alice's, Sam knew that Clive had got it just as bad, if not worse.

"Wow! Great jacket!" said Alice. "Can I try it on?"

So Alice and Clive swapped jackets for a couple of hours. Sam knew what that meant. They had swapped skins. Clive would get Alice's scent. And ever afterward that lunacy-inspiring glandular pipe bomb would continue to detonate just under his nose and yet just out of range.

Clive had gone over; and from that day Alice might choose to snuggle up to, or link arms with, or even nuzzle against, any one of the three of them. She called them her three "protectors" and distributed her favors in almost equal measure. But if extra favor was to be apportioned anywhere, it went to Terry. Sam wondered, in the private, aching chambers of his heart, if Alice had shown Terry the secret of the Gossamer.

One Saturday morning Sam thought an episode in his life was being replayed. The only difference was that Connie and Nev were out shopping when the doorbell rang and Sam answered it to two oddly familiar faces.

"Mornin'!" said one of the two men, picking up a bottle of milk from the doorstep. "Your parents in?"

The two had put on weight, and one had grayed around his sideburns, but Sam recognized the two police detectives who had turned up at the house some years ago to ask questions about vandalism. "No. They're out shopping."

"Can we come in?"

But the second detective intervened. "He's a minor," he said in a low voice.

The first one smiled at Sam affably. "Look. You don't have to say yes if you don't want to. But could we sit in our car and have a chat?"

Sam put on his shoes. As they walked down the garden path one of the policemen said, "Have we met before?"

"Don't think so," said Sam.

"Explosions," said the first detective, as the car door clicked shut. They sat in the front, Sam in the back. The driver watched Sam through his rear-view mirror. "They make us nervous."

"Yes."

"You know what a terrorist is?"

"Yes."

"How old are you?"

"Fourteen."

"Fourteen. Well, you don't look like a terrorist to me. But Ma Casey didn't look like a bank robber. And causing explosions is a serious offense. What could you get for causing explosions, Bill?"

The second detective continued to look at Sam through his mirror. He whistled. "Ten years. Fifteen years."

"As much as that? As much as fifteen years? That's longer than Sam here has been on this earth."

"Serious offense," said Bill.

"Know anything about explosions, Sam?"

"No. I wouldn't know how to make a bomb."

"Oh, so they're bombs, are they? What sort of bombs?"

"I don't know what sort. If there are explosions, they must come from a bomb." Sam couldn't stop himself exhaling a huge breath of air.

"No, you get all sorts of explosions, don't you, Bill?"

"All sorts."

"See, Sam, someone thought they saw you. Though they admit they might have been mistaken. Do you think that was it? They were mistaken?" Sam nodded. "You saying you weren't there that night?"

"What night?"

The big smile suddenly went from the detective's face. He stared at Sam without a word for some time. Sam was sitting on his hands and they were sticking to the leather upholstery. The detective leaned over the seat and opened Sam's door. "Okay."

"Can I go?"

There was no answer from the unsmiling detective. Sam got out of the car and walked up to the house without looking back. Slamming the door behind him, he ran to the toilet and was violently sick. After he'd cleaned himself up, he sneaked a look through his parents' bedroom window. The car with the two detectives was still parked outside the house. They waited there for half an hour before driving away.

Sam pulled on his jacket and hurried up to the pond. He wanted to find out if any of the others had been visited. At first he thought none of his friends was around, but as he approached their hideaway he heard the low murmur of voices. Backing off, he crept around the bushes. There he had a full view of Alice and Terry sitting on the slashed Morris Minor seat. They were talking in hushed, intimate tones, Terry's lips hovering inches from Alice's.

Then Sam noticed Terry's hand. Crab-like, it rested casually over her left breast, the fingers flexing lightly as Terry and Alice continued to talk. For the second time that day Sam's stomach turned over.

Backing, unheard, out of the bushes, Sam raced across the field and cleared the gate. He marched across the neighboring fields in bitter blindness, wiping his glasses on his shirt, blinking at the clear September skies. His feet marched him in the direction of the woods, not slowing until he reached the trees' perimeter. He ducked into the woods, following twisting paths almost sightlessly, wanting to break into a run, his breath coming short. He had to fight down a tightening in his chest, a constriction that threatened to climb into his throat and strangle him.

Finally his raging emotions flung him, like a stone from a catapult, into a familiar clearing. There he saw a hollow stump stuffed with ferns and broken branches. A sinister, purple flower grew from out of the stump, its vulgar, thick, white stamen nodding lightly in the breeze. He approached slowly.

The flower was rooted in a rich mulch of leaves, decomposing under the branches that he, Clive and Terry had heaped over the deep hollow. This time there was no mistaking the location. Somewhere under there was Tooley's rotting corpse. Sam plucked up a broken branch of elm. Trembling, he poked at the leaf mulch moldering at the base of the plant.

His stick turned over a dark and juicy pap of rotting leaves, revealing, as it did so, a puffy yellow fungus beneath. A host of wood lice, mites and black beetles spilled out, crawling over the spores of the corrupt-looking fungus. A glistening grub with skin like white leather sucked on the root of the plant. Disgusted, Sam let his stick fall, and stepped back. He scowled again at the plant the Tooth Fairy had called a carrion flower. The purple-black and nightshade-blue petals were tightly wreathed, and the fat, white stamen was dusted with touch-me-if-you-dare saffron pollen. He wanted to recover his stick and slash the plant to the ground, but he was reluctant to handle the elm branch again, as if it had been contaminated. He was afraid that the plant somehow possessed preternatural powers of retribution. Moreover he sensed that the Tooth Fairy was there in the woods, watching him.

Sometimes it seemed as if she was always, always with him.

At last he came to his senses and went home.

Sam lay on his bed all afternoon. When his mother eventually tapped on the door, he pretended to have been sleeping. He ate his tea in silence and then told Connie he was going to spend the evening studying the stars through his telescope.

Which is what he did, knowing he could lose himself in the galaxies. The telescope seemed even clearer since it had been repaired. The night sky was cloudless, and the constellations were strong, and he didn't have to think about Alice and Terry. He trailed a satellite, and watched a meteor shower, and made notes in his book.

"Come down," said a voice in his ear. "Come down a little to Andromeda. I want to show you something beautiful."

He didn't even remove his eye from the viewfinder. He altered the angle of his telescope as instructed.

"Hold it there—perhaps another degree. So. Am I forgiven yet?"

"You did hurt me. You hurt me badly."

"I've decided I'm going to help you. I've always paid you, haven't I? From the first tooth? Come here. Lie down with me."

He took her hand, and she led him to the bed, and they lay down together. She cradled him in her arms, whispering, whispering. "I'm going to smooth away all obstacles. I'm going to help you with Alice."

"How?"

"I'm going to help you. Terry won't lay his hand on her again. You'll see."

He fell asleep in her arms. When he woke in the middle of the night she was gone, but his window was open, as it always used to be when he was a small child.

THIRTY-TWO
Ripples

The next day was a Sunday. Sam decided he'd better tell Clive and Terry that he'd been visited by the police. First he went to Terry's house. Halfway up the path he could smell breakfast cooking, and in the kitchen he found Terry's Uncle Charlie, unshaved and still in his vest, poking slices of bacon around a frying pan. "He's messing about in the garage," Charlie said sleepily, without looking up.

Sam, hearing the dull clonk of activity within, tried to let himself into the garage. It was bolted from the inside. He tapped on the door and announced himself. There came the sly whisper of a bolt withdrawing on the other side of the door before Terry let him in.

"Bolt it after you," said Terry.

There was a workbench at the end of the garage. Terry had a rag wrapped around one end of a length of plumbing pipe. "Looks like a hefty piece," Sam said, eyeing the pipe bomb.

"Alice is going to love this one," said Terry. He picked up a hammer and brought it down on the rag-end of the pipe.

Sam thought Terry's technique a bit dangerous, and said so. "Shouldn't you use a vise to close that?"

"Too thick. Needs some wallop." Terry swung his hammer down on the pipe. There was another dull clonk.

"Listen, Terry. The police came round to my house. About the bombs."

Terry lowered his hammer, letting it dangle at his side. He looked at Sam in astonishment.

"Yesterday."

Terry's eyes fell to the hammer in his hand and then to his bomb. He weighed the hammer before giving the tail of his bomb another swipe. "Suppose we'd better give it a rest, then."

"Suppose so."

"Maybe make this the last one for a while."

"Better not to do any more at all."

Terry looked sadly at his latest model. He hadn't even had time to come up with a name for it. He turned back to the workbench. Holding the bomb steady with his left hand, he tried to compress the near end of the pipe with a series of vigorous short, sharp raps. Sam noted how Terry's fingers closed delicately over the other end of the pipe bomb, the way they'd fastened over Alice's breast.

"I'm going to tell Clive," said Sam. "You coming?"

"I'll finish up here. I'm meeting Alice up at the pond at twelve. See you there later."

Sam shrugged and left. As he passed by the kitchen window Charlie, still in his vest, offered him a mock farewell salute. Sam could still hear Terry tapping away in the garage.

Sam had gone less than a hundred yards when he heard the bomb explode.

Sam, Alice and Clive sat by the pond that afternoon. After the bare facts had been established, they sat in utter stillness, each cocooned in a private and eerie silence. They gazed into the pond, watching fine concentric circles, almost invisible, rippling slowly out from the center of the pond and breaking at the clay bank. It seemed astonishing that such ripples could be generated without even a pebble being tossed into the water, and yet there they were, barely discernible yet undeniable, as if answering some deep and unknowable disturbance at the very heart of the pond.

They sat from three o'clock in the afternoon until twilight began to descend, slowly, in graded installments. The water sucked gently at the dusk, dark calling to dark, until the blackness itself seemed to creep out of the pond and make its way on land, until the water of the pond and the land surrounding it had reached an equivalence, an uneasy truce.

"It's getting dark," one of them said. It could have been any of them, it didn't matter. But the words spoken seemed to radiate in concentric waves from a still, small center, traveling to some bleak, unknown and terrifying shore.

THIRTY-THREE
Cucumber Rings

One week after Terry came out of hospital, Linda left home for London. The event of Terry blowing off his own left hand eclipsed some of the leave-taking and the drama which might have occurred. As it was, there were tears and tribulations and misgivings and last-minute doubts. But now, in the grand scheme of things, cast against a background of juvenile boys blasting off their own limbs, a young woman leaving home seemed so much less to get upset about. After all, she was over eighteen. After all, she was of age. After all, London wanted her.

The recriminations about Terry's accident had still not ended when they assembled at Linda's house to wave her goodbye. Charlie had polished his car, all ready to drive her to the station. Derek, deprived even of that last privilege, had had to say his goodbyes up the country lane the evening before. He cut a sorry figure, standing slightly apart from the rest of the assembled group, like a bit actor with no lines. Clive, Sam and Alice, all unbearably subdued, had come along at Linda's request. They leaned against the gate, making weak jokes and trying not to look at the cauterized and bandaged stump of Terry's wrist. Connie and Nev, always friendly with Charlie and Dot, had also turned up for the send-off.

After the nature of the accident and the circumstances of the bomb-making had been unraveled, people had reacted differently. Clive's father Eric slammed Clive up against the wall and hit him, hard, bruising the boy's cheek. It had been only the second time he had ever, in anger, laid a hand upon his son. Nev, however, went strangely quiet and took to staring at his son as if Sam were the most loathsome species of insect ever hatched out by the perversity of Nature; Connie meanwhile interrogated him, uselessly, and sometimes hysterically, and above all interminably.

Yet while most bewildered parents might try to explain an offspring's delinquency in terms of the mesmeric evil of peers, Charlie and Dot never seemed to reserve any blame for either Clive or Sam. One night, while Terry was still in the hospital, Sam drank three bottles of cider and turned up, blubbering, on Charlie's doorstep, claiming exclusive responsibility for the accident. Charlie took him in and, unable to make head or tail of Sam's wild stories or even to fathom why exactly Sam felt personally responsible, he offered Sam a cigarette and talked him down. After that he took Sam home and privately suggested to Nev that he go easy on the lad, that the boy was suffering badly.

"Suffering?" Nev had shaken his head. "Suffering? He should suffer."

"That boy feels a lot, Nev. He feels things."

"He should feel my fists, that's what."

"No, Nev. You've got it wrong."

After Terry had come out of hospital, Linda cried for him every night. The effort of trying to pretend that everything was still exactly as it was before was too much for her. Consequently she was pink-eyed for the big day of her departure, which didn't bode well. Dot had made her lie down with cucumber rings pressed on her puffed eyes and seemed heartless to Linda when she said, "Terry's done it: he'll have to live with it." It didn't seem right to Linda. When someone you love blew off their hand, it didn't seem right to mess around with cucumber rings. But Dot was firm, and her stoicism carried them all through.

Linda eventually appeared in a shocking-pink suit with her hair cut short in a fashionable, scooped wave. She kissed and hugged everyone with excessive enthusiasm, and it was not until the moment before her departure that Sam realized she'd always been there, in the foreground or in the background, a quietly reassuring presence, and he really was going to miss her. He glanced at Derek, standing back from the chatter and the unusually demonstrative behavior, and he felt a pricking of sympathy.

Linda kissed Clive and Alice, but before hugging her mother and climbing into the car with her father, she took Sam and Terry to one side. "Terry," she said softly so that the others couldn't hear. "I want you to take care of Sam. You're all stupid, all of you, but Sam's the most stupid, and I worry about him more than any of you. So you've got to promise me you'll look out for him. Promise me?"

Sam was surprised by this. He wanted to protest. He wanted to say, "Look, he's the poor fucker with one hand," but instead he colored and said nothing. Terry, embarrassed, brushed his nose with his bandaged stump and looked away.

"Promise me?" Linda insisted.

"Sure," said Terry. "Yes."

Then Linda kissed them both before going to Derek. A final hug with Dot, and she climbed into the car. Everyone waved, everyone shouted, everyone blew kisses. Linda was gone.

The adults filtered away, except for Derek, hands in pockets, gazing down the road after her.

"She'll be back," Alice said brightly.

"Not as if," Terry offered, "you weren't going to see her again."

Derek looked up. There was malice in his eye. "What do you know about it?" he spat bitterly. "You know nothing. You're just kids. For you I'm just Linda's boyfriend, someone to try to take the piss out of. But she's away, and that's it. I can't compete where she's gone. I'm out of it. I can't compete." He got into his Mini, slamming the door. The engine revved angrily and the tires squealed as he spun the car in the road. Derek accelerated away from them, very fast.

THIRTY-FOUR
Yer Blues

"You've got to understand something, lad," Skelton was saying. "You just don't have that kind of power. You don't have it. I don't have it. Nobody has it."

Skelton was trying, and not for the first time, to unburden Sam of his guilt over the business of Terry's hand. This was not his first appointment with Skelton since the pipe-bomb accident. Indeed, a regular pattern had established itself in Sam's life. Sam had an annual appointment with his psychiatrist. Skelton had determined that meetings of greater frequency were unnecessary. "We just want to measure your skull," he'd joked, "and keep everyone else happy." However, any incident in Sam's life, from being caught smoking to involvement in bomb construction, resulted, through Connie's insistence, in a further appointment.

Sam had explained the entire business of the evil hand and of the Tooth Fairy's promise of retribution.

"Coincidence!" Skelton hissed. "Though I'll happily assert that you may have had some special insight into what happened before the event. By which I mean you *knew* there were dangers. You *knew* how these damned stupid things are made, presumably by holding them still in one hand and hammering the ends with the other. You *knew* all this. You foresaw it. That's just intelligence at work, not some supernatural power. You are *not* responsible!"

"What about when Terry's father shot himself and his family?"

"Maybe you saw something there too. You sensed some danger for your friend, something about his father's behavior that was deeply disturbing. You wanted him out of there. The mind is an incredible measuring instrument, Sam. It knows more than you think. It knows more than it should."

"How do you know all that?"

"It's my job to know."

"The Tooth Fairy said Terry owed me his life anyway."

"And therefore could afford a hand?"

"Yes. That's what the Tooth Fairy told me."

"Sod the Tooth Fairy!" shouted Skelton, at the end of his patience. "Why don't you get that Tooth Fairy and give it a good shagging!"

"I do. Sometimes."

"Yes yes yes. I know you do. You've told me. I'm just running out of ideas."

Skelton was brutally honest with Sam about the limitations of his ability to deal with Sam's problem. For the psychiatrist, Sam was a unique case. Skelton had encountered plenty of children and adult patients with dangerous imaginary friends, but in his experience these entities either disappeared one day and never came back or developed into classic symptoms of paranoia, schizophrenia or other self-sustaining delusory conditions. Sam seemed to operate perfectly normally except for this one conviction. He had, Skelton had reported a long time ago, never been a danger either to himself or to others. So far.

"And what about this wonderful . . . Alice, was it? Alice? I'm certain that when you lie down in the grass with this wonderful Alice, you'll not see this Tooth Fairy again."

"How do you know that?"

"How do I know? I'm paid to know! It's my job to know! And I don't mind telling you, I'm disappointed with your progress there. You've got to *try,* son. *Try.* Do you know the secret of success when it comes to women? To *try.* You may get your face slapped. You may endure the occasional stinging rebuke or withering humiliation. But if you want some apples in your barrow, you've got to put your barrow under the apple tree. See? You've got to *try!*"

"It's more impossible than ever now."

"Why? Tell me why." Skelton was almost crying with frustration.

"Because that's what this was all about. Between me and Terry. We both want Alice. That's why Terry's hand got blown off."

"And that," screamed Skelton, "is why I said to you that you just *don't have that power!* God give me strength!"

"On television," said Sam, pushing his spectacles up the bridge of his nose, "psychiatrists don't get all worked up like you do."

Skelton bared his nicotine-stained teeth. "I'm coming to your house with a brick. And I'm going to throw it through your television screen. Now off you go. Make another appointment with Mrs. Marsh on the way out. Don't make any bombs. Have a good year."

"Any news on the Interceptor?" Sam said, as he got out of his chair.

"Eh? Oh, nothing to report. Everyone I've mentioned it to thinks it's clever but too fanciful. I'm still trying."

"You know, I don't want it patented for myself. I want it for Terry's father. He invented it."

"I knew that."

"How? How did you know that?"

"Get out of here," said Skelton.

Sam spent a great deal of time walking in the woods, trying to figure it all out. He knew he should avoid the site where Tooley's corpse lay moldering, yet the extraordinarily radiant presence of the carrion flower drew him like a beacon. Sometimes he would stand at a distance of twenty yards, observing the flower from behind a tree; occasionally he would approach it, circling it, peering at the base of the hollow trunk from which it grew. He wondered which particular part of Tooley's corpse succored its roots, whether brains or guts.

One day Sam felt oddly energized. He stood close to the plant, inspecting the purple leaves and the white stamen. It seemed to have reached a certain maturity and, Sam felt, was about to make a spectacular transformation. The fat stamen was ready to burst. The air about it quivered.

Sam experienced a stab of impatience, almost as if it was communicated directly from the plant. He felt drawn to helping Nature along. Using a stick to scrabble among the leaf mulch at the base of the plant, he uncovered the puffy, poisonous yellow fungus beneath. It had swelled considerably since he was last there and had grown to the size of a small skull. Sam touched his stick to it. The tumorous white sac responded to the pressure with a wheeze of air and swelled visibly. Sam dropped the stick in surprise and stepped back. There followed a second consumptive sigh of air as the venomous sac puffed up still further. The short blasts of air began to accelerate, and slowly the fungus swelled like a football inflated by a bicycle pump. The puffball continued to wheeze and inflate with increasing rapidity, until it began to resolve into an identifiable face. Tooley's. It was sallow, jaundiced and poisonous, cheeks horribly scarred, eyes oily with hatred.

Still hyperventilating, each breath coming like a sobbing wheeze, Sam jerked up in bed, the crocodile clip of the Nightmare Interceptor tearing from his nostril.

The pond was bulldozed, as threatened. One day two giant yellow earth-movers came in, frightened the fauna, flattened the field and pushed a huge pile of earth into the pond, reducing it to a third of its recent size. It was all over in a day. The Moodies went up to survey the damage.

They looked on in silent dismay. They felt an inadmissible sense of personal violation. As if someone had stolen something intimate from them while they'd been sleeping. Like a vital organ, such as a lung. Or perhaps a tooth.

Even their old hideout had been destroyed. The place where they had spent so many afternoons, in fair weather or foul, was now a flattened plane of red earth imprinted with thick caterpillar tracks. The trees formerly overhanging the pond were uprooted and piled high for burning. The old Morris seat, springs now exposed through the torn leather, had been casually slung on the top of the pyre. The water in the small pond that remained had been stirred the color of stewed tea. It seemed impossible that it could continue to sustain the myriad forms of pond life it had supported for years: herons and moorhens and swifts, perch and pike, toads and newts, dragonflies and water-boatmen, snails and spawn, duckweed and spyrogyra.

"They were only supposed to fill in half!" Alice's voice, though subdued, burned with indignation. "Surely they can't get away with that!"

"What do you suggest we do?" Clive said bitterly. "Dig it out again?"

No one mentioned anything about bombing any more.

Somehow it was more than just the pond that had been taken away. None of them could say what it was exactly, but the event rang for each of them like a bell marking a stage in a terrible race. Something like a whisper, more of a warning signal than a voice, sounded out of the cracked, tracked, hard-packed earth, saying, *This is how it is, this is how it will be, I can change anything at any time, and there is never, ever, any going back.*

"Hey, Clive," Terry said. "This is yer blues."

Clive had become a living authority on pop music. He'd discovered it was more socially acceptable to show off about the rhythm and blues antecedents of the Rolling Stones and the Yardbirds than it was to exhibit comprehensive knowledge of calculus and atomic theory. He didn't stint himself. He traced lines of influence back to the Delta blues and to Mississippi sharecropper tunes. Whatever it was that the Cream had laid down or John Mayal's Bluesbreakers were getting on, Clive knew the source. "Yeah, but you see, that was a Blind Lemon Jefferson composition . . ." "Oh, yeah, the Robert Johnson number . . ." "Uh-huh, Josh White did it first . . ." "Who? . . . No, you're probably thinking of Howlin' Wolf."

It was exasperating for Sam and Terry to be told they were mistakenly thinking of someone they'd never even heard of in the first place—Howlin' *who?* But they knew better than to argue. Clive was never wrong about these things, and he had an entire thesis running in his head. He started buying the music magazines, *Melody Maker* and *New Musical Express,* just to pick arguments with the rock journalists. He sent vitriolic and sarcastic letters to these journals on a weekly basis, undeterred by the fact that not once did they get published. He also collected in a big way, building up an impressive library of blues records. He took a job pumping petrol after school to pay for the habit. Clive became the boy you never saw without the trademark album sleeve under his arm.

Of the others, it was Alice who was most impressed by his encyclopaedic knowledge of the genre. He loaned his records to her, and they would discuss the stuff for hours, humming tunes, tossing hook lines back and forth. It was deeply irritating to Sam and Terry.

"It's pure mood," he condescended to explain to them. "That's why Alice and I like it. Deep Mood. It's Redstone music." The casual reference to "Alice and I" went a long way.

Clive's acne hadn't disappeared; Thomas Aquinas failed to produce the desired miracle. It had subsided, however, leaving him with a face permanently inflamed and prematurely aged. When Terry said to him, as they looked upon the filled-in pond, "Hey, Clive, this is yer blues," and Clive lifted his face in wry recognition, it was Sam who thought how extraordinarily old Clive looked. And when he came to scrutinize Terry and Alice, they too seemed suddenly aged. Not deeply aged, and no older than mid-teenagers should look. But it seemed to Sam as if one moment they had all been fresh-faced children, and life had been irresponsible and adventurous, full of implacable, long hot summers and inconsolably brief, freezing winters, and now suddenly everything you said and did *counted* for something.

He wasn't sure that he was happy with the change.

THIRTY-FIVE
New Activities

"Finished," Alice casually announced on the bus home from school one day, referring to her boyfriend. "We're finished."

Seated behind Sam and Alice, Clive's ears pricked up. Sam's attention was fixed on Alice, so he couldn't possibly see Clive's ears, even so he knew instantly that his friend's ears had stiffened with interest. Perhaps the air around Clive quivered slightly and became hotter, or cooler, by one degree. It was just one of those things it was possible to know.

Sam was no less interested. He wanted to ask whether this meant that Alice's mother had also "finished" with the sports-car-driving boyfriend from London. Instead he asked, "Did you finish with him, or did he finish with you?"

"Mutual agreement," Alice said, looking out of the window. "We both thought it was for the best." Then she glanced back at him with a look that told him she'd been dumped.

Sam thought the proper thing to do was to mouth some words of sympathy, but he couldn't because his heart was inexpressibly gladdened. His blood started singing in his veins. He readjusted his glasses on his nose and tried to disguise the faint twitchings of a smile. "You're better off without him. He was too old for you."

Alice said nothing. Clive didn't know Sam had once encountered Alice's boyfriend. "You've met him?"

"Yeah."

"What's he like?"

"What *was* he like, you mean. A rodent. A weasel."

Alice said nothing. "You never told me you met him," Clive
protested.

"No," said Sam. "I never told you."

It had been his secret. He collected secrets about Alice the way
some people collect matchbox labels. He hoarded scrupulously all
small intimacies and confidentialities concerning her but was not
above releasing small examples of privy information to Terry and
Clive, to confirm his superior bonding with Alice. He'd never told
them that he'd met this boyfriend, or that he'd once read snippets
of a letter, or that he'd found evidence of a gossamer nature or, indeed, about the bizarre triangular relationship—which he himself
didn't even understand—involving Alice's mother.

"What about your mother?"

Clive's interest fibrillated again. A damp, homicidal film
formed over Alice's eyes. "It's all over," she said meaningfully to
Sam. *"All* over."

Now that this new development had been announced, he understood exactly why he had been so guarded about all this information. It wasn't simply respect for Alice and protection of her
private matters that had guided him: he'd been motivated by advantage. As the bus sped home that day he knew Clive would soon
tell Terry what he'd just heard, and that between the three of them
the gloves would come off, and that it would be *game on* for Alice.

Sam made a sly assessment of her as she gazed sadly out of the
window. She was not strikingly beautiful, yet she was irresistible:
her dark hair tumbled over an ivory-pale neck, reaching almost to
the half tennis-ball convexity of her breasts. Something about the
school tie knotted carelessly at her throat made him want to cradle
her, and her teasing habit of tracing her slender white fingers along
her black-nylon-clad thighs provoked him beyond all endurance.

It didn't seem at all ridiculous to him that he wanted nothing more than to marry Alice.

And so, he suspected, did Terry and Clive.

Alice, however, was keeping her options open. It was never certain that she even considered Sam, Terry or Clive as conjugal options.

"Do you want to come with me to a football match?" Terry asked her one day.

She squinted at him doubtfully. "Football? Are the others going?"

"No."

"Then I don't think I'd like it."

"Let's go to your place and play some blues records," Clive suggested.

"Okay. Get Terry and Sam to come too."

"Oh. Why?"

"It'll be more fun."

Sam remembered Skelton and took a deep breath. "Want to go and see a film on Saturday?"

"Have you asked Terry and Clive?"

"Well, no."

"You mean just me and you in the back row or something?"

"Or something."

"Hmm. Fruity."

Which wasn't a no, but it wasn't exactly a yes either. While the three boys watched each other like nervous hares around Alice, she seemed quite dexterous at avoiding the conferment of particular favors or finding herself alone with any one of them. They, on the other hand, were prepared to jump through hoops of fire to be with Alice or simply to ensure none of the others enjoyed the advantage of being alone with her. Consequently they found themselves involved in activities alien to the very fibers of their souls.

"Pull it! Just pull it back!" Alice screamed at Terry.

"I'm trying! It's not easy with one hand!"

Clive's horse seemed to want to go home. "No! Not that way! Make it come round!" Alice was almost at the end of her tether. Their ineptitude dismayed her.

Then Sam's decided to sit down. "It doesn't want to go," he said lamely.

"*Make* it fucking go! You have to *make* it go!"

She turned her own horse and trotted back to Sam's gray mare, thwacking its haunches with her riding crop. The mare got up. "Don't let her do that again!" Then she cantered off after Clive, grabbing the reins of his chestnut mount and bringing it back in line. Meanwhile Terry's dun was still munching grass from the hedgerow, unchecked.

Fifteen minutes into the hack and they'd only managed to cover a few hundred yards. Alice had been careful to find quiet nags for all three, but none of the horses were accustomed to trekking, and she'd underestimated the terror and incompetence of teenage boys in the face of livestock.

"What is the matter with you? I've taken seven-year-old girls out on these horses! You have to *make* them do what *you* want to do!"

"WHOA!" screamed Terry when his dun stopped chewing grass and tried to take a bite out of Clive's chestnut.

The chestnut wheeled round in a tight circle. Clive dragged the bit too hard to his left side. "Fuckfuckfuckfuck!"

"Calm down! Don't panic it!"

"You said control it!"

"I didn't say rip its mouth out with the bit!" Alice was leaning precariously from her own horse, holding Terry's reins in one hand and grasping Clive's in the other. Sam's horse at least was now standing upright again and waiting obediently. Alice's riding hat fell off and bounced on the tarmac of the country lane. Her hair fell forward and across a face pink with exasperation and exertion. Her pert buttocks, delineated by tight-fitting jodhpurs, rose out of the leather saddle and were offered to the air as she struggled to bring the other two horses under control. The sight of Alice's bottom so presented gave Sam an instant and unexpectedly ferocious erection.

While he was still considering what he would like to do to Alice, someone leapt roughly on his horse from behind, hugging Sam at the waist and violently kicking the horse in its flanks. The gray reared in the air, whinnying and snorting, before galloping two hundred yards along the country lane, breaching the hedgerow and racing into a small copse. Terrified, Sam let go of the reins and knitted his fingers in the horse's mane instead. It only seemed to make the horse bolt faster.

"I LOVE HORSES!" shrieked the Tooth Fairy over his shoulder. Twisting branches lashed at Sam's face as they thundered through the thickening copse. The Tooth Fairy squealed with laughter, reaching a hand for his groin and pushing her wet tongue in his ear. Sam saw a low branch flashing toward him at head height. He ducked, flattening himself against the horse's stretched, thick-veined neck. The Tooth Fairy sprang out of the saddle and grabbed the onrushing branch. Sam looked back to see her swinging herself up on the branch, laughing and shouting something incomprehensible, her words lost to the wind in his ears. The horse swerved suddenly, and Sam felt himself pitched out of the saddle, speeding through the air and coming to a sudden stop at the base of an oak.

Badly winded, he must have passed out for a moment because when he came to, Alice was dismounting and hurrying toward him. His own horse stood idly nearby.

"Are you all right? Are you hurt?"

"I'm all right."

"This is a disaster," said Alice. "A disaster. I'm not bringing you three riding again."

Sam was still too winded to say what he would have liked to have said.

But the pattern was repeated. When the school organized a caving expedition in the spring term, available to both third- and fourth-formers, Sam and Clive found themselves crawling through slime and freezing waters in the sinkholes of the Derbyshire Dales. Neither of them had any particular fascination for grubbing around in dark, wet underground cavities, but Alice had wanted to go. Luckily for Terry, he was excluded from joining in this particular trip, but Sam had been marshaled by fear that Clive might go with Alice if he declined, and Clive too had to go, knowing that Sam would if he didn't.

Even though it was springtime, it was very cold wriggling through the potholes of the Dales. They spent most of the time crawling on hands and knees, with the nose of one or other of them just inches behind Alice's bottom. Alice, of course, delighted in the caving experience. Clive had a moment of terror when he became wedged in a narrow shaft, unable to move forward or backward. Sam too had a nasty scare when he was separated from the others and his carbide lamp went out, and he had no means of relighting it. He consoled himself that at least the Tooth Fairy wasn't there, gloating in the darkness of the cavern. And then Alice reappeared to light his lamp, and he remembered why he was in that awful place.

That summer Alice introduced a new element into the proceedings. They sat around what was left of the pond. Some of its flora and fauna had revived, but it had nothing of its original character. It had lost the ability to distill the atmosphere around it, to draw from the air and offer back tranquility. The pond was still alive, but it was in a state of shock. They rested on its warm clay banks one early evening after school, and Alice produced a small, foil package.

"Where did you get that?"

"My boyfriend left it behind. I don't think he's coming back for it."

"Have you done it before?"

"Sure. It's no big deal."

Terry shook his head doubtfully. "No. Not for me."

"Me neither," said Sam.

"Definitely not," said Clive. "I've heard too many stories."

Alice shrugged. "Don't mind if I do, eh?"

No one said anything. They watched, spellbound, as Alice stuck three cigarette papers together, split a cigarette, unwrapped the foil to produce what looked like a shiny chip of boot polish, singed it with her cigarette lighter and crumbled some of the stuff into her reefer. She neatly finished off crafting a slim, elegant product by popping a piece of cardboard torn from the cigarette-paper cover in the end of the joint. It was so expert, it looked like she'd been doing it for years. Something "glooped," unnoticed, in the pond. Alice shrugged at the boys. "I make them for my mother."

"For your *mother?*"

Alice lit up. "She loves it." Puff, puff, wince. She held the smoke back in her lungs and croaked, "She says it helps her to write the romantic verse on the greeting cards." Then she exhaled mightily, holding the smoking joint out for one of the others to take.

"No," said Terry.

"Count me out," said Sam.

"Absolutely not," said Clive.

Clive went ghostly white and curled up on the bank; Terry was virulently sick into the pond; and Sam, flushed, feverish and feeling he had to get away from the others to straighten out his head, took a walk across the field, his feet seeming to lift too high each time he took a step. The last thing he heard before leaving them was Alice saying, "I suppose you three don't want me to roll another one?"

Sam found a clump of deep, sweet-smelling grass and sprawled in it. He felt nauseous, and his heart thumped unpleasantly. But he was overwhelmed by the rich, fresh odors of the earth: hayseed and dandelion, mushroom and dew, soil and root and the spangled green grass.

"I told you," said the Tooth Fairy. "She's dangerous, that Alice. I warned you years ago. You think I'm trouble, but watch out! She'll lead you over the edge of a cliff."

Sam squinted up. The Tooth Fairy was smiling down at him, chewing on a blade of grass. She was completely naked, and her skin was tinged green, reflecting in a polished sheen the brilliant clarity of the grass.

"And you're dumb enough to follow her over in the hope of a kiss on the way down."

Then Sam perceived that the Tooth Fairy was composited from grass and wasn't made of skin and bone at all. She lay on her back, blending perfectly with the dry, herbal stalks and the pricking ears of yellow-green grass until finally it was impossible to distinguish her from the vegetation itself. Sam sat upright, feeling the vomit rising from deep in his gut. When it spewed forth it looked as if he'd been eating grass. The Tooth Fairy was gone, and he heard Alice calling his name.

THIRTY-SIX
Zoot Salem

"Unbelievable," said Clive.

"What a thing to do."

"Senseless."

"That's love," said Alice. "It gets hold of you. It makes you do things. You want to do things like that when you love someone."

Sam knew all about that. He accepted the roach-end of the weak joint she handed him. After their first experience of smoking cannabis resin, it was surprising that they should want to sample the weed ever again. But Alice assured them it only made you sick the first time, and so they persisted. At least, they persisted whenever they could get hold of the stuff, which was so infrequent that talk of it becoming habit-forming was luxurious. Alice's "ex" did occasionally make a flying visit, depositing a gold-foil package in his wake, and Alice was sometimes able to shave a portion from her mother's supply. Alice and Clive always rolled the joints: Terry couldn't for obvious reasons, and anything constructed by Sam tended to disintegrate or flare alarmingly early in its career.

The effects, it has to be admitted, were much milder than everyone had anticipated and no more sensational than speed-drinking bottles of Woodpecker cider. But it was different, it was mellow. Except for Sam, that is, who seemed extremely susceptible to its best effects, who took to wandering off at odd moments and who was occasionally caught holding conversations with unseen entities. Privately Sam started to develop the notion that the stuff could act to keep the Tooth Fairy at bay: even though she might appear to him when he was slightly stoned, she tended to leave him alone at most other times. Sam thought about how he might share this idea with Skelton.

"So he just drove his Mini straight into a wall?" Clive wanted to know.

"That's it," said Terry. "Killed outright."

It had been well over a year since Linda had left Derek to go to London. He'd seen her only a couple of times since that day, and his prediction that she'd left him behind had been entirely accurate. He'd been seen sitting alone one night in the lounge of the Gate Hangs Well, drinking heavily. The landlady of the pub, Gladys Noon, had spotted him clutching his car keys at closing time and had tried to dissuade him from driving. But he had gone from there, climbed into his car and put an end to it.

"That's odd," Nev Southall said, when his son reported what Terry had told him. "I was drinking in the Gate Hangs Well that night and I saw him drive off. But he had someone with him in the car."

"Are you certain?"

"Positive."

Sam suddenly felt very strange. "Who was it?"

"I don't know. I saw her snuggling up to him in the pub at the tail end of the evening. A queer-looking girl. She seemed to be whispering in his ear all the time. Then they got up and left together."

"What did she look like?"

"Small. Curly hair, jet-black. Gypsy-looking and a mouth full of shiny teeth. As I came out of the pub they roared out of the car park. Almost knocked me down. She was in the passenger seat, still talking in his ear. But he was looking dead ahead, as if he was trying to ignore her. Then they sped off down the road."

Sam felt a cold sweat bubble on his back. He said nothing.

"The thing is," Nev said, "there was no mention of any passenger when they scraped him out of the wreck."

Sam winced.

"Did you kill Derek?" he asked the Tooth Fairy in the dead of night. "Did you?"

"What do you care about Derek?" she answered, sneering.

"Did you? Did you kill him? I have to know."

"When Linda was here, you spent all your time wishing Derek was out of the way. You and your cronies never stopped giving him a hard time. You hated Derek. If I did or if I didn't, what's Derek to you? If I did it, I was doing you a favor."

"Did you tell him to kill himself? Did you?"

The Tooth Fairy wouldn't answer. She hugged her knees in the dark and curled her lip at him. Her face looked pale and sickly. There was an air of contagion about her, a whiff of carrion. Sam felt an Arctic thrill of fear for everyone around him. It pierced his bones.

"You keep away from me," said Sam. "I want nothing more to do with you. Do you hear me? Nothing! Nothing!"

The Tooth Fairy only hugged herself harder and narrowed her eyes at him.

Some time later Linda made one of her rare visits to Redstone. The mood after Derek's demise was subdued. No one blamed Linda, but there was some resentment from Dot and Charlie that Linda didn't honor them more often. Nevertheless, beyond the first evening, after they'd discussed Derek in hushed tones, the old warmth and familiarity soon returned to the hearth. Linda chatted away happily about her exciting new life in London, scattering celebrity names like confetti at a wedding. Most of the names were lost on Dot and Charlie, but they listened attentively, trying to frame a picture of Linda's milieu.

"Pippa says I should move to a flat in Mayfair. Pippa says I can afford it, so why not?"

"Is that better?" asked Charlie.

"Mayfair, Dad, *Mayfair,* as in 'Monopoly.' "

Charlie colored. "I know, I know. I'm just asking if it's better, that's all."

"Pippa says you need to live in a place where you might get spotted. Pippa says anybody who's anybody lives in Mayfair right now."

"Not Redstone?" said Terry.

"You're wearing a lot of makeup these days," Dot observed.

"Not more, just different. Pippa said I had to change the way I did it. She said my old makeup style made me look like a barmaid in a working men's club."

Dot, who'd taught Linda how to use makeup, sniffed at that.

"It seems to me," Charlie snorted, "that Pippa's got a lot of soap and water up her arse." He got out of his seat and left the room.

Dot looked meaningfully at Linda.

Several weeks after Linda had returned to London, a picture of her wearing only a man's collarless shirt appeared in a tabloid newspaper. Her breasts were partly revealed, although the open shirt front decorously covered her nipples. A tantalizing glimpse— but no more than that—was offered of the aureoles of her breasts. Charlie raged and had a day off work. Never again, he said, would he be able to look his workmates in the eyes. Sam, in the privacy of his room, clipped out the photograph and pinned it to the wall over his bed.

About that time a new English teacher took up a post at Thomas Aquinas. As teachers went, Ian Blythe had uncommonly long hair and a taste for unconventional, herringbone sports jackets. He stopped Clive in the corridor one day. "What's that?"

"Sir?"

"That! Under your arm!"

"Sonny Boy Williamson, sir."

"Give me a look at it! Original American pressing? I had one of these. Got warped in my student days. Any chance I could borrow this to make a tape recording?"

And so began a friendship, based on the blues, between teacher and pupil. Mr. Blythe had a collection of records and tapes exceeding even Clive's. He also ran, fronted and played at a monthly folk-and-blues club in the back room of the Cock Inn in nearby Frowsley.

"You can come if you like, but you can't drink," Blythe said firmly.

Clive dragged Sam, Alice and Terry along, and they compensated for not being allowed to drink alcohol by smoking pot *en route* to the event and by chain-smoking tobacco during it. Some nights the performers were dazzling, some nights they were stinking, and they always had to leave before the end to get the last bus back to Redstone. But it was better than hanging around the streets and infinitely preferable to the desperate remedy of attending a youth club.

Blythe himself played a respectable blues guitar; only his voice let him down. Clive came dangerously close to getting a crush on the man, so much so that his English, dragging behind his extraordinary ability in maths and the sciences, suddenly caught up. All of his teachers, including Blythe, wanted to propose him for early Oxford entrance exams, but, with his father's support, Clive steadfastly resisted any new attempt to separate him from the common herd.

One evening, as they were coming out of the Cock Inn to make their way to the last bus, they were set upon in the dark by six or seven Frowsley youths in a completely unprovoked attack. They had been laughing and joking as they left the pub, and it was Sam who heard someone shout, "Fuck off back to Redstone," before he felt a half-housebrick rammed into the side of his face. He went down, vaguely conscious of the ensuing scuffle. On his knees, he spat blood and a tooth to the ground. Though dizzy and unable to see clearly, he recognized a familiar face appear before him in slow motion, grinning evilly and reaching for his tooth.

"I'll have that," the Tooth Fairy whispered in his ear.

Sam was astonished. The Tooth Fairy was one of their assailants. He staggered to his feet and waded in to try to help his friends. Glass broke. Somebody's nose squelched under his fist before people came running out of the pub to stop the fracas. In the blur of fists and toecaps he saw the Tooth Fairy flailing at Alice. The unknown attackers peeled off into the night. It was all over in under fifteen seconds.

It was an ugly incident. Alice emerged with a split lip and a bloody mouth. They made their way to the bus shelter still looking over their shoulders. Only Terry was confident they wouldn't be attacked again. His good fist and his shirt front were covered in blood, and it wasn't his own. They all felt that they had at least dealt out a return. Sam knew he'd broken someone's nose and Alice felt she'd given as good as she'd got. Clive had probably taken more punishment than any of them, but he remembered scraping his boot so hard down someone's shin that he'd felt the skin rip.

Then the bus driver, frightened by their bloodied condition, refused to allow them on the bus. They had to walk off their adrenaline on the road back to Redstone.

"I'm sure it was a girl," Alice said for the fourth time. "I'm sure it was a girl who punched me in the mouth."

Sam knew exactly who it was. *I need to talk to Skelton,* he thought. *It's spilling over again. It's getting out of hand.*

The upshot was that the landlord of the Cock Inn banned them from going to his pub ever again, as if they'd been the cause of the brawl. Blythe defended his pupils staunchly—so staunchly that the landlord told him to take his folk-and-blues club elsewhere. Eric Rogers, picking up on the problem, mentioned to Clive an unused back room at the Gate Hangs Well and promised to have a word with the landlady. So Blythe came over to Redstone one evening, charmed the widowed Gladys Noon, and the Frowsley Folk Club became the Redstone Folk Club. Blythe landed a coup on the opening night. Some legendary Black American blues musicians had started to come to England after the Yardbirds had done an unheard-of thing in bringing over Sonny Boy Williamson. Bottleneck guitarist Zoot Salem was billed to appear on opening night. Clive and Alice took money at the door; Terry and Sam were recruited to collect glasses and help with equipment.

The legendary Zoot turned up in a hired Ford Capri, with no assistance, one guitar and a small PA system, which Sam deferentially carried into the pub. Zoot, still on the road at eighty years old, was a thin, wiry man with a leathery face. Sad, heavy pouches hung under his eyes, and he had a disconcerting habit of frequently putting his hand to his mouth as if to pluck some tiny but irritating object from his tongue. A good-sized audience turned up, and the old man's bottleneck guitar playing was masterly. Clive, in particular, was mesmerized.

Sam was enraptured too, but toward the end of the set something happened which made him feel faint. Introducing his next song, Zoot Salem seemed to fasten on Sam with particular intensity. Perhaps Sam imagined it, but Zoot appeared to stare right at him when he said, in a deep and barely coherent Southern drawl, "This hyeh song I wrote long time 'go. This hyeh song call 'The Toof Fereh.' " Zoot launched into a foot-tapping twelve-bar routine, growling into the microphone, making the strings of his guitar shiver and squeal in protest.

For Sam the sound receded for a moment, and he felt badly disoriented. Surely he'd misheard? But, no, Zoot had a refrain between each verse in which he chop-muted a chord, stopped playing, closed his mouth around the microphone and rasped, "Yo! Yo just a toof fereh, yo!"

The audience got the idea, joining in the refrain every time it came around. But to Sam it seemed like Zoot was speaking to him, even mocking him. It appeared too that the audience were in on the joke, picking up the line with gusto every time it occurred. He felt hot. He needed air. He had to go outside.

Sam sat down on one of the unseasonal benches, blinking up at the evening sky. It was a clear, cloudless night. A silver scythe of new moon was bright in the sky. Mars twinkled, orange-yellow, close to the constellation of Leo. He felt better. The song could not have been about him, he decided, since they had continued to sing it long after he'd left the room. He remained outside for a while, breathing steely night air, hearing rapturous applause as Zoot closed his set. Alice came out while Zoot played an encore.

"Here you are." She sat down beside him, laying a hand on his arm.

"Here I am."

"What's wrong?"

Sam tapped the side of his head. "It's this. It's no good."

"Yes. It's a problem. That head of yours."

"Don't take the piss."

"Why don't you tell me about it? Why don't you? You never tell me about it."

"It's too . . . It would take too long." He wanted to tell her that it was too scary to talk about. He thought he would tell her, one day. But not tonight. He looked up at the sky. "Stars are bright."

"Change subject on me, would you?"

He looked back at her. "I love you, Alice. But you know that."

Her eyes searched his face. Then she stood up. "Come back inside. Hold my hand."

Zoot was well into his third encore. The evening had been a wild success, the landlady was making good sales, the club was up and running. After Zoot denied the crowd a fourth encore, and the drinkers scrambled to the bar for last orders, Sam went to help the old musician with his gear. He needed to get near to the man.

"Why did you write that song?"

"Which song you say?"

" 'The Tooth Fairy.' "

Zoot put a huge, leathery hand on Sam's shoulder, cocked his head to one side and smacked his lips. "Well, I was a-dreaming . . . ummm, ummm. That's right. This toof fereh come take mah toof.

I said, no, you don't take mah toof . . . ummm? No, sir. I want this here toof for mahself. I wrote the song. Heh, heh, heh!"

Sam gazed back at the old man. Then Zoot was beleaguered by admirers who pressed forward to talk to him. Before turning away, he said, "I thank you kindly, young man, for carrying mah guitar."

"What did he say?" Clive was frantic to know. "Tell me what he said."

"Nothing."

"Come on!"

"He just said he wrote the song."

THIRTY-SEVEN
Condom

"Actually, Sam, you're not the first person to believe in fairies. Sir Arthur Conan Doyle, he was a great believer. You and he would get on like a house on fire. He even wrote a book about it."

Sam had never seen Skelton looking so haggard, so tired. He'd mentioned to Sam that he was approaching retirement, and Sam had noticed a carelessness about him recently, an untidiness in the office that wasn't in evidence when he'd first visited Skelton several years ago. Mrs. Marsh, his faithful secretary, had lately adopted an air of exasperated patience. Skelton was like a man who, somewhere along the line, had lost the faith and didn't know why.

Sam was now old enough to understand too that while he had his Tooth Fairy, Skelton was tormented by his own imps and demons and that they were let out of a bottle called Johnny Walker. Drink never made Skelton dysfunctional or inattentive, but his face was now permanently flushed, and his eyes had a rheumy look. He was also less discreet about taking a drink in his study if the fancy took him. He'd given up pretending. Disappointingly, all plans for the Nightmare Interceptor had long been forgotten.

"He was taken in you know, Conan Doyle. Two little girls faked a photograph of fairies and he believed them. Who'd have thought it? A clever fellow like Conan Doyle."

"I've seen it. It's rubbish. Anyone can see the picture's a fake."

"Not Conan Doyle. Because he *believed,* Sam. He had the belief, and if you've got the belief, you can see anything. God. Communism. Fairies. Psychiatry. We fake our own photographs, do you see? And it seems the cleverer we are, the cruder the forgeries we're prepared to accept."

"Look," Sam protested, "I know what you're saying. But fairies don't look like flimsy-winged pixies with names like 'Peapod' and 'Butterscotch.' "

"Correction. *Yours* doesn't."

"But I'm trying to tell you, other people are seeing it and are being affected by it. My dad saw her in the car with Derek. Alice got a punch in the mouth from her. Terry saw her through my telescope. And then Clive and Terry saw . . ."

"Saw what?"

"Nothing."

"I've told you about that 'nothing.' " Skelton had. He'd taught Sam that when people say "nothing," it was always to hide a highly significant "something."

"Clive and Terry saw it once when we were in the woods."

"You're holding something back."

"I told you about it once. You rubbished what I'd told you."

Skelton bared his teeth and searched his memory. He shook his head slowly from side to side. Then he suddenly remembered. "The Dead Scout? Are you talking about the Dead Scout?" Sam nodded. "Do you remember when you used to come here and draw me pictures of gravestones and bats and whatnot?"

"It's not like that." Sam knew it was useless to argue. His entire relationship with Skelton had been like walking through a hall of mirrors where illusion and reality reflected back at each other, infinitely. Dead Scouts could not be distinguished from Tooth Fairies in Skelton's vision of Sam's world.

"Sam, I'll tell you, I'm worried about you. I'm more worried about you now than at any time. I've never used words on you before. I avoid psychiatric terms because they're a kind of incantation which stops people from having to think further. But all this time

I have thought this *projection* of yours was harmless. Fucked-up, I suppose, in your language, but harmless. Now you're starting to exhibit signs of *paranoia*. Do you know what that is?"

"I think so."

"You're a bright lad, Sam, always have been. Look at this story you told me about the old musician. Can you see how your mind picks up on a coincidence and goes belting down the wing with it? Eh? This is a pattern you must resist.

"I was hoping when I retired next year to close the book on you, without having to pass you on to someone else. Now I'm not so sure. Maybe another head would help. It's just that you're so damned different from every other case who ever walked through my door, and I'll be the first to admit you've got me stumped."

"Sorry."

"Don't say sorry. I care about you, Sam. I do."

Sam looked up at the ravaged old face glowering at him from the other side of the desk. He believed Skelton. "You haven't asked me this time."

"Asked what?" said Skelton.

"About Alice."

"Hallelujah! Don't tell me you've gone and done it? Not finally done the deed?"

"No."

"For God's sake!"

"It's just that you didn't ask. And you always ask."

"I've lost hope in you in that department." He tapped his pencil on his desk blotter. "By the way, have you ever told Alice about your Tooth Fairy?"

"No."

"Perhaps you could give it a try."

"She'd think I was mad."

"The idea!"

"She'd laugh."

"Give it a try."

"Why?"

"It just occurred to me. The little girl who tricked Conan Doyle with the photograph was called Alice. If she could trick him into seeing fairies, maybe your Alice could trick you into not seeing 'em."

"Paranoia," said Sam.

"Get out of here, you young horror. And mind how you go."

Sam found himself with more time alone with Alice. Clive, who after Zoot Salem's appearance had gone around faintly disgusted that he hadn't been born black, as if nature had spitefully denied him his rightful ethnic heritage, spent more time visiting jumble sales and second-hand stalls and collector's fairs, digging out obscure albums and 78 rpm slate singles. Terry's football consumed his weekends; he turned out now for Redstone FC on Saturdays (having found himself back in favor with a new coach) and on Sunday afternoons for the Gate Hangs Well pub league, where he shone against big-bellied men who fueled their football with five pints of bitter and twenty cigarettes before the game.

So, having the time, Sam told Alice. And when he told her, he left nothing out.

"You're mad," said Alice.

"Probably." They were at her house one Sunday. Alice's mother was in her room with the curtains drawn, "resting," which meant enduring a Cyclopean hangover.

"I mean it. You're barking mad."

"I told Skelton I shouldn't tell you."

"No, I'm really glad you did. It makes a lot of things suddenly clear. What does Mr. Skelton say you should do?"

"He's tried all sorts. Mostly just talking, telling me not to panic whenever it comes. He gave me some pills once."

"You kept that quiet."

"Well, with you lot around . . . Anyway, the pills just put everything in a cotton-wool fog, and the Tooth Fairy still came along.

Skelton also told me I should find a girl to do it with. He said that was the best thing for it."

"What? He said doing it with someone would make the Tooth Fairy go away? I don't believe you!"

"It's true. Well, to be fair, he said it would help. That's all. He said it would help."

"I think you're making it up."

"No. Honestly. He explained it to me. It's like a poison if it gets trapped."

"It?"

"Sex. It gets all blocked up and messes up your brain. Something like that, anyway. I couldn't make too much sense of it."

Alice gazed at him with fascinated, horrified eyes. She reached out and casually brushed her fingers across his chin. Then she stared at the carpet, deep in thought. Sam was about to speak when Alice got to her feet, left the room and tiptoed across the landing. She looked inside her mother's bedroom before quietly closing the door on her snoring mother. Returning at last, she gently clicked her own door shut.

She stood over Sam, looking grave. Her cheeks were flushed, her eyes deep-set. "Swear you're not making this up just so's you can fuck me."

"I swear," Sam croaked.

Alice nodded. Then she lifted her white T-shirt over her head and tossed it aside. She wore no bra, and her small breasts quivered slightly as she stood over him, breathing deeply, never taking her eyes off him for a second. Her skin had a sallow sheen. There was a small mole underneath one of her breasts.

My God, thought Sam, she's going to let me do it out of kindness. Out of kindness.

Alice kneeled beside him and kissed him. Still kissing, Sam took his glasses off. He touched her breasts, and the dark buds of her nipples stiffened under his fingers. His cock strained inside his jeans, trying to force a route through the tough denim fabric. He quickly peeled off his own T-shirt and the sweet, penetrating sting of her skin on his almost made him swoon. Her arms enfolded him. He was irradiated by the Alice-scent, that utterly personal signature-smell of hers that had hooked him long ago. He was dangerously aroused and yet paralyzed with excitement as she fumbled with the button of his jeans.

There was a movement in the next room, and a creak of floor-boards. Alice jumped back, grabbing her T-shirt. The bathroom door closed, followed by the rasp of the latch. Alice sighed and put her shirt back on. "Not here. We'll have to find somewhere else."

Sam quickly put his T-shirt and spectacles back on, blinking at her.

"Mum, I'm going out for a while," Alice called through the bathroom door. A small groan was offered by way of answer. "Come on."

It was a warm spring day. They walked arm in arm from Alice's house without talking, overloaded by anticipation, their brains clouded with a distilled expectancy.

Inevitably they gravitated toward the pond, where the shrubs and bushes erupting from the clay bank offered plenty of cover. But a group of children were gathered there, throwing stones in the water. Sam sighed.

"The woods," said Alice.

Sam scratched his head. "I don't like the woods."

"Where else?" Her question seemed to say, do you want to or not? He shrugged, and they moved toward the dense line of trees. "By the way, have you got something?"

"Something?"

She grabbed his arm and stopped him in his tracks. "I don't want to get pregnant."

He was openmouthed, then it dawned on him. "Light filmy substance. Floating in calm air or over grass. Something flimsy. Delicate gauze."

"What???"

"Gossamer. No."

"Hell. I had one in my room. I didn't pick it up."

Sam had an idea. "My place is closer. I know where there are some."

"Sam, I'm not walking to your house and chatting to your mum while you get a dobber."

He was afraid she was changing her mind. "Wait here. I'll go and get it. I'll run."

"Oh, God!" said Alice.

Sam was already jogging down the road. On his way home he tried to short-cut through a field. Climbing a stile, he slipped, going down on one knee into some soft black mud. The thick, rich earth molded itself to his jeans.

"Why are you in such a state?" Connie, in gardening gloves, said as he flew past her.

"Forgot something."

He raced upstairs. His father was in his parents' bedroom, tying a tie in the mirror. "Aye, aye," said Nev.

Sam muttered a reply before stumbling into his own room, sitting on his bed, trying to recover his breath. His father was obviously getting ready to go out. He waited.

And waited.

Finally Nev went downstairs. Sam heard the door close and listened to voices in the garden outside. He crept into their room. Nev and Connie were standing at the bottom of the garden talking about standard roses. If they looked up, they could see into their bedroom. He crouched on all fours and crawled to the far side of the bed. Slipping his hand between the mattress and the base of the bed he made a sweep back and forth. There was nothing. He pushed his arm farther in, sweeping frantically now. Still nothing. He dug his hand closer to the pillow end of the bed and his fingers fastened on what he was looking for. Withdrawing the packet, he found it contained only a single condom.

One. Would his father miss one? Of course his father would miss one. Nevertheless, he kept the single condom and returned the empty packet under the mattress, hoping Nev would simply think he'd been mistaken.

"Not a good idea," said the Tooth Fairy.

Sam recoiled in shock. The Tooth Fairy sat on the bed, shaking her head. "Go away," said Sam. She gestured at something on the floor. He looked down. Mud from the knee of his jeans had scored a dirty trail on the beige carpet. "No no no no no!" He leapt to his feet and ran to the bathroom, returning with a damp rag, trying to mop up the faintly glistening, giant-slug-like trail.

"This is going to cause all sorts of trouble," the Tooth Fairy insisted. "For both of us. The consequences of this are going to be enormous."

Sam finished wiping up the mess. He jabbed a finger at the Tooth Fairy and said, "Paranoia." To his surprise, the Tooth Fairy disappeared instantly.

Wondering if Alice would still be waiting for him, he raced down the path. His mother called him back. "Where are you going?"

"Nowhere."

"Well, if you're going nowhere, there are things I want from the corner shop."

"I can't. I'm going somewhere."

"You just said—"

"WHAT? WHAT IS IT?" Connie was astonished by his vehemence. "Sorry. I mean, what do you want? From the shops. What?"

"I made a list. It's in the kitchen."

Sam took a deep breath and jogged back to the kitchen. There he leaned his head against the wall for a few seconds before snatching up the note from the table. Then he was off again, running up the road to find Alice.

He found her sitting on a fence near the entrance to the woods, smoking a cigarette. "I was just about to go. You look all in."

"Don't ask," he said, producing the condom from his hip pocket.

Alice looked as if she'd had second, or even third and fourth thoughts about the matter in the intervening period. Almost wearily she took Sam by the hand and led him into the woods. It was bluebell time all over again. Bluebells scintillated like pools of shallow water among the trees.

He didn't like the direction in which she led him, though he stifled all protest. When she settled on a secluded spot, Sam had the uncomfortable impression that it was very close to the mortal and presumably putrefying remains of the Dead Scout. Still, he said nothing. The trees gathered around them to witness the act; tangled bushes crowded in; leaf mold and new ferns scented the air; bluebells chimed with a chorus of color.

Alice stepped out of her jeans, laid them on the ground between some tall ferns, and sat down on them. Then she slipped off her knickers and pressed her knees shyly together. Sam tugged off his own jeans. His erection bobbed angrily, already having found a way outside his underpants. They kissed. Alice put her hand on his engorged cock, and he thought he would ejaculate immediately.

"Don't come," Alice said, removing her hand. "Don't come yet."

He was mesmerized by the nut-brown triangle of pubic hair at the top of her long, slender legs and by her creamy, flat belly. He detected the source of the scent which had had him in a noose since the first day she'd collided with him in the school bus queue. He whipped off his underpants. Then he remembered the condom. She watched him expectantly, her lips parted slightly as he rooted through his pockets for the condom. He tore open the foil packet, and the lubricated rubber slipped into his hand.

A bird broke from the thicket suddenly. Sam looked up. A short distance away, half-hidden by the giant ferns, a strange trumpet-shaped purple flower grew out of the hollow of a tree, similar or perhaps identical to the one shown to him by the Tooth Fairy. Its white tuber-like stamen jiggled suggestively in the breeze. Sam unraveled the condom a short length and tried to fit it over the straining helmet of his cock. He seemed to have the thing twisted inside out. Alice relaxed back, parting her legs a little. At the periphery of his vision the unpleasant, fleshy white tuber jiggled distractingly. Tooley's Revenge, he thought. *Tooley's Revenge.* As he struggled with the condom, he prayed his father wouldn't guess who'd stolen it. Then he remembered the muddy trail on his parents' bedroom carpet and instantly regretted not making a more thorough job of cleaning up behind him.

His cock softened slightly as he tried to fit the condom the other way, but the teat end wouldn't come clear. The smell of latex was distractingly strong. He thought of both the Tooth Fairy and the Dead Scout grinning over his shoulder, mocking this ineffectual fumbling. He looked at Alice. She raised her eyebrows at him, a gesture which didn't help.

His mother's shopping list came back to him, and again the thought of the Tooth Fairy, and then briefly—and appallingly—of his mother and father copulating. The white tuber inside the purple-black flower waved provocatively. By now his cock had softened and the rubber refused to unroll the length of his penis. He took it off and tried again. With the thing half unrolled the results this time were worse than before. Sam looked about him in desperation. The white tuber inside the purple flower was quivering with merriment in the breeze, almost as if it was being shaken by an unseen hand. Defeated, he snapped off the rubber and tossed it into the ferns before cradling his head in his hands.

Alice said nothing. She sat up and dressed quickly. After a while she put her hand in his hair. "Put your jeans back on," she said. "We'll just lie here together for a while."

And they did, lying amid the scent of ferns and bluebells until the twilight settled upon them and over the aromatic woods.

THIRTY-EIGHT

Announcement

Terry left school that summer. He had little interest in studies, and Redstone Secondary, where he'd been streamed from the age of eleven, had been designed to ensure things stayed that way. The loss of toes and a left hand showed no sign of restricting his footballing prowess; he had found his way on to the books of Coventry City FC, and neighboring Aston Villa were sniffing around with suggestions of an apprenticeship.

Terry's Uncle Charlie was realistic enough to ensure that the lad took a trade apprenticeship. Charlie had been the one to encourage Terry's footballing interests ever since Terry had been spared Chris Morris's killings and suicide. Charlie knew football. "The beautiful game, Terry. There are more disappointments in the beautiful game than there are in life itself. Get a trade."

That wasn't so easy, what with only one hand; and after Terry had been rejected for several tool-making apprenticeships, Charlie called in a few favors and got Terry fixed up in the paintshop at the car factory.

Meanwhile in Sam's household there was an announcement.

"I don't know what to say," said Sam.

"Well," said Connie, "we're as surprised as you are."

"What . . . ?" said Sam. "When . . . ?" He just about stopped himself from saying, "How . . . ?"

"February," said Connie. "It's going to be around February."

"Look," Nev put in, himself still somewhat shell-shocked, "it wasn't something we expected, but there it is and that's the way it is. So we're pleased about it. We think."

"We *are* pleased," Connie corrected.

The Tooth Fairy appeared to Sam that night. She was wearing a pale-blue cap, like a flower head. "What do you think of this?" she said. "I thought it looked kind of traditional. For a fairy." Sam looked closer and saw it was a giant bluebell. She moved her head this way and that. "Well? Maybe I should have a name like Herb Twopence. I got it as a souvenir of that afternoon you were in the woods with Alice."

"You put your mark on that, didn't you?"

"I'll admit I was watching. Though I did warn you. I said this was going to lead to trouble."

"Trouble?"

"What's the matter with you? Can't count? Your mother said February. So that's May, June, July . . ."

Suddenly it dawned on Sam. The stolen condom. He slumped on to his bed, pressing his fingers to his temples, the Tooth Fairy counting through the months in exaggerated style.

"I do hope it's a girl," said the Tooth Fairy.

Sam looked up suddenly, through the jail bars of his fingers. "What do you mean?"

"You'll be leaving here soon. Going away. Leaving me trapped here. But I could have so much more fun with a girl. I would start earlier than I did with you. Females are so much more suggestible. So seducible. I could *create* her. Oh, I really do hope it's a girl!"

Sam thought his head would burst open. He could see no way of preventing the Tooth Fairy from daggering a newborn baby. He was horrified at the implications of what he'd done.

"Hey!" she said suddenly. "Your dad doesn't have any problem getting it up! Not like you! Your old man fucks your mother until her teeth rattle! Ha ha!"

Sam leapt from the bed, aggressively jabbing a finger in the Tooth Fairy's face. "Paranoia!" he shouted, and she disappeared.

Sam and Clive moved up into the sixth form at school. Sam studied physics, chemistry and biology at A-level. Clive's genius was detected to have been slowing down. He'd been persuaded to sit, during the summer holidays, A-level exams in applied maths, pure maths and physics. Something went "badly" wrong with the pure maths, and he passed with only a B grade instead of an A. Still, he and his father were united in staunchly resisting all pressure for him to go early to Oxford or Cambridge. The Epstein experience had frightened both of them, and Eric Rogers was adamant that Clive's education should not be speeded up beyond the norm. Even so, Clive was scheduled to take four more A-levels, making a total of seven to Sam's three. Along with Terry, they grew their hair long, took to wearing army-surplus greatcoats and looked more moody around Redstone than ever before.

They continued to help Ian Blythe run the Redstone Folk Club. Sixth-form status conferred on them the privilege of calling Blythe by his first name and of being able to drink (now only slightly underage) in his presence. Clive pestered him into changing the name to the Blues and Folk Club and had a say in booking the acts. Some of the old folkie purists objected to the inevitable swing toward the electrical, but every Friday night the back room at the Gate Hangs Well was stuffed to capacity.

Around Christmas of that year they saw Blythe get blindblazing drunk. He didn't seem to care that three pupils from his school witnessed the spectacle of him falling from his stool while trying to play a song in between two guest spots. Sam and Clive helped him outside, where he promptly threw up. But nothing he did could diminish him in their eyes. They were forced to admire the style with which he wiped his mouth, took a deep breath of air and said, "God bless you, gents," before going back inside to introduce the next act.

"I think his wife just left him," whispered Alice, who was in his upper-sixth English class. "He said something when we were doing *Othello.*"

They could tell Blythe most things, and they generally respected his advice when he gave it. They once tried to tempt him with a ready-rolled joint, but he declined it ruefully. One night, when again he'd imbibed a gallon of bitter, it seemed as though something darkly amorous was shaping up between him and Alice. The other three saw what was going on. Blythe must have noted the expressions of hurt and confusion and betrayal in their eyes, or perhaps he just thought about his position. Whatever it was, he sensibly backed off.

"What is it about you and older men?" Sam wanted to know, while Blythe was busy paying the band.

She thought hard about it. "I don't know myself well enough to answer that question."

"Know thyself," bellowed Clive, eavesdropping over the pub talk, with the bell clanging loudly for last orders. "That's what was written over the oracle at Delphi. 'Know thyself.' "

Alice, Sam and Terry stared at Clive for a moment. "Fuck off!" they said with one voice.

Toward the end of February, Sam's sister was born. Sam went to the hospital with Nev to visit Connie and the baby. All Nev could say, over and over, was, "She's gorgeous! Look at her, Sam, she's gorgeous!"

Sam had to agree. He was overwhelmed by the miniature perfection of the new arrival, by the fact that the baby could be born with fingernails, nostrils, toes and ears all on such a miraculously tiny scale. It was like seeing the Lord's Prayer written for novelty on the back of a postage stamp.

He also carried with him the burden of knowledge of the

stolen condom. It was impossible that Nev or Connie remotely suspected it; but the fact remained that Sam, by his actions and by his intervention, was responsible for the birth of this shiny new human being.

"You're miles away, Sam," Connie was saying, all proud smiles, hugging the baby to her breast. "I said me and your father want you to name her."

"Name her? Gosh. I can't! I mean, why me?"

"Don't panic. You don't have to come up with a name this instant!"

There was, it was pointed out, one slightly unusual feature about the baby. "Look," said Connie, gently prising open the baby's mouth with her finger. "She was born with a tooth."

Sam gazed in horror at the baby's tiny, pink mouth. The minute pearl of an incisor was visible there. Sam grasped the hair at the side of his head. "My God! A tooth! My God!"

A nurse standing beside the bed scoffed at him. "It's not so uncommon," she chided. "It's unusual, but it's not unheard-of. Some say it's good luck."

"And some say it's bad luck." Nev laughed.

Connie laughed too. "Sam, you've gone white as a sheet."

"Look at her, Sam," Nev said oafishly. "She's gorgeous!"

Sam looked. The baby opened its brilliant blue eyes for him and stared back, as if stunned by the horrifying sensual beauty of the universe into which it had been delivered without consultation. There, reflected in the mirror of the baby's tiny black pupil, was the yellow-eyed Tooth Fairy, gazing out at him. Sam's fear for his sister's innocence was glacial. He had done something to mark her, to bring trouble and difficulty to her, to invite wicked fairies to gather at the foot of the maternity bed.

All attention was on the baby. Sam turned to see the Tooth Fairy waiting, unnoticed, behind them all, arms folded. Sam wanted to ask what this new thing meant. He was prepared to make a deal that would allow him to sacrifice himself in order to protect his sister.

"Paranoia," said the Tooth Fairy, and disappeared.

Later Sam left the hospital and went looking for the Tooth Fairy. He'd never been able to make her appear at his bidding. She came whenever she wanted to come and always on her own terms. He had no way of changing that. His search took him back to Chris Morris's locked and abandoned workshop. He remembered that the Tooth Fairy had once appeared there, although with disastrous consequences, and he wondered if she would do so again. Waiting until dusk, he slipped unseen down the side of the garage, swung open the loose window frame and climbed inside.

Terry had been correct. Any of Morris's remotely valuable gear had been sold off. Only junk remained. Sam folded an old sheet, and sat down in the dark. Dust settled, and after a few moments his eyes adjusted to the available light.

The workshop still reeked of Morris's brittle, neurotic energy. Sam imagined too that he could still smell the man's hair oil and his tobacco. But it had been almost a decade since Morris had taken his shotgun to his family. The wall bracket where the shotgun had been mounted was still intact.

"I hate this place. Why do you bring me here?" The Tooth Fairy was crouching under the shotgun bracket, shivering.

"You have to leave her alone. My baby sister, I can't have you going near her."

"You put her there, Sam. It was your doing."

"Why the tooth? Why did you do that?"

"It was one you gave me, a long time ago. You took it back. Never really let go of it, did you? Why didn't you just let go of it, all those years ago, instead of keeping me here?"

"I don't keep you here. And if you don't stay away from her, I have the solution."

The Tooth Fairy froze. Then she smiled. "You'd do that? You're prepared to do that to yourself to keep me out of it?"

Sam nodded.

"You don't understand anything," said the Tooth Fairy. There were tears in her eyes. "You don't dream me. I dream you. You're *my* nightmare, Sam. Please let me go. I hate this place. Morris is here. Please let me go."

Exhausted, confused, Sam closed his eyes. When he opened them again, the Tooth Fairy had gone. He shuddered. He was losing himself. He hardly knew whether the conversation had taken place at all. But the Tooth Fairy was right. Morris's breath was on the place. He was afraid that if he stayed, he would certainly encounter Morris's ghost. In one specific way, he felt he already had. In one precise way, Morris had already spoken to him.

He got out the way he came in. On returning home he said to himself, "I think we should call the baby Linda Alice."

In the moments between sleeping and waking, in the airless workshop where thoughts are forged into words, there came to Sam a voice, speaking out of the dark, intimate, reassuring, reasonable. Suicide, said the voice from the dark, suicide.

Linda came home again the following spring. People started to remark that she was looking a little tired. She'd lost weight, and she turned up in an Afghan coat, which Charlie detested. Charlie asked her if she'd slaughtered the garment in one of the nearby fields, and he made other hurtful comments about her appearance, the true meaning of which was obvious. He didn't like what he was seeing. He wasn't happy that his daughter appeared to be turning into "some sort of hippy." She was twenty-one years old, and it broke Charlie's heart that she had a life of her own.

It was unusual for Sam to find so much tension in the generally warm household, but relations became more strained with each visit. "Get me out of here," Linda said to Sam and Terry one evening. "I need a drink."

The gang was called together, and they took Linda into the city for a night out. For them the evening had a gala air about it. Linda's name had been romantically linked in the press with Gregg Austen, lead guitarist and front man for the Craft. She'd been pictured with him, and Clive in particular couldn't wait to pose a mouthful of questions.

She bridled. "He's a shit, Clive. Some of these people are not as interesting as they look. Let's just leave it at that."

So they left it at that. Sam observed that Linda's hands had developed a slight tremble as she drew hard on her cigarette. She told them about London and she dropped famous names—not to impress them but to offer a flavor of her lifestyle—and they all realized how much they'd missed her. Terry took a chance and tapped her knee, offering her a small joint under the table.

"My God," she said, accepting it, "civilization has come to Redstone."

"Don't slag off the place," Terry said.

"I think if I had to live here all my life," she said breezily, "I'd get a gun and blow my head off."

Everyone tried to avoid looking at Terry, whose eyelashes fluttered madly. He was struggling to control the tic that had been with him since he was seven years old. Sam heard the shotgun blast somewhere far off, and he looked desperately at Linda.

"I can't believe I said that," Linda said. "After all this time of not . . . I can't believe I said that." She tried to recover the situation with a mirthless laugh and, almost by way of apology, fished a small, golden snuffbox from her handbag, flipped it open and placed it on the table. It contained a dozen or so pink pills. "Be my guest, everyone."

They gazed at the pills but didn't avail themselves.

"No?" said Linda, taking one for herself and snapping the box shut. "Hey, let's go to a nightclub. Come on, I'm paying."

In the nightclub Linda was in a dancing mood. She danced frenetically with Sam, with Clive, with Terry and with Alice. They couldn't keep up with her. She bought rounds of Buck's Fizz. Her mood was as buoyant under the pink and ultraviolet lights of the nightclub as it was flat in her parents' house. She repeatedly kissed them all and told them, individually and collectively, how much she loved and missed them. She disappeared into the toilets with Alice and the two came out giggling hysterically. She fell into conversation easily with anyone and everyone but used the group expertly to fend off the fascinated attentions of other men.

Sam wanted to slow-dance with Alice, but Terry grabbed her first. Instead Linda grasped his hand and led him on to the dance floor. She smelled of some wildly expensive perfume.

"What about Alice?" she asked, laughing.

"What about her?"

"Who is she with? You, Terry or Clive?"

"It's a moot point. She keeps us all at arm's length."

"She's too fast for all of you."

"Do you dislike her?"

"Dislike her? I love her! I love all of you! You're wonderful young people! I wish, I really wish, you would all come to live in London with me."

The thought seemed to make her sad. Then she cheered up suddenly, skipped to the bar and returned with yet another round of Buck's Fizz. At the death of the evening she danced a final slow dance with Sam, almost falling asleep in his arms. Suddenly she stopped dancing and looked at him through half-closed eyes. "There are demons," she said.

"What?"

"In the woods, in the trees. At night. I've seen them in the bushes. In Redstone. In London too, probably."

"I don't follow."

"Who are we anyway?" she asked dozily.

"Eh? I'm Sam. You're Linda."

The music stopped, the disc jockey wished everyone a safe journey home. "No. I mean, who are we?"

Sam shrugged. "We're the Redstone Moodies."

She looked at him as if this remark was profound, philosophical and apposite to everything in her experience up to that point in time. Grabbing his collar, she threw her head back and cackled loudly. "That's right!" she screamed. "We're THE REDSTONE MOODIES!" Then she laughed again, leaning back on her heels and dragging on Sam's lapels. "THE REDSTONE MOODIES!"

An irritated bouncer in an evening suit and bow tie marched

across the dance floor. "Haven't you got homes to go to?" he bellowed.

While they waited in the taxi rank, Alice admired Linda's Afghan coat. "It's gorgeous!"

Linda took the coat off. "Have it. It's yours."

"I can't take your coat!"

She draped it over Alice's shoulders and kissed her passionately on the lips. "I want you to have it. I love you. I love all of you."

The taxi dropped Linda and Terry first. Linda paid, tipping overgenerously. As the cab moved on, Clive said, "Anyone know what was in those pink pills?"

THIRTY-NINE
Ghosts

Sam made three feeble efforts to fix an appointment with Skelton, as the voice whispering in the dark appeared with greater frequency. He couldn't speak about his feelings to anyone else. Certainly not to his mother or father: he didn't want them burdened with any new anxieties about their daughter, and yet he was terrified by the idea that he had blighted his tiny sister's life. And not to Alice, who distanced herself from him when he was subject to morose moods. With her he struggled to keep things light, bidding all the time for an easy humor he didn't feel. Clive and Terry, as potential sympathetic listeners, were beyond the pale.

"What's the matter with you lately, Sam? Get a grip."

"Yeah, get sorted out, for chrissakes."

He took to watching over his baby sister for signs of the Tooth Fairy's threatened transfer of attention and became obsessed by the shocking vulnerability of the small child. He scoured the house looking for sharp objects, broken glass, pins which he might remove from her path; he wedged doors open so that she might not trap her fingers; the sight of boiling water made him feverish with alarm for her. The entire home was a rigged and booby-trapped maze of hazards. A stinging lash lurked behind every seemingly innocent chair and cushion.

Each time Sam had tried to telephone Skelton, something in Mrs. Marsh's voice on the other end of the line had made him hang up without speaking. Finally, without permission, he took an afternoon off school and went to Skelton's offices.

Mrs. Marsh was absent from her usual place at the reception. Her desk was cleared and spotlessly tidy, as if she too had taken the afternoon off. Sam went to Skelton's room and listened outside the door. With no sound of any session in progress, he turned the handle and quietly opened the door.

Skelton was at his seat but slouched with his head on the desk blotter. An empty bottle of scotch and a glass stood on the table beside his head. Noiselessly closing the door behind him, Sam crossed the room and took his traditional seat opposite Skelton. He gazed at the sleeping figure for some time.

"He's too far gone," said the Tooth Fairy. "Do you want me to wake him up?"

"Yes," said Sam. "Wake him."

The Tooth Fairy moved over to Skelton and put her mouth close to his ear. She spoke a single word, unheard by Sam, stepped back and dragged a second chair across the room so that she could sit beside Sam.

Skelton twitched. His eyes opened. Slowly lifting his head from his desk, he smacked his lips and focused his rheumy gaze on Sam. Then he looked at the Tooth Fairy with a quizzical expression, and then beyond her, as if the room was full of strangers or as if he had been shanghaied and brought to this place against his will.

"What?" he said. "What was that?"

"He's in danger," said the Tooth Fairy. "He's in danger of killing himself. He wants you to talk to him."

"What? What's that, laddie?"

"I didn't say anything," said Sam.

Peering hard at them, Skelton rubbed the back of his neck. "Sam? Is it that time of the year already?"

"No. I needed to see you."

Skelton scowled at his empty whisky bottle. "Did you see Mrs. Marsh? No one gets past Mrs. Marsh."

"She's gone."

"In disgust, no doubt." He gestured at the Tooth Fairy. "Who's this?"

" 'Who's this?' indeed," sneered the Tooth Fairy. "To think I used to be afraid of you."

Skelton stood up slowly, still massaging the back of his leathery neck, squinting from one to the other of them. "I hope this isn't who I think it is."

"Who?" said the Tooth Fairy. "Who do you think I am?"

From behind his desk Skelton came prowling with a lion's stealth. His stride was superbly slow. "Stop this, laddie," he whispered. "You'd better stop this now." He paced warily behind the Tooth Fairy, watching her with a baleful, glittering eye. He swayed dangerously. Then he moved behind Sam's chair. Sam could feel the man's breath on his neck, savor the rot of whisky.

"He's contemplating suicide. He's come to you for help. But you're a drunk. You've lost the faith. You're history."

"Stand up!" Skelton barked at Sam. "Stand up, laddie!"

"Don't," said the Tooth Fairy quietly, as Sam made to move. Sam flinched. "I said, *stay where you are!*"

The Tooth Fairy was metamorphosing by the second, from female to male, becoming ugly. At standoff, Skelton regarded her/him steadily. A blister of sweat appeared on his brow. "Clever. Very clever. Do you make this come on whenever you want?"

"I don't have any say in it," Sam said.

"This is a waste of time," said the Tooth Fairy. *"He's* supposed to help *you?* I warned you a long time ago about these people."

"I'm ordering you out," Skelton growled. "For the last time. Out."

"Drink your drink," said the Tooth Fairy bitterly. "Talk your talk."

"It gets violent," Sam warned Skelton. "Very violent."

"Not with me it doesn't. Watch this." Skelton crossed to his desk, opening a drawer and fumbling inside. He returned extending an empty palm. "Remember this?" He held his fingers like a gun. "See? I load it with a silver bullet. Like so." He swung perilously close. "Here. Take it. Fire it at this abomination before you."

"I can't," said Sam. "I can't do it."

"Then I will." Skelton stepped back, leveled careful aim at the Tooth Fairy and fired. There was a blast of white heat and a muffled report as the room imploded, shattering like a windscreen, reassembling itself almost instantaneously. Sam saw that the Tooth Fairy was stunned: wide-eyed with horror. Slowly, a malicious smile curved across its lips. Grinning, it revealed a silver bullet, caught neatly between its teeth.

The Tooth Fairy plucked the silver bullet from its mouth and displayed it in a mallet-sized fist. Then it stood up. The smile evaporated. Two feet taller than the sweating psychiatrist, it towered above him, exuding palpable malice and a stench of venom.

"Now it's my turn," said the Tooth Fairy. It brought the massive hammer of its fist across Skelton's face in a backhand swing. Skelton was thrown off his feet, dashing his skull on the corner of his oak desk. The Tooth Fairy turned to Sam. It raised an imaginary gun to its lips, blew smoke from the barrel and offered Sam a conspiratorial smile.

Terry and Sam were delayed one Friday evening on their way to the Blues and Folk Club at the Gate. Sam had called round for Terry, only to find Charlie and Dot in a state of agitation while Terry was talking to Linda on the telephone. Linda was upset about something, but no one could determine the nature of her problem. Both Charlie and Dot had tried to talk to her, without penetrating the mystery, and now Terry was having a go.

Terry held out the phone for Sam. He'd mentioned to Linda that Sam had arrived and was waiting in the hall, and now Linda wanted to speak to him, urgently it seemed. Linda was obviously in tears on the other end of the line, but she wasn't making any sense. This went on for some time. Eventually Sam handed the phone on to Charlie.

"Look, my darling, you can always come home, any time you like," Charlie soothed. "No, my sweetheart, no one's saying you've *got* to come home. I was just . . . No, my flower . . . No . . . your mother never said that . . . and she never said that you said that . . ."

"Come on," Terry whispered to Sam, "let's get out of here."

The club was already filling up when they arrived. A three-piece electric band of drums, bass and organ was setting up battered amplifiers on the tiny stage. Alice and Clive were busy taking money at the door.

"Late for class," said Ian Blythe. "Could you two set up a couple more tables at the back? We might have a crowd in tonight."

"What's the band called?" Terry wanted to know. Band names had gone crazy back in the late sixties; he was compiling a list of the worst ones who'd appeared at the club, to compete with How in the Blitz and Yampy Cow.

"Spy V Spy. From London."

Blythe was right. The club filled to capacity again, and it was standing-room only when Spy V Spy broke into their first number. It was standard gut-bucket blues with pitched vocals and some filigree organ effects. Fine, Clive would say, but not worth bringing all the way from London. Sam noticed some people he wanted to talk to in the corner of the room, and ten minutes had gone by before Clive came over to him and yanked his arm.

"Come here," Clive hissed in his ear.

"What's the rush? I'm talking."

"Come here!"

Clive had turned very pale. His eyes had a strange cast, and Sam knew he shouldn't argue. Excusing himself from his company, he followed Clive to the door.

A desk and two chairs were set up at the entrance. Terry was waiting for them there. His face was white. "What is it?" Alice was saying. She appealed to Sam. "What's the matter?"

Clive ignored her. He grabbed Sam's wrist, hard. "What do you see?" Sam looked around. Everyone in the club was intent on talking, buying beer or watching the band. It seemed, by all accounts, an average night at the Gate Hangs Well, everyone enjoying themselves.

"Will someone tell me what the hell is going on?" Alice protested.

"No," said Clive. "The band! Look at the band!"

Sam squinted between the bobbing heads of some youths standing forward of the entrance area. He saw nothing remarkable about the trio on stage. The organist's tight blond perm looked suspiciously like it might have been dyed or highlighted. The bass player pursed his lips unpleasantly as he worked his fingers up and down the frets. There was little to note.

"The *drummer!*" Terry shrieked in his ear. "Look at the fucking *drummer!*"

Sam looked but still couldn't see anything remarkable. The drummer was a fat guy with a beard, drumming competently, if a little lazily, relying perhaps too much on the snare. Then he looked up, flashing a gap-toothed smile at the audience, and the light caught a certain degenerate expression in his eyes. *No,* thought Sam. *It can't be.*

Clive sidled up. "Take away the beard."

Alice had given up and had gone to talk to Blythe.

"It's not possible," Sam spluttered. "It can't be him."

"It's him," said Terry. "It's him all right."

Sam visualized the face without the beard. A sharp smell of the woods in autumn cut through the pub tang of sour ale and dead nicotine. There was no mistake. Now he could see that leering face in a scouting beret and with a neckerchief at the throat. "This means . . . What this means is . . ."

"Yes," said Terry.

"Yes," said Clive. "He must have crawled away from it."

"What is it, boys?" Ian Blythe wanted to know. He regularly treated them to a couple of beers out of the takings, and he was offering three foaming pints on a tray. Alice stood behind him, look-ing suspicious. "You all look like you've seen a ghost."

"What do you know about this band?" Sam said quickly.

Blythe shrugged. "Not much. Got 'em through the usual newsletter. Drummer told me he's a local boy, first time back since he went to London some years ago."

The boys stared in disbelief. After muting his organ and re-peating a couple of chords, the permed organist leaned forward and began to introduce his band. "We got Chaz Myers on bass . . ." A polite ripple of applause encouraged Chaz to launch into a tedious bass solo, running his fingers up and down the frets as organ and drums dutifully faded. "And we got Tooley Bell on drums . . ." Another polite ripple as Tooley grinned happily at the audience, an upper canine missing. Tooley bashed happily away for his moment of limelight.

"Hey, where you going?" Blythe shouted, as Sam pushed his way out of the room. Terry and Clive followed quickly behind. "What about this beer?" Blythe called after them.

The Gate Hangs Well had a lawn in front, with a phoney gazebo and rustic tables and benches for the summer months. Sam flung himself, facedown, on the damp grass between the tables. His body quivered.

"You all right?" Terry asked, worried.

"Sam, come on," said Clive.

But Sam was sniggering. Then he snorted violently, and his sniggering turned into full-throated, manic laughter. He rolled on his back, kicking his legs in the air, laughing like a man in a padded cell. Terry fell to the ground, hugging Sam with his one good hand, wrapping his legs around Sam's and laughing with him. Clive dived on both of them, and in a second the three were rolling round on the grass, hugging each other and roaring hysterically.

Blythe came outside with Alice. Spy V Spy were building up to a standard blues climax for one of their numbers. They could hear Tooley artlessly bashing his cymbals on the Big Finish. The thought of him lashing out with his sticks only made them howl with vicious merriment. "What have you been taking?" Blythe said disapprovingly. The question only made them laugh louder, more uncontrollably. They squeezed their ribs, gagging for breath.

"Stop!" squeaked Terry. "Stop!"

"Can't," Clive gasped. "Caaaaaaannnnn't."

"Hooooohooohooohooo," went Sam.

"You guys want to be more careful. I'm serious. This drugs business is no joke," Blythe said sharply. Then he turned and went back inside.

Alice waited patiently until the hooting and the laughter had subsided. Eventually the three of them were able to draw themselves partially upright, leaning against each other like defeated marathon runners. "So? Are you going to let me in on it?"

Sam looked at Alice. Recovering his breath and his composure, he managed to tell her, "The drummer. He's the Dead Scout."

And the hysterical laughter started up again.

FORTY

White Cube

It was a considerable relief to be acquitted, by events, of being a murderer. For Terry and Clive the commencement of that summer seemed particularly heady, balmier than all summers hitherto, benign, scented and laden with extra promise. Alice, unfortunately, was encumbered with having to revise for her final A-level exams, but for the others dark chains had been taken from their backs.

But not, for Sam, the darkest and heaviest chain.

No longer in fear of tripping over a corpse at least, Sam enjoyed solitary walking in the woods again. He found the place where the original incident had happened and speculated that Tooley had only been unconscious when they'd dumped him in the hollow stump. He'd obviously recovered, gone home to lick his wounds and decided to make the break for London, just as his sidekick had suggested at the time. That night at the Gate, when they'd recovered from laughing, Clive, Terry and Sam had deliberately pressed in on Tooley to see if he recognized them. Terry even presented him with a pint of beer at the end of the evening, chatting genially. It was agreed that he did eye Sam strangely as the band's equipment was carried out of the pub, but nothing was said.

Before leaving Tooley had looked back at Sam, holding his head to one side like a puzzled dog, but then he'd climbed in the van with the other members to return to London.

Meanwhile London was sending back another of its migratory children. The first time Charlie and Dot understood the nature of Linda's predicament was when they were telephoned by a Harley Street doctor. He had been treating Linda for exhaustion, he explained, and recommended that Linda come home for complete rest, where she could be properly looked after.

"Exhaustion?" Charlie had managed to ask.

"I don't like the expression *nervous breakdown,*" the doctor had said suavely. "I don't find it helpful."

Charlie and Dot went to meet Linda from the train at Coventry station. Dot burst into tears when Linda stepped down from the carriage. Looking painfully thin, her hair hanging limply at the side of her gaunt face, she stood on the platform trying to tug her heavy suitcase behind her. What had London done to Linda? Her eyes were devoid of sheen, her skin had given up its ambrosial glow. She looked old and yet girlish at the same time. Her golden crown lay in twisted fragments on the platform at her feet. Choking back a huge stone in his throat, Charlie stepped forward and hugged her.

He took charge. He picked up her suitcase and led her and Dot along the crowded platform and out to his waiting car. They asked no questions of her, having been advised by their local GP, in whose care she was placed, not to press. After a few days a bill arrived from the Harley Street doctor, addressed to Charlie. He opened it, and his stomach turned.

"What is it?" Dot wanted to know.

"Nothing to worry about."

Charlie brooded on it for some days. He calculated that if he took out all of his savings and sold his car, he might be able to cover half of the bill. Then he got hold of Linda's address book and rang her agency. He was put through to Pippa Hamilton.

"Is that Miss Pippa?"

"Speaking."

A curve in the woman's voice had him incandescent with rage before the conversation had even begun. "I'm Linda's father."

"Linda? How is the poor darling? I *do* hope she's better."

"Is she owed?"

"I beg your pardon?"

"Has she got any money due to her? From the agency?"

"I'm afraid not. She is rather a *silly* with money."

"A bill came. From a doctor in London."

"Yes, he's a friend, actually. We were lucky to get his services."

"How long had he been seeing her?"

There was a pause. "Quite some time. Actually."

Something in that last word sent Charlie cold. "I'm going to come and see you."

"There's no need—"

"Yes. I'm coming. And after what I've done to you, the only use you'll be to anybody is if one of them fancy models of yours wants to wear you up on the catwalk." There was a silence, and he put the phone down.

After his hands had stopped trembling, he took the bill and wrote on it "To be paid by the Pippa Hamilton Modelling Agency," addressed an envelope and took it out for posting. Charlie knew that Pippa Hamilton had sensed this was no idle threat. He never heard anything about the bill again.

It slowly emerged that the high life and the low life made bedfellows in Linda's celebrity world. After an unhappy love affair, she'd started using slimming pills with an amphetamine base, and someone had taught her how to pop barbiturates to offset the sleep disruption caused by the uppers. More significantly, Linda had been carrying a huge burden of unexpressed guilt over the death of Derek. The champagne-and-pills parties were an effective way of blotting out her desperate unhappiness. Most of her pills were obtained from the very Harley Street doctor who had telephoned her home when the crisis occurred.

These were the explanations offered concerning Linda's "exhaustion." But Sam recalled the day Linda had won her first beauty-queen title, and he remembered the Tooth Fairy reaching out to touch her with a fetid hand.

He wanted to see the Tooth Fairy. He wanted to interrogate her, to ask what putrid influence she might have exercised over Linda's life in London. He was still convinced that his "affliction" was always capable of leaking into the lives of those people he cared about most. But he didn't have—had never had—the ability to summon the Tooth Fairy at will. She came when she wanted to, and these days she came more erratically than ever. He remained terrified of the malign influence she might have over the hitherto unblemished life of his sister Linda Alice. On bad nights the voice still came, darkly offering him a solution.

"So, then, it's goodbye, Sam." Skelton thrust out a bear-like paw that wanted shaking. His other arm was in a sling. He still had a large plaster on the side of his head.

Signs were that the psychiatrist had already started packing. Files were stacked on chairs; journals had been lifted down from the oak bookcase and dumped in cardboard boxes. He had opted for an early retirement. "I've been letting one or two people down lately," he said. "Particularly that last time you came in. I had a bit of a fall. Don't remember a deal about it, to be honest."

"You can't remember anything?"

"You know what they say: when the drink's in, the wits are out."

"Perhaps you don't want to remember?"

"Well, you've a learned a bit of psychology from me, if nothing else. Eh, laddie? Anyway I thought I'd better get out. Let someone in who knows what they're talking about. I'm no use."

"You were a lifeline," said Sam.

"I really did enjoy our wee sessions. Though I don't say I've been the slightest help to you in your plight."

"You have."

"I'm rather sorry I never found a use for that Nightmare Interceptor contraption of yours. Do you still have the thing?"

"It's around."

Skelton scratched his head with his good arm. "It has a certain potential, one feels. Hang on to the thing. I wouldn't want you to throw it away. Still, dreams have been a wee bit out of fashion lately. There's a younger chap coming in here. Different ideas. Neurophysiology—know what that is? Me neither, and I don't care to. I've passed on your case notes, and I've indicated that it may be necessary for you to see him. He'll look at the file and decide."

"I don't much fancy seeing someone else."

"I know what you mean. Gets to be a cosy habit, doesn't it, these little meetings? I sometimes wonder if that's part of the problem. Yes, I wonder if we keep our demons in orbit for each other."

Glumly Sam thought of his own demon. "Paranoia?" he asked brightly.

"Aye, we support each other's paranoia. Listen, there's not a lot wrong with you, son. Deep down, I mean. Let's just say you're different."

"I almost forgot." Sam reached inside his sports bag and produced a boxed gift for Skelton. It had been Connie's idea.

Skelton opened the box and withdrew a bottle of Johnny Walker. He examined the red label as if it was a work of art, then held the bottle up to the window. "Look at the light in that, Sam. Look at the amber light. See what I mean?" he said, spinning the top off the bottle and pouring them both a small measure. "About keeping each other's demons in orbit? Only yesterday I decided to go teetotal."

It was Clive who managed to obtain the stuff, through his music-collecting contacts.

"Oh, it's you three. I shouldn't let you in because she's studying for some exam or other." Alice's mother, still in her dressing gown and smelling of sleep, pushed a straying gray curl out of her eye.

Leaving the door open, she turned her back on them, calling over her shoulder. "She's in her bedroom."

Alice sat cross-legged on the bed. Her hair was tied back in a ponytail. Schoolbooks were strewn over the bed. "I'm so fed up. Just look what a beautiful day it is outside, and I've got to do this."

"Leave it. Come with us."

"I've got an exam next week."

"You don't want to do too much," said Terry.

"Can't pour a quart into a pint pot," said Sam.

"What you need is a break," said Clive. "Something to take you out of yourself." He opened his fist and presented, on the flat of his palm, four sugar cubes.

Alice peered closely at the sugar cubes. They looked entirely harmless. "I've heard it's a long trip," she said doubtfully.

"Only eight hours," Clive said brightly.

Terry was first to snatch up one of the cubes. "Down the hatch," he said, and popped it in his mouth.

"I keep trying to count us," said Alice. "And every time I count us I get five."

Clive tried. He got the same result. "Wait a minute!" he giggled, counting again. Again he got the same result. "Wait! Wait! This is ridiculous!"

Terry tried. He also came up with five. He shook his head and started over. "But there's me and Sam and you two, and that's four."

"Obviously."

"Obviously."

"So how come I keep counting five? Ha! Ha, ha! Wait, I'm going to do it again . . . Four . . . five! It can't be! Ha, ha, ha!"

The knot of anxiety in Sam's stomach was swelling. He knew that the Tooth Fairy had appeared in their company about half an hour after they'd all swallowed the sugar cubes at Alice's house, and that was three hours ago. He'd sensed her presence, though he hadn't actually seen her. Somehow the others were seeing the

Tooth Fairy now, but they were only seeing her in the form of one of the others. Perhaps Terry saw her as Alice, Clive as Terry, Alice as Sam.

They'd made their way to the football field, and they were sitting beside the pond. It was a warm day, but the sky was broken by a warning of herringbone clouds. It had taken them some time to recover from the shock of color. Everywhere color leaked, oozing like a substance not yet dry on the canvas. Light pulsed. They'd passed through a period of uncontrollable hilarity and elation, followed by a long period when no one spoke. The warm air breathed sensually on the backs of their necks. The earth streamed rich perfumes, and the grass and soil were an impossible tangle of runes and spirographic designs, as if the universe had been put together by a crazed geometrist.

Sam had himself tried to count, and he too arrived at the figure of five. There were five in the company. Five. He counted again. It was maddening. Yet the only others apart from himself were Terry, Alice and Clive.

"I've got the answer," Terry offered. "Stop counting."

Alice waved a dismissive hand through the air, and her arm fanned out like the exotic feathers of a great bird's wing, a staggered image arching through the air. The birds in the bushes and trees around them flitted from branch to branch, sketching intersecting parabolic trails in the air behind them.

"Know thyself," Alice said for the third time.

"Why do you keep saying that?"

"Clive said it, ages ago. It was written on the sugar cubes at Dolphin."

"Delphi," Clive corrected.

"Delfever . . . Delve free . . . Deal fee."

"?"

"The oracle."

"Horror-kill," said Alice. "Horror-cull . . . Whore-call . . ."

"If you were a fruit," the Tooth Fairy said to Alice, "what fruit would you be?"

Sam blinked. He'd distinctly seen the Tooth Fairy sitting upright, grinning at Alice. But now it was Clive asking the question
and not the Tooth Fairy at all.

"Huh?"

"It's a game. What fruit? You?"

Words were slipping away from them, unraveling on the
tongue, becoming redundant. Paradoxically, communication
seemed easier, richly telepathic. Sam suddenly felt hot. His anxiety
was mounting. Then he saw the Tooth Fairy putting the same
question. "If Sam was a fruit, what . . . ?" But before the question
was completed, the Tooth Fairy had become Terry. ". . . what fruit
would you be?"

Sam counted his companions again. Still five in total.

"Sam would be a lime." Someone chortled.

Sam's skin greened over. His body inflated to roughly spheri-
cal form. A thick, protective rind formed over his skin, and he
sensed the rich, pulpy effervescence of his internal mass. He inhaled deeply, enjoying the bittersweet tang of his own citrus. He
pressed his skin, and a fine zest burst forth, falling in a light, fragrant shower around them.

Laughter from the others brought Sam back. He extended his
body and returned to normal.

"Getting strange, isn't it?" said the Tooth Fairy.

"You're not helping," said Sam.

"Who's not helping?" Alice wanted to know.

"Alice would be an orange," said the Clive Fairy.

Or the Tooth Terry.

Sam shook his head vigorously. His grasp of events was falling
apart. He seemed unable to hang on to a thought for more than a
moment. One second Terry and Clive seemed to be only inches
away, the next moment they were blasted a hundred yards across
the field. He desperately wanted to hug Alice, to find infant comfort at her breast. But every time he crept toward her, he seemed accidentally to telegraph his intentions, and Terry would inch closer
in competition. Then it occurred to him that Alice was manipu-

lating them all so that they would fight over her. A dirty wave of hatred washed over him, and yet he simultaneously found himself wincing at the corrupt depth of this emotion.

"Don't panic," said the Tooth Terry.

Sam pointed his finger. "Paranoia."

The Tooth Fairy smiled but didn't disappear.

"Paranoia," Sam tried again.

The Tooth Fairy shook its head. It was mutating now from its female to its male aspect. Its face had a poisoned, blue sheen. " 'Fraid I tricked you on that little paranoia number. Won't work here."

Sam felt a hot flush rising, and then a hand stroked the scruff of his neck, grabbing his hair and tugging it. It was naked fear. "Leave us alone. Just leave us."

"Sam," said Alice. She too was having problems with her words. It was all she could say. "Sam."

"Good idea of yours," said the Tooth Fairy, "to name your kid sister after Linda and Alice. Fair trade."

"Don't be jealous. There's no need for you to be jealous."

"I told you the kid was for me, didn't I? Well, you win some and you lose some. I've already had some payback from Linda. Now it's time to give Alice a taste."

The Tooth Fairy sprang over to Alice, put its mouth close to hers and breathed hard in her face. She leapt back.

Sam's words were gone. He found he could use telepathy to talk to her. *It's the Tooth Fairy I told you about.*

Clive and Terry still seemed to be deeply engaged in conversation a hundred yards away. Alice spoke back telepathically. Her lips shaped different words to the ones he was hearing, like a film soundtrack out of synch. *My God. Is this what you see? I never realized.*

"Now you know."

"You see this all the time? But it's so ugly! It's ugly!"

"You'll pay for that." The Tooth Fairy grimaced. "I owe you one."

"Paranoia," Sam tried again.

"I told you already I only let you think that would work on me. Just remember. This is my dream, not yours."

"So ugly," Alice repeated.

"If you were a fruit, what fruit would you be?"

Alice recovered her ability to speak normally. "I'm an orange," she said. "I'm an orange."

The Tooth Fairy reached for a rusting razor blade embedded in a tree. "Know thyself. Peel thyself."

Sam gasped, feeling himself zoomed hundreds of yards away from where Alice sat. Then the clouds aligned in a menacing pattern of wicked chevrons, and the sky was filled with screaming, like the shrieking of a thousand strange birds, their wings interlocked to comprise the sky itself. And Sam realized that the screaming was coming from his own throat.

FORTY-ONE
Aftermath

Sam, Clive and Terry spent the next three days trying to piece together the events of that afternoon: why Alice did what she did; when the ambulance arrived; who summoned it. Police wanted to know. Doctors wanted to know. Parents wanted to know.

The difficulty was that they were all so far out of their heads at the time, they found it difficult to distinguish real, horrific events from the three hours of hallucinatory nightmares which followed. It emerged that Terry had almost killed himself by sprinting to the road and leaping out in front of a car. Babbling incomprehensibly, he'd managed to terrify some family who were out for a Sunday drive, but they'd understood enough from him to call an ambulance.

To the squeal of the ambulance siren was added the migraine-flash of the police car's blue light. Sam was still vomiting from the sight of so much blood when the uniformed officers arrived. Clive was shocked into a state of paralysis, while Terry tried to make a run for it. He would have made it too but, having reached the safety of the woods, some impulse of surrender made him abandon the idea of escape, and he turned back to share the fate of his friends.

Once the ambulance crew had dragged out of them information about what Alice had taken and in what quantity, they left the
young men to the police. Still hallucinating wildly as the ambulance
sped away, the three were driven to a police station in Coventry.
There they were isolated, interviewed and examined by a doctor.

"Any history of mental illness?" Sam was asked, and the question made him laugh hysterically. When he recovered he told the
doctor about his contact with Skelton, about the Nightmare Interceptor, about Skelton's whisky demon, about Skelton's secretary
Mrs. Marsh, about neurophysiology and—

"I'm going to give you a sedative. Is that acceptable?"

"Yes."

Sam was quizzed over and over about exactly where he'd obtained the psychedelics. The "stranger-in-a-pub" routine angered
the interrogating officers, but he stuck with it because he knew
Terry and Clive would do the same. This was only a bust if he
could just keep his head. Eventually the sedative smoothed the
edge off the hallucinations. By midnight the effects of the drug
had almost worn off. A police officer cheerfully informed him that
Drugs Squad officers had been dispatched to each of their homes
to search for more drugs. Sam despaired

It was in the early hours of the morning when he was taken to
a room already occupied by Terry and his Uncle Charlie, Clive
and Eric and Betty Rogers, and his own father.

When he walked through that door, his father gave him *the
look*. Sam had been relegated from the status of insect. Now he
was some species of insect larva.

The recriminations were endless. None of their parents actually banned them from seeing each other, but any hint that they
might so do produced reactions of astonishing vitriol. All contact
was out of the question. Telephone calls were proscribed. His own
parents, and he suspected the same would be true of the others',
swung wildly between viewing him as the villain of the piece and
the innocent lamb led astray by the influence of vile friends.

Worse still, they couldn't seem to get any information about the fate of Alice. Finally it got too much for Sam, and he plucked up the courage to go to her house.

Alice's mother answered the door, wearing a threadbare housecoat, her hair in curlers. She'd taken her dentures out. Her mouth puckered and she looked confused when she saw Sam. For a moment he thought she'd failed to recognize him. Her face, bruised with alcohol, was streaked with juniper-colored shadows.

"I came to ask how Alice is. Is it possible to see her?"

Alice's mother made a gargling noise at the back of her throat. She twisted her head from side to side. Then she came at Sam like a hissing snake. "How *dare* you show up at this door! How *dare* you! It's unspeakable that you should show your face at this door! Unspeakable!"

"I just want to know how she is!"

Alice's mother jabbed a nicotine-stained finger in his face. "I TRUSTED YOU!" she shrieked. "All of you! I gave you your freedom, and this is how you pay me back. I TRUSTED YOU!"

Sam was taken aback by her vehemence. He retreated, but after taking only a single step some instinct made him face her again. "You're wrong. You didn't trust anyone. You just didn't give a damn. You didn't even care about her and that *boyfriend* of yours. That's not the same as trust."

"MONSTER!" she screamed. She hurtled down the path in her carpet slippers, launching herself at him, her arms flailing wildly. "YOU MONSTER!"

Sam dodged to safety and jogged away from the house. Even after he'd put two hundred yards between them he could still hear her screaming. He walked back through the fields, hot tears of indignation stinging his eyes.

Only yards from the place where it had all happened, Sam saw Linda leaning against the fence. She was out walking Titch, their whippet-cross. Titch barked in recognition, and Linda turned.

"Sam!"

Reluctantly he crossed over to her. He didn't know whether she blamed him, like all the other adults.

"You look a lot better, Linda." It was true, Linda was recovering, but there was a flintiness to her now. Tiny chips of ice in her eyes suggested that the sweet provincial girl would not be seen hereabouts again.

"Never mind me: what about you? You look terrible."

"Alice's mother won't let me see her. She blames me. They all blame me."

"Terry feels the same. He asked me why everything he touches turns to shit."

"Why does it, Linda? What's wrong with us?"

She took his arm and stroked it, her face suffused with sympathy. She could see a boy who needed to cry but who couldn't break the taboo. "It's not like that. Look at me. Am I any better? Didn't I fuck things up too?"

"Sure. But then you're also a Redstone Moodie."

"Am I? I never thought I was in."

"No, Linda. In fact, you were the original Moodie."

Linda laughed, but it was a bitter laugh. "See? We can cheer each other up, can't we?" Sam hung his head. She rested her cool fingers against his cheek, and he remembered another time when she'd done the very same thing. "I'll go to Alice's this evening. Her mother won't chase me away. I'll find out how she is and I'll let you know." She linked arms with him. "Come on, walk down with me."

FORTY-TWO

Farewell Moodies

Blame, like water, levels out. The police failed to prosecute, having found no evidence on which to do so, their midnight searches notwithstanding, though all involved were officially cautioned. After the summer had passed, they had their final exams to think about. If Sam and Clive got their heads down to study that year, it was all in deference to Alice.

Because of her self-inflicted injuries, Alice missed her exams, so she was set back a year to re-sit them at the same time as Clive and Sam sat theirs. Her wounds healed with time, but they didn't look pretty. At least the brutal stepladder series of gashes on her left forearm and over the left side of her rib cage could be covered up most of the time. The point was that Sam and Clive somehow felt that they should initiate a mood of serious study to help Alice through.

It worked because they all passed their A-levels with more than respectable grades. It was a relief all round that something had finally worked out for them. Though it had never been in any doubt, Clive was going to Oxford to study microbiology. Sam was on his way to university in London to study astrophysics—if he could abandon his young sister to fate. Alice had suspended her academic career for a while, even though she had secured a place at a teacher-training college in Sheffield. She talked frequently of taking some time off to travel.

Terry didn't make it as a professional footballer, slipping off the books of both Coventry City and Aston Villa, but he was remarkably sanguine about the business. He enjoyed the feeling of having money in his pocket from his paintshop job and was generous when it came to buying rounds at the Gate Hangs Well Blues and Folk club. Ian Blythe was the only adult who never actually condemned them for what had happened, though he did proffer some advice one night as they stacked chairs after closing up the club.

Befuddled himself from several pints of Guinness, he assembled the four of them. "Listen," he said. "Listen. Look at me. Most drugs make most people stupid. That's it." Then he nodded judiciously, absolutely in concurrence with this opinion of his, burped and staggered to the toilet.

What was to be the last summer in Redstone passed in a haze and a heatwave. The four of them went on holiday together, to a caravan in Norfolk, scrupulously to ignore Blythe's edict about drugs. Clive wanted to try some of the stuff that had caused all the trouble.

"Just to find out what went wrong," he said when Alice was out of the caravan.

Sam and Terry answered with hostile glares.

"Okay," said Clive. "Just a thought."

Sometimes Sam genuinely didn't know if he was dreaming the Tooth Fairy or if she was, as she claimed, dreaming him.

"Do you still think about killing yourself?"

"Yes," said Sam. "Because it would kill you. And in doing so, it would protect other people. Now I've seen how you do it. You talk people into destroying themselves. You probably told Terry's father to kill himself and his family. You told Derek to kill himself. You told Alice, and she would have done it if the ambulance hadn't arrived."

"You're wrong. You were responsible for what happened to Alice, not me. You handed her the blade."

"That's a lie," Sam whined. "I saw you give her the blade."

"But I only act on your directions," said the Tooth Fairy. "Right then you hated Alice. She made you jealous. I responded to that. Look back at all the times I came to you when you were angry, or afraid, or hurt."

Sam was looking back. "You feed on these things? Like you feed on a lost tooth?"

"It's a trade-off. You always get something in return. But it's an unfair partnership, Sam. You never give of yourself. That's why it often goes wrong."

"What? What exactly am I supposed to give?"

The Tooth Fairy shrugged. "Teeth. Soul. Love."

He looked at the Tooth Fairy sitting on his windowsill. She looked sad. Exhausted and miserable.

"In all the times I've given myself to you, how often have you been content just to have me? I lay down in your bed. Be Linda, you say. Be Alice. Be this one, be that one. You never want me to be me. And every time your need calls me, I come. I'm chained to you, Sam. I've told you before: you're my nightmare."

"But if I'm your dream, where are you when you are awake? Where do you go?"

"That's just it. You won't give yourself to me. So you would never come to the place I go."

"That's not true."

The Tooth Fairy sat upright. She seemed suddenly to grow in strength. "You would? You'd come with me? Now?"

"Yes. I would, yes."

And the world inverted. And the world reinvented itself.

Sam found himself in Wistman's Woods. But they were changed. Instead of trees through which to wind a path, there were tree-shaped pillars of white light—brilliant as a magnesium flare—through which to walk, and the space which should have existed between the trees was impenetrable. He could move by leaping from point-of-light to point-of-light. And the ferns, the unwalkable paths, the leaf mold floor and the space between the tree-shaped pillars were lilac and mauve. If he tried to step beyond the pillars of light, his way was barred and the color rubbed off on to his skin until he too was lilac and mauve.

He felt a claw of anxiety in his bowels. He could sense the Tooth Fairy close by, but he couldn't see her. And his teeth felt weighty in his mouth. They felt like some strange metal wedged in his lilac gums, and when he touched his tongue to them, he knew they were sharpened to points.

At last he found her, illuminated within another tree-branched pillar of light. She smiled at him, and the dagger points were gone from her own mouth. She was radiant. He had never seen her looking so unambiguously beautiful. The clothes which had seemed so shabby in his world were now pristine and resplendent, strobing with iridescent threads. She beckoned him to follow.

They moved through the woods, springing from point-of-light to point-of-light. Then she stopped and, taking him by the hand, gestured at a strange flower growing from a broken bowl of light. The long-stemmed flower was trumpet-shaped and acid-white. Inside the trumpet of petals was a tuber-shaped stamen, the color of a lilac shadow. On the anther of the stamen was some venomous-looking yellow dust. The Tooth Fairy reached over and grasped the lilac tuber, collecting the yellow dust on her forefinger. Looking at Sam, she put her fingers to her mouth, shyly licking them clean. She collected more on her hand, offering it to him.

He licked her fingers clean of the substance. It fizzed on his tongue. The Tooth Fairy cocked her head to one side, delighted by his surprise. She collected more of the weird pollen for him, and again it effervesced in his mouth. This time he began to feel fumes ascending to his brain.

Laughing, the Tooth Fairy stepped out of her clothes. Taking coy steps toward him, she undressed him. Shaking more pollen from the flower, she smeared it across his chest and arms, and smoothed it on to his thighs. Then she inserted some of the stuff into her vagina. Sam felt himself becoming aroused, but as he did so his whole body became tumescent, as if his entire skin were engorging with blood.

The Tooth Fairy pressed her body to him. Her skin rippled with light, hot against his. "Who do you want me to be?" he heard himself say. His voice sounded like a strange wind.

"Just be you." Her nipples stood erect, like twin blades, and as she pressed herself to him, he felt them puncture the pumped-up skin of his own chest. There was a sudden release of pressure, and he panicked. He felt betrayed, and suddenly he was paralyzed with fear. The blades of her nipples tore open his skin as she maneuvered her breasts down the length of his torso. Late in realizing his terror, she stopped, looking gently into his eyes, her sweet face anxious to reassure him. The incisions stung, but only momentarily. Blood bubbled at the wounds, but only minimally. She continued to open up his skin from his breastbone, down the entire length of his trembling body, over his thighs, ending only at his toes.

When she'd finished, she proceeded to flay her own skin with her sharp fingernails. Then she stepped out of her skin, revealing a new but identical version of herself, softly luminescent, glowing dully and with virginal purity. Turning to him, she helped him out of his old skin as if it were a suit of clothes. In a state of shock, he complied. The epidermis underneath could hardly bear the whisper of a faint breeze, so sensitive was it. His new skin effervesced.

Then the Tooth Fairy kissed him a full-mouthed kiss; and with the deft steps of a ballerina, she climbed on him, slowly impaling herself on his stiff cock. Inside she burned. The honey-like fire of her was overwhelming, unbearable, like a searing, sweet energy rampant in his brain. She bucked on him, urging him to thrust deeper into her, and he found they were rising slowly from the floor of the woods. Sam laughed uncontrollably, hysterically, demented with pleasure. At last he ejaculated inside her. Some thousand-year-old longing within him came away like a pulled tooth.

"You gave," she whispered in his ear, shuddering and weeping with joy. "You gave."

He lost consciousness.

When he came to he was lying naked on the carpet of his bedroom floor. He was weeping and his nose was sore from the crocodile clip of the Nightmare Interceptor. The alarm on the end of the wire was ringing. He had no recollection of attaching the thing to himself.

A couple of weeks before Clive and Sam were due to leave Redstone to take up their studies, Blythe announced that he'd arranged something special for a farewell night. Landlady Gladys was putting on sandwiches; staunch club supporters were exhorted to be there; even parents were invited to come along. "We'll give you a good send-off," promised Blythe.

Come the night, a huge banner decked the back room of the Gate. Daubed in red paint, it said FAREWELL MOODIES. The banner had been painted and hoisted by Alice and Linda. The club was already full when Sam arrived. The beer flowed quickly, sandwiches were passed around on huge ceramic plates and a couple of early floor singers paid tribute to "the young boys and girls who really ran the club while Ian Blythe sat on his arse and drank the profits."

Not fair, said Blythe, pointing out in good part that he'd gone to a lot of trouble for once to get some decent musicians for the evening. And he had, in an Irish folk band called Deviltry, hugely respected on the circuit.

"Couldn't you get a blues band?" Clive said ungratefully.

Blythe only laughed and patted Clive's face before going to introduce the band.

Deviltry tore the place apart. With guitar, banjo, fiddle and a bodrhon they played spirited, fast-paced jigs and reels that kept the beer tap vibrating in time. Foaming pints of ale floated in on trays for Clive and Sam, to be consumed almost as fast as they appeared. Deviltry stopped for a beer-break of their own.

"You don't have to drink it just because it's there," Connie said in Sam's ear.

"Mum! Glad you made it! Is Dad here?" Aunt Madge had been recruited into baby-sitting service to look after Sam's little sister. "Have you met Ian Blythe?"

Sam left Blythe listening to his mother. "I was just saying, he doesn't have to drink it just because it's there," Sam heard her say as he moved off. He was looking for Alice. She'd been staying pretty close to Terry these days. He had things to say to her before he left.

"Your mother says to tell you," said Alice, "that you don't have to—"

"I know, I know."

"Look at Linda!" Linda had joined Ian Blythe at the bar. Together they were giving a good listening to Connie's recommendations. Linda, flushed with drink, was leaning in on Blythe. "Do you think those two are going to get together?"

"I think you're right," said Sam. "Have you noticed how he's cut down his drinking? He's trying to make a decent impression."

"I need to talk to you," said Alice.

"Sure."

"Outside."

Long before they reached the beer garden Sam had a flat feeling it was not going to be what he wanted to hear.

"I wanted to tell you," she said. "Terry and me. We're planning to go away together. To travel. To Greece or India, or somewhere like that."

Sam looked down. Already a dew had formed on the grass. "You chose Terry. Somehow I always thought you might."

"You're not upset, are you? He's worried you might be upset."

"Part of me is upset, disappointed. Part of me is pleased for you and Terry."

"I still care for you. We both do."

"Can we go back inside now?"

"You *are* upset."

"Don't torture me with it, Alice!"

The band started up again inside, and Alice kissed him passionately on the mouth. Then she led him back inside by the hand. Sam avoided Terry and made for the beer. Clive meanwhile seemed to be drinking himself into a stupor.

Sam downed another pint and wiped a moustache of foam from his lip. The fiddler fiddled a high-pitched reel; the pace of the war-drum hotted. The music tricked his heart into missing a beat. Then the fiddle hit a high, skirling note that had him wincing with pleasure. The combination of infused ale and the reeling, squealing fiddle stung his blood and set up a tickling in the back of his brain.

Someone near the band started jigging in the small space between the band and the forward row of tables. In moments half of the audience was up on its feet, swinging back and forth in an ecstatic jig. A braceleted arm reached out and grabbed him; his beer slopped as he was dragged into the dancers. It was Linda. He managed to aim his glass into a passing hand as she swung him round, both locked at the crook of elbow. When she released him he catapulted across the floor, only to be borne up by Ian Blythe, clenched again by the crook of his elbow.

Gladys Noon was exhorting all the dancers to stop. "I haven't got a license for dancing!" she protested, a remark which for some reason everyone found hilarious. Ian Blythe released Sam and swung up with the landlady, who stopped complaining and joined in, throwing her free hand into the air. Sam was dizzy. He gazed across the seething heads of the dancers. Either he was hallucinating or a heat haze was rising from the throng. Alice jigged with Terry, and Linda reeled with Clive. His mother danced with Betty Rogers and Nev was kicking up his heels with Terry's Aunt Dot. Shaking his head, Sam battled to the bar and ordered another pint. The fiddle squealed and dipped, and the sweet sting of music braced his blood. He took a mighty gulp of beer and rejoined the fray.

He was flung from one jigging partner to another, ale swim-

ming in his head. Alice linked arms with him, eyes sparkling, hair
sticking to the side of her face. She released him, and he sailed free
to find his arm picked up by his mother. Nev's face ballooned by;
and Clive's sweating, drunken features; then he was swung by
Terry's good arm; and by Linda; and then out of the crowd loomed
the Tooth Fairy, jigging, grinning, locking him at the elbow. "See
you later," she whispered in his ear.

He stopped, releasing himself, stepping out of the unruly
crowd of dancers. The Tooth Fairy had gone again.

Faces swung back and forth, swollen-lipped, bulbous faces,
puce, perspiring and distorted in the amber light of the pub. He remembered stumbling into a table full of glasses, hearing them
crash, before all sound became a dull roar in his ears.

When he came to, he was sitting in the beer garden outside.
Alice was loosening his collar. Terry and Clive were propping him
upright.

"Deep Mood," said Sam.

"Come on," said Terry, hoisting Sam to his feet. "Let's walk it
off. You two go back inside."

"You sure?" said Alice.

"Yeah. Let me and Sam walk it off."

So with Terry supporting him, Sam lurched away from the
pub. Terry led him on a circuit down the lane and behind the
houses. Sam stopped to piss in the bushes.

He looked up at the night sky. "Stars are brilliant," he shouted.
Terry said nothing. "Hey! You don't mind leaving Clive and Alice
together?"

"Nope. I wanted her to have a word with Clive. Like she's had
a word with you." Terry was poker-faced, his clear eyes piercing.

"Fuck you. I love that Alice."

"We all do. Funny, isn't it? So now you hate me, do you?"

"Yes. No. Oh, I dunno." Sam squatted in the lip of the ditch at
the side of the road and fumbled for a cigarette. Terry kneeled beside him, offering a light. "Terry, don't you feel like we're on a
long, strange journey?"

"Getting stranger all the time."

Sam let out a plume of smoke. "No, I can't hate you, even though I've tried. I'm just so jealous, I could cry. Nothing goes right for me."

"For *you?* Nothing goes right for *you?*" Terry's eyelashes started fluttering, the way they always did when a certain thought crossed his mind. Then the fluttering stopped, and Terry was wide-eyed and angry. He was on his feet, and he was raging. "A pike bit off half my foot. Then my father blew my mother's head off. Then the twins'. Then he blew his own head off. Then I blew my hand off. And *you* say nothing goes right! Sam, I've lost things all my life, and now my number's come up for once. Don't begrudge me Alice!"

Sam stared in astonishment at his friend. It was the first time Terry had made open reference to any of these incidents. It left Sam speechless.

Terry was still quivering with rage. "And now I'm losing you and Clive!" he said bitterly.

"You're not losing us."

"Yes, I am. Have you noticed something about this place? They took away the brightest and the best and the most beautiful. They took Linda away, didn't they? And now they—"

"Don't—"

Terry cut him short. "Hear me out. This is our last night together, and I want to say this, whatever you think. You and Clive are going away to college. I'll see you from time to time, and after a year or two you'll start coming back with some big words and some new ideas, and if I'm lucky, no, if I'm *very* lucky, you two won't look down your noses at me and—"

"Terry!"

"—you might not look down your noses at me and we might talk about the old days, but things will be different between us forever. I know this. All my life I've had to get used to things falling away from me. Life is not something you can keep in your hand. You have to get used to losing things. It's the one thing I know everything about. And now I'm losing you, and all I ask is you remember this conversation."

Now Sam couldn't look Terry in the eye. He pretended to look up at the stars. "Oh, shit, Terry."

"Don't cry, man. It's only the booze. I'm just trying to keep a bit of you, that's all. Oh, bollocks." He got up and yanked Sam to his feet. "Let's get back before they finish. There's a lot of people want to say goodbye to you."

They trooped back to the pub in silence. Deviltry was still whipping up a storm in the back room, and the dancing showed no signs of exhausting itself. "Don't start drinking again," was Terry's parting shot as he left in search of Alice. Instantly someone clapped Sam on the back and pressed a glass of whisky into his hands.

"Down the hatch," said Sam, to no one in particular. Then the landlady jigged by. She thrust her hand in the air and waggled her head inconsequentially.

A lattice of cool fingers spread themselves across his cheek. "Are we going to see each other in London when you go to college?" It was Linda.

"Of course. I mean, you're going back there?"

"Sure. I can start again. I'll do it differently this time. God, Sam, to think I used to take you three to school."

The lights flashed on and off. "Last orders. Let me get you one, Linda."

The band played an encore. There was raucous applause. Finally Gladys Noon got people to leave. Sam's mother wanted to walk him home, but he declined. Too drunk to be useful, he hung around while the band were paid and their equipment was carried outside. He watched them roar away in their van. Alice and Terry, Linda and Ian Blythe all offered to walk him home but he resisted. He didn't want to go home. His mind was spinning; he wasn't ready for his bed. The others left together, and he walked back from the pub with an equally inebriated Clive, the pair almost leaning together to remain upright. A light shower of rain was falling. Clive stopped to rummage in his pocket. He produced a squashed, fishtailed ready-rolled cigarette.

"One for the road?"

A gust of wind blew the rain in their faces. Sam had an idea where they could go. "Come on."

He led Clive to the place where Terry had once lived in a caravan. The cottage was in darkness, as was the driveway. Clive followed blindly. When they reached Morris's old garage-workshop, Sam told Clive to wait. He forced his way down the side and entered by the rickety window. He unlocked a side door to admit Clive.

"You been here recently?"

"Some time ago."

They sat on the floor in the dark, and Sam offered a flame from his Zippo lighter. The place was as quiet as the dust. For some time there was only the sound of rain on the roof, of sucking on the lighted joint and of the exhaling of lungfuls of smoke.

Sam broke the silence. "Deep Mood. All those years ago. You painted the walls, Clive."

Clive snorted. "So what. How did you know?"

"Paint pot in your garden," slurred Sam. "You put it there, so's everyone would think it too obvious to be you. You wanted us to think Alice had planted it on you. Y'outsmarted yourself. Always trying to be one chess move ahead."

" 'Strue," said Clive. " 'Strue. I overestimated everyone's dumbness."

"You pretended to be furious with Alice. As if she'd stitched you up." Sam saw that Clive was dozing. "You were hiding your true feelings."

"Let's keep off Memory Lane, shall we?"

A fresh gust of wind swept rain across the leaking roof of the old garage. Something breathed sourly in the dark, and Sam stiffened. Reaching for his Zippo lighter, he spun the milled wheel and the tiny explosion of light chased the blackness back a few feet. There was Clive, sack-like, hunkered against the cold wall, his eyes closed. The hand-crafted cigarette, still clenched between his knuckles, had gone out. The puttering lighter illuminated the immature peach-fuzz moustache lining Clive's upper lip. Sam advanced the flame dangerously close to his friend's weak moustache, and Clive, opening his eyes in time to see the flame coming, interpreted it as an invitation to relight his cigarette.

"You fell asleep," Sam slurred. "You're drunk."

Clive smacked his lips, trying to moisten a furred mouth. He looked about uneasily. "I don't like this place. I never did. Why did you make us come here?"

"She's had us all, you know. One way or another."

Puzzled, Clive took a deep pull on his cigarette. "I'd give you some of this," he croaked through crowded lungs, "but you've had too much. Let's go."

"She's had me. She's had Alice. Terry. Morris. Linda. Even Derek—remember him? Skelton, too. And she's had you. That school exam thing, when you flipped out? That was her."

Sam flicked his lighter again, catching the bitter gleam in Clive's eye. Clive stubbed his cigarette out on the sole of his boot and got up unsteadily. Rain lashed at the shed roof. "I'm going. Don't stay here. It's like a tomb."

"I'll be all right."

"Go home, Sam. Don't fall asleep here."

Clive shuffled his feet before turning decisively, pushing his way out of the door. His presence in the shed was replaced by a draught of rain-bearing cold. Sam was afraid to stay there alone but knew it was the only place where he would find an answer. It was in there somewhere. The answer had to come from Morris's old workshop.

His senses were alerted by a familiar scent, a whiff of someone else in the shed with him. A blend of tobacco, whisky and hair oil and of another more elusive odor he associated with Morris's mind working at speed. Sam felt himself drifting into sleep. And as he did so, he sensed something out there, waiting, hovering, as if motionless under the surface of a familiar stretch of water.

He shifted himself. He remembered having a conversation with Clive, but he couldn't recall what it was about. Then Clive was gone, and he couldn't remember seeing him go. He felt only that he had some question to ask of the fattening dark.

Sam closed his eyes and let sleep overtake him. He didn't know how much time had passed before he was roused by a faint stirring at the far end of the shed. The air was suddenly chilled and fetid, like that of a newly opened tomb. Someone was in there with him.

A faint glow came from the desk. Half in shadow, a man sat at the table, working, drawing with geometrical instruments. Sam recognized the shape of Chris Morris, Terry's father.

"Mr. Morris," he breathed.

Chris Morris laid compass and ruler on the desk and turned slowly. Seeing Sam, he put a finger to the side of his head, like a gun. As Sam gazed back in awe and horror, Morris brought his hand round, extended his finger and thumb, and gently pinched the side of his own nostril.

"Suicide," Sam uttered in a tremulous voice. "You also had a Tooth Fairy. That's why you did it. Is it the only way out?"

Morris opened his mouth and worked his jaw slowly, but no sound came out. Finally he made a winding motion with his hands, and for the second time pinched his nostril with thumb and forefinger. In the next moment a low buzzing sound emerged from somewhere behind him. Then Morris was gone, as the buzzing became louder, furious, ear-splitting. Sam saw that it was coming from a jamjar standing on the desk where Morris had been. The jar crawled with live, angry wasps. Almost instantly the noise and the vision of the jamjar was gone, and Morris was back again. He made an O of his mouth, as if it was painful to work his jaw. *Let them out,* a voice said. *They get in but can't get out.* Morris suddenly looked horribly bewildered, and the apparition faded.

Sam gagged before his limbs unlocked. He scrambled to his feet and got out of the shed quickly. Outside the rain was still falling in a light shower. Shuddering, he turned up his collar and made his way home.

In the dark of his bedroom, the Tooth Fairy was waiting for him. She looked exhausted and depleted. Her clothes seemed more ragged and threadbare than at any previous time. He wondered if their last encounter, in her world, had done that to her. "I thought you'd never get home," she said softly.

"It's been a long night. But I'm glad to see you here," Sam whispered, beginning to undress. "That last time. In your world. Did I dream it? Or was that real?"

"How many times, Sam? How many times will you ask me that?"

"Not many more times. This can't go on, can it?"

"No."

"No," Sam said soothingly. "It can't. You know, tonight has been a night of goodbyes. To Alice and other people. Will you get into bed with me?"

She complied, stripping off her ragged clothes, her tunic and her mustard-and-green tights, and stood naked before him. Her smooth skin glowed blue-white, exaggerating the dark vine of her pubic hair. Sam took her hand and breathed deep the sexual, earth-raking odor of her, and they lay down together.

"All along people have been telling me what to do to be rid of you. But even though I thought it was not entirely in my power, I never really wanted to, did I?"

She said nothing. Her dark eyes were starbursting as he stroked her and whispered to her. "Even you told me, didn't you? That's why you took me over to your world. It was our last time, wasn't it?" She closed her eyes and he held her until he sensed her falling asleep in his arms, as she'd done so many times before.

"I never realized how I was holding on to you. At least not until that time in your world, when I finally let go."

Reaching under his bed, his hand found the clock of the Nightmare Interceptor. He lifted it carefully, wires trailing. Its crocodile-clip sensor was padded with cotton wool. "And I have my little sister to think about. After all, I helped make her. And even if I go away, she would tie you to this world, wouldn't she? You understand I have to let you go, don't you? For Linda Alice? I couldn't let her go through all of that."

The Tooth Fairy was asleep. "You told me how when you said you weren't my dream, but that I was yours. I just wasn't listening properly. And tonight Chris Morris showed me how."

He opened the spring of the crocodile clip and let it close gently, not on his own nose but this time on the Tooth Fairy's nostril. "All this time I've been trying to wake up from my nightmare. And I'd got it wrong. Now it's time for me to let you wake up from yours." She stirred slightly in her sleep but didn't awaken. Sam carefully trailed the wires from her and set the clock by the bedside. Then he put his head on the pillow and held her until he himself fell asleep.

In the morning he woke to find the Nightmare Interceptor clip in his bed, wires trailing from the pillow where her head had been. The impression of her body was still on the bed. The scent of her was left on the pillow. He thought he remembered the alarm triggering at some point in the night. The window to his bedroom was firmly closed.

He knew he would never see the Tooth Fairy again.

FORTY-THREE
Star

The following evening Sam was packing his suitcase, preparing for departure the next morning. Connie fussed around him, ironing shirts, sewing on buttons, folding trousers. "Astrophysics," she kept saying as she bustled about. "Astrophysics." It was as if she'd discovered a liking for the taste of the word in her mouth.

Sam had already bidden farewell to Clive that afternoon. He'd left for Oxford a day early. Everyone had been at Terry's house immediately prior to Clive's departure, and they all made promises about writing and being serious about staying in touch. London was going to be the location for a full-battle-dress rendezvous, since both Sam and Linda would already be there and it was on hand for Clive. Their enthusiasm about the perpetuation of the Redstone Moodies almost outweighed their unspoken instinct that the fellowship was finally being broken.

Sam blabbered Clive's secret from years ago, about daubing the walls with graffiti. Clive loudly denied it, but only for five minutes, and mainly because Dot and Charlie were present. Finally he admitted it. Charlie innocently asked him why he'd done it.

"Brainstorm," said Clive.

"Deep Mood," said Sam.

Alice, who'd been the main suspect all along, only shook her head in astonishment. Then, amid gales of laughter, they told Dot and Charlie the saga of the Dead Scout, after which it was Charlie's turn to shake his head. "You all want locking up," was his only comment.

Then Clive had to go, and Dot was dabbing her eyes while Charlie told her not to be so damned silly. Sam didn't stay much longer. Alice and Terry had promised to go with him to the station in the morning, and he told them he had his packing to do, but his main reason for following Clive out of the door was because he couldn't stand dragging out the farewells.

Linda stopped him at the door and planted a special kiss on his cheek. "I don't feel worried about you any more," she said.

"What do you mean?"

"I mean, I've always felt concerned for what happened to you above all the others. Now you're moving on, and I don't feel worried any more. Strange, isn't it? You'll be all right."

"Thanks," he said ironically.

She laid her hand on his cheek again, and then she let him go.

Later that afternoon, alone and trying to walk off a certain mood just as he always used to do, Sam made his way toward the pond. He was simply out to kill time. He had to get away from people: the affection of everyone was almost bruising in its intensity. Approaching the pond, he considered how often he had been drawn to this place. This womb-opening in the earth had always been there and had always found a way of speaking to him, though with an ever-diminishing voice. He fondly recalled the days when the pond seemed to stretch—at least to a small boy—like an ocean across the land.

Now the pond was a poor reduction of its former mysterious and life-breathing self. As he stood on the bank and sighed, something floating on the still, slightly scummy water caught his eye. It was the carcass of a pike. The dead fish was perhaps two feet long. He knew nothing about the average life span of a pike, but he thought it couldn't possibly be the same creature which had stripped Terry of two of his toes one day long ago. In any event, that original pike had been a monster—or so it had seemed at the time. Surely that king of a mythological realm hadn't been reduced to this?

"Or maybe," Sam said aloud, "this pond just got too small for you."

The pike, dead in the water, gave no answer.

Sam went home. He thought about it all while he was packing a few last things in his suitcase. He thought about three small boys running wild in the early morning, collecting cobwebs from a hedgerow blanketed by a pearly mist.

"Are you taking this with you?" Connie stood by the windowsill. The curtains of his bedroom hung open to the evening twilight, and behind her early stars were breaking out in the sky.

"Sorry, Mum, I was miles away."

"I said, are you taking your telescope with you? Will you be wanting it in London?"

"No. There's too much light pollution in London. Loss of stars, Mum, the effect is loss of stars. It's a condition of—"

"Just as you like." Connie turned away and busied herself with his suitcase.

Sam moved over to the telescope. It was angled low in the sky. He squinted into the eyepiece. The telescope was already trained on Sirius. The great, mythical star scintillated in the twilight; glimmering, iridescent in the lens; unattainable, impossible to know, and yet generating endless delight in its singular capacity to shine.